A quintet of bikeroos pedaled past, each one blasting away. Bullets pinged all around him. Civilians were across the street, behind the thugs and close to his line of fire, so he took careful aim. The Eagle screamed twice. A pair of bikeroos jerked from their mounts. Their compatriots kept on going.

Back on his feet, Noah made certain the shooters weren't coming back. He looked over the pigeons he'd plucked. They weren't going anywhere but the morgue.

That's when Marilyn came running up—if you could call what she did in those heels running. She had the sonic stunner she'd been issued in her hand but looked dazed.

"You can put that whistle away," he told her, gesturing toward the two bodies. "Looks like I've made the Blue Scorpions' hit parade."

"The Blue Scorpions? That's the same gang that was involved in the incident where Inspector Budd was killed."

"Yeah," Noah said, holstering his weapon.

"But why?" Marilyn asked, still looking stunned by the whirlwind violence.

"Payback, street cred—who knows. But if they're shooting at you, you know you're doing something right."

If you enjoy this book…

Milky Way Marmalade by Mike DiCerto

Metered Space by M. D. Benoit

Meter Made by M. D. Benoit

Synergy by M. D. Benoit

BETTER THAN CHOCOLATE

BY

BRUCE GOLDEN

ZUMAYA OTHERWORLDS   AUSTIN TX

2007

This book is a work of fiction. Names, characters, places and incidents are products of the author's imagination or are used fictitiously. Any resemblance to actual persons or events is purely coincidental.

BETTER THAN CHOCOLATE
© 2007 by Bruce Golden

ISBN 13: 978-1-934135-46-4
ISBN 10: 1-934135-46-1

Cover art and design by Cerberus Inc.
and Martine Jardin

Look for us online at http://www.zumayapublications.com

Library of Congress Cataloging-in-Publication Data

Golden, Bruce, 1952-
Better than chocolate / by Bruce Golden.
     p. cm.
ISBN-13: 978-1-934135-46-4
ISBN-10: 1-934135-46-1
1. Police--California--San Francisco--Fiction. 2. San Francisco (Calif.)--Fiction. 3. Murder--Investigation--Fiction. 4. Virtual reality--Fiction. I. Title.
PS3607.O452B48 2007
813'.6--dc22
                              2007015568

1

DIAMONDS ARE FOR NEVER

"...THEN SHE SAYS SHE DOESN'T THINK SHE CAN TAKE IT ANYMORE. SAYS IT'S TOO INTENSE. So I say to her, you just keep wiggling that thing, I'll let you know when you can't take it anymore. So she did, and I did, and it was a slice of heaven with cheesecake on the side. I mean, for at least a few glorious moments there, she was on a different plane of existence...if you know what I mean. Now she wants the pow-whammy every time she sees me. Not that I *don't*, but a man's got to share the wealth. It wouldn't be right for me to deprive the other flowers in the garden." Noah cocked his head and locked his combustible blue eyes on his partner.

Cyrus shook his head slowly, like a father who didn't know what to do with his prodigal son. "Dane, you're a walking erection. Someday that salami of yours is going to get you into serious trouble."

"It can't help itself—it has a split personality."

"What?"

"It's both obsessive and compulsive."

"Yeah, right."

Noah laughed. "Hey, I say give me pleasure or give me death."

"Yeah, you're a regular Patrick Henry."

"Who's he?"

Cyrus shrugged in response, so Noah took another bite of his taco and scanned the street outside their pod. There wasn't much to see. Certainly nothing out of the ordinary. He noticed a fellow in a dark business suit carrying a briefcase emblazoned with the neon slogan PEPSI THE DRINK OF A NEW GENERATION and wondered how much product placement credit the guy was

1

paid. Probably more than *he* took home in a month.

Eventually, the suit and his annoying iridescence blended into the crowd near the juice bar across the way. That was the pseudo-health pub their targets were known to frequent. A frosty spot for a cool drink and molten merchandise like idisk blinds and fresh falsefaces. Right now, though, nothing smelled of trouble.

Next to the juicer was a clothing outlet-cum-art store for the avant-crud crowd, and beside it was a little sex toys boutique, the Erotic Emporium. It had been around for years, so Noah was surprised to see a sign in its window that read GOING OUT OF BUSINESS SALE. Strange. Most of the markets and shops in the area seemed to be thriving.

He scratched his chest and wondered how you could mismanage a business that catered to mankind's most basic appetite. Well, he had no head for business, so what would he know.

There was nothing out of the ordinary. The usual assortment of citizens made their way up and down the busy commercial boulevard, stopping here and there at public grid screens to focus on some matter or another that caught their attention. Most were walking, some were silently motoring by on their movers, while the rest pedaled their way on bicycles.

There were more and more bikes on the roadway all the time—not that Noah was worried about spotting their suspects. The bikeroos they were waiting for stood out like peacocks in a pigeon roost. If the Blue Scorpions tried to move their contraband today they were going to need their own going-out-of-business signs.

A pair of trolls passed by, but he didn't give them a second look. They'd become commonplace, despite their enormous ears and bluish skin. The barefoot alien immigrants had proved to be nonviolent types, though he once saw one so hopped up on jazz juice it took four uniforms to subdue him. That was right after the Troloxians arrived and were still naive concerning the dangers of assorted human vices. Nevertheless, they didn't seem to possess any criminal instincts, so he rarely concerned himself with them.

Noah shifted in his seat, trying to make room for his considerable bulk. "I swear these damn pods were designed by a dwarf with a nasty sense of humor."

"It's not like you couldn't afford to lose a few pounds," Cyrus replied. "That gut of yours is downright retro."

"Hey! Look who's talking about vast waist lands." If Noah was starting to get a little thick around the middle, then Cyrus was downright pudgy. "I can't help

it that I'm a large man," Noah added. "I think six-six, two-twenty, is just right."
"Two-twenty? You haven't weighed two-twenty since you were linebacking for the Bulldogs. Two-forty's more like it."
Noah made a noise that was part grunt, part grumble.
Outside the pod, up above, something caught his eye. He stuck his head out the window and saw a holoboard hovering overhead. Rapid-fire editing flashed 3-D images emblematic of romance, mystery and danger, all set in exotic locales. Those scenes were replaced by a model with more cleavage than Noah felt the average man would have known what to do with. Seductively the model covered her eyes with a visor that was a sleek variation of a single-lens pair of sunglasses. The orange tint of the horizontal lens transmuted into a red glow, and above her appeared the colorful words GET REAL WITH V-REAL. She smiled that dreamy smile women get right after it feels so good it hurts, and the scripted message morphed into IT'S BETTER THAN CHOCOLATE.
Noah pulled his sandy blond crewcut back inside the pod. "You sure you don't want one of these?" he asked, unwrapping the grease-soaked paper from another taco.
"Thanks, but no thanks," replied Cyrus, "I'll stick with this sandwich Debbie made for me."
"How *is* the missus, and the kids?"
"They're great—I'm taking little Dan and Denise to the new Galactic Miniature Golf Park after I clock out today. And Debbie wants me to have you over for dinner again soon."
"She's probably got some new marriage-minded harpy lined up for me to meet. Doesn't she know I'm a lost cause? I've fumbled away two marriages already. What makes her think the third time will be charmed? That's like sticking your hand in the snake pit after it's already full of puncture wounds dripping venom."
Cyrus laughed.
"You know me, Cy. Positioned properly, I think women are great—the hottest thing since Cro-Magnon man discovered fire. I love them—love to make each and every one feel like they're the Empress of Orgasms. What I don't like is when I become a pain in their ass—as my ex-wives will attest I eventually do. If at first you don't succeed, try again—then give up."
"Speaking of hot—see that, Dane, I'm changing the subject—it's damn hot today." Cyrus wiped his hand across his damp forehead, emphasizing the point. "It seems like lately it's always either too hot or too cold. San Francisco wasn't like this when we were kids. Not this time of year anyway. It was windy

and rainy but never this hot and humid. Hell, it seems like every other week we're setting some new record."

Noah looked at the sky as Cyrus continued.

"Half the state's drying up like a desert, but it's like we're living in the tropics. Either that or freezing our asses off due to some rogue arctic front."

"You think it's going to rain?" Noah asked with some trepidation. "It smells like rain to me."

Cyrus smiled at his partner's unease. "Yeah, there's going to be a downpour with thunder and lightning and—"

"All right—very funny. Enough with the weather report."

"Come on, Dane, you know I like to get in a few jabs when I can. We've all got our little phobias—yours is just stranger than most."

"Yeah, yeah, yeah, I've heard it all before. How's IRIS doing? Has it spotted anything interesting?"

They looked down at the pod's monitor and watched the scene pan back and forth across the street as the remote sentinel's camera scanned the crowd for their suspects.

"Not even a sniff yet," said Cyrus.

"These techno-gadgets aren't worth the sweat off a baboon's ass." Noah reached inside his coat and adjusted his shoulder holster, reassuring himself of the weight there. "I never met a robot, droid or drone that was half as good as its hype. Worse than that, you can't trust them. Not like a human partner who you know has your back."

"What are you going to do?" Cyrus said with resignation. "Someday, we'll all be replaced by machines."

"Yeah, that'll be a hell of a world, won't it? Count me out. Hey! What was that? On the monitor."

Cyrus rechecked the system. "There's no alert from IRIS."

"Shows you how much it knows. Quick, play back the last forty seconds."

Cyrus complied, and they both studied the recorded images.

"Hello, mama. Look at her, will you."

A tall, amply endowed young Asian woman on rollerblades passed through the sentinel's remote video scan.

"Put it back in your pants, Dane."

"I told you, there's just some things a machine can't do for you. I'm going to go question a potential witness."

"Dane, we're on a stakeout. You can't go chasing down a skirt."

"I don't think that little thing she has on qualifies as a skirt, partner."

4

"Dammit, Dane, at least check your com before you go running off for some burntail."

"You're so sweet to worry about me, partner," Noah said as he pressed the hatch release and stepped out. "Thanks to you, I may live to be an old man yet," he said, pinching his left earlobe. "Com check, this is Dane."

The reply came as clear as if Cyrus were whispering in his ear. *All right, Dane, I've got you. Now try to stay out of trouble, and keep your com active.*

The pod closed behind him, and Noah was off down the street, making his way through the human traffic. He had to move it if he was going to catch up to her before she got too far—she was rolling through the crowd at a brisk clip.

Even before he reached his objective he caught the scent of her perfume. At least, he was convinced it was hers, though a dozen bodies swarmed within range of his sensitive nostrils. It was something sweet, like candy—maybe cherry.

"Hold up there, miss. Yes, you on the rollerblades. San Francisco Police, miss."

The woman turned to look at him, surprised at first, then curious.

"Could you skate your way over here, please?"

He saw as she made her way toward him that she was a real fineline for sure.

"What's wrong, officer? I wasn't speeding, was I?" she asked in jest, brushing her long dark hair away from her face.

"It's inspector, miss, not officer. Inspector Noah Dane. And no, you weren't speeding. But I'm afraid I'm going to have to place you under arrest…for being absolutely too incredibly sexy."

She smiled, and so did Noah.

"What's wrong?" she asked coyly. "Is my outfit breaking some kind of law?"

"No, but I'm certain that body of yours is illegal in several states. However, I'll have to examine it more closely to—"

Dane, we've got trouble.

"Just a moment, miss." Noah pinched his com. "What is it, Cy?"

Three Scorpions just biked up to the juice bar and went inside.

"Did IRIS make them?"

No, but they're packing heat. Handguns shoved right in their belts like they were as legal as slingshots.

"I'll be right there. Wait for me." Noah left the com hot and turned to the rollerblader. "Sorry, miss, duty calls. Some other time maybe."

Before he could turn around, he heard muted gunfire.

"What's up, Cy?"

I don't know. Two other guys just ran out of the juicer and took off down the street. The Scorps are right behind them. I'm in pursuit.

"Dammit, Cy, wait for me."

The baseball-size IRIS swooped overhead, and he heard the droning buzz as it turned in response to the alarm. Noah followed, moving at a trot now, trying to dodge pedestrians and bicyclists alike. He collided with several but didn't waste time on apologies. He could barely keep the sentinel in sight.

Can't wait, partner, get here quick.

Noah heard more shots and held up momentarily to get his bearings. He caught a glimpse of his partner and the shooters as everyone with half a brain hit the deck or ran for cover. He pulled his Mark XIX out of its holster and took off at a sprint.

The bikeroos were easy to spot with their chrome chains and scraps of gaudy blue clothing. Noah came up parallel to them, but they were already hunkered behind a delivery truck outside the foodplex. They fired carelessly in the general direction of the pair they'd been chasing, their little guns popping like toys. The other two, he was surprised to see, were armed with some weapon he'd never seen before. Ray guns? Even the thought sounded silly. Lasers, probably.

Whatever, there was suddenly a lot of firepower on one street, especially considering civilian ownership of firearms was outlawed. Not that it mattered, because everybody and his little sister seemed to have something that went bang.

But he didn't have much time to ponder how two street rats could've gotten their hands on such high-tech hardware, because Cyrus had somehow gotten himself positioned between the two factions and was caught in the crossfire.

Noah assessed the scene in an instant, realizing his partner was in a seriously risky spot. He cursed himself and opened fire on the Scorpions. That got their attention immediately—his .50-caliber Desert Eagle was a cannon compared to their smaller weapons. They turned their fire on him, and he took cover. That freed up Cyrus, who, seeing his partner, moved in on the other two.

Noah tried to keep one eye on Cyrus as he continued to blow good-sized holes into the truck the bikeroos now cowered behind. A searing blast burned a patch of concrete Cyrus had only recently vacated. His partner returned fire on-target and dropped one of the shooters. The fellow's confederate began a retreat, and Cyrus moved to pursue. The guy turned, and Noah got only a quick glimpse before he fired.

Too late he called out, "Get down, Cy!" The incandescent light caught his partner in the chest, full-on.

Noah erupted with a roar, charging out from his protective cover like an enraged bull elephant. The trio of Blue Scorpions seemed momentarily stunned, amazed he was out in the open, coming right at them. They recovered quickly enough, but the sight of him must have shaken them because every shot they fired missed. Noah squeezed his trigger once, and the closest bikeroo was propelled backwards, the large slug tearing through his sternum. Two more quick shots took care of his buddies.

He didn't waste any time with the gangsters. He ran to his partner, determining as he did that the remaining shooter had fled.

"Cy!" He pulled out his pad as he ran and signaled officer down. "Cy..." He choked off any more words as he saw the carnage that had been inflicted. A hole the size of his fist had burned through his partner's chest, incinerating a good portion of the heart and cauterizing the wound. Cyrus was gone.

Noah's expression hardened as he stood. He looked down at his partner but didn't speak. A brick-like knot constricted his throat. He made no attempt to contain the rage swelling in his gut.

His gun still hanging loosely in his hand, he walked to the shooter Cyrus had nailed. The body lay on its stomach, but the head was turned so that Noah could see where Cy had shot him. The face was a fright mask of bone, blood and mangled skin. Noah couldn't have cared less. He wasn't about to waste a twitch of disgust on this street rat.

He stuck his foot under the corpse's hip and kicked it over. The body flopped onto its back and a black vinyl bag that had been clutched by dead hands broke free and spilled its glittering contents across the pavement.

For a moment, he didn't believe his eyes. How would a rodent like this have gotten his hands on such loot? He couldn't be certain of course, but to Noah they looked like diamonds.

2

WHEN IT RAINS...

THE RAIN EVOLVED IN MOMENTS FROM HESITANT DRIZZLE TO AGGRESSIVE DOWNPOUR, but Noah's sense of time, his usual steady grasp of reality, and even his normally acute awareness of his environment were skewed. He fought against the fear, the irrational terror that had been his burden since that single, terrifying incident as a child.

The reflex horror of being outside in a storm struggled with his reluctance to move closer to the door—to do what he had to do. He stood there, his clothing drenched, his mind racing nowhere and everywhere.

Still he didn't move from the walkway where he had planted himself, or notice the robot toy left lying on the well-manicured lawn. Even his usually overactive sense of smell was a blank. He stood staring straight ahead at the off-white, colonial-style door, its pseudo-brass fixtures and inlaid pane of rose-tinted glass.

It wasn't until the door opened that any sense of place or purpose returned to him.

"Who's out there?" A woman's voice cut through the deluge, and the fog that clouded his brain. Hesitantly, he started up the walkway. The porchlight flicked on and blinded him.

"Noah, is that you standing out there? You're soaked." The woman smiled at what he thought must have been a pathetic sight. "You crazy man. What are you doing? Where's Cyrus?"

He had no words to answer her, but the look on his face must have said enough.

In one jarring instant of revelation, her smile morphed into an expression of anguished terror. She staggered, backpedaling into the house as Noah climbed the porch steps.

"No. No. I don't want to talk to you," she said, tears already forming in her eyes. "Go away."

Noah stepped to the door. She looked ready to collapse, so he grabbed her and held on, her delicate shift saturated by the contact.

"I'm sorry, Debbie. I'm so sorry."

HE PUT DOWN THE BOTTLE LONG ENOUGH TO TAKE OFF HIS LONG BLACK COAT, SHOULDER holster and shirt, exposing his hairy torso. His shoes and socks were next, but he left on his still-soaked pants.

Outside, the rain continued its onslaught. He heard it pounding on his roof, streaming rivulets racing down across the asphalt shingles to the quagmires forming in his yard. Inside, it was only raining whiskey.

Noah downed another swig and mindlessly watered his patchouli blossoms. His grid screen was on in the next room, audio up, but he wasn't listening. He wasn't thinking. He wasn't feeling.

His bulky form moved with gentle precision through the exotic jungle that overran his residence—a water container in one hand, bottle in the other. He checked the soil of each, examined leaves where necessary, and pulled away withered petals. He'd made the little arboretum out of what once might have been a sewing alcove or sunroom, but his cherished greenery had begun to spill out into all corners of his home.

His door chime sounded. He ignored it. It rang again—then several more times until he reluctantly conceded to the irritation. He put down the water, held on to the whiskey and went to the door.

It was an old house, with no homeminder or even sensors. He didn't want one of those "smart homes" you had to talk to. He'd never bothered installing so much as security cams—he considered there to be more than enough cameras in the world already. You practically couldn't take a shit these days without some cam recording it for posterity. He didn't like them. He didn't trust them.

He opened the door to a heavyset woman in a long, sack-like dress embossed with wild paisley designs and surreal clock faces melting into nothingness. Her face had a doughy consistency, while her neck was a roadmap of wrinkles. Her hair had been dyed a bright red-orange and was curled onto a dozen rollers. She was trying to close her umbrella but having a devil of a time doing it.

"Mrs. G, what are you doing out here in the rain?"

She pushed her glasses back against the bridge of her nose and inspected him. His neighbor was the only person he knew who wore such antiquated corrective lenses. Once she apparently reassured herself who he was, she tried to crane her neck so she could see around him.

"Do you need something, Mrs. G?"

"I thought I saw a mutant come in here," she said, still searching the room behind him.

"No, Mrs. G, it was just me."

"Are you certain? You can't be certain, you know." She pointed at him as she spoke. "They're everywhere. You know mutants took my Charlie," she said, as though it were a startling bit of new information.

It wasn't. He had heard the story many times. He'd even looked into it—unofficially.

"They took him away and never brought him back," she continued. "That's why you've always got to be on the lookout. They're everywhere, you know. Are you sure there aren't any mutants in there?" she queried, her head bobbing and weaving like a fighter as she tried to get a clear look behind him. "I thought I saw one come in here. I was afraid they might get you."

"No, Mrs. G, I'm fine, I swear. There aren't any mutants here. Just me and Jack Daniels," he said, holding up his bottle. "You'd better put that umbrella back up and go home now."

"All right. All right, if you're sure." She almost sounded disappointed. "I do want to get back in time to watch *Bizarre del Mundo*. They've got ballet-dancing Siamese clones tonight, and they're bringing back the guy who catches flies with his tongue. I heard they also might have some of those cute little blue aliens doing something.

"Well, you be careful now," she said, opening her umbrella. "And don't forget the rent. The rent's due, you know. I don't want to have to toss you out in the street. No, I don't. Not in this weather. Not with all the mutants about."

"I won't forget."

His deluded neighbor thought she was his landlady, and he'd long ago stopped trying to correct her. He watched as she made her way back to her own home.

He closed the door, dropped into his favorite overstuffed chair and stared at the grid screen. He raised the bottle to his lips once more and upended it. Poor Mrs. Grabarkowitz, he thought. What had really happened was that Charlie Grabarkowitz had run off with another woman more than two decades ago. His wife had gone off the deep end and never come up for air. Her demons had become "mutants," and she saw them everywhere. He sat there for some time, drinking, not noticing what was on the screen until big bold red letters flashed NEWS ALERT. He coaxed up the volume.

"Authorities warn that an attack by the Icelandic terrorist group Loftur is likely imminent." The superimposed letters faded to a scene of emergency crews and hospital rooms. "It was just four months ago in Texas that toxic chemicals were found in Houston's water supply. How the chemicals got into the water was never determined, but government officials have attributed the threat to the terrorists. A spokesperson for the Office of Homeland Security reports they have no specifics as to the nature of the threat at this time, and deny rumors of some new strain of sexually transmitted disease. However, they warn all citizens to be on the alert. Keep an eye on your neighbors, watch your co-workers, check your surveillance systems and be certain to submit to all bioscanners to affirm your identity."

The video cut to a scene of two young children, a boy and girl, playing with an older girl. The staccato voice of the male newscaster also changed, replaced by the pleasant, cheerful tones of a woman, accompanied by light, breezy music.

"This news alert was brought to you by Cyber Sister. She's a companion for your kids, a nanny for little ones, a helper around the house. And now, to make your home complete, there's also new Cyber Brother for that pseudo-male influence. Cyber Sister and Cyber Brother are products of Droidco, a division of General Motors."

Noah poked at his pad to change the link and took another swallow from his bottle. Before he could even see what program he had linked to, the audio faded and an insert of the on-file picture of his ex-wife Sheila invaded the screen, along with her relevant information.

"You have an incoming call. You have an incoming call. The caller has been identified as Sheila McIntire, formerly Sheila Dane, formerly Sheila Anne Wentworth. The caller has designated this communication urgent."

Everything was always "urgent" with Sheila, thought Noah, taking another drink. She probably wants one of her husbands arrested for leaving the seat up.

"You have an—"

"Open the call," he commanded, and the frantic face of his ex replaced the program video. Her long blond hair was tied back, and though the image was only from the shoulders up, he could tell she'd put on some weight.

"Noah, Catherine's gone."

"What do you mean she's gone?"

"I mean she didn't come home tonight when she was supposed to. She was supposed to be home at nine."

He checked the time. "Hell, Sheila, it's only eleven-thirty. She just might be late."

"No, no, I think she's run away again. You have to find her."

"What is it with you two? I thought mothers and daughters were supposed to get along. What happened this time?"

"Nothing happened," she declared defensively. "Don't try to blame this on me, Noah Dane. I'm here every day, taking care of her."

"Yeah, you and your five husbands and—how many co-wives is it now?"

"It's a perfectly legitimate polyamoristic family group. That has nothing to do with it."

"It doesn't? I doubt that's how Cat feels."

"How would you know?"

He could envision the fumes starting to spiral out of her head.

"When was the last time you saw your daughter? I mean in person. When was the last time you took her somewhere, sat down and really talked with her? When was the last time you were a father to her?"

"I'm in no mood to argue, Sheila. If she's not home by morning, I'll put out a DIRS alert."

"By morning—"

"Disconnect," he ordered, and his ex's bitter image was replaced by previous programming.

He glanced at the videograph of his daughter that hung on the wall. It looped a scene of her playing frisbee, her lanky frame running only to fumble and drop the disc; trying to push her stringy strawberry-blond hair out of her face; a closeup of her freckled smile. He couldn't remember the last time he'd been with her. He didn't think it had been that long, but exactly when it was or what they had done he couldn't recall. Even the videograph was a couple of years old.

She was sixteen now—almost a woman. He was sure she didn't need an old leadfoot like him around. What good was he to her? She had a big family now—an extended family, not that she seemed to care for it. But it was better than what he had to offer.

He turned his attention back to the screen and tried to lose himself in whatever inane program happened to be usurping his grid link at the moment.

"...that may be true, Ms Blume, but since prostitution was legalized in 2021, there has been a remarkable decrease in both sex-related crimes and sexually transmitted diseases."

"Isn't it possible, Professor Hayward, that reduction in diseases could be explained by medical advances, and that the decline of sex-related crimes is linked directly to heightened security measures, specifically bioscan technology and the digital imaging recognition system?"

"I'm afraid that's a rather simplistic way of looking at it, and doesn't account for the cause and effect factors which—"

"Isn't it true, Professor, the sexual act itself, factored by jealous rages and primitive territorial instincts, has been the cause of countless acts of violence throughout history? And isn't it also true that if humanity had channeled the mental and physical energy it has squandered on sexual recreation, we would have long ago found a cure for cancer and explored the heavens beyond our own solar system? Doesn't the legalization of prostitution only condone that waste?"

"I fail to see the relevance of..."

Noah listened to the contentious prattle but didn't absorb it. Involuntarily, he had flashed back to the scene in the street, remembering the way it had played out—the gunfire, the positioning, trying to reach Cyrus, and the still vivid image of his partner burned down by a flash of crimson light. Near to the surface of this fresh memory was his own dereliction. He should have been there. He should have been with his partner. He should have been the one to take the hit.

"You're watching Gridspeak with Chastity Blume, brought to you tonight by V-Real and its latest alternate reality, *High Castle*, where you can experience firsthand the glory and splendor of medieval chivalry and close combat warfare. Don't wait, order yours on the grid right now. It's your turn to get real with V-Real."

Noah took another drink and stared blankly at the screen. It was getting harder to focus. It occurred to him that if he drank enough, he wouldn't be able to see at all—not the grid screen, not Cat's videograph, and not the scene that played on a continuous loop inside his head.

3

SOME LIKE IT BOUGHT
& SOME LIKE IT NOT

THIRTY SECONDS TO LIVE," CALLED THE DIRECTOR IN HER EAR. "EVERYONE ON SET." Chastity straightened her tepid-blue skirt and fidgeted with the hem. She adjusted her matching jacket and took one last glance in the mirror before hurrying back to her chair. She realized she wasn't as focused as she liked to be for a show.

She also knew why. She'd much rather be out investigating the so-called Loftur terrorist group or the rumors of a grid poll scandal at City Hall instead of tallying more face time. But that wasn't to be. Not yet, anyway. Right now, she had a show to do. She had to get her mind straight, stay on subject, not let up.

We're live in ten…nine…eight…seven…six…five…four…three…

"Welcome back, and if you've just scanned in, I'm Chastity Blume and you're linked to a special live edition of *Gridspeak,* the true voice of the people." She straightened in her seat, cleared her mind and drew on her assertive cloak. It was showtime.

"Our topic tonight is legalized prostitution, and the spurious claims that it has actually proved beneficial to our society. My guest is Dr. Raymond Hayward, a professor of sexology at the University of California, Berkeley, and author of *Outlaw Sex: The Dark Ages,* a book that, I must say, looks back almost in anger at

15

the time in this country before prostitution and other deviant sexual practices were legalized under a politically charged and nefariously comprehensive ruling by the Supreme Court."

"Thank you, Ms Blume, and yes, you could call it anger. I think any rational person would be angry looking at the history of sexual condemnation. First, though, I must take exception to your use of the word *deviant* to describe any form of consensual sex. An individual's right to his or her sexual preferences and ideology, no matter how bizarre-seeming to others, is akin to the right which guarantees religious freedom. This concept was at the heart of the court's ruling. By law, and by the very ideals on which this country was founded, there is no such thing as a deviant sexual practice."

"Are you saying, Professor, that our Founding Fathers would have condoned the rampant carnality which afflicts us today?"

"Condoned publicly? No. But privately they most definitely engaged in it. It was a different time. What was done in privacy was not flaunted. But, yes, in spirit, I do believe they would have agreed that the freedom of the individual is tantamount to a healthy society. If I may paraphrase Thomas Jefferson, many of the worst abuses of law enforcement stem from political wars on vices. Government power must be limited to protecting citizens from other people's aggression, not from their own stupidity or weaknesses."

"Well, Professor, I'm no expert on Thomas Jefferson, but doesn't prostitution perpetuate violence against women?" Chastity caught herself staring at the professor's trim white beard and trying to picture the old goat actually engaging in sex. Subconsciously, she pulled down on her skirt. "Isn't it degrading in the way it reduces women to chattel?"

"I don't believe you can make this a woman's

issue. After all, there are male prostitutes—a rapidly increasing number of them, I might add. As for violence, legalizing prostitution has reduced the threat. Legal brothels have tight security measures and provide an outlet for the sexually frustrated who may, without this option, become violent sexual predators.

"When you account for the cost and futility of enforcing laws against prostitution and other sexual acts, the burden on the judicial and penal systems and the lack of regulation concerning health matters, I don't know how any reasonable person cannot agree with the court's ruling. I believe time has proved the wisdom of that decision."

She paused a moment, considering his words, and meditatively put her hand around her throat.

"That may be true, Professor, I won't concede or debate those points right now. However, didn't the Supreme Court's ruling proliferate the fallacy that sex, aside from its obvious procreative function, is a necessary, even indispensable avocation?"

Her guest chuckled, finding some perverse humor in her comment. Chastity was not amused. Her eyes flashed like incandescent emeralds under the glare of the camera lights.

"I think, Ms Blume," he said, smiling as if at some joke she wasn't privy to, "that most people find it a *pleasurable*, if not indispensable, pastime."

"Wrap it up, Chastity," directed the voice in her IFB. "Close on two."

"I'm not certain, Professor," she said stiffly, her indignation held professionally in check, "that you are the best spokesperson for 'most people.' It is a fact that you don't speak for me or for the thousands, or should I say millions, of others who don't share your prurient views.

"However, I thank you for joining me today." She turned toward a secondary camera. "I hope you'll link in to our next program when we'll talk with a young couple who, unlike Professor Hayward and his people, have dedicated their lives to sexual abstinence. I'm Chastity Blume, and you're watching *Gridspeak*, the true voice of the people."

"Stayed fixed to this link, Chastity will be right back with a story about a smalltown boy, his dog and a harrowing journey that nearly spelled disaster for both."

4

TEAM CHEMISTRY

THE WIND BLUSTERED AND SWIRLED AS IF IN ANGER. NOAH HELD HIS COAT AROUND HIM and hustled up the Hall of Justice steps. It was a massive gray building, nondescript except for the product placement screens that were so familiar he didn't waste a glance.

The morning sun had emerged to scare off storm cloud stragglers, but the streets were still painted with damp. The Mag had been delayed by some nebulous Loftur threat and he was late. He wasn't sure what was riding them, or what they wanted, but those Loftur types were becoming increasingly annoying. Of course, their threats had given the legislature the ammo it needed to slap down civil liberty concerns and make DIRS a reality. That was good coming out of bad, he guessed.

It had been a rough night, though he didn't remember much of it. He woke with a headache and shredded remnants of remorse. However, bolstered by an ample dose of Hangoverin, he replaced the specter of yesterday with the resolve of today. There was a killer to hunt down. Cyrus's killer. That was something he could get his hands around—a mandate conducive to his instincts and training. Leave the ghosts and guilt for someone else to sweep up. Retribution was an easier vein to tap.

He flattened his hand against the idisk, stated his name aloud and scowled at the security cam as the biometric scan compared fingerprints, vocal intonations and body odor with his facial features. The reinforced shieldglass doors parted, and he marched straight to the desk sergeant.

On the wall above the desk was a vid placement he hadn't seen before. It looped an action sequence starring the SWAT guys scaling a building with

19

ropes and was accompanied by a crawl that read SAN FRANCISCO'S EMERGENCY RESPONSE TEAM IS BROUGHT TO YOU BY REDWOOD. WHEN YOU WANT TO GET IT UP AND KEEP IT UP, TAKE THE LITTLE PILL WITH THE POWER OF A PRIMEVAL FOREST.

"Dane." The sergeant nodded in recognition. "Sorry to hear about Cy. He was good police."

"I need to put out a DIRS and idisk alert for this girl," Noah said abruptly, handing the sergeant the videograph of Cat he'd brought from home. Sheila had called an hour ago. He didn't take it, but the message was clear. Cat hadn't come home.

"Sure, Dane, but DIRS has been bugged-up. Now it's backlogged—not that that's a gridflash. Damn thing is a thorn up my butt."

"Well, put a priority on this one, it's my daughter. The name's Catherine Anne Dane." The sergeant looked at him like he wanted to ask, but didn't. "Just file it as a missing person, possible runaway."

"Is this a recent videograph?" the sergeant asked, already inputting the relevant data.

"No," said Noah, chagrined, "it's a couple of years old. Check education department records, they should have a new one on file. Oh, and make a note—she's always dyeing her hair something different. Who the hell knows what color it is now."

"I'll take care of it."

"Thanks," Noah replied, already on his way around the desk and into the station.

It was the same way he went every day, but today the walls seemed closer, the space just a little tighter. The faces, at least, were familiar. If you were looking for a cross-section of the city, here's where you'd find it. The department had all shapes, sizes, and ethnocentric bents—the way it should be.

Only today when some of those familiar faces looked up and saw him, gazes were averted, eye contact avoided. A few acknowledged him with a quick nod and went right back to work. No one spoke. He knew what they were thinking—knew they were trying to come up with the right thing to say and deciding silence was safer. He'd been there himself.

Someone had a grid screen on a news link, up full volume. Noah heard the reporter say something about a shortage of the latest V-Real adventure, and then he noticed Brunelli headed his way. He braced for some caustic remark that would force him to deck the ugly little pug, but Brunelli simply gave him a look, like heartburn on steroids, and walked right past him.

Noah reached his desk, activated his screen and dropped into his chair. He could tell someone had been fucking with his *Rubra oxalis*, so he moved it back where it belonged and straightened the leaves. First thing up on the screen was a message in blazing purple font to REPORT IMMEDIATELY to the captain. Well, he'd expected that—standard obtuse procedure. The sooner he got it over with the sooner he could get on the trail of that scummer who burned Cyrus.

He glanced toward the captain's office and caught the tail end of some daftly overdressed blonde walking away. Wackadoo or not, he had to admit it was some potent pow-whammy.

Let's get it over with, he thought as he shot out of his chair and stalked straight to the box—"the box" being how the squad endearingly referred to the captain's office, especially when a lecture of some sort was expected. Noah started to knock then hesitated, his fist poised over the gold inscription reading CAPTAIN LING ZHAO RAEVSKI. He shrugged his shoulders, gave the door a couple of quick raps and stepped in without waiting to be invited.

Captain Raevski, her black hair scored with gray and pinned up in haphazard fashion, regarded him without comment and returned to what she had been studying on her grid screen, her face scrunched up like an old blouse. Noah stood there, ignoring the worn vinyl chair beside him. He didn't say anything, he just waited, noticing the captain reeked of cannabis, as she typically did.

Not that he'd ever seen her partake on duty, or that she ever would, but his incomparably cogent snout could always smell it on her person. Whether it was her clothes, her hair or her aura, he didn't know. He just knew she must indulge frequently. Who wouldn't after a day in this place? He'd tried it a few times after it had been legalized, but even as a teenager it wasn't his cup of hemlock. He was a whiskey man, born and drenched.

He waited, stared down at his diminutive boss and realized what she was really doing. She wasn't studying any report, she was deciding what to say. He opened his mouth to break the silence then thought better of it. Instead, like any good detective, he searched her desk for clues. Nothing out of the ordinary was apparent. Just her laser bug-zapper and the usual assortment of pizza crusts.

When he started to play with her desk nameplate, she looked up at him with those soul-blunting Asian eyes of hers.

"You really fumbled the ball this time, Dane. This isn't the wild west you know. We're a damn modern police force. We use forensics, surveillance technology, investigative methodology, prosecutorial law. We don't stage gunfights in the middle of the street."

He met her glacial stare with one of his own. "It seemed like the thing to do at the time."

The captain glowered. "Sit down."

Noah sat.

"I'm sorry about Budd. I know you two partnered for a long time. You had good team chemistry."

"It was my fault, Cap, I—"

"Don't give me any of that fault crap or I'll bench you. Tell me how it went down, play by play."

So he told her.

"What happened to the other shooter?" she asked, reaching for her zapper.

"Gone," he replied with a shrug.

The captain pivoted her chair, aimed the tiny laser and fired. Noah saw the beam burn into a brown-shelled cockroach making its way along the floor molding. A wisp of smoke rose from its charred carcass.

"Game over, you degenerate little scumsucker," she said, spitting the words out like they'd left a bad taste in her mouth.

"Hey, Cap, is this bug roasting thing some kind of ancient family tradition?"

"The only family tradition I remember is my father sprawled on the couch with a Budweiser and a bag of chips watching the Niners. And don't try to change the subject.

"Your IRIS recorded most of what happened, and I can tell you management is not happy about the playback. Five dead bodies, including a San Francisco police inspector, and a killer on the loose with a sophisticated weapon. The grid polls are screaming like a baby with a bad case of colic. It was all I could do to keep you off the trading block, Dane. What do you think was going down?"

"I don't know, Cap. Those diamonds make it look like either a sale gone bad or an outright ripoff."

Raevski nodded.

"By the way, I don't want you to put anything about that roller girl in your report. Don't argue!" she snapped, anticipating his objection. "Just say you and your partner got separated in the crowd. That's true enough, and I don't need any surplus problems right now. All I want is an easy three-up and three-down. Get my thirty in, retire and spend time with my grandkids. So don't cause me any grief." The captain swivelled in her chair and dropped her zapper back on the desk. "You're running a little hot right now, so I want you to take some down time. Then, when you feel like coming back, I'll assign you a new case."

Noah reached into his coat, pulled out his SFPD badge and slapped it on her desk. "There's your down time." With some reluctance he pulled out his Mark XIX 50-caliber Desert Eagle and gently placed it next to the badge.

"Don't pull this tired old cliche on me, Dane," she said, standing.

When he turned to leave, she called, "Timeout, timeout."

Noah wheeled around with a steely-eyed stare. "I'm going to find the guy who burned my partner—with or without a badge."

"For the love of Jerry, Dane," she said in a high-pitched snarl. "As it is, I'm catching hell along with the rest of the department because violent crimes are off the graph. Homicides, muggings, beatings, armed robberies, fistfights, hate crimes of all kind—everything but rapes are multiplying like roaches. It's as if people got nothing better to do than pummel each other into stickum. You're my go-to guy, Dane. I need you out there."

Noah just stared at her.

"Okay, you can stay on this case, though I'm going to catch hell for it. But there's one thing."

The captain got out of her chair, walked partway around her desk and looked through the transparent partition. Noah saw something was bothering her—something she didn't want to tell him. He took the opportunity to retrieve his badge and gun. He didn't feel balanced without that weight in his shoulder holster.

"I wanted you to take a breather before you had to deal with this, but…I'm assigning you a new partner. Shut up and listen," she said, stopping him short him again. "You know the rule book as well as I. You've got to be partnered-up. And I'll tell you right now, you're not going to like this. I don't like it either. But it's not my call. This play comes straight from the booth up top. Yesterday's debacle left you a marked man. So you can either stick to the game plan or find yourself back on bike patrol."

"Hell," wondered Noah aloud, "who is this new partner, some sort of mental defective? I know. It's a troll, isn't it? I'm not working with some alien midget."

"That's not it, though I almost wish it was." Captain Raevski walked back to her chair and sat. "You remember last year's celebudroid craze?"

"Sure. All those robots made to look and act like famous dead people. They were everywhere, hired out for parties, mall openings..."

"Yes, well, the fad faded away quicker than a lame-armed quarterback. Celebuwares went bankrupt, couldn't pay its taxes, and the city came out of the scrum holding its assets."

"What in the name of Jack Daniels does that have to do with me?"

"It was in a local grid poll, didn't you see it?"

"I don't vote."

"You should. The public decided it wanted to recoup its losses and have the celebudroids retrained, or reprogrammed, I guess you'd call it, for a variety of municipal tasks. Some jerkoff bench jockey in City Hall decided to see if one of these droids could do police work."

"Don't tell me." Without taking his eyes off the captain, hoping for a telltale sign it was an elaborate gag, Noah dropped back into the chair.

"Yes. This particular droid has been reprogrammed with complete law enforcement and police academy training. It's passed all the written and physical tests."

"No."

"Now I've been ordered to take it into the squad and make it part of the team. Specifically, I've been ordered to make it *your* partner."

"No."

"I know. At first I thought it was somebody's idea of a joke, too. Now the joke's on you, Dane."

As Noah tried to harness the rather schizoid engrams running amuck in his brain, Captain Raevski did something with her desk screen. A few seconds later, there was a knock on the door.

"Enter," she said officiously.

Noah turned and saw the front view of the blonde he'd eyed before. She was every bit as impressive from this angle. Rich honey-colored hair, bedroom eyes, lacquered nails, a tiny mole on her left cheek, luscious lips—though a touch heavy with the lipstick, he thought—and an hourglass figure that cried out for a full-body inspection. She had on this one-piece all-white outfit that was belted in the middle and tight in the ass. It covered her from neck to calf and left most everything to the imagination. That was okay. He had plenty of imagination.

Then a string of cerebellic goup snapped, and he realized he'd seen this tasty pow-whammy before. It occurred to him he recognized her from several pieces of pop art he'd chanced on in some store. The realization slammed him to the mat.

"Inspector Dane," said Captain Raevski formally, "let me introduce you to your new partner, Detective Special Class Marilyn Monroe."

5

THERE'S NO BUSINESS LIKE
POLICE BUSINESS

OPERATING STRICTLY ON REFLEX, NOAH STOOD AS THE CAPTAIN INTRODUCED HIS NEW partner. He stared with dismay at the blonde bombshell who had inconveniently sauntered into his life. But it wasn't only her shrapnel he was worried about. He couldn't smell her. His impeccable proboscis always knew, but now it was sniffing up a vacuum. She didn't smell like a woman. And if he couldn't smell her, he couldn't trust her.

"A pleasure to meet you, Inspector, I'm sure," she said, holding out her hand.

Still stuck in polite mode, he reached out and took the hand, but didn't know what to do with it. It certainly felt real enough. However, the thought that it wasn't real caused him to release it rather ineptly.

"I understand Detective Monroe has been enhanced with augmented reality software," spoke up Captain Raevski, trying to disperse the awkward moment.

"What's that?" Noah asked, still unable to take his eyes from the celebudroid.

"For the love of Jerry, Dane, don't you keep up with anything? It means she has direct access to the grid within her own circuits. She can establish any link, collate data, deliver communications, even control certain systems—all while still functioning in the physical world. Is that correct, Detective Monroe?"

"It certainly is, Captain. I'm told I see a visual representation of the grid in my mind's eye. I like to think of it as my third eye." She giggled and looked at Noah.

"Great, she's got three eyes," he said, finally wrenching his gaze from her to look at Captain Raevski.

"Go ahead, Monroe," the captain said, "show him that thing you showed me."

"All right."

As soon as she said it, the grid screen on the captain's desk winked out. It came right back on, but the lights in the room flickered several times.

"See that?" the captain declared. "She can even get to our power controls."

"Captain, could I have a word with you, in private, if…*Detective* Monroe doesn't mind?"

The captain sighed. "Please wait for us outside, Detective."

"I can't wait to work with you, Inspector. I've downloaded your recent case files and it all sounds so exciting."

Noah didn't respond. He waited for her to leave and closed the door behind her.

"Don't even bother, Dane."

"Cap, she's not a detective, she's a walking pinup. She doesn't even sound like police. Did you hear the voice on her? She sounds like she should be on the *Talk Dirty To Me* link. You've got to make this go away."

"Sorry, Dane, that's the way it is. If you want to work this case, you'd better get on the same page as management. It's a whole new ballgame now." She spotted something on the wall behind Noah and reached for her zapper. "It's up to you to break her in, so to speak. Teach her the fundamentals like you would any rookie."

"Rookie? She's a grid link with tits! She's just going to get in my way."

Ignoring him, Captain Raevski's eyes tracked the downward movement of her prey. "Oh, and another thing before I forget. You're going to have to spend some time with the department theratech. Don't make me give you chapter and verse. You know it's mandatory when you, you know, lose a partner like you did. Not to mention dropping three bikeroos."

"Great! Just great. I not only have a package of pistons and plugs for a partner, I've got to be analyzed by a bucket of bolts. Do you have *good* news for me?"

"Yeah," she said, taking aim with the zapper, "the clock's ticking. It's the fourth quarter and management wants this cop killer in the bag before the final buzzer. So get your game face on and dazzle me with some fancy police work." She fired the laser, missed her target, then fired again. "Got you! In your face, you filth monger."

WITH A LOATHING JUST NORTH OF NAUSEA, NOAH STALKED OUT OF THE CAPTAIN'S OFFICE and stared at his new partner. She had a compact out and was arranging her hair, unaware half the squad was gawking at her.

"Let's go, Monroe," he growled as he whipped by her.

She stuffed the compact into an unwieldy shoulder bag and scampered after him.

"Where are we going?"

He ignored her, but increased his pace as if somehow he might lose her. It wasn't going to be that easy, though. She was right behind him when he pulled into a room off a long, dim corridor. The muted sound of Ray Charles singing "This Little Girl of Mine" added a hint of life to the room's otherwise sterile feel. Noah spotted an ebony goddess in a white lab coat and took a millisecond to admire the voluptuous form barely concealed beneath it.

"Excuse me, can you tell me where George is?"

She turned, tossing her long black locks over her shoulder with one hand. Her coat was open, and Noah stifled an exclamation when saw the ample cleavage revealed by a low-cut blouse at least two sizes too small.

"What's the matter, sugar, don't you recognize me?"

"George?"

"It's officially Georgia now." She held her arms out and spun around. "What do you think?"

Noah shed his surprise, as well as his carnal designs, and let out a quick laugh. "Well, I see the operation was a success. I didn't know you had, uh…gone in for it."

"Yes, yes, yes, sugar," she said, throwing her arms around him. "I couldn't wait."

Noah tried his best to ignore the nipples pushed against his chest, but he didn't stand a chance. So he separated himself as Georgia noticed the celebudroid behind him.

"My, my, aren't you a dish of honey and cream. Who's your friend, Noah?"

"This is…" He paused, not quite sure how to put it. "…my new partner, Marilyn Monroe."

"Marilyn Mon—"

"Don't ask," shot back Noah, cutting off the question. "Monroe, this is George…I mean Georgia Browne, the department's top forensics specialist."

"Pleased to meet you, sugar…I guess." Georgia looked from Marilyn to Noah and back again, not sure of what to make of the pair. "I'm sorry about Cy, Noah. Is that the shooter I've got in there with the three bikeroos?" she asked, motioning toward a small bank of morgue drawers.

"No, but it's his buddy. Cy nailed him before he went down. Tell me what you've got so far."

"I was just about to have some breakfast," she said, grabbing a glazed chocolate doughnut from a large box. "Want one?" Noah shook his head. "What about you, sugar?"

"Oh, no, thank you."

"Watching the calories, dear?" Georgia used her free hand to pull open one of the drawers. Noah noticed there was nothing feminine about her arms. They were still fleshed out with male muscle. "Me, I can eat all day long and not gain a pound. Just a lucky girl I guess." She pulled back the plastic sheet, and a startled Marilyn choked off an exclamation.

The faceless body, sans oozing blood, looked like what Noah remembered. He experienced a fleeting bit of grim satisfaction that the sight shook his new partner. But he had to admit, up close, after the adrenalin had stopped flowing, the mangled visage was tough to take.

"Cy hammered him good," Georgia noted, her voice taking on a more professional tone. "Death was instantaneous. He's had a print job—a good one—and what's left of his face isn't going to be much help. We've got width and shape of the lips, curvature of the ears, the pattern of one eyebrow, but not enough for the biometric ratios DIRS needs. Though you might get some images from the scene before he took that shot to the chops. By tomorrow I should have a DNA ident for you, unless he's a blank."

"I didn't notice this before," said Noah, pointing at the corpse's neck. An inch-wide tattoo of fanciful swirls, drunken dashes and other odd geometric shapes encircled his neck like a collar. "Is this some sort of gang tat?"

"If it is, it's not one I've seen before," Georgia said, taking another bite of her doughnut. "It's an unusual design. It looks like Azteca art, or maybe cuneiform."

"What's that?"

"Ancient Persian writing."

"Put a good close-up in the case file and I'll see if I can identify it."

"There's nothing else to tell you, sugar. No other physical evidence on the body that will help much. His weapon is something, though. I've never seen anything like it. A handheld laser with the capability of burning a hole through metal is definitely not standard street thug issue. I couldn't find any manufacturing codes, but it has a serial number."

"Looks military to me," Noah said. "I'll run the number past the DoD."

Georgia swallowed the last bit of pastry and began licking her fingers. "I've got the stones you found, too. Haven't had a chance to analyze them yet. Offhand, I'd say they're exactly what they look like—high-grade uncut diamonds."

Baffled by how these diverse pieces fit into any kind of puzzle, Noah scratched the spot he favored just above his sternum and turned to his partner for feedback. But instead of reliable old Cyrus, he saw this pneumatic blonde doing her best to avert her gaze from the grisly cadaver.

"So, *Detective* Monroe, do you have any thoughts on this case? Any insights you'd like to share?"

"It's awful, isn't it? I mean, to be dead like that."

"You'll get used to it, sweetie," Georgia said, pulling the plastic sheet back over the body and pushing in the drawer.

"That's it?" asked Noah with mock astonishment. "That's all you have to say? 'It's awful?' Where's all that fancy programming? Do you know anything about tattoos? What about diamonds? Do you know anything about diamonds?"

Marilyn thought a moment. "I know they're a girl's best friend."

"That's just beautiful," Noah replied with no small helping of sarcasm.

"I can grid-search diamonds, if you like."

"Yeah, you do that." He turned back to Georgia. "Do you think after you have those stones analyzed you can tell me where they came from?"

"Not likely, sugar, but I'll see what I can do."

"I could check to see if there have been any recent thefts of precious stones," offered Marilyn tentatively.

"Yeah, brilliant. Why don't you go plug yourself into the grid and do that. And while you're at it, download the IRIS so I can take a look at scene vid." She looked at him like she didn't comprehend. "You know—IRIS. The Independent Remote Identification Sentinel?"

"I'm familiar with the acronym," she responded, sounding aggrieved. "However, I don't have to go anywhere to connect with the grid. Don't you remember Captain Raevski explaining about my augmented reality link?"

"Yeah, yeah, whatever. But go anyway. Go to your desk, if you've got one, and I'll check with you later. Go, go."

"Suits me, Inspector," she replied coldly.

Noah watched her leave, and discovered his gaze fastened to her jouncing derrière. Somehow, it conjured up the image of spring-loaded Jell-O. Just looking at her made him want to grab the engineer who designed her by the lapels, shake him senseless and ask what the hell he was thinking.

"I think sweet Georgia senses a great big, fuzzy ball of sexual tension between Inspector Dane and his new partner. Want to talk about it, sugar?"

"Sexual...with that wirehead? She's a droid—a celebudroid of some cinematic ghost."

Georgia finger-flipped her hair and reached for another doughnut. "An android? I thought she was just a fetisher with a good surgeon." She changed her mind about the doughnut and instead put her hand on Noah's shoulder. "But a big, strong, sexually charged bull like you has got to have himself a way to relax." She ran her other hand down her newly shaped body. "Do you think you could ever get into this?"

"I'm, uh, not really into gender-benders."

"Are you sure?" she asked, taking hold of both shoulders now. "Variety is the spice of life—and I should know. I could make you forget all about George."

Noah eased out of her grasp and moved toward the door. "You look great," he said. "I'm happy for you and all that drudge. But I don't think I'm ready to forget George yet. Let me know as soon as you get the ident on our phantom in the box."

Once back in the corridor, he felt like he needed to sit a moment and reload. He'd had about all the mind-twisting revelations he could take for one day. But he couldn't sit. Not now. Not yet. He had to shrug them off. They were distractions. He had to concentrate on what was important—getting his hands around the neck of Cy's killer.

6

ABSTINENCE MAKES THE WORLD
GO DOWN

"...AND THEN BILLY HAD TO BLOW HIS NOSE, AND WHILE I'M TAKING CARE OF THAT, Shannon sticks her hand into the spaghetti sauce. Luckily, it wasn't hot yet. So, while I'm cleaning that mess, I hear crying from the other room. Well, it..."

Tanya was rambling on about her family again. Chastity tried to listen, to feign interest, but her producer's family exploits stirred up too many conflicting emotions. She wasn't certain whether she should be envious or repulsed.

The strange thing was, even when her anecdotes bordered on chaos, Tanya was always smiling as she relayed them. Chastity couldn't understand that. She tried, but she couldn't fathom the depths of such illogical joy. She stared at the desk videograph of Tanya's three kids, and found herself trying to imagine what it must be like for them to grow up with their mother always around.

"...I tell you, I was so happy when Will got home. After we put the kids to bed, we just cuddled for an hour."

"That's nice," Chastity replied as if punctuating her producer's narrative. "Are we ready for air? Are our guests prepared?"

"I've already spoken with them," Tanya said, shifting gears into professional mode. "I understand they had some trouble getting into the network because of the security upgrades, but I straightened it out."

"Security upgrades?"

"Yeah, because of the Loftur threat, IGN has increased security everywhere."

"I didn't notice."

"I've got to get out there and do a quick run-through with Vince. It should be a good show." She looked at her watch. "You've got about twenty before we need you on set."

Chastity was checking herself in the decorative wall mirror even before Tanya was out the door. She needed to stop by makeup for a quick fix before she went on. She turned one way, then the other, reaching down to adjust her placid-pink Candeur skirt. She fondled her purity chain as she contemplated her appearance. Her immaculately manicured fingers slid down the silver chain and idly began to play with the inverted triangle and its inner crucifix.

After a moment, she realized her mind was wandering, and put an end to it with a disgusted little shake of her head. She grabbed her notes and was on her way to makeup when she spotted Leeland approaching. As much as she tried not to, she couldn't look at him without thinking about how handsome he was. His mere presence tended to overwhelm her. He was tall, with dark, wavy hair and piercing eyes she imagined were the color of freshly blued steel. More than that, he carried himself in a way that shouted *I'm smart, I'm powerful, and I know it.* The fact he was her provisional supervisor only complicated matters.

"You're looking striking today, Chastity. Ready for another engaging show?"

"I'm ready," she gushed, pulling down on her dress. "Actually, I'm on my way to makeup."

"I don't think makeup can improve upon perfection."

"Leeland," she replied, admonishing him.

Gently, he took her by the shoulder and pulled her aside. She felt a flutter deep in her stomach as he touched her.

"Why don't we have dinner later tonight?"

"I...don't know," she said, her mind already bogged down with self-debate.

"We had a nice evening last time, didn't we?"

It had been nice. And though he'd been a perfect gentleman, Chastity knew he wanted more. More was what made her hesitate. More was wrong. It went against everything she believed in. She wasn't ready for more. She wasn't sure if she ever would be.

"I've got too much work to do."

His expression didn't change, but Chastity could see him switch gears. He wasn't the type of man to plead his case.

"All right. Some other time."

"Yes," she responded a little too quickly, "some other time."

"Have you seen the numbers today?"

A shake of her head said no.

"That new GridVid show is coming on strong."

"You mean *Bizarre del Mundo?* It's a freak show."

"Maybe so, but freaks sell. We'll keep an eye on it. Likely it'll peak soon and those boys at GV will have something new to throw at us. I'm not worried. Your point of view is ripe. The tide of cultural dynamics is flowing in your direction. It's my job to understand these trends, and it's obvious there's a growing swell of dissent, a backlash against blatant sexuality. For some time now, the viewing public has been leaning the other way—your way. Timing is what makes a show a hit...or a dud. Not that your own, irrepressible personality hasn't played a major role. Just keep it up.

"Meanwhile, I'm going to have to speak with someone about your workload." He flashed a big, fleeting smile, then sobered. "Have a good show," he said, and walked away without waiting for a response.

She half wanted to slap herself for a being a fool. The other half felt relief. IGN executive Leeland Powell was attracted to her—she'd even say intrigued—and what was her reaction? She had too much work to do. They both knew that was a lie. He was just mature enough not to call her on it. What was she waiting for?

SHE WAS STILL THINKING ABOUT LEELAND, BOTH CENSURING AND SALUTING HERSELF, AS her two guests took their seats on set and she turned her attention to them.

"I want to tell you both how much I admire you, and thank you for being on our show."

"Oh, we just love your show, Chastity, don't we, Miguel?" The petite young blonde turned to her boyfriend, who nodded in agreement.

"Oh, yeah, we never miss it."

"And we love you, too," the girl added.

"Well, thank you."

"Thirty seconds, Chastity."

"Okay, we're about to start," she told them and settled back in her chair. She noticed some movement off-set, and glanced over to see two anxious women standing there. The teenagers' mothers, no doubt, from their proud but nervous expressions.

The familiar pristine theme music came up in her IFB, and Chastity prepared her persona.

Live in ten...nine...eight...seven...six...five...four...

"Welcome, everyone, to another edition of *Gridspeak*, the true voice of the people, and a show that not only examines the wretched afflictions of society but offers valid solutions and healing hope.

"I'm Chastity Blume, and visiting with me today on *Gridspeak* are Valerie Grant and Miguel Rivera."

As she introduced them, Chastity saw the teens reach out and grab hold of each other's hands. Their fingers seemed to touch with both eagerness and reluctance.

"Valerie and Miguel are here today to talk about something that is important to them.

"What would you two like to tell our audience?"

They looked at each other and Valerie shyly deferred to Miguel.

"Uh, well, we want to tell the world that abstinence is a beautiful thing."

"Explain to everyone out there what you mean by abstinence, Miguel."

"Uhmm, well, even though we love each other, we believe, Valerie and me, that we shouldn't have sex until after we're married."

"And then only to make babies," Valerie interjected.

"Right." Miguel looked at her and went on. "We just don't think sex is that important."

"Tell us, Valerie, why do you and Miguel feel this way?"

The young girl shifted in her seat. "I think—we think—that our love is more pure, more spiritual without all that nasty...well, you know. And we think everyone, especially other teenagers, should know about this. So that's why we're here—to tell them."

"You travel all around the country spreading your message, don't you?"

They both nodded.

"We also visit nursing homes to, you know, cheer them up," said Miguel.

"We do other things too," Valerie added, "like reading stories to little kids as part of our church's literacy program."

"So, you both believe that abstinence makes you more productive, more spiritually concerned citizens?"

"Yes...Yes, it definitely does."

Chastity wondered at how they seemed so sure of themselves. They were such innocents, like she was once. She could see herself in Valerie. Only she'd never been so certain, or so pure.

"I think what you two are doing is absolutely wonderful. You're sincere, solid role models for the youth of this country—for the youth of the entire world.

"We're going to take a short break now, but when we come back, we're going to ask Valerie and Miguel about kissing and touching. What they do, what they don't do, and why. Please stay linked, we'll be right back."

"You're watching *Gridspeak with Chastity Blume*, brought to you by V-Real. Get real with V-Real. It's better than chocolate.

"Be sure to link in to *Gridspeak* next week, when Chastity examines a topic close to us all, in her special series *Masturbation: Gentle Delusion or Crisis of Misconception*. That's next week on *Gridspeak*. Chastity Blume will return in ninety seconds."

7

A SNIP IN TIME

NOAH HAD MANAGED TO AVOID HIS NEW PARTNER FOR MOST OF HER FIRST DAY, BUT NO doubt she'd be waiting for him this morning. Did she even leave the station? Did they give her a room somewhere? A closet? Did she even need to sleep?

He didn't know, and he didn't care. He'd already decided he wasn't going to let her bother him. She could act like his partner all she wanted. He was going about business as usual. Nothing was going to get in his way—nothing was going to slow him down.

He started up the Hall of Justice steps but stopped when he spotted Snip sitting across the street in her usual spot, still half-tucked into the thermal bag he'd given her. She saw him coming and freed up a rare, if brief, smile.

The poor little defective had been on her own ever since she escaped from wherever it was they'd bungled her creation. Her face was a juxtaposition of opposites, with the distorted mongoloid features and missing ear of her right side clashing with the pixie-cute adolescent on the left—a pitiful but prime example of why human cloning had been outlawed almost a decade ago.

Her genetically flawed half had only four fingers and four toes, and she was missing a breast as well. She sported a ragged, partially graying Mohawk Noah believed was a futile attempt to draw attention away from her imperfections.

"What's the sliggy, PD man?" she called to him as she worked her wiry little frame out of the bag and stood. Her clothes were wrinkled and stained.

"What are you doing sleeping out here, Snip? I thought you were going to stay at the shelter."

Still a dozen feet away from her, he was hit by a wall of foul odor. There were times that sniffer of his wasn't a good thing.

"Only take so much preaching, singing and praying. It's drudge. 'Sides, I like loning it. Don't need nobody else. Regular folks don't care for me—I don't care for them."

Noah didn't believe she really liked being alone, but he wasn't about to say anything that would mess with her acquired defenses.

"You know, you could really use a bath. Why don't you at least go back there long enough to clean up. You can always leave again."

"S'matter? I don't perfume up like your regular pow-whammy? I can bath…you bath with me."

She was always flirting with him like that, but she was just a kid—a kid he tried to look out for. She reminded him of Cat, in a way. For all he knew, his daughter was out sleeping on a street somewhere right now.

"Lay off that, Snip. You know we're friends."

"Could be friendlier. Could be some fun."

She liked to tease him, but he knew when she hung out around the PD it meant one thing.

"Are you hungry?" he asked.

"Cheeseburger with extra picks?"

"For breakfast? Sure, let's do it."

"Crucial."

As they headed for the nearby Smokey Joe franchise, Snip put her hand in his. He knew she craved whatever affection she could get, not ever having any to speak of. But he didn't have much to give, so he looked out for her, made sure the other badges did the same and bought her a burger now and then.

"Gots to warn you," she said conspiratorially. "Streetword says Blue Scorps painting a target on your head. Pissing acid, they is. Guess you clipped their tails, somehow. Better keep low, stick to the shadows."

"Thanks for the warning, Snip, but I'm not going to sweat beads over a bunch of bikeroos."

The woman inside the kiosk was in mid-conversation with another customer, so Noah waited, listening but not paying attention. He was anxious to get back to work—back on the trail of his partner's killer.

"…not that I mind that much," said the customer as she stated her name and placed her hand on the idisk to pay her tab. "It's just so strange that my Hank doesn't want it anymore, because he always wants it. I mean, before this, I couldn't keep his hands off me."

Noah spotted his reflection in the mirrored wall behind the counter and realized he was staring at his hairline. Damn thing was receding more every day.

"I don't know what to tell you, Liz. Men get that way sometimes." The server turned to Noah, but then noticed the street clone behind him. "You can't be in here," she said, throwing her arm out as if to shoo Snip away. "Go on, get out before I—"

"She's with me," Noah said firmly, reinforcing the statement with a stare that meant even more.

"Oh," was all she said. She gave Snip another disapproving look then responded coolly, "What can I get you?"

Snip pushed in front of Noah and made a point of slapping both of her unwashed hands onto the counter. Her rheumy eyes stared razors.

"You gots cow milk?" she asked the server.

"Yes, we do."

"I don't want any milk," Snip said, turning away from the counter.

The server glowered at her until Noah stepped forward.

"I want you to give this girl your biggest cheeseburger with lots of extra pickles, and one of those large bottled waters." He put his own hand on the idisk and voiced his name as the server diffidently turned to fill the order. "I've got to get going, Snip."

"Sure, you gots to slither on. I'm tiptop," she said with exaggeration.

Noah knew her bluster was a well-honed act.

"You take care of yourself, and give that shelter another try."

"No drudge on you, PD man. I'm tiptop and ready to shop. You keep eyes back of your head."

Her concern for him was a role reversal he wasn't used to, but you didn't need eyes in the back of your head if you weren't planning on turning around.

INSIDE THE SQUADROOM, MONROE STOOD OUT LIKE A BEST-OF-SHOW POODLE IN A PIT BULL arena. When he saw she was sitting at Cy's old desk, Noah had to turn around and take a deep breath. He wasn't going to let this pseudo tail get to him. He had a job to do.

He didn't know if she'd spent the night here or not, but she'd changed her outfit. The change hadn't made her look any more like police. In fact, to Noah, she couldn't have looked any prissier. She had on a tight little kelly-green skirt and a matching jacket, topped off with a white beret he thought made her look like some kind of amusement park guide.

He made it to his desk, and she looked up as though she expected him at that very moment.

"Good morning, Inspector Dane. It's such a yummy day, isn't it? I just love days like this, after the rain when the sun first comes out. It's just dreamy."

"Look, you can call me Noah or you can call me Dane, but knock off that 'inspector' drudge, all right?"

"Sure, well, gee, if that's what you'd like. If you don't mind, I'll call you Noah. Just 'Dane' seems so impersonal—so plain. I think Noah has a nice ring to it. I could—"

"Anything new on the case?" he asked, successfully punctuating her ramble. He activated his screen. "What have you got for me on the diamonds?"

"I've finished my grid search and catalogued the analysis. I can now answer any questions you may have regarding diamonds and other precious stones."

"Any heists?"

"There have been no reports of any diamond thefts in the city or its surrounding regions over the last six months. Do you want me to increase the parameters of my search?"

"No, we're looking for something recent. But if they weren't stolen, where did those street thugs get the rocks?" he asked, talking more to himself than to his proxy partner. "Could they have been ripped-off from some industrial stockpile without anyone realizing it yet?"

"That's very unlikely, Inspector—I mean, Noah. Security for industrial-grade diamonds is very rigorous."

It was one thing to have to look at this sexed-up droid, but even her voice was getting to him.

"Do you have some kind of respiratory problem?"

"Whatever do you mean?"

"I mean, do you have to talk like that?"

"Talk like what?"

"The way you talk, all breathy, like you aren't getting enough air."

"That's silly. I simply don't know what to tell you about that. My vocal intonations are built into my system, and reinforced through the use of archival films and interview clips."

"Films?"

"Sure. Much of my primary programming included exposure to all known cinematic and documentary video files of the original Marilyn Monroe. Everything that's recorded about her, every line of dialogue she ever spoke, is a part of me. I am her, to the extent of what was known about her. My voice is her voice."

"All right. If you say so."

A flashing icon alerted Noah to an incoming message. He pulled it up fullscreen and saw the smiling face of George—Georgia, he corrected himself.

"Hi, sugar. I've got the ident on your faceless phantom."

"Who is he?"

"Born one Timothy Lee Huang. He's got no criminal record—not much of any personal record, either. His grid account shows an address, but I can't promise it's current."

"Good work."

"Good enough for a kiss?" Georgia puckered up and closed her eyes.

"No, but you can go with me—" Noah checked himself, looking up at his partner. "…with us to check out that address. Meet us at the pod launch in ten."

"Just give me time to powder my nose and buff my bouffant, sugar."

BETWEEN HIS FLASHY BLONDE PARTNER AND HIS FORENSICS SPECIALIST IN HER MINISKIRT and gold lame top, Noah conjectured he resembled some rube going upstairs with a pair of hookers. It didn't help that this hovel looked like the kind of building that would attract such activity. In fact, the morgue was a step up for this Huang guy.

Trash littered the hallways, graffiti splashed the walls, and a population of creepy-crawling squatters that would have drained Captain Raevski's zapper appeared to have the run of the place. However, for some reason, the guy had bioscan security on his door. Unusual for such a dump. Noah wondered what he was trying to protect.

"I'm afraid the PD override isn't linking up with this old model biolock," Georgia said after several attempts to open the door.

"Don't be discouraged. I'll do a grid search for the building's owner," Marilyn suggested. "Maybe we can locate a building superintendent to—"

As she spoke, Noah stepped in front of the door, leaned back and kicked it. The door jamb shattered into splinters, and the door cracked as it flew back on its hinges.

"Oh, sugar, don't spend all that testosterone in one place."

Noah had his gun out as he entered the room but promptly holstered it. There wasn't much to see—a bed, a chair, a beat-up dresser and a tiny wallscreen that looked inoperative. There was a bathroom and a small closet, but no other rooms, and only a two-by-two sealed window. Like the hall outside, the place was a sty. It stank so atrociously his nostrils burned.

"What is that odor? Do you smell it?"

"Well, it's not my Ricardo Andante, I can tell you that," Georgia said, opening her forensics case.

"I can't smell anything," replied Marilyn.

"You're kidding, right?"

"No, honest," she answered, making a sniffing noise to prove her point, "I don't have a sense of smell. No sense of taste, either—of course, I don't eat—and only limited tactile sensations. I guess my designers didn't think they were necessary."

"'Jectures," Noah grumbled. "You're lucky you don't smell this. I'm stepping out for some air. I'll check with the neighbors, find out if any of them have seen this guy. You and Georgia find what you can in this dump."

"I'll turn my little dustbunnies loose and see what they can suck up," Georgia said as she placed a pair of evidence-gathering autovacs on the floor and activated them. They scurried off in different directions, one moving east and west, the other north and south, hovering on a cushion of air an inch above the floor, collecting for analysis every trace of skin flake, hair and dehydrated spittle they could find.

There weren't any neighbors, or at least any who'd answer their doors. Noah didn't blame them—not in a place like this. Downstairs, he looked outside and saw the wind was blowing good. It was starting to rain. It looked like another big storm coming through. He shivered involuntarily and felt the goose bumps spread across his hairy arms like a virus. He moved back away from the entrance and tried to shake loose from the reaction he so despised.

Sometimes he controlled it better than others. This time it seized hold of him with wrathful intensity. He had to concentrate on something else.

It occurred to him he hadn't checked with Sheila to see if Cat had gone home. Of course, if she had, she certainly would have been identified by DIRS and he would have been notified. Still, he 'jectured he'd better check in with Sheila.

The look on her face, as tiny as it displayed on his pad, told him everything he needed to know.

"Why haven't you called me?" she scolded. "Catherine hasn't come home. I couldn't link with your pad but I left messages. Where have you been? What are you doing about Catherine? What if something's happened to her?"

Noah had long ago registered a block-out on his pad so she couldn't link in and annoy him.

"I've been working a case, and you know as well as I do that Cat's run off with some friends. DIRS is searching for her, and when she bioscans anywhere, which she'll have to do eventually, we'll find her. If there was anything else I could do, you know I would."

Sheila's expression softened. "What am I going to do with her, Noah?" She sounded close to tears.

"You'll do what you've always done—the best you can. When we find her, I'll talk to her. Don't worry. I've got to go, Sheila. I'll keep in touch—I promise."

He looked up from terminating the link and saw Marilyn and Georgia descending the stairs.

"Anything?" he asked, clearing his throat.

"A couple of empty jazz juice vials and this." Georgia held up a holocard ID. "An employee security badge from the V-Real Corporation. I've got some fiber, mineral and hair samples I'm taking in for further analysis, but I doubt there's anything here to get hot about, sugar." She finger-flipped her hair over her shoulder and dropped the badge into her bag.

"Analyze away. I want to talk to someone who knew him. Doesn't V-Real have some kind of corporate headquarters in town? Or is it just a factory?"

Marilyn paused a moment before answering. "I've got it. The address for the V-Real Corporation is 769 Vallejo Street."

"Isn't that in Chinatown, sugar?"

"Used to be," Noah replied. "Now it's part of Trolltown."

"Trolltown?" wondered Marilyn. "I'm finding references to that name, but no officially designated district."

"It's Trolltown, Monroe, take my word for it. Let's get out of here."

They could hear the rain even before they reached the entrance. A boom sounded in the distance and Noah pulled up short of the doorway.

"Was that thunder?"

"It sounds like it's still far off, sugar."

Noah stepped out to the edge of the rain and stood there.

"Forget something?" asked Georgia, wondering why he had stopped.

He didn't hear her. He was in his own little space right then, bracing himself, gathering his courage. He could do it, he knew he could. It was just rain—just water. He didn't see any lightning. He could make it.

"Inspector Dane?"

His new partner was eyeballing him. He had to go.

"Noah?"

He was ready. He should go now—right now. Ignoring his own inner commands, he hesitated then took off running, straight for the pod.

8

DAVID, DADDY AND THE BEAVER

A S THE CAR ROUNDED THE CORNER AND SHE CAUGHT SIGHT OF HER BUILDING, SHE LET
out a sigh. It was a relief to be home.

The towering glass structure used to be her window to the world, but since celebrity had crept up to her doorstep she'd opted to keep her windows opaque. She couldn't wait to relax in her sanctuary, away from the demands of the show, the obsessive fans who craved pieces of her—any pieces—and the men who ogled her and whispered behind her back.

She knew what they were saying. She knew what they were thinking when they looked at her. She knew what they all called her—her fans and detractors alike. She should have found it appropriate and endearing. She should have savored it. Yet she didn't—she couldn't. She knew the truth of it, and the truth kept her contrite. Image was one thing, reality was another.

She opened the door before the driver could, thanked him and climbed the steps to the entrance under his watchful eye. She laid her palm flat on the illuminated idisk, stated her name and looked into the lens affixed above the entrance. The door opened, and she offered a cursory wave to the guard in the elevated booth.

Someone was coming down the entry corridor toward her, and her feeling of relief curled into a fetal fist. When she realized it was David, she relaxed again. The building's maintenance man was the nicest guy she knew. He was a bit withdrawn, but always friendly with her, his expression festooned with a perpetual smile. He was pushing his bike—probably headed home for the evening.

"Hello, Ms Blume. How are you tonight?"

He stopped as Chastity approached. He was so much taller than her, she had to look up. He was a big-boned man, but with small features that conveyed a kind of suppressed longing. Chastity was particularly drawn to his large hands. She often caught herself staring at them. Long, thick fingers, as dark as chocolate. The fingers of one hand were wrapped around a book. Though he never gave the impression of being well-educated, he always seemed to be reading something.

"I saw your show. It was a good program. You looked real good."

"Thanks, David. I'm always nervous before a show, so I never know how I look."

"You sure don't look nervous. You looked real nice."

"What are you reading there?"

He glanced at the book he was holding. "It's called *Of Mice and Men*. I just started it."

"I've read it. I think you'll like it."

"I don't know—it's different from what I'm used to. I usually like to read, you know, fantasy stories."

"Well, give it a chance."

"I will. But I have to get going. My mom is expecting me."

"How's she doing?"

"You know," he said, looking at the floor, "she has her good days and her bad days. She needs help with lots of things."

"She's lucky to have a son like you who takes care of her."

David looked at her and smiled. "I like to help. But I better get going now."

"Goodbye."

Watching him mount the bike and pedal through the door, Chastity felt a brief surge of envy. David was off to see his mother, to take care of her. The simplicity of it was bliss.

SHE'D BARELY HAD A CHANCE TO CLOSE THE DOOR AND PROMPT THE SECURITY NODE WHEN Angel greeted her with an accusing *merrow*.

"Did you miss Mommy?" Chastity inquired, bending down to stroke the snow-white fur. "I think you just want to be fed. Suzette, does Angel need food?"

"Its receptacle is empty, Ms Blume," answered the penthouse's homeminder. "Would you like me to feed the cat?"

"No, I'll do it myself."

Affectionately, Angel pummeled Chastity's legs as she prepared her meal, but deserted her as soon as the feast was laid out. Chastity started undoing her dress, but reconsidered.

"Suzette, would you activate my kitchen screen, please."

The homeminder complied, and the screen came alive. Chastity reached for it then hesitated, her hand hovering in the air like a reluctant hummingbird. With a resigned shrug of her shoulders she touched the screen and designated her father's office link.

She'd given up trying to contact him at home. It seemed he was never there—or simply never responded to calls there. She waited, nervously tugging down on her dress.

When his dour countenance appeared on the screen, she tried to mask her surprise. His response to recognizing her was a familiar frown.

"Father, how are you?"

"I'm busy, Chastity. What do you want?"

"I've been wanting to talk with you—to ask you something. I thought if—"

"I can't talk now. I have someone in my office. We'll talk later."

With that he severed the link, leaving Chastity staring at her tropical beach default image and wondering about her father. He'd never been a person she'd described as genial, yet lately he'd undergone a change. He was more withdrawn, more sullen than usual. Whatever it was that was bothering him, it was unlikely he'd share it with her. They didn't have that kind of relationship.

He'd always been driven—so much so that she rarely saw him as she was growing up. She was raised by a succession of nannies and chaperones. Their faces were a parade of interchangeable images. It had always seemed that just as she began to trust and enjoy the company of one of her caretakers that person was replaced. It had made for a lonely childhood, but one she'd adapted to.

Still deep in thought, she wandered into her closet and undressed. She took off everything but the triangular medallion around her neck and put on a robe. Once back in the expanse of her sitting room, she fell into her lounge chair and took a piece of chocolate from the candy dish. Its sweet essence had a calming effect on her. She took another and picked up the book she'd been reading—*The Rapture of Celibacy* by Dr. Rebekah Redstone.

"Please adjust the lighting so I can read here, Suzette."

"Certainly, Ms Blume."

"Thank you, Suzette."

The high minister looked extraordinarily beautiful in the photograph on the book's back cover. Not that she wasn't. Despite her usual modest demeanor, Minister Redstone was a stunning woman with fantastic cheekbones and the most exquisite long raven-black hair Chastity had ever seen. She wondered if Redstone had written the book before or after she'd become high minister.

She tried to read, but her mind kept wandering. After several failed attempts to immerse herself in the philosophical jargon, she gave up, put the book down and picked up another piece of candy.

"Suzette, would you activate the main grid screen and access my sitcom collection?"

"Having trouble reading, Ms Blume?"

"Yes. I guess I'm too tired."

"I know how much you love your vintage comedies. I'm sure you'll enjoy watching them. Which show would you like to start with?"

She didn't even feel like making a choice, but maybe *Leave It To Beaver* would straighten out the tangled web of introspection that preoccupied her.

"Any episode of *Leave It To Beaver*, Suzette. You decide."

9

WHAT GOES UP...

NOAH TOOK OFF HIS COAT AND DRAPED IT OVER THE BACK OF HIS CHAIR BEFORE SITTING. He wrapped his woolly arms behind his head and stretched. The stress kinks in his back served as a reminder.

It had been sixty-three hours. Sixty-three hours since Cy had been taken out. And what did he have? He had drudge. He needed to kick himself into gear, get this case moving.

"Dane, I got a message for you."

It was Harper, Brunelli's partner. Noah felt sorry for him on that score, because he was new and seemed like a good guy. It wasn't his fault he got partnered-up with a genetic aberration.

"Damn, Dane," he said, looking at Noah's holstered weapon, "you still using that antique?"

Noah pulled out his gun and brandished it for effect. "You can keep your tasers, your lasers, your phasers, your sonic stunners—I'll stick with my Desert Eagle."

"What the hell is that, a .44?"

"Hmmph," Noah sniffed as if he'd been insulted. "This is a .50-caliber Mark XIX."

"Don't you think that cannon's a bit of overkill?" Even has he said it, Harper was admiring the weapon.

"Harper, you'll find out after you've been out there a while, you can never have too much firepower," Noah said, reholstering the gun. "Besides, the sound alone scares the crap out of the bad guys."

Harper laughed.

"You know, they're talking about restricting us to using only stunners."

Noah harumphed. "That's the day I toss my badge in the recycler and go home to my bougainvilleas. So, what's this message you've got?"

"Captain Raevski had to leave, and she was afraid you wouldn't check your date file. She wanted me to remind you about your appointment this morning with the theratech."

"Going to get your screws tightened?" It was Brunelli, smiling like he'd won the grid lotto.

Noah didn't bother looking at him. "Blow it out your ass, Brunelli, then maybe someone will listen."

"Let's go, Harper," Brunelli growled, his upper lip twitching. He walked away then turned, grinning. "Tell me, Dane, have you pushed your new partner's buttons yet? A little motor oil and you're in business, right?"

Normally, he would have torn into the little miscreant, one way or another, but he wasn't in the mood. He kept his head down and sucked it up. He had higher priorities than that anus pucker.

"He was talking about me, wasn't he?" Monroe appeared next to him, frowning in the direction of the departing Brunelli. Noah opened his mouth to speak but was distracted by her get-up. She had on this tight red sweater, a white pleated skirt and scarlet pumps. Add the white scarf tied casually around her neck, and she looked like she was ready for a ride in the country.

"Forget it. We've got work to do," he grumbled. "Show me what we got from IRIS."

Marilyn worked her hand across his screen as though she'd been doing it all her life—which Noah realized wasn't all that long. Still, she knew exactly how to call up the video she had already collated and edited at his request. He allowed himself a grunt of surprise then focused on the video.

The relevant action had been plentiful and dispersed over a wide area, but the remote sentinel had managed to record most of it by flying to a higher elevation. It was a simple enough matter to zoom down on the various scenes—a detail his new partner had already taken care of. But only one frame interested him.

"Give me a close-up on the shooter that burned Cyrus."

She made a few more adjustments to the pixelator, filtered the distortion and adjusted the resolution until the picture was clear. It didn't mean anything to him, though. He'd never seen the face before. But now he'd never forget it.

"We need to run this through the database."

"I've already done that," said Marilyn. "His face isn't on file. I hope you don't mind, I also went ahead and put out an alert with the Digital Imaging Recognition System."

"Why would I mind? DIRS is proper procedure, isn't it?" he growled, upset but not all that surprised his suspect was a blank.

"Look here, there's something else." She zoomed in on a tiny area above the suspect's collar and adjusted the resolution some more.

"A tattoo?" wondered Noah.

"I can't say for sure. That's the best picture we can get. But it could be the same as the one on Huang's neck."

"All right, we've got a face but no name, so we're going back to basics. The first thing you need to learn is that you can't count on machines to do your police work for you." She didn't react, she just looked at him. He realized what he'd said. "You, uh…know what I mean.

"Anyway, what would you say our next step is, *Detective* Monroe?"

"Well, we have a connection through our deceased shooter with the V-Real Corporation. I think we should follow up by speaking to them," Marilyn replied stiffly. "And, by the way, I prefer that you not refer to me as 'detective' if you are going to take that snide tone of voice that says you don't really think I *am* a detective. I'm not stupid, you know. And I do have feelings."

"Feelings?" Noah found that more implausible than her actually being his partner.

"Sure. The complex molecular-chemical reactions of my biochips allow for a full range of emotions."

"Okay, whatever you say. Right now we need—"

A message alert chimed from his screen, and Noah accessed it. It was a reminder from the adminisphere about his imminent appointment with the theratech. Raevski wasn't about to let him forget.

"We're going to have to hold off on that while I take care of this drudge, Monroe. Why don't you spend the time looking for anything on this Timothy Huang and collect an overview on V-Real in case we need background. Also, do a search of all the digital imaging systems in the surrounding areas, and see if you can find out anything about the previous movements of Huang and his pal. Maybe we can backtrack them. That should keep you busy."

"Of course," she replied brusquely and returned to her own desk.

"Feelings, huh?" Noah mumbled to himself as he noticed the attitude in her walk. *Maybe she's the one who should get shrinkwrapped by the theratech.*

IT WAS LESS THAN A ROOM, MORE THAN A BOOTH. ONCE HE GOT INSIDE HE REALIZED IT WAS only a bee-sneeze larger than the videograph kiosks he'd sat in to make funny faces as a kid. Had he been prone to claustrophobia he might have had trouble breathing. As it was, his neck itched, and he could smell the perspiration of the previous occupant.

As soon as he sat in the thickly cushioned pseudo-leather chair, the display in front of him activated and the chair tilted back at a slight angle. The screen projected a product logo with a message superimposed over it.

THIS THERATECH SESSION IS SPONSORED BY NEW PHASE III.
REMEMBER, A PHASE A DAY KEEPS THE DOLDRUMS AWAY.

The commercial catchphrase and its attendant logo were replaced by an efficient-looking older woman who glanced up at him from her prop desk.

"Please identify," she instructed matter-of-factly.

He rested his hand on the built-in idisk. "Noah Dane."

It took only seconds for his identity to be confirmed.

"Inspector Noah no-middle-name Dane, badge number three-six-nine. You are four minutes late for your appointment," responded the secretarial image.

"I can leave if you'd like to move on to your next case," he said, showing his willingness to rise from the chair.

"Your session will proceed as scheduled. I am required to advise you that doctor-patient confidentiality is applicable to your session, excluding any responses that fall under Section Eight of the state medical code. Now, would you prefer a male analyst or a female?"

"I always go with the female of the species," he responded flippantly.

The screen went dark for a moment and then reactivated, displaying a new face. It was a professional-looking face—a woman wearing a modest indigo pantsuit, her lackluster brunette hair tied up in a bun. Not especially attractive, but with potential, thought Noah. Definitely not the same representation he'd seen the last time he was here. The display had been upgraded, but he reminded himself it was still a machine, not a real person. The model hired for the video representations and vocal intonations didn't know any more about theranalysis than he did. She was just someone they used to humanize the circuits behind the screen, the programming that would do the real head-shrinking. He wasn't about to let it fool him, or mess with his mind.

"Good morning, Inspector Dane. Do you mind if I call you Noah?"

"Call me whatever you want."

"Good."

"What'll I call you?"

"You may refer to me as Doctor, or, if you prefer, I can provide you with a listing of names to choose—"

"How about if I call you Gertrude?"

"If that's what you'd like, Noah, that would be acceptable. Tell me, was your mother's name Gertrude?"

"No," replied Noah with no small amount of irritation, "her name was Jane. Her stage name was Velvet. I thought this was supposed to be a sophisticated program. But here you are, going right for my mother. What could my mother possibly have to do with this?"

"Nothing, really, Noah. I was only attempting to make conversation. However, your reaction leads me to believe we should consider pursuing the matter further."

"Believe me, my mother has nothing to do with why I'm here, so let's get on with it. I've got a case to solve."

"Yes. I believe the case concerns the suspect who killed your partner."

"You don't believe—you know it does," retorted Noah, not bothering to disguise his resentment. "My files have been accessed by your program. You know everything about me down to the last time I scratched my balls, so don't pretend you don't."

The theratech hesitated a moment before responding.

"I don't believe such hostility will prove to be constructive, Noah. I think it would be best if you were to disregard my actual state of being. Free yourself from it and try to think of me as Gertrude—someone who just wants to help."

He relaxed back into his seat. "Sure, whatever you say, Gertie. Standard obtuse procedure. Go ahead. I want to get this over with."

"How do you feel about the three suspects you killed?"

"I don't feel anything. They were street scum—bikeroos who chose to live on the razor's edge. They were trying to turn me and my partner into mulch. They got what they deserved. Next subject."

"You feel no remorse for their deaths?"

"None, zero, nada, bupkis."

"I see."

He watched the theratech image's lips move, and its facial expressions change, but he knew no real emotion existed behind that face. It didn't care about him. It couldn't care. What's more, he couldn't smell it. If he couldn't smell it, he wasn't about to trust it.

"How are you dealing with Cyrus's death?"

"How do you think? I was there, I saw him go down."

"How did it make you feel?"

"Feel? I was his partner, his friend. I should have…"

"You should have what?"

"I should have been there for him. I should have protected him. I should have been the one to…"

"You should have been the one to die?"

Noah didn't respond. He wasn't about to open that psychoanalytical door.

"So, you feel a sense of guilt over your partner's death."

"Of course, I do!" he said, slamming his fist onto the upholstered armrest. "That's what happens when your partner goes down. Any real police would feel the same."

"Yes, I'm sure they would," consoled the theratech. "What would you tell Cyrus if you could talk to him right now?"

"What would I tell him? You're kidding, right? What could I tell him? Keep your ass down next time? What a stupid fucking question that is."

"I think it's important, Noah, that we attempt to conduct these sessions in a constructive manner."

"What do you mean sessions? You're not saying I have to come back here again?"

"Yes, that's going to be my recommendation to your superior officer. I believe there are some issues you need to work out. However, as long as you keep your appointments, I'm going to allow you to remain on active duty."

"*You're* going to allow me?"

"Yes. At this time, I feel you are no danger to yourself or your fellow officers."

"Gee, thanks for that. Just how many more sessions are we talking about?"

"That's difficult to say, Noah. We'll have to see what kind of progress we make."

"I got your progress right here," he mumbled under his breath as he grabbed his crotch.

"I'm afraid I couldn't hear that, Noah. Could you speak up please?"

"It was nothing. Just readjusting the equipment, Gertie."

"I'm afraid the time allowed for this session has elapsed." Noah's seat resumed its original angle. "Please confer with your supervisor and then be certain to schedule another appointment within the week."

"What if I'm busy working this case and forget."

"Automated reminders will be transmitted. If you fail to appear for a session within the allotted time, your official and personal identifications will be suspended, thereby—"

"I know what happens then," he said, standing. "I guess I'll be interfacing with you again soon, Gertie."

NOAH DECIDED TO FOREGO THE ELEVATOR AND HEADED FOR THE STAIRS—HE FELT THE need to work off an excess of frustration. A brisk jaunt down five flights would clear away the drudge and get his mind breathing right again.

"Hey, there, marathon man. Where are you going without even saying hi?"

Noah recognized the voice even before he turned. It was Heather, a sizzling pow-whammy he'd shared a shudder with on more than one occasion. She had the pouting lips of a porn starlet but the forlorn eyes of a lost puppy. She was gorgeous, bright enough to work with the DA and, as far as he could tell, insatiable. As she approached him, it was as plain as the swivel of her hips she had one thing on her mind.

"Where have you been hiding yourself, Inspector?"

Before she got within ten feet he smelled that wonderful perfume she always wore, and like Pavlov's dog, he came to attention.

"I haven't seen you since—well, let's see, since that night on my terrace."

"It's always good to see you, Heather." As if to reinforce his compliment, his gaze devoured her. She noticed and seemed to appreciate it.

"I heard about Cyrus. I'm so sorry."

"Yeah," he replied, not wanting to encourage the subject.

"I'm sure it's got you down," she added. "I wish there was something I could do to make you feel better."

Noah knew what she had in mind.

"Why don't we go into my office and discuss it?"

"I don't know, Heather," he said with uncustomary reluctance. "I've got to get back to work."

"Just for a few minutes," she pleaded. "It'll give you a whole new outlook on your day."

"Well..."

Normally, he wouldn't have thought twice, but his mind was on the case, on Cyrus, on a dozen different things. However, he soon became aware he was inside Heather's office, with his lips locked on hers and one hand full of soft tit. Heather moaned loud enough to be heard out in the corridor and began tearing off her own clothes. She was halfway there when Noah turned her around and grabbed hold of both breasts from behind as his tongue did a dance across her back. She was squirming in a near frenzy already, her ass grinding back against him.

Only his reaction wasn't what it should have been. He realized his resolve was less than firm, and for some reason, that made him think of Cyrus. He flashed on the memory of his partner sitting in the pod, saying "Someday that salami of yours is going to get you into serious trouble." The memory had an even more debilitating effect.

With a look of perplexed concern on her face, Heather turned in his arms, gave him one of those you're-mine-right-now-and-nobody-else's kisses. Noah tried to delete the image of Cyrus from his mind and concentrate on the incredibly juiced pow-whammy right in front of him, but even the effort felt foreign to him. Heather broke the kiss, briefly stared into his eyes then descended to her knees, undoing his pants as she went.

She seems determined, thought Noah, as he relaxed and gave in to the mounting sensations.

10

CHASTITY GIVES GOOD GRID

I KNOW YOU'RE NOT PARTIAL TO THIS ASPECT OF THE BUSINESS, BUT I NEED YOU TO SMILE and make nice with these people," Leeland instructed as he guided her through the immense structure. Workers, a good many of them Troloxians, went about their business all around them. "It's no big deal. Right now you're better grid than night flames, so the time they're buying is worth every centavo. But they're our biggest sponsors—they're *your* biggest sponsor, so let's put on our kissy faces for ten minutes and we'll be out of there."

"I can handle it," Chastity replied. "Like you say, it's part of the business. I can do my job."

She wasn't too worried about the meeting with the V-Real executives. She didn't think Leeland was, either. He knew V-Real was a division of the Lucidity Corporation, whose founder and majority owner was her father. She figured Leeland assumed that was why they had become the primary sponsor of her show. She doubted it. Her father was not a fan of her celebrity. He'd come to accept it, but she was certain he wouldn't go out of his way to promote it.

"You look great. You'll knock them out."

As if on cue, she adjusted her soft-yellow skirt, pulling it down at the hips.

Leeland changed his tone and slyly inquired, "Did you finish all of your work last night?"

"As a matter of fact, I did," she answered impassively.

"Maybe then we can...oh, we're here."

An assistant lackey in a smart suit stood as they entered the outer office.

"Mr. Powell, Ms Blume, Mr. O'Toole is in a meeting. I'm sure it'll just be a minute." He disappeared into the inner office, but in less time than promised was holding the door open for them. "Please, come in."

Three men and one woman were sitting inside. All wore the same model of V-Real visors she'd seen so many people wearing lately. Trying out a new program, she guessed.

"Mr. O'Toole, Ms Chastity Blume and Mr. Leeland Powell."

As soon as they were announced, the quartet removed their visors and stood to greet them.

"Ms Blume, Mr. Powell, welcome to V-Real." The oldest of the four, whom she assumed was O'Toole, the company's chief executive, shook Leeland's hand and took hers lightly. "It's so nice to finally meet you, Ms Blume. I'm a big fan of your show."

"Thank you, Mr. O'Toole."

"Call me Jack, please."

"All right, Jack," she said as he released her hand. "Then you'll have to call me Chastity."

"Fine! Let me introduce everyone."

As he made the introductions, Chastity noted their names, designated a certain phrase to each one to remember them by association—a technique she found worked for her. But she noticed something else, something unusual. They all were pleasant enough, but the three men didn't look at her. Not like men usually looked at her. She found it refreshing, if a bit odd.

Even when they were doing their best to be polite, men looked at her in a specific way—at least the heterosexual variety. It was the way their eyes would dart about, expeditiously focusing on her various attributes. It was possible all three preferred boys to girls but unlikely.

Once the introductions were over, she spoke up. "I want to thank you all for allowing me to do my show here at V-Real today."

"Not at all," O'Toole assured her. "We're honored to have you here. We've been looking forward to it. Not to mention it's great publicity."

Everyone laughed. Chastity contrived a smile.

"I also wanted to thank you for arranging for me to interview Mr. Kess," she said. "I know that most Troloxians shun any notoriety."

"You'll find Mr. Kess exceptionally outgoing and eloquent for a Troloxian," said the woman whom Chastity had designated gargle-and-ski because her last name was Garganski. "He's really quite interesting, and an excellent representative of the Troloxian people."

"I look forward to meeting him. I know that V-Real employs many Troloxians, both in the factory here_and elsewhere. What is Mr. Kess's position?"

O'Toole cleared his throat and responded, "He has many responsibilities. He's one of our vice-presidents, and the de facto foreman of the factory, but his duties here encompass quite a number of tasks. I would have had him here to meet you, but Mr. Powell said you prefer to meet your interview subjects for the first time when the actual interview begins."

"Yes, Chastity can be hardheaded about certain things," Leeland interjected.

"My producer and I prepare thoroughly for our interviews," replied Chastity, "but I find the discussions to be fresher, more frank, if I'm meeting my guests for the first time. And speaking of preparation, there are some final items I need to go over with my producer—make certain there are no problems with the remote production equipment and such. It was a pleasure to meet all of you, but I'm afraid I'm going to have to leave you with Mr. Powell. I'm sure you have business to discuss."

"I look forward to your show, Chastity."

Once in the outer office she realized she didn't know which way to go.

"Excuse me," she asked O'Toole's assistant. "How do I find the staging area for tonight's show?"

"It's easy, Ms Blume. Just go out the door and to the right down the corridor. When you come to the large advertisement on the wall, take the corridor to your left. That will lead you straight to where your people are setting up."

"Thank you."

It turned out not to be quite as long a walk as she expected. The ad she'd been told to look for was impossible to miss. It covered the wall with its image of a larger-than-life model wearing a V-Real visor, the fiery red glow of its lens confirming activation. Chastity couldn't help but notice the way the model's lips parted, and the slight turn of her head, as if she were transfixed with rapture. Below her ample bosom was the company's newest catch phrase, "It's better than chocolate." Chastity had never tried V-Real, but she doubted it was more enjoyable than a cinnamon ganache.

She came to a checkpoint where a guard hurried to pull back a corded barrier and let her pass. As she walked through, she saw an unusual couple, plainly not employees, coming toward her. The woman was one of those flamboyant blondes whose restrictive red sweater and tight white skirt did little to disguise her outright voluptuous charms. Her face was familiar, but Chastity couldn't recall why.

The man was a big, brutish sort of fellow with a fleshy nose, wearing a long black coat over a simple dark-blue collarless shirt. He had a short, sandy-blond brush cut that accentuated his square jaw, but it was his eyes that beckoned her. Pugnacious, belligerent blue eyes that seemed to stare straight into her soul. Or were they just trying to look beneath her blouse? No doubt he was taking her full measure—sizing her up for God knew what kind of libidinous perversion.

She wouldn't let herself admit it, she disavowed the feeling as soon as it swept through her; but as much as she was repulsed by him, she couldn't deny a certain animal attraction. She could, however, ignore it.

11

THE TWAIN SHALL MEET

NOAH SPOTTED HER RIGHT AWAY. SHE WAS A LITHE LITTLE THING, BUT WITH CURVES IN all the right places. However, that banana-colored getup of hers looked like something you'd wear to church. Which he figured was about right when he got close enough to see the symbol hanging from her neck. That's when he recognized her—the planet's most famous member of the Church of Transcendental Platonics. Too bad, because those green eyes of hers were killers, and she smelled of lilacs—his favorite.

She looked like she was going to walk right past, so he stopped in front of her.

"You're Chastity Blume, aren't you?"

"Yes. Can I help you?"

"I thought you were her. I've seen you on the grid."

"That's nice," Chastity replied, waiting for Noah to move out of her way. When he failed to move, she continued. "You don't look like a fan."

"I'm not. I could be, though. I have to say, you're definitely a more delectable dish of cream in person."

"Well, thank you for the lovely coffee room metaphor."

"I'm Inspector Dane, San Francisco PD. This is my partner, Detective Monroe."

"I'm very happy for you both. Now, if you don't mind stepping aside, I—"

"You don't really believe in that abstinence crap you preach, do you? It's just hype right? A gimmick for ratings?"

"Excuse me?" Chastity's annoyed amusement flared to open hostility. "Do you have any official business with me, Inspector? Do I need a lawyer? Maybe

60

you'd like to hear from a lawyer. My network has several to choose from."

"No need to get all hot and sweaty, there, Ms Blume. I was just making conversation."

He stepped aside, and Chastity continued on her way.

"Didn't mean to upset you, Ms Blume," he called after her, "but I always say abstinence makes the hard grow longer."

"Who was that?" Marilyn asked. "Is she one of your old girlfriends?"

Noah snorted. "Girlfriend? Her buns are screwed on way too tight for me. Don't you know who that is? No, you wouldn't. That's America's Favorite Virgin—the sweetheart of the lonely hearts."

"I don't think she likes you."

"You could be right there, Monroe. Then again, she may be all wet and gooey for me and is just trying to hide it."

Marilyn glanced at him. "I don't think so."

"Forget that fembot, she's walking freezer burn. Come on, we've got work to do."

The gray-suited guard held his ground as they approached, so Noah flashed his badge. The fellow wasn't impressed.

"We're with the SFPD. We need to speak with..." He looked at Marilyn.

"Jonathan O'Toole," she finished for him.

"Mr. O'Toole doesn't speak with anyone without an appointment," said the guard, then added with a sneer, "especially anyone with a badge."

Noah stepped toward the guard as if he were considering tossing him aside, but Marilyn edged between them.

"Now, boys, there's no need for this." She moved closer to the guard and read his ID. "Sean, we could have our captain or maybe the precinct commander call and bother Mr. O'Toole, or we could even get a warrant to search the premises, but that would mean closing down operations for a good part of the day. I don't think Mr. O'Toole would like that. I wonder if you could just check with his office and find out if he'll see us. We just have a few quick questions for him about one of his employees, a Timothy Huang."

Noah could have sworn he saw her bat her eyelashes at the dope behind the rope.

"All right," replied guard, "you both wait here."

He moved to a nearby grid screen, and Noah flashed his partner a look of skepticism.

"Sometimes men find it very difficult to say no to me," explained Marilyn. Then she got this look on her face, as if she were straining hard to remember something.

"You all right?"

"Yes. It's just that as soon as I said that, I got the feeling I'd said the exact same thing before. I don't know when."

"Hmmph," grunted Noah. "Who knew droids got déjà vu."

The guard returned, looking chagrined.

"Mr. O'Toole will see you," he said reluctantly. "But you've got to wait here. They're sending someone down for you."

His partner broke out in a big smile, looking, he thought, like she'd picked the winning lotto numbers. Noah ignored her childlike glee and shuffled his feet impatiently.

THEIR GUIDE INTO THE INNER SANCTUM WAS A WEASEL-FACED CHARACTER WHO CALLED himself O'Toole's "executive assistant." His politeness was strictly superficial, and Noah got the distinct impression the glorified secretary considered himself above dealing with two ordinary police. He delivered a perfunctory apology, saying he had to convey the envelope he was carrying to another department before he could take them to V-Real's chief executive, who was otherwise occupied at the moment, anyway.

He proceeded to lead them on a circuitous route Noah noted took them down two levels to a below-ground factory. Through an open door, they spied row upon row of blue-skinned alien immigrants doing close work with tiny instruments. Noah was astonished by the lack of space each worker was given. They had packed them onto the factory floor like busy little sardines. He was about to say something, but his partner beat him to it.

"My goodness, they seem to barely have room to breathe down there, let alone work."

"Everyone who visits remarks upon that," said the weasel indifferently. "They actually prefer to work in cramped, poorly lit spaces. Troloxians are light-sensitive and somewhat agoraphobic. They can become agitated in large open areas."

Noah was about to make a flippant comparison to a mythical North Pole workshop when he detected a peculiar aroma. It was distinctive, not particularly pleasant and definitely coming from the troll-crammed chamber. Apparently, their body odor was as alien as their oversized ears and ruby-like eyes.

As strange as it was, he thought the smell was somehow familiar. Was it the same stench that had forced him out of the dead perp's apartment? It seemed similar, but he wasn't sure.

Weasel made his delivery, and eventually, they were shown into the spacious office of V-Real's chief executive. However, O'Toole wasn't alone. When Noah and Marilyn entered, he was talking with a Troloxian. The squat alien obviously wasn't just any Troloxian. He must have been almost five feet—tall for one of them—and he wore a fancy dark-gray suit that complemented his pale-blue face. He was also the first troll Noah had ever seen wearing shoes. They must have been size 20-triple E extra-extra wide.

"Inspector Noah Dane and Detective Marilyn Monroe," announced the weasel, showing them in.

"Inspector Dane, Detective Monroe, please have a seat."

"We won't be taking up that much of your time, Mr. O'Toole," Noah said, making no move to sit.

"Fine," replied O'Toole. He gestured toward the alien. "Let me introduce you to one of our VPs, Walter Kess."

The troll stepped forward and put out his hand in a very human gesture. Noah took it without hesitation but found the four-fingered grip unsettling. Kess had that alien smell, too, though on him it seemed subdued.

"Walter Kess?" Noah inquired as the Troloxian shook hands with his partner. "That doesn't sound like a very Troloxian name."

"What's in a name, Inspector? 'That which we call a rose by any other name would smell as sweet.'" Kess paused as if waiting for a reaction. When he didn't get it, he continued. "Shakespeare, Inspector Dane. Truly humanity's most brilliant literary figure, don't you concur?"

"Yeah," Noah replied, "I'm familiar with him."

"As for my name, many of my people have adopted more human names in an attempt to integrate ourselves into your societies. Those that landed in Norway and have taken up residence there are beginning to use Norwegian names. The same in Kazakhstan, Argentina and elsewhere. We are a very adaptable species. However, I'm certain your investigative instincts yearn to know my true Troloxian name. It's Kessssmet."

It sounded like a snake hissing.

"Let's get on with why you're here, Inspector," said O'Toole, handing a data disk to Marilyn. "Here's what little information we have on Timothy Huang. He was not employed here long."

"What was his job?" asked Noah.

"He was a courier. He made deliveries both internally and externally. However, his performance was deemed unsatisfactory, and he was recently terminated."

"Yeah, he was," Noah said dryly. "Are you aware of any other employees he might have associated with?"

"I have no idea. As I've told you, what little we know about Mr. Huang is on that disk," said O'Toole in a regal tone that announced he was cutting short the audience he had granted. "Now, if there's nothing else, we have work to do."

"So do we, Mr. O'Toole. That's why we're here. We're just doing our job, trying to track down a cop killer. You understand what that means to us?"

"Certainly, Inspector. But I don't know how else we can be of assistance."

"If you don't mind," said Marilyn, trying to charm him with courtesy and a smile, "we'd like to speak with Mr. Huang's supervisor, and anyone else he worked closely with."

"Of course. I'll have my assistant direct you."

"That's just peachy, Mr. O'Toole." Marilyn deposited the disk in her purse. "Thank you ever so much for your time."

"Yeah, thanks," added Noah.

"Good luck with your investigation," said O'Toole.

As they turned to go, the Troloxian proclaimed, "'I see you stand like greyhounds in the slips, straining upon the start. The game's afoot!'"

Noah glanced at the troll. He couldn't decide if that glint in Kess's red eyes was a trick of the light, or if it meant the little blue mump was cracking wise at their expense.

THE QUESTIONING OF SEVERAL V-REAL EMPLOYEES PROVED FRUITLESS. IT SEEMED NO ONE knew Huang very well, or would admit to it. As a courier, he hadn't worked closely with anyone else. He picked up his packages and made his deliveries. Nobody socialized with him. Nobody knew where he hung out.

"So, what do you think?" Noah found himself asking his partner, more out of habit than any expectation. It was getting late, and he was tired.

"I think," Marilyn said, "we'll have to start over, go back to the evidence and see where that leads us."

Noah 'jectured his ears were deceiving him. She was actually starting to sound like real police. Of course, she still looked like...well, like *that.*

Marilyn continued. "I think the diamonds are still our best clue. If only we could find out where they came from."

Noah had to agree—but he wasn't going to. Still, it was time to stop letting this celebudroid distract him from the case and make the best of a singularly weird situation.

"O'Toole was lying when he told us about Huang being terminated."

"How do you know that?" Marilyn wondered.

"He looked up and to the right when he said that. He was accessing the creative side of his brain to lie."

"Are you sure?"

"No." He answered flatly. "It's not foolproof, but it's one of several telltale signs."

"Why would he lie about that?"

"I don't know. Big business executive—could be he just lies about a lot of things out of habit."

"What about Walter Kess?"

"The troll? I don't know. I don't know how their brains work, and I couldn't read his face."

"He seemed genuine."

"Yeah, genuinely slippery." Changing his tone, he said, "I'm going to get out of here, get me some tacos and head home. Where can I drop you? Where does a former celebudroid, now a police detective, live?"

"I don't...have a place," replied Marilyn. "I stay at my desk in the Hall of Justice."

"Your desk? Don't you—" A vibration in his coat pocket interrupted him. He pulled out his pad and activated the link. It was Georgia, looking garish in a chartreuse-and-lavender outfit that was only partially concealed by her lab coat.

"I've got some interesting results for you, sugar. How's Mama's big boy today?"

"Wound tighter than a politician's asshole. What have you got for me?"

"You certainly have a visceral way with words, sugar. Oh, hi, there, Marilyn, honey. You're looking faboo today."

"Georgia!"

"All right, all right. Can't a girl even be mannerly? I can't help it if I'm a people person. Nothing I found at the apartment sent up any red flags. It was the usual assortment of hair and epithelials, all matching our DOA's DNA. No blood, no semen, no unusual bacteria of any sort, no—"

"Get to it. You said you found something interesting. What?"

"You're not going to believe this, but there were traces of guano Chiroptera on the floor of the apartment, and on the bottom of a pair of shoes I found under the bed."

"What the hell is that?

Georgia let loose with a big ear-to-ear grin. "Bat shit."

"Bat shit?"

She nodded her head, still smiling.

"Bat shit?" Noah repeated it as if he couldn't believe his own voice. "Where in the hell in San Francisco do you find bats?"

"Not my department, sugar. I've got to run now. I've got a date with a good-looking hormone therapist, and I'm hoping for more than just the usual injection, if you know what I mean." Georgia bounced her eyebrows conspiratorially and terminated the link.

"Bats?"

"I'm checking the grid," said Marilyn.

Even though her eyes were still focused on him, he could tell her mind was augmented into a different reality. It didn't take long for her to come up with something. He had to admit, she saved him tedious fingerwork when it came to grid searches.

"There are at least sixteen varieties of bats in the greater San Francisco area," Marilyn reported. "They're nocturnal creatures that roost by day in buildings, wood piles, rock crevices, caves and abandoned mines. Many species forage for insects near bodies of water, and some live in colonies of a thousand or more. Their lifespan can—"

"Okay, okay. Is there anywhere, specifically, in the city where bats hang out?"

"No. According to the information I've accessed, there are likely hundreds of bat colonies of all different sizes in the area."

"That's about as much help as a fan in a windstorm."

Forgetting that his partner could have done it with a thought, Noah fumbled for his pad and opened the pod's doors. He took the pilot's seat and checked the hydrogen powercell levels.

"You know," he said, looking at Marilyn, "it's ridiculous for me to take you back to the Hall just so you can sit at your desk all night. Bureaucrats got all the brains of a windup toy. Why don't you...Heck, why don't you power down at my place for the night? It's got to be better than your desk. I'll keep the pod signed out, and then we can get an early start in the morning."

Marilyn's demure smile was so potent he caught himself staring.

"That sounds just creamy to me," she said.

"What?"

"Oh, that was a line from *How To Marry a Millionaire*. Sometimes my old movie dialogue kind of slips out."

"Okay. If you say so."

12

ASK NOT FOR WHOM
THE TROLL TOLLS

WELCOME TO A SPECIAL LIVE EDITION OF GRIDSPEAK, THE TRUE VOICE OF THE PEOPLE. I'm Chastity Blume, and tonight we're broadcasting from the heart of the V-Real Corporation. We're here because this is where our most unusual guest is employed, along with hundreds of his fellow Troloxians. Joining us now is Walter Kess, whose official title here at V-Real is Vice-president in Charge of Production.

"Thank you for consenting to be a part of our show, Mr. Kess."

"I'm happy to be here as a representative of my people, Ms Blume. It's nice to meet you."

Chastity noted that, despite his unusual features and heavily wrinkled, bluish skin, he looked like any executive. His suit was well-tailored and expensive, and, unlike every other Troloxian she could remember seeing, he wore shoes. Extraordinarily large shoes to be sure, but stylish, nevertheless.

"Is it true that this is the first official interview that you or any of your people has granted the media?"

"To my knowledge, that is true."

Chastity found herself staring at one of his enormous ears and redirected her focus to his eyes. "I understand that it is inherent in the Troloxian people to shun notoriety of any kind, so I thank you for choosing *Gridspeak* as your first public forum. But nine years is a long time to remain silent. Why have you chosen to speak publicly now?"

"Nine years as your calendar tracks time is but a brief interval for us, Ms

Blume. We are a long-lived and persevering people. It's true that the precepts of our race do not condone celebrity. However, it's not because we have anything to hide, as some fringe elements of your society have suggested. It was because of these disturbing fabrications that it was decided I should step to the forefront, as it were, and dispel any misgivings that may linger.

"I think it's essential that everyone understand it took us years to adapt to your various societies, and even longer to absorb the nuances of your myriad languages. Many of my people still struggle to speak even a single Earth dialect."

"Well, I must say your English is profoundly erudite."

"Thank you. The point I want to establish is that, as a people, we've been reticent about speaking out until we were more certain what we were saying, and how it might be accepted. Our race is a model of forbearance. Your Shakespeare once wrote, 'Have patience and endure.' Patience is something we have in abundance.

"You must appreciate that, at first, we were simply grateful your world accepted us, for the most part, with open arms."

Chastity realized focusing on his eyes had been a mistake—those twin red orbs had a hypnotic effect after a while. She pretended to glance at her notes just to break the spell.

"The reason your first ship ventured to Earth nearly nine years ago is widely known, but since you're here tonight, I'd like you to tell us about that in your own words."

"Simply put, we were forced to flee our home world because of religious intolerance. Though our sect was an ancient one, an alteration to the presiding political power structure led to new leaders who condemned our beliefs. The persecution became so vehement we were forced to flee and search for a new home. Our journey took many decades, but we never lost faith that we would find a home."

"And you found one."

"Yes. Once our lead ship descended just outside of San Francisco, and we established a relationship with your authorities, our other vessels landed in several different nations, so as not to overburden any single region. We do prefer cooler climes, which is why none of our ships landed in any domains near your equator."

Chastity realized that what she thought were sporadic little tufts of hair on his head and hands were more like feathered down.

"Except for that regrettable incident in Germany, the people of Earth have proved to be very gracious hosts."

"What can you tell us about your religious faith?"

"I'm afraid our theological beliefs are a very private thing. By tradition, we don't speak of them in public, or with outsiders."

"That must make it difficult to recruit new members."

"Recruiting an outsider into our faith would be an extraordinarily rare event. For the most part, we are born to it."

"All right, we'll respect your privacy and move on to another topic. There are those who are concerned that you may be pursued, and that your pursuers may not be as peaceful as you've proven to be."

"I can state categorically that there is no reason for anyone to pursue us. Our persecutors actually aided our departure, finding that to be the most politically expedient course for their own machinations. Even if there were to be a reversal of reasoning, they'd have no idea where to find us. It's a big galaxy, Ms Blume."

"Speaking of which, can you tell us why all attempts at adapting Troloxian technology to human spacecraft have failed? There were hopes when you first arrived that your ability to cross such vast stretches of space would enable mankind to do the same."

"We have allowed complete access to our ships, but I'm afraid I can't explain why your engineers have not been able to adapt the technology. I am not an engineer myself, and to my knowledge, none of those who emigrated here to Earth were involved in the construction of the ships. It took intensive training for a few of us to simply learn to operate them. Had repairs been necessary, we would have been, as you say, out of luck."

"Very well. How would you say the integration of your people into human society has progressed?"

Kess pondered the question for a moment. "For the most part, I believe we have adapted quite well. I do sometimes worry that, as my people become acclimated to human cultures, learn human attitudes, that we may begin to lose a little of ourselves, our traditions. I often regret that. However, mankind is a unique species. To once again quote Shakespeare, 'What a piece of work is a man. How noble in reason. How infinite in faculty. In form, in moving, how express and admirable. In action how like an angel. In apprehension how like a god. The beauty of the world. The paragon of animals.'" The alien's serious expression succumbed to a brief grin. "So how can we reproach ourselves if, on some levels, we imitate such a noble beast."

"One notable area in which you don't imitate humans," Chastity interjected, "is that of reproduction. Is it true that Troloxians are sexless?"

"Our race is, indeed, parthenogenic. That is, we procreate asexually."

"That's fascinating. Are there male and female Troloxians?"

"No. Unlike humans, we have only one sex, and neither male nor female sexual organs. Neither are we encumbered by the mating rituals that consume much of your time and energy."

"As our regular viewers know, I certainly agree with that assessment. To think of all you are able to accomplish without that...burden."

"But what of love, passion, romance, Ms Blume? So much of your literature, your cinematic creations, your music are based upon such concepts. We have nothing that compares. Where would you as a species be without those ideals?"

Chastity put her hand around her throat and fingered her purity chain. She found it awkward the Troloxian was defending humans, and that she'd somehow ended up on the other side of the issue.

"You're certainly right about that, Mr. Kess. It's definitely food for thought.

"Speaking of food," she said quickly, changing the subject, "let's talk about what Troloxians like to eat, and what Earth foods they've developed a taste for."

13

NOT ALWAYS WHAT THEY SEEM

THEY HADN'T TAKEN TWO STEPS FROM THE POD WHEN HIS DAFT NEIGHBOR DARTED OUT at them from behind her hedge.

"Who's this?" she asked, gesturing at Marilyn. "I don't know you, do I?"

"This is my partner, Mrs. G. Don't worry, she's not a mutant."

"Of course, she's not," said the older woman, inspecting her all the same. "Mutants aren't this beautiful."

"Thank you," responded Marilyn, looking puzzled.

"You sure look familiar, dear. Do I know you?"

"I don't believe so. My name's Marilyn, what's yours?"

"I'm Fran Grabarkowitz. Call me Frannie."

"It's nice to meet you, Frannie."

"I'm sure I know you from somewhere," said Mrs. Grabarkowitz, walking back toward her house as if she'd forgotten they were there. "I'll remember eventually—yes, I will."

Once inside, Noah activated his grid screen out of habit and dropped his food on the table. He reached for the shelf where he kept his libations and retrieved the first bottle he put his hands on. But as he was about to sit, he realized he'd grabbed the Single Barrel Tennessee Whiskey that Cy had given him facetiously to celebrate their eighth anniversary of partnering. It was a special blend of Jack Daniels, hard to find and expensive. He stood there, staring at it for an uncomfortably long moment, placed it back on the shelf and took another, nearly empty bottle.

Marilyn, meanwhile, was wandering around his place, looking at everything.

"You have so many plants. I think it's just elegant. It must take a lot of your time to take care of them."

"Yeah," he said as he pulled a taco out of its wrapping and took a bite.

"Your home is so cozy, it reminds me of…well, isn't that funny? I'm not sure what it reminds me of."

"You sure you don't want some of this, or something else to eat or drink?"

"No, thank you."

"That's right. For a second there, I forgot you were…that you don't eat."

"It's funny, though," she said, still surveying his place, "sometimes I get this absolutely uncontrollable craving for matzoball soup. I really don't know why. And even though I know I can't eat it, I still feel like I want it. Isn't that peculiar?"

"Uh-huh," he murmured as he chewed.

Of course, he speculated as he ate, being a droid who thought she was a cinematic legend, she already had the peculiar market cornered. Not that she seemed to realize it. In fact, he had to remind himself every now and then that she wasn't real—not *real* real. On the other hand, he'd met plenty of humans he could say that about, too.

After he washed down his first taco with a drink straight from the bottle, he turned his attention to the grid, where a talking head was rambling on—something about Valentine's Day.

"…a significant decline in sales of candy, flowers and even greeting cards compared with recent Valentine's Day figures."

The screen cut to a two-shot, revealing the mouthpiece's female counterpart.

"That's certainly odd, Brian. Do you think it has anything to do with the economy?"

"There's nothing wrong with the economy. It could just mean that people are buying fewer traditional gifts this year. My girlfriend gave me a V-Real visor with the newest programming. It's better than chocolate, you know."

"Maybe that explains the downturn in candy sales." She tittered the way newscasters do, and continued. "Now for the latest statewide grid poll results. By a four-percent margin, California voters have selected the death penalty over life in prison for Justin Boyle, who was convicted last week of killing his wife and mother-in-law. It's not known whether the voters' decision will be appealed.

"Today's nationwide grid poll asks voters to determine whether DNA testing and cataloguing should be mandatory for all citizens at birth. You may vote now by using the selections on your screen, or by linking with your designated polling site. Relevant facts can be accessed at that site, or through the 'Put An End To Blanks' link. The polls on this issue close at—"

Noah poked his pad, shifting the link, did it once more then tossed the pad to Marilyn.

"Go ahead, watch whatever you want," he said, going back to his meal.

"Aren't you going to vote?"

"I don't vote," he muttered. "People manage to screw up everything easily enough without my help. Do you want to vote?"

"I'm not eligible to vote," Marilyn said as though the fact were an embarrassment.

Noah snorted with contempt. "Too bad. You'd probably do a better job of it than most. Hell, you can use my vote if you want."

"No...no, thank you," she said, shifting the link again. "Maybe someday I'll have my own vote."

Noah looked up from his food to see if she was serious. Her attention was focused on the screen.

"Program this link, and return tomorrow at eight when we'll tell you what you need to know, what you'll need to do, in order to survive a biological terrorist attack. Until then, ask yourself: Are you prepared for a viral assault?

"Now, don't touch that pad, because coming up next on GridVid...it's strange, it's outlandish, it's fantastic, it's *Bizarre del Mundo.*"

"I guess that's one thing you don't have to worry about—viruses, that is."

"No, not biological ones," she replied. "Do you think Loftur is a real threat?"

"It's hard to say. Never met one myself, though plenty of people are afraid of them." Noah swallowed the last bite and pushed aside the refuse. "Things aren't always what they seem. That's the first lesson you need to learn as a detective." He scratched his chest, took another swig from the bottle and pulled the Desert Eagle out of his shoulder holster. He grabbed his kit and proceeded to clean the gun as he spoke.

> > "One time, Cyrus and I were investigating this string of homicides at a hospital. Five patients had died on the same floor in a two-week period. Now, all of these patients were really bad off. A couple were terminally ill. So, we 'jectured it was some doctor or nurse who believed in euthanasia and thought they were doing the poor bastards a favor. We were in there every day for week, sweating the likely suspects, and then a sixth patient died unexpectedly. We finally sent another detective in undercover as a patient.

"It turns out the cleaning lady was coming in every other night and pulling the plug on somebody's life support system so she could plug in her floor buffer."

"Oh, my," responded Marilyn.

Noah finished with his gun, replaced it in the holster and stood to unstrap it.

"What happened?"

"You mean to the cleaning lady? Nothing. 'Tragic accident,' they called it. Now, of course, those systems have backup alarms."

Noah took his coat and holster and hung them in a closet. When he closed the closet door he looked in the mirror hanging there. He turned profile and inspected his bulging waistline, tilted his head and ran his fingers through the spot on top that was thinning. "Yeah, things aren't always what they seem to be at first glance."

He realized he was staring at himself and turned away. He was relieved to see the droid wasn't looking at him. She'd gotten up from her seat and gone over to his arboretum. He couldn't help but notice that unconscious wiggle in her walk. He reached for his bottle and took another drink.

He felt a sense of pride when she remarked on how beautiful his *Mimosa pudica* was. She bent to get a better look at the blossoms, and he discovered he was enjoying her delight. He was also enjoying the magnificent ass that beckoned him from behind her tight white skirt. If only…

What was he thinking? Mentally, he slapped himself and turned to look at the grid screen.

"Do you have to dress like that?"

"What?" She straightened up and looked at him. "Dress like what?"

"Like…Like that."

"You don't like my outfit?"

"Me? No, I think it's great," he said, adding under his breath, "if you're looking to stop a runaway Mag-Lev."

"I'm terribly sorry. I was given a limited wardrobe. All my clothes are reproductions from my films. I guess the dungarees I wore in *The Misfits* or *River of No Return* would be more suitable, but there was no real call for a celebudroid to dress that casual, so—"

"What do you mean you wore?"

"Oh, silly me. Residue from my original programming gums up the works sometimes. I mean what the original Marilyn Monroe wore in those movies."

"Yeah, silly you."

He had to watch his step. He had slipped into accepting this zaftig droid as a person, and she wasn't even able to uncross her own wires. He couldn't let her soft, sexy exterior and provocative blue eyes bamboozle him. She was a machine, and a schizoid one at that.

14

GOING DOWN?

Deciding what to wear had been a decision she just didn't want to make, and, as a result, Chastity was way behind schedule. She was trying to get an early start because of a meeting scheduled with a group of advertising and marketing consultants. God knows what kinds of changes they will want to make now, she thought. They always wanted to fix something, no matter how good the ratings were. Change was their lifeblood. Consultants had to make changes to justify their jobs. She'd handle the consultants, mollify the ad execs and placate Leeland Powell, but choosing an outfit for the day was something else.

She was still in rush mode when she dashed out her door and into the elevator. The panels slid shut, and she was about to relax when she realized the car was on the way up instead of down.

"Damn!"

She took hold of her crucifix, closed her eyes and mentally repeated a calming mantra as she waited for her carriage to complete its ascent. When the elevator came to a stop and its doors parted, she opened her eyes and saw David. He was about to wheel his maintenance cart in when he saw her and wavered.

"Ms Blume, what are you doing up here?"

"Hello, David. I uh, took a wrong turn. I wanted to go down."

"Me, too."

"Come on in. We'll go down together."

Before he could move, the doors began to slide shut. Chastity and David both reached out to stop them. She was quicker, and as she grabbed one of the panels, his hand landed firmly on hers.

The chance touch, the feel of his large brown fingers over hers, sent a shiver down Chastity's arm that carried all the way to her belly. The contact was momentary, but in that brief instant her thoughts strayed. A seditious image of those hands touching her, roving softly over her body, presented itself, only to be swept away by denial.

The elevator doors reversed their direction, and Chastity gently disengaged her hand from David's. She observed him as he wheeled his cart into the elevator, seemingly unaffected.

"It's nice running into you, Ms Blume," he said shyly. "You're one of the nicest people in the building."

"Thank you, David. I like you, too."

The doors slid shut, and Chastity struggled to think of something else to say, something that would derail her insistent train of thought.

"How do you like *Of Mice and Men* so far?"

"I like it. I'm at the part where Lennie and George first start working on the farm. I really like George because of the way he takes care of Lennie. I guess it reminds me of the way I take care of my mother."

"Damn!"

Startled by her sudden outburst, David asked, "What's wrong, Ms Blume?"

"Oh, I forgot to water my plants again. I always forget, even when I remember to remind Suzette to remind me. I haven't watered them in weeks. I guess I need to buy an autosystem."

"Who's Suzette?"

"She's my...or I should say *it's* my homeminder. You know, the artificial intelligence-equipped—"

"Sure, I know," David blurted, as though the need for an explanation was demeaning.

"Of course you do, David, what am I thinking. You probably have to repair those things all the time."

"That's not really my job, Ms Blume. But I can water your plants for you. Plants will die if you don't water them regularly."

"I couldn't ask you to do that," Chastity said. "You've got plenty of other work to keep you busy."

"No, I'd like to do it," David replied eagerly then, realizing he was staring at her, averted his gaze. "Everyone—I mean everything needs a little loving care now and then, some nurturing, don't you think?"

"I'm sure that's true, David. All right, you can water my plants if you promise to stop calling me 'Ms Blume.' From now on call me Chastity."

"Okay, Ms—I mean, Chastity."

The elevator doors opened, and Chastity stepped out onto the main floor. David followed, pulling his cart with him.

"When you go up to water the plants, just tell Suzette I said 'Angel Eyes,' and she'll let you in. That's our code."

"Okay, Chastity," David said, enjoying each syllable of her name. "Don't worry. I'll take care of all your plants, and make sure they're watered good."

Chastity wasn't concerned about David taking care of her plants. Her anxiety was rooted elsewhere, and nurtured by the vague notion he was capable of more—much more.

15

STREET PUISSANCE

NOAH SET THE POD ON HOVER AND SCANNED THE STREETS BELOW. HE KNEW BINK usually set up in the Haight somewhere. If he was out and about, he wouldn't be hard to spot.

"What are we looking for?" asked Marilyn. "Maybe I can help."

"Not what, who," Noah responded, maneuvering the pod to a different vantage point. "Just sit tight. If he's out here, I'll find him."

"I can't help with the investigation if you don't let me know what we're doing."

"Don't get your fiber optics in a bunch. You'll know what you need to know when you need to know it."

She turned away from him, pouting, and something caught his eye. It wasn't who he was looking for; it was a massive holoboard in the shape of an inverted pyramid—the trademark of the Transcendental Platonistas.

Its dazzling luminosity was distracting, even in daylight. Inside its giant mauve neon border, where normally you'd see the symbol of the cross, was an image of the sect's current leader, Rebekah Redstone. Noah was no true-believer, but the Platonic high minister was a familiar sight. Those full lips, Cherokee cheekbones, and that silver headband of hers were everywhere you looked these days. She had the kind of volcanic charisma that made her the darling of the grid.

No audio emanated from this particular holoboard, and no script was superimposed across its screen. It was a simple visual, made all the more powerful by Redstone's prevailing celebrity. It began with her on her knees, in prayer, forming the inverted pyramid with her thumbs and forefingers over her groin. She rose from her knees, standing tall and straight, her breasts, evident even beneath her white robe, thrust out proudly. She tilted her head back, her long black hair flowing behind her as she looked skyward as if for guidance, slowly spreading her arms wide until she assumed the posture of a cross. Her image froze in that position for several seconds before not-so-subtly transposing itself, back and forth, with an actual crucifix. Then it all began again as she knelt to pray.

You had to admire her showmanship, thought Noah, not to mention her heavenly body. Too bad her idea of spiritual purity precluded the sort of divine rapture he had in mind.

"There he is," he said, more to himself than to his partner.

The standard prerecorded warning cleared the area, and Noah set the pod down like an egg on foam core. They were mostly ignored by passersby as they left the pod and he sealed it. The wind was blowing so ferociously he had to hold his coat closed. When he turned to his partner, he saw she was fighting an updraft that had blown her pleated white skirt above her waist, revealing her plain white underwear. She stood there in her high heels, grabbing at the hem and trying to force the dress down until the breeze subsided.

"You really do need to get some new clothes. Come on, he's over this way," he said, motioning for her to follow him.

Marilyn recovered, straightening her dress and adjusting her belt. "I'm coming."

By the time she caught up with him, Noah was exchanging greetings with his skinny little acquaintance, who had set up shop on the street corner.

"Hey, Bink, what's the word?"

"The word is ebullience, dear Noah, as in the abundance of joy I am experiencing at your unexpected appearance."

"Likewise. Bink, this is my new partner, Marilyn Monroe. This is Buddy The Magnificent Binkowski."

The street artist was draped in an emerald shirt splattered with ivory and lavender designs resembling various punctuation marks. Arranged on easels and mobile shelves all about him were garish surreal paintings, works of clay, feathered jewelry and an odd assortment of gewgaws and trinkets.

Bink dropped to a knee with an exaggerated flourish and took Marilyn's hand. His ash-colored hair was thinning at the crown. He looked up at her in all sincerity from under eyebrows unruly as birds' nests and said, "Madam, the moment of our meeting is a prodigious and profound event I will recall vividly until the time of my demise." He kissed her hand succinctly, stood and said to Noah, "The force is strong in this one."

"Uh, thank you ever so," stammered Marilyn. "Why 'magnificent?'"

"Why indeed. Because, fair maiden, modesty is the opiate of the mediocre. And because," he said, producing a crimson rose from behind her ear and offering it to her, "my powers of prestidigitation surpass that of mere mortal illusionists."

"Bink's a magician," Noah said as Marilyn accepted the rose. "He used to headline all over the world."

"Why...?"

"Why do I now confine my extraordinary skills to this obscure corner of the universe? A man's fate is not necessarily his calling. Mine is a sad and sordid tale of an illusion gone awry. Some day, perhaps, I will summon the fortitude to render its telling to you properly. Currently, my consciousness is preoccupied by meanderings of Loftur conspiracies and a diabolical fungus which plagues my nether regions in perpetuity. Whether to itch, to scratch, or to once again call for a futile fungicidal assault, these are—"

"What have you heard about Loftur?" Noah asked, interrupting what seemed destined to be an interminable rant.

"Nothing. Naught. Nil. I know what you know. I'm familiar with the accounts that taint the grid, nothing more. Even the streets are silent of rumors. It's as if the Nordic terrorists did not exist at all. Perhaps their illusion is the greatest one yet.

"However, it is not the threat of Loftur which distresses me as much as the deterioration of the planet's primal orgasmic puissance."

"Its what?"

"I don't know if I can explain it rationally. I can feel it, though," Bink said with a look of apprehension Noah had never seen on his face before. "There's a tremor in the very quintessence of mankind's carnality, a preternatural occurrence, a metamorphosis. The world is in a state of flux—veering frantically off course."

"If you say so, Bink. Try not to lose any sleep over it, though, okay?"

"You are, of course, correct, my friend, and wise beyond your IQ. Agonize not over what you are incapable of controlling. I recall the indomitable Cyrus once espousing words to that effect. Where is your comrade? Has he been reassigned?"

Noah's chest felt tight, and he turned his head as if scanning the street for something.

Marilyn spoke for him. "Inspector Cyrus Budd was...killed in the line of duty."

"My heartfelt lamentations to you and his family, Noah. What a paralyzing stroke this must be for them. I had no knowledge of this. It is, indeed, a harsh reality we inhabit. If there is anything I can accomplish..."

"Yeah, there is something," Noah said, pulling out his pad. He accessed a pre-set file and passed it to Bink. "This tattoo, have you ever seen anything like it?"

The Magnificent One studied the picture a moment. "I don't recognize the motif, but I'd conjecture that it's an imprint—not the work of a true artist."

"You mean a machine job?"

"Yes, it most definitely looks like a work of mass production."

Noah reclaimed his pad and pondered how Bink's deduction could further the investigation. Bink, meanwhile, never one to miss an opportunity with an audience, set about entertaining Marilyn with some sleight-of-hand.

"Tell me, Ms Monroe, have you ever indulged in the hokey-pokey?" he asked as a pigeon materialized in his hands and flew off.

"The hokey-pokey? I don't think so."

"Then that is an oversight we must remedy without delay, for I am a hokey-pokey aficionado nonpareil. First, you put your right leg in..."

Noah had hoped Bink would recognize the work of a particular tattoo artist, giving him some kind of connection—a trail to follow at least. Now he had nothing. He was facing a dead end, twiddling his thumbs. None of their clues, if they were clues, had any connection. At least, no connection that was evident so far. A bizarre machine-imprinted tat, a bag full of uncut diamonds and bat shit.

As he was contemplating how the pieces might fit, he caught a whiff of an irresistible familiar scent. He turned his head and spied a dynamically-endowed redhead sauntering by. He knew right away it wasn't her perfume he smelled. She was in heat, primed and ready, and he had just the hose to cool her down.

His partner was occupied—entranced, really—by Bink's old levitation trick, so he followed his nose. When the fineline made an abrupt turn into an enclosed public grid booth, his first reaction was to follow her in. He stepped up to the enclosure, took hold of the door latch...

But before he could give it a tug, he had second thoughts. They were queer, conscience-rending notions, as alien to him as cactus to a carp. They squawked and squealed that he couldn't leave his partner—not again. Even if she was some cybertoy.

He turned away from the booth, grumbling to himself. As he stalked back toward Bink and Marilyn, he heard a pop and something flew by him. The glass store window behind him shattered, and in a single motion he ducked, rolled and had his Desert Eagle in his hand.

A quintet of bikeroos pedaled past, each one blasting away. Bullets pinged all around him. Civilians were across the street, behind the thugs and close to his line of fire, so he took careful aim. The Eagle screamed twice. A pair of bikeroos jerked from their mounts. Their compatriots kept on going.

Back on his feet, Noah made certain the shooters weren't coming back. He looked over the pigeons he'd plucked. They weren't going anywhere but the morgue.

That's when Marilyn came running up—if you could call what she did in those heels running. She had the sonic stunner she'd been issued in her hand but looked dazed.

"You can put that whistle away," he told her, gesturing toward the two bodies. "Looks like I've made the Blue Scorpions' hit parade."

"The Blue Scorpions? That's the same gang that was involved in the incident where Inspector Budd was killed."

"Yeah," Noah said, holstering his weapon.

"But why?" Marilyn asked, still looking stunned by the whirlwind violence.

"Payback, street cred—who knows. But if they're shooting at you, you know you're doing something right."

16

VIRGINITY SELLS

CHASTITY DIDN'T KNOW WHAT IT WAS THAT MADE HER THINK ABOUT ACCESSING THAT OLD vid. It was the one of her playing in some nameless park when she was a little girl. She munched on a handful of chocolate drops and smiled involuntarily as she watched.

She had only been five then—no six—and she looked so happy, so irreproachable as she spun around in a circle until she became so dizzy she tumbled to the ground. The little girl in the vid laughed out loud, straightening her dainty chiffon dress around her knees. She began playing peekaboo with the camera. She covered her eyes with her hands, giggled then pulled them away squeaking, "Peek!"

When was the last time she had laughed out loud, or even giggled? Chastity couldn't remember. Her hand found its way to her throat as she tried to recall that day in the park. Her fingers stroked her neck absentmindedly. Had her father been behind the camera, or was it one of her nannies? It was too long ago, too many memories ago.

She popped another drop into her mouth and felt the chocolate begin to melt away. She paused the vid, reached to access another link with the thought of calling her father then balked. She took a deep breath, gathered her thoughts and was about to make the call when an incoming message diverted her. It was her producer, Tanya.

"Chastity, good, you're there," she said, out of breath.

"You sound busy. What's going on?"

"We had another Loftur false alarm, at the airport this time. And when it came in I was in the middle of making arrangements for us to go to Merced."

"Why are we going to Merced?"

"Not us—I mean, not you. Will's got a big family reunion down there next week, and we're all going. You don't know what it's like—planning, packing, hauling three kids with you. Lucky for me Will is pretty good with Shannon and Billy, so I mostly have to deal with the baby."

"That's nice, Tanya. Sounds like a…fun trip."

"I don't know about fun, but Will likes to be around his family when he can. I'm the same way, but our clan isn't nearly as big as—"

"Did you call me for a reason?" Chastity asked a bit too abruptly.

"Oh, yeah! Gee, I almost forgot. Mr. Powell says they're ready for you now. They're in the main conference room. I'm so sorry, I was preoccupied, then I got distracted. I hope—"

"It's okay, Tanya. They'll wait for me."

Chastity cut the link with a swipe of her hand across the screen, glanced in her mirror and took a deep breath. Time to play the game, she thought.

SHE SLIPPED INTO THE ROOM UNNOTICED AT FIRST, CATCHING THEM IN MID-CONVERSATION.

"…used to be that you could put a pair of breasts or a six-pack of abs on the screen and guarantee at least a fifteen-percent upswing in sales, but lately it seems as if the holy quaternary of tits, tots, pets and sunsets has lost its sex appeal."

"I don't believe that. Sex always sells—always has, always will."

"I would have said the same—"

"Come in, Chastity, come in." Leeland was at one end of the oblong conference table, which was otherwise populated by half a dozen dark-suited execs—four male, two female. "I think you've met everyone before. Have a seat."

She tugged at her skirt, selected a chair at the other end of the table and sat.

"We've just been discussing some general marketing trends," Leeland said, "but I wanted you here before we turned to more specifics concerning your show."

"I appreciate that," Chastity responded, trying to make quick eye contact with everyone in the room. "I realize sales and marketing are key to the success of my show…just as my show is key to the network's ratings clout."

She glanced at Leeland, who smiled, accepting almost with pride how she had turned the tables to assume the status role in the room.

"Chelsea, why don't you go ahead with your group's proposal concerning

Gridspeak." With that, Leeland sat back in his chair looking relaxed, ready to observe every nuance of the meeting.

A dark-haired woman Chastity remembered meeting briefly some time ago called up something on the imbedded screen in front of her and cleared her throat. She was attractive, in a stark, professional way, and not much older than Chastity herself. Chastity recalled the mnemonic she'd given the woman to help remember her name—Chesty.

"First, let me say that *Gridspeak's* latest insta-market results have been very steady, though not quite as vibrant as this time last quarter. Of course, a leveling-off is always to be expected. However, it's often advisable with a popular show to alter its marketing strategy before it begins to fade, as opposed to waiting until the slide has begun. And now that its number-one status is being threatened by GridVid's *Bizarre* show, we believe the timing is right to make some changes in *Gridspeak.*"

"What kind of changes?" Chastity inquired apprehensively.

"Not to the show itself." The man across from Chesty/Chelsea spoke up. He was older—Chesty's superior on the executive food chain, as Chastity remembered. His name was Sully or Sorry or Sullen—she couldn't recall. "We want to be sure you understand we're not looking to mess with a good thing, Ms Blume. You'll still produce your show as you always have. What we want to do is use a little more razzle-dazzle in promoting it."

Chastity noted his eyes lit up when he said "razzle-dazzle."

"We want to revamp the promotions for your show to use a new catchphrase," Chesty/Chelsea added. "Something that people are already familiar with—something they relate to, that will remind them to link with your show."

"We want to make some promos that feature the popular phrase *America's Favorite Virgin,*" Sorry-Sullen-Sully said.

There was a momentary silence, then Chesty/Chelsea blurted out, "And to coincide with those new promos, we'd add the phrase to the show's title—*Gridspeak with Chastity Blume, America's Favorite Virgin.*"

A wave of contradictory emotions swept over Chastity. She wasn't sure if it was embarrassment or guilt.

"Just one minute," she said forcefully. "I have no intention of turning my program into some kind of freak show."

"That's not what we're suggesting," offered another one of the execs, and Chastity realized she wasn't _here for a discussion. They'd already made up their minds.

"This is just a way of drawing more viewers to your show," said Triple-S. "It will have no effect on content. You'll always have final say on your subjects and subject matter."

In Chastity's gridcast experience, "always" lasted about as long as your next show. "I don't like the idea of identifying my show with some street label."

"It's not just street talk, Chastity," Leeland said. "Like it or not, it's who you are to the viewing public."

She knew he was right—she'd heard the term often enough herself. She despised it, even when its use was endearing. She loathed it because it made her feel like a huckster, a peddler of snake oil trying to pass off tonic water as a mystical cure-all, a traitor calling for others to rally round the flag.

"All right," she said, standing. "If you think these promos will increase ratings then go ahead. Call me whatever you want. But I'm not changing the name of the show. The show is me, it's personal, and I won't change that. The promos are you, so do whatever you'd like with them. If you change the name of the show, I walk."

The faces around the table expressed surprise and a touch of awe at her forcefulness—all except Leeland's. He was still smiling, almost as if he'd won some wager.

"I want to thank you all for the time and thought you've invested in the success of my show. Is there anything else, Mr. Powell?"

"No, I think that's it, Chastity."

"Good day, then. I've got work to do."

The room was still silent behind her when she closed the door.

17

LIZARD KINGS AND SCORPIONS

I FINALLY HEARD BACK FROM THE DEFENSE DEPARTMENT ON THAT LASER'S SERIAL numbers. It is one of theirs—US Army, not standard issue. Apparently, until I called them, they didn't even know it was missing." Noah shook his head in mock disbelief.

"Do they have any idea who took it?" Marilyn asked.

"They're *investigating,*" he replied with more than a hint of sarcasm. "Said they'd let me know if they find anything."

The pod was pulling to the right, so Noah landed it in the maintenance bay. He explained the problem to the mechanic on duty, whose dull response was "Sure."

He and Marilyn were on their way up the stairs to the Hall's rear entrance when something stopped her.

"What is it?"

"I see an old friend," she said, pointing at some guy who was connecting a long thick hose from a truck to some refuse bins.

"An old friend?"

Marilyn was already bouncing down the stairs.

"How could you have an old friend? You're, like, four years old." Noah shrugged his shoulders and halfheartedly followed her.

"Jim? It *is* you," Marilyn squealed with glee.

The guy was a skinny little mump with a pointy chin and gaunt face. When he got closer, Noah saw he was wearing tight black leather pants. The getup, along with his shoulder-length curly hair, gave him a decidedly girlish look.

"Marilyn baby! What's happening? How's my 20th Century fox?"

They hugged, and Noah cringed. He could smell the stink of garbage on this fellow from twenty feet.

"You haven't been in my head in a long time, girl. Where've you been? Chaplin's been asking about you. What's happening?"

"I know, sorry I didn't make contact. I couldn't for a long time. I was undergoing some new programming. I'm a police detective now. I work here, in the Hall of Justice."

The long-haired fellow shook his head in dismay. "They made you a pig? Man, that's really uncool."

"It's better than being a garbage man," Noah responded as he forced himself past the stench to move closer.

The fellow turned to look at him, and Noah was aware of the intensity of his eyes. It felt for a moment as if they were staring straight into his soul.

"I prefer the term 'Shaman of Sanitation.'"

"Jim, this is my partner, Inspector Noah Dane. Noah, this is Jim Morrison. He was one of the celebudroids I worked with. I'm just crazy about Jim."

"Never heard of him."

"I'm a wild child, full of grace, savior of the human race."

"Sorry, there, Jimbo, but we've got to get to work. I'm sure you've got some trash that needs sanitizing, so we'll link you later."

Marilyn flashed Noah a look of displeasure and turned back to her friend. "I'm terribly sorry, Jim, but we do have to go."

"I can dig it. You've got, like, important police work to do."

Noah noted the sarcasm in the droid's voice, considered grabbing the little mump by the scruff of the neck, then saw Snip standing near the main thoroughfare, watching something on the grid screen mounted there.

"You two go ahead and exchange programmed pleasantries, or whatever it is you do. I've got to see a lady about a tramp. Snip!" he called as he got closer.

"How you lurking there, PD man?"

"I need you to do me a favor."

"Your favor's my flavor. What's the drudge?"

"You know where the Blue Scorpions hang?"

"They're here, they're there. I can scope 'em, but I won't turn 'em."

"I'm not asking you to. I just want to talk with their leader."

"Thrashmaster may not want to talk. He may want to slice and dice."

"Tell him I want a truce. He's lost five of his bikeroos. He may be feeling a little light."

"I'll slither on and pass the word. Still being careful, you are."

"Don't worry about me, Snip, I'm a big old ball of caution."

"YOU'LL LOVE THIS ONE, DANE."

Before he could even get to his desk, Harper was telling him about a report he'd gotten.

"This woman calls, all upset and everything. She wants to report that her husband doesn't want to play hide the salami anymore."

"Shit and frijoles," Noah replied, "what did she want us to do, arrest the poor bastard?"

"I should have given her your link, eh, Dane?"

"Don't do me any favors, okay, Harper?"

His partner was already at her desk. He could tell she was making a point of ignoring him. Nevertheless, just as he was thinking he didn't give a rhinoceros crap what she did, she looked up at him, her sensual baby blues full of indignation.

"That was very rude of you."

"Rude? What are you talking about?"

"The way you treated my friend Jim. You embarrassed me."

"It seemed like the thing to do at the time."

"You...oh, you! You can act like a crabby old man all the time if you want, but don't expect me to just smile and say 'Yes, sir,' and not care what you do. Because I do care. I have feelings, too, you know."

Her vehement diatribe startled him, and despite himself, he felt guilty. He might be crabby but he wasn't old—not that old. Yeah, life had taken a spastic turn, but he shouldn't be taking it out on her.

"Listen..." he started, then paused. "I'm sorry I blew off your garbage man friend. I just—"

"Well, if it isn't the fastest gun in the West."

The grating voice of Brunelli interrupted his apology, but he kept his eyes trained on Marilyn. Brunelli kept talking.

"Hey, quick-draw, I heard you mulched a couple of really dangerous desperados riding bicycles. That's what happens when you've got an itchy trigger finger. Don't worry, though. This time if you lose your partner they'll just build you another one."

He hadn't even finished the sentence before Noah was out of his chair, an exploding human projectile hurtling toward him. Fortunately for Brunelli, Marilyn and Harper were between them. They intervened, both grabbing hold of Noah before he could close in. His eyes, however, were locked on target and radiating venom.

Brunelli, braced against a desk, his lip twitching strobe-like, was silent, his self-preservation instinct somewhat tardy.

"We know he's an asshole, Dane," grunted Harper, straining to hold back Noah, "you're not going to prove anything."

"Captain Raevski wants to see you," Marilyn said. "Maybe this would be a good time to take care of that."

Noah didn't react; he continued to burn a pair of eyeball-sized holes into Brunelli. He grunted, eased back and walked away. It was a slow, measured walk, and by the time he reached the box he was relatively calm. The captain's door was closed, so he took a moment to compose himself. Just as he was ready to knock, the door opened and Heather nearly bumped into him.

"Heather, what are you…what are you doing here?"

"I do work with the DA, remember?"

"Sure, but…" That great perfume of hers hit him, but instead of firing the pistons of his lust, the scent pushed his anxiety button.

"Just a little prosecutorial business," she said. "Don't worry."

"I'm not worried."

"You should see the look on your face. You look like you think I'm telling bedtime stories. Speaking of which, have you got a minute or twenty to come up to my office for a little law and order? You make the law and I'll give the orders."

"I, uh…I'd better not."

"What about tonight? My place?"

Ordinarily, his response wouldn't have required even conscious thought. However, his usual firmness of purpose was beset by doubt. He flashed on their last encounter, and his procreational instincts began to flag.

"I can't. I mean, I could, but I've got this case I'm on. It's not a good time."

Heather looked at him with surprise, then concern. "All right. You've got my link. Take care of yourself, okay?"

"Always."

He watched as she walked away, metaphysically smacking himself upside the head as he followed the jaunty rhythm of her memorable derriere. What was wrong with him? And why, all of a sudden, was everyone worried about him? He wasn't worried. He'd find that gutter perp and make him pay for Cy. Then there wouldn't be anything to worry about.

"Dane!" He heard Raveski screech. "Are you going to stand there all day, or are you going to get your trouble-making butt in here?"

Okay, maybe there was a little to worry about.

18

PLATONIC ASYLUM

D ENSE CLOUDS THREATENED A DOWNPOUR, AND THE ONSLAUGHT OF THE WIND GAVE wings to anything that wasn't fastened down. Chastity held her coat over her head, partly to protect her hair but mostly for anonymity. She had her driver drop her off a good distance from her destination for that reason. Her public excursions had been that way for some time now, moving surreptiously through the streets, sneaking into back doors, outfitted with assorted scarves, sunglasses, hats and veils. It was the one aspect of her success she regretted.

Even worse than the chance of public recognition were the snoop cams. Armed with digital recognition files of the faces of politicians, sports figures, grid personalities and the like, they roamed the city, often at random, in search of celebrity prey. Used by so-called professional journalists and amateur enthusiasts alike, it took only one significant piece of video sold to the grid's highest bidder to pay off the investment in equipment.

When Chastity reached the Platonic sanctuary, she had to pass by the busy main entrance in order to slip around to the side door where the idisk would allow her entry. She was surprised to see ongoing construction. Workers were in the final stages of installing a massive holoboard. Even more surprising was the board's message. Though not yet fully functional, Chastity could read the words in the now fixed image. *V-Real, One Step Beyond Reality, One Step Closer To Heaven.*

It wasn't the display so much as its location that was unsettling. Such product placement was everywhere these days, even within the walls of her own studio. But on the face of the sanctuary? And the reference to heaven? It seemed almost sacrilegious.

After identifying her, the automated door controls allowed entry, and she hurried inside. No one was in the immediate area, but then, Minister Redstone knew she was coming and had likely notified her staff of her guest's desire for privacy. Of course, with the entryway camera focused on her, Chastity doubted her arrival went unnoticed. She folded her coat, set it on a shelf near the door and straightened her timid-green frock.

Though she was aware of Minister Redstone's affinity for cleanliness, she still marveled at the hospital-like sterility as she passed through various hallways on her way to the high minister's office. Such devotion to detail was something Chastity could relate to.

The high minister's personal secretary was not at her desk, so Chastity took the liberty of opening the office door and peering inside.

"Chastity, my dear, come in, come in," Minister Redstone instructed upon seeing her. "I've been waiting for you. Did you have any trouble getting here?"

"No, Minister. It was uneventful."

"Good, good." Minister Redstone came forward to greet her and gestured toward her couch. She had abandoned her official white robe and donned a vermilion jumpsuit of some velvet-like material. A headband of the same cloth, imprinted with the church's logo, held her long hair at bay. "I must say you're looking quite fetching today. That's an interesting, if subdued, outfit you have on."

"Thank you." Chastity ran her hands down her dress as if to smooth the wrinkles as she moved toward the white leather couch.

"Oh, my! Look at the filth on the back of your dress."

Chastity strained to look but saw only a tiny smudge. "I must have brushed up against something."

"We can't have you wearing that in here. Take it off, and I'll find you something else."

Chastity hesitated a moment then shed her modesty along with her dress. Nevertheless, she found it disconcerting that the high minister stood there watching as she disrobed. When only her simple white undergarments remained, she fought the impulse to cover herself with her hands. Minister Redstone produced a plastic bag and held it open.

"Put your dress in here, and I'll have it cleaned."

"That's not necessary, High Minister, I—"

"I insist," Redstone said in a tone that demanded obedience. "It will be clean by the time you're ready to leave."

Chastity did as she was told, but felt unworthy watching the high minister carry her dirty laundry out the door. When she returned to the room, she handed Chastity the gray robe of a deaconess.

"Is it okay for me to wear this? I mean, I haven't taken any vows or been consecrated or anything."

"Yes, dear, it's absolutely okay. After all, in way, you're one of the church's most prominent missionaries."

"I never thought of myself as a missionary," Chastity said, feeling more secure now that the robe was snug around her.

"Come, sit down." Redstone again motioned to her couch, and they both sat.

"High Minister, I noticed the new holoboard outside the sanctuary, and I—well, I guess I was wondering why you would allow such a thing."

The high minister's dark brown eyes flashed momentarily with what Chastity interpreted as indignation.

"The church is endowed by many patrons, my dear. We welcome them all with open arms, and praise the economic efficacy which allows us to spread our message through the multitudes."

"But V-Real? That seems an odd choice to—"

"We don't choose our benefactors, God directs them to us. Besides, isn't V-Real one of your own sponsors?"

"That's true but—"

"Now they've chosen to sponsor the tenets of the Platonic faith. Is that not as worthy an ambition as sponsoring *Gridspeak with Chastity Blume?*"

"Of course it is," responded Chastity, shamed by her doubt.

"The V-Real Corporation has been very generous with its donations, and its leaders have convinced me _their alignment with our church is based as much on spiritual concerns as those more monetary."

"I'm sorry I questioned you, High Minister. You're absolutely right, of course."

"There's nothing wrong with questions, my dear. Life begins with questions. My calling here on Earth is to help as many souls as I can to find the right answers.

"So, tell me, what questions, what crisis of the soul brings you here today?"

"It's not really a...What makes you think I have a crisis of the soul, High Minister?"

"I know you, Chastity, better perhaps than you know yourself. What's troubling you?"

"I've been thinking more and more about my mother recently. I don't know why. I never even knew my mother—not that I remember. All my father has ever told me is that she's dead. The subject seems to upset him, so I haven't brought it up in years. Not since I was a little girl. But now…"

"Now you'd like to know who your mother was," Minister Redstone said, finishing the thought.

Chastity nodded.

"I think it's wonderful that you want to know about your mother, Chastity. You must approach your father, gently but firmly, and let him know how important this is to you. I'm sure he'll understand."

"You don't know my father."

"How could a father deny his little girl," asked the high minister, smiling, "especially one so pretty? Still, I sense that's not the only thing weighing on your mind. What's really troubling you?"

Chastity glanced down, her eyes searching the immaculate white floor for nothing in particular. Her hands fumbled idly with her robe. "I'm having certain thoughts, High Minister. The kind of thoughts I shouldn't be having."

"Lustful thoughts?"

Chastity looked up at her spiritual mentor. "Yes. How did you know?"

Minister Redstone allowed herself an unrestrained chuckle, tossing strands of raven silk hair over her shoulder. "It's only natural, dear. You're a twenty-six-year-old woman, primed for childbearing. Such feelings are a normal part of life."

"But the teachings of the church…"

"The teachings of the church require us to harness those primitive urges and direct such energy toward more civilized pursuits in order to become productive human beings. There's nothing sinful about having such thoughts. I myself have been tempted by the pursuits of the flesh on many occasions. Even the Most Pristine Plato was burdened by such urges." Minister Redstone placed her hand atop Chastity's, patting it gently. "It's not what you think, my dear, but how you act that's important."

It was her actions, both past and potential, that distressed Chastity. It was one thing to believe in something, another to abide by those beliefs. She prayed she had the strength.

"So tell me, Chastity dear, just woman to woman now. Who is it that's kindling these lustful thoughts?"

19

MY DAUGHTER,
THE TRANSCENDENTAL TUBER

S HE LOOKED EXACTLY THE SAME. SHE HAD ON THE SAME DARK-PURPLE PANTSUIT, HER hair was tied up the same way and even the dull expression on her face hadn't changed.

Except "she" was really "it." Noah had to keep reminding himself the image he saw was make-believe. It was a machine talking through video lips.

"Good afternoon, Noah, or should I say good evening? You're late again," scolded the theratech.

"Yeah, police business. Didn't you get my message?" His tone oozed sarcasm.

"No, Noah, I received no message. Let's proceed, shall we?"

"Fire away, Gertie."

The vid representation pretended to look at the notes on her pad, but Noah knew the real "doctor" had gigabytes of data available without refreshing its memory.

"How is the case coming along?"

"Like a garden snail on dozers."

"How does that make you feel?"

"How does it make me feel? It pisses me off. It frustrates the drudge out of me. It makes me wonder why the hell I'm wasting my time sitting here when I've got real work to do."

"I see. I understand you have a new partner. How are you adjusting to the change?"

"I'm adjusting fine," replied Noah, shifting in the cramped seat to find a more comfortable position.

"What's your impression of your new partner?"

"Oh, you'd like her. She's just like you."

"In what way?"

"Why is it, Gertie, you insist on asking questions you already know the answer to?"

"Don't you, as a detective, ask suspects questions you already know the answer to?"

"Sure. But that's just to take their temperature, see if they're prone to lying."

The theratech image patted her brunette bun as if to be sure it was in place. "Then let's just say I ask those questions sometimes to take your temperature. So, in what way is your new partner like me?"

"She's a machine. What did you think I meant, that her ass was the same size as yours?"

"How do you feel about having a partner that's, as you call her, a machine?"

"Look, I admit I wasn't wild about the idea at first. I still don't think droids will ever make good detectives. Let's just say I've gotten used to her. She's okay—I could've done worse. Shit and frijoles, she's even staying with me."

"How are you, Noah? Are you experiencing any anxiety, any misgivings, any overwhelming emotions or distress?"

Noah hesitated. The memory of his encounter with Heather surfaced.

"Nope, no problems."

"That's good to hear," responded the theratech. "Now let's talk about—"

"Hold on a second, Gertie," interrupted Noah as his left ear began to itch, "I've got incoming."

He pinched the lobe and was half surprised to hear Marilyn's voice. He shouldn't have been. His partner was the only one who'd be on his direct com frequency, but part of him still expected to hear Cy's graveled tones.

Noah, the Digital Imaging Recognition System has recorded a positive hit on a Catherine Anne Dane—ninety-seven percent probability. I thought you'd want to know right away.

"Where and when?"

A stationary cam picked her up in Union Square ten minutes ago. An IRIS was dispatched to the location, but so far, it hasn't detected her.

"Meet me at the pod launch and route the video to my pad." Noah deactivated his com and bounced out of the padded chair. "Sorry, Gertie, I've got to fly. Police emergency."

"All right. Shall we meet again tomorrow at the same time?" There was no response. The theratech's sensors focused on an empty room. Noah was already gone.

HE SPOTTED THE MOB FROM ABOVE—AT LEAST, IT LOOKED LIKE A MOB. THERE MUST HAVE been thousands pressed together. He had no idea what it was all about, but that crowd was going to make it more difficult to locate Cat—that is, if she was even still in the area. No wonder the IRIS hadn't found her yet.

"You know I'm fully qualified to operate a pod," said Marilyn as he chose a landing spot on the periphery of the throng. She'd been yapping about why he wouldn't let her fly since they'd taken off. "I've flown dozens of simulations without a mishap."

"Well, simulate silence for a while, okay? I need to concentrate."

Marilyn got that pouty look on her face and turned away from him as he landed the pod. She was still ignoring him when they got out, and that was fine with him. He was preoccupied anyway, trying to see every face that passed. Scores of people were still streaming in, immersing themselves in a crowd that was predominantly young girls. That was going to make it even harder to pick out Cat. He'd already seen half a dozen that looked like her from a distance.

"Damn, it's hot and humid out here."

"Yes, it…that's strange."

"What's strange?"

"The funniest thing just popped right into my head. When you said 'it's hot,' I thought when it's hot like this I put my undies in the fridge. Isn't that silly?"

Noah didn't know whether to laugh or frown. "Yeah, you're a real wackadoo there, Marilyn."

He noticed newscams from various outlets making their way through the swarm, not that anyone bothered to notice. There were few places in the city you could go without being the star of your own little mundane drama these days. Still, it looked like the media thought this was a happening worth covering.

"If we split up, we can cover more ground and have a better chance of finding her," he said, still searching for the face of his daughter.

"Regulations stipulate that in a potentially chaotic situation such as this law enforcement teams need to remain in visual contact at all times."

Noah flashed her a disgusted you're-quoting-regulations-now look and threw his arms in the air. "Fine! Whatever. Just keep those droid eyes of yours on the ball, would you? You know what she looks like, let's get in there and find her. You there. You." Noah poked a passing girl, who turned and smiled. "What's going on here?"

"It's Chastity Blume. She's doing her show live inside, but she might come out later."

"That's what this is all about?"

"Chastity's the greatest," said the young girl, focusing on Marilyn for the first time. "I know you. My grandmother collects old films. She's got hundreds. You're Marilyn Monroe, aren't you? Will you autoprint my pad? Please? My grandmother would love it."

"Sure," Marilyn said, taking the pad from the girl and placing her fingertips on the screen.

"I want to get Chastity's print later, if I can."

"You know she's not the real Marilyn Monroe, don't you?" asked Noah.

The girl stared at him like she didn't know what he was talking about. Marilyn frowned at him. When the girl hurried off, she said to Noah, "That was the cruelest thing you've said yet."

"What are you talking about?"

"Saying I'm not real, especially in front of that young girl."

"Well, you're not, are you?"

"That doesn't give you the right to be mean about it."

"Okay, okay, I'm sorry. I'm a little distracted right now. Could we please start searching for my daughter?"

Marilyn didn't respond. She stalked off into the fringes of the crowd looking hurt. Noah mumbled a curse at droid engineers everywhere and followed her.

He spotted a pair of satellite trucks, barricaded to keep away the overly enthusiastic fans. Cables from the trucks snaked their way inside the Galleria where, no doubt, America's Favorite Virgin was holding court. Giant grid screens were set up for those who couldn't get inside, but currently they only displayed a variety of music vids.

Boisterous hucksters of all types were taking advantage of the grid star's draw. Among them, Noah saw several shirtboarders sandwiched with pulsing neon verbiage promoting the latest virtual reality experience. *Get Real with V-Real.* The palpitating lights were almost mesmerizing. *It's Better Than Chocolate*, they proclaimed over and over.

Bikes and movers were parked everywhere, and not only in the specified stalls. There were too many people. Noah thought of alerting riot control, but then saw a group of uniforms carrying sick sticks and 'jectured he'd let them deal with it. He needed to find Cat.

As he and Marilyn continued their search, a chant began somewhere off to his right. He couldn't understand it at first, but it gathered momentum, virulently sweeping through the multitude.

"We want Chastity! We want Chastity! We want Chastity!"

The swell of adulation was almost deafening, yet Noah sensed no anger or even dissatisfaction in the mass acclamation. No threat of violence was hinted at by their cry, simply communal devotion. Still, the chant sent a chill of apprehension through him. He wasn't certain if it was the single-mindedness of the crowd he found so disquieting, or the fact that a passionless talking head like Chastity Blume could muster such a following.

When it seemed like the chanting would go on forever, a trio of glittering flatbeds pulled up to the outskirts of the gathering. Heads turned to look at the flashing displays, and gradually the shrill chorus died. What now, wondered Noah as he did his best to examine each young girl's facial features. He had to keep reminding himself to look at the dark-haired girls instead of the blondes. The DIRS image had revealed Cat had changed her hair color again.

A large portion of the throng began moving toward the flatbeds, and he overheard enough shouts to realize what the new fuss was all about. Some genius had decided this was the perfect time and place to stage a product giveaway. Workers on the flatbeds were overwhelmed as they attempted to parcel out V-Real visors to all comers. They began throwing handfuls of the devices over the heads of those closest in an effort to keep the mob back. Noah pitied the uniforms doing crowd control. The giveaway was rapidly turning into one hell of a clusterfuck.

"Noah," called Marilyn over the clamor, "your daughter—over there."

Noah whipped around and looked to where his partner was pointing. It was Cat, no doubt about it, despite her new dark auburn hair. She was sitting with a group of other kids in a small entry alcove, away from the heart of the crowd. She looked up at him in recognition.

"Hello, *Daddy*," she said, the irony in her voice making him look uncomfortable. "What are you doing here?"

"I'm looking for you, that's what I'm doing. Your mother's worried herself into a frenzy over you."

"What about you? Were you worried? No," she said, answering her own question before he could, "you were too busy chasing bad guys, weren't you?"

"Sure I was worried. But let's face it, this isn't the first time you've run off. I 'jecture you know your way around by now. What should I do, Cat, call out the National Guard? Cry myself to sleep? What is it you want?"

The lanky, freckle-faced teen remained silent for a moment, unable or unwilling to respond.

"Let's go, Cat. Get up. Say goodbye to your friends. It's time to go home."

"My name's not Cat," she said peevishly.

"Okay, then, let's go, *Catherine*."

"My name's not Catherine, either, it's Callisto."

"Callisto?"

"Yes," she said defiantly. "I changed it when I joined the Platonians."

"Are you talking about those transcendental tubers?" Noah practically spat the words out. "Is that what this is all about? You let yourself get mind-drudged by a bunch of fanatical religious pecans?"

"There's nothing wrong with my mind!" she snapped as she stood to face him. "We're not fanatics. We believe in Minister Redstone's teachings. But you wouldn't know what I believe, would you? You don't know me, so don't pretend you care."

The verbal slap caught Noah unaware. He opened his mouth to answer, but his rebuttal was nonexistent. He turned around to collect himself, knowing his daughter's accusation was at least partially true. He hadn't been around enough to know her. Who was he to play daddy dearest now? Still, he couldn't believe she'd hooked up with the Platonistas. He'd rather she'd shacked up with some guy.

Regardless of how she felt about him, he had to take her to her mother. He looked at Marilyn. She had hung back and stayed quiet, waiting for him to deal with his daughter on his own.

He resolved to be firm, and turned back to tell Cat she could play Transcendental Platonics at home. However, as he did, a singularly sexy woman sheathed in red leather sauntered by. He gave in to the automatic impulse and was in the process of devouring her from tip to toe when he spotted the tattoo. He only had a quick glimpse before she moved deeper into the crowd, but it was wrapped around her neck, and he was sure it was the same design as Huang's.

"Grab her!" he called to Marilyn. "The one in red. She's got the tat."

"The what?"

"The tattoo—the same tattoo!" Noah turned to his daughter. "Cat, you wait here, don't move. I'll be right back."

He was behind and to the left of Marilyn as they waded through the press of bodies. It wasn't until he broke through the outer rim of the throng that he spotted the woman in red again. She didn't appear interested in either the V-Real giveaway or the virgin Chastity. Apparently, she was just passing through the hubbub on her way to somewhere else.

"Excuse me, miss," Marilyn called out. "We want to talk to you. We're with the police. Please stop."

The woman looked back and saw them coming after her. She stopped, and Noah saw her shoulders sag as if in annoyance. Then he saw something else and lunged at Marilyn.

The tattooed lady had a weapon in her hand when she turned. She fired, and a beam of hot white light sliced through the cool night air about ten inches above where Noah lay atop Marilyn. Fortunately, the laser's path to the crowd was blocked. It burned into a grid kiosk behind them, sending sparks flying.

Noah held on tight to his partner as he rolled both of them over and behind the cover of a concrete garden wall. Marilyn squealed as she was flung over for the second time and hit the pavement with him on top of her.

He was on his feet, his Desert Eagle in hand, almost before she realized he was off her. By the time she scrambled up and pulled out her sonic stunner, Noah was holstering his gun.

"She's gone," he said stiffly.

"She had the same weapon as—"

"Yeah, I know."

"Shouldn't we search for her?"

"She's history. But go ahead and put out a DIRS alert. We may get lucky. I've got to get back to Cat."

"You saved my life," Marilyn said, as if she'd just realized it.

Noah grunted. "It seemed like the thing to do at the time."

CAT WAS ALREADY GONE, AND SO WERE ALL OF HER FRIENDS. NOAH WASN'T SURPRISED. HE hadn't expected her to wait so he could haul her home. Marilyn wanted to search for her, but he knew it was useless. At least now he had an idea of how and where to find her—and who to ask.

"What have you got there?" he inquired, seeing Marilyn fiddling with something.

"It's one of those V-Real visors," she said. "Some nice young man gave it to me."

"You can play with it later. Let's get out of here."

20

THE STORK WAS A MOCKINGBIRD

I'M SORRY THAT IT'S TAKING SO LONG, MS BLUME, BUT THERE WAS A HEIGHTENED terrorist alert put into effect this morning, so security measures have been more stringent."

"Does this alert have something to do with Loftur?" Chastity asked the gate guard.

"I don't really know, ma'am. It probably is. I'm sure security will clear you in just a minute."

"Thanks."

It was a brisk morning, and Chastity was sorry she'd sent her car away. She rubbed her hands together and paced behind the gate to keep warm. She had decided on the spur of the moment to go see her father, striking while her courage was hot. Usually they'd let her right in—not that she had dropped in unannounced to see him much in recent years.

These Loftur terrorists had everyone on edge. She'd heard various rumors about the group's agenda but wasn't positive what it was they wanted, or what they were against. All she knew was they were a Scandinavian group. Not knowing went against her journalistic grain. She told her staff she wanted to devote a program to the terrorists, but they were unable to collect any substantiated data or, for that matter, find anyone with the government or law enforcement who was willing to be interviewed as an expert on the subject.

The guard leaned out of his gate and waved for her attention. "Ms Blume, they say you don't have an appointment, and aren't on any of the guest lists."

"I don't need an appointment to see my own father," she replied angrily, her face turning red to complete the patriotic theme of her powder blue-and-white outfit. "You tell whomever you're talking to that I'm not a terrorist, and if you don't let me in immediately to see my father, who's the chief executive officer of the Lucidity Corporation, certain people are going to lose their jobs." She didn't usually play the daughter-of-the-CEO card, but the cold was making her irritable.

The guard pulled his head back inside and conversed with someone for a minute. She heard the pneumatics of the gate stir into action.

"I'm sorry for the delay, Ms Blume," said the guard. "You can go on in now."

She passed through the gate and marched up to the main building, her annoyance withering as she anticipated confronting her father. She was resolved. She wasn't going to wilt this time. She was going stand her ground and get an answer from him. At least, that's what she kept telling herself.

When she reached his outer office, she was greeted by her father's long-time executive assistant.

"Good day, Ms Blume," he said, rising from his chair behind an expansive cherrywood desk. "I'm so sorry you had trouble gaining entrance. I took care of it as soon as I was notified. These days you just can't be too careful."

"Apparently, Michael. Is my father in his office?"

"He's in a meeting, but it shouldn't be much longer. Please have a seat." He hurried to brush any unlikely dust off the leather sofa and straightened the magazines on the table. Michael had always been a bit fussy—for an android. "Can I get you anything to drink, Ms Blume? What about some breakfast?"

"No, thank you, Michael. I'm fine. I'll just have a seat and wait."

"Very good then. Let me know if there's anything I can get you."

He returned to his seat behind the desk and resumed whatever he'd been working on.

"It must be an important meeting if he closed his office door." Her father had always had a mysterious aversion to closed doors. Every door inside their house when she was a girl was always open, even if just a little.

"I couldn't say, Ms Blume."

Not two minutes passed before Chastity heard what sounded like an argument coming from her father's office. It got louder. She recognized one of the voices as her father's. The recognition sent an anxious flutter careening about her stomach as the door opened.

A younger man, thin and dressed casually, burst out of the office with a frown. He glanced at Chastity as he stormed out.

"Have a nice day, Mr. Hutchinson," Michael called after him, oblivious to any altercation that might have occurred.

Her father followed several paces behind his departing visitor as though to chase him down, but stopped short of the outer hall. He turned and marched directly back his office without even noticing Chastity. His stride was steady, but the hunch in his posture was revealing. He looked smaller than she remembered, and much older, she thought, than a man of sixty-seven should. Michael stood. "Mr. Blume, you have a visitor."

When he turned and saw her, his face morphed into what was, to her, a familiar frown. Resolutely she stood, tugging her skirt down as she did.

"Chastity. What are you doing here?"

"Can't a girl come visit her father?"

The skepticism on his face was pronounced. "Come in then," he said, opening his office door and proceeding in without waiting for her.

She followed, and Michael, dear that he was, patted her on the back and said, "Have a nice visit, Ms Blume."

Henri Blume stalked across the room to his desk but didn't sit. Instead, he stood behind it, rigidly staring out his spacious office window at a tiny uniform courtyard.

"So, what's this about?" he asked brusquely, then continued before she could respond. "Are you still involved with that religious group?"

"The Church of Transcendental Platonics, Father. Yes, I'm still a member of the church."

"Waste of time, that. Superstitious nonsense, you know."

"If it's such nonsense, then why is one of your companies supporting them?"

"That's a business matter," he said flatly. He moved a few feet behind his desk but remained standing. Still gazing out the window as though he were avoiding looking at her, he asked, "So, do you have some sort of man in your life?"

Chastity was taken aback. He'd never inquired into her personal life before. In fact, he'd treated the subject like it was a virus.

"I have been seeing someone on occasion. Leeland Powell, he's vice-president in charge of programming at IGN. It's not serious, though."

He turned to look at her as if to determine the veracity of her statement.

"Sit, sit," he ordered, pointing at the chair facing his desk. She did, and he reached into a drawer, pulled out something in a plastic wrapper and handed it to her. It was a V-Real visor, still in its original packaging. "You can access our newest virtual adventures with that. You can climb to the top of the pyramids or fly to Lunar Colony. It's the very latest technology."

Chastity accepted the visor without comment and set it in her lap.

"Father, I want to know who my mother was." She'd said it. She'd rushed it, but now the forbidden subject was out there, and there was no retrieving it. Henri Blume looked like he'd been punched in the kidneys or had swallowed a burr spiked with Tabasco. He ran his hand through what was left of his thinning white hair and pulled out his chair so he could sit. He didn't respond right away, as though he were deliberating various scenarios.

"I'm sorry if it hurts you to talk about her," Chastity began, "but I want to know who my mother was. I want to know all about her. You've never told me anything. I don't know the first thing about my family. You always changed the subject, or told me you'd tell me some other time, or shushed me. I won't be shushed this time, Father. I have a right to know about my mother. I don't even know what her name was."

"Neither do I."

The words escaped her father's mouth like steam escaping a long-sealed pressure valve. Chastity fell silent, momentarily bewildered as she attempted to interpret and reinterpret his statement. Henri Blume stood and turned to the window again.

"What do you mean?" she blurted.

"I mean your mother's not dead, or she is dead—I don't really know. I told you she was dead because I didn't want to tell you the truth."

"The truth about what?"

"The truth…The truth is that you are a product of in-vitro fertilization. You never had a mother."

"What?" Chastity gripped the arms of her chair and labored to think clearly through the haze that enveloped her. What was he saying? How could she not have a mother?

Her father sat back down, sighing as if a torturous burden had been levitated off his shoulders. "I was forty years old, the grid had been established as the ultimate means of communication, making me more money than I could ever spend, and I decided I needed an heir. Someone to oversee the company I had created after I was gone. I wouldn't—" He cut himself off as though he were about to say something he didn't want to reveal and visibly shifted gears. "I didn't have anyone. I never wanted to marry. I'm a scientist, so I turned to what I knew—technology. The technique had been perfected long ago, primarily for infertile couples. So I used it.

"An intermediary arranged, through an assortment of rather exorbitant fees, to harvest the eggs of a woman who was genetically and medically certified. I was never allowed to know her name, and she never knew mine. You developed and were born from an artificial womb, so this woman didn't actually carry you. She was just an egg donor.

"That's why I always told you your mother was dead. Because you never had a mother—not truly. But you do have a father. One who's always looked out for you. That's more than I had. My father disappeared before I was three. He left me to…" Her father seemed to catch himself. He wavered, lost in some distant memory. "You've always had a father who cared about you, took care of you."

Henri Blume stared at his daughter expectantly, but she remained silent. What could she say? How could she respond to being told something like that? Was it better than thinking a mother she never knew was dead? Was it worse than knowing nothing?

"You know, at first, when I thought of an heir, I thought of having a son, naturally. But something changed my mind. Something told me to create a little girl. And at the last minute, that's what I did. I created you, Chastity. I gave you life."

Chastity moved her head side-to-side in disbelief. She had no concept of how much time passed before she reached a decision and stood. She pushed her chair back and tossed the V-Real visor onto her father's desk.

"I don't have time for any virtual realities, Father. I think reality itself is going to be quite enough for me right now."

She turned and walked out. Afterwards, she couldn't remember how she got home.

21

BUBBLE GUM, BUG POISON
AND THE SPIRITUALITY OF KEY LIME PIE

T HE SUN WAS STILL FIGHTING FOR A TOEHOLD ON THE DAY WHEN NOAH BULLED HIS WAY into the office of the Platonic high minister. Getting there proved easier than actually seeing the grand poohbah herself. The secretary stationed outside the massive chrome double doors said Minister Redstone was out of the sanctuary today, wouldn't be back and never granted an audience to anyone without an appointment anyway.

"I don't want an audience with her majesty. I want to talk to her—now."

He slammed his open hands onto her desk, but the secretary stood firm.

"I'm sorry, Inspector. You'll need to make an appointment."

"Look…" Noah glanced at the nameplate on her desk. "…Ms Pearce, if I don't speak with Minister Redstone sometime in the next sixty seconds, I'm going to call for a full raid on this sanctuary of yours. That means a couple dozen ham-handed police officers going through every room, every cabinet, every drawer. Then I'm going to handcuff you and take you in as an accessory."

"Lord, no!" gasped the woman.

"Just call me Noah."

"Please wait a moment. I'll see if I can locate the high minister."

He backed away from her desk and went back to where Marilyn was waiting for him.

"You don't have the authority to search this church, or any evidence that justifies the arrest of that woman," she said quietly.

"She doesn't know that."

"Still, whoever she's calling probably does."

"Doesn't matter. Sometimes just the threat of a fuss can gain you a little cooperation."

"Inspector Dane," called the secretary, "if you'd like to wait inside the high minister's office, she'll join you shortly."

"I'll do that." To Marilyn he said, "See what a little bluster can accomplish? File that away while you wait out here for me."

"If you think that's best."

"I do."

Redstone's office was Spartan but stylish—that is, if you were color-blind. Everything inside was either white or chrome, and that included the alabaster floor tiles. The brightness of it all was dazzling. Noah presumed that was the calculated celestial effect. The room was almost antiseptically clean, though an odd odor pervaded the place. As soon as he walked in he smelled it. It was a queer combination of bubble gum and bug poison.

"Good day, Inspector." High Minister Redstone suddenly appeared where there was apparently nothing but a seamless white wall. More holy hocus-pocus for the true believers. She gave him the traditional Platonic greeting with her hands held down below her waist, forming the inverted pyramid with her thumbs and forefingers. She was dressed in the same ceremonial white robe and silver headband he'd seen her wearing on that holoboard representation.

She moved behind her highly-polished metallic desk with perfect posture, carrying herself with the poise of a dancer. Noah realized for the first time how tall she was.

"I certainly hope this is as urgent as you make it out to be, Inspector."

"Yeah, I'd say it's urgent. I want my daughter."

"Your daughter?" She seemed taken by surprise, but he'd expected that. "I have no idea what you're talking about."

"My daughter ran away from home and was persuaded by you people to join up."

"So, your daughter is a believer, and I take it that you're not."

"My daughter's sixteen."

"There is no age requirement for enlightenment. Many young people today have accepted the word, even if it remains beyond the comprehension of their parents."

"I'll tell you what this parent comprehends. My daughter might believe in you today, but tomorrow she's going to believe in see-through sandals, and the day after that it'll be the spirituality of key lime pie. She changes her beliefs the way she changes her hair color."

Even as he spoke Noah found himself distracted by Redstone's calm sensuality. Regardless of this disruption in her routine, she remained poised. Her mahogany eyes beckoned him despite their aloofness. She was gorgeous, no question. She had a stately beauty that was almost unreal. He wondered for a second if she could be wearing a falseface. No, he didn't think so. The boom in pop religions being what it was, he was sure she could afford the real thing.

When he found himself imaging the sleek limbs, the smooth bronze skin that lay hidden beneath her robe, he shook his inner self. This was no time to be appraising her pow-whammy potential. Not that it mattered. Apparently, the attraction was purely a one-way link. He didn't perceive even an ember of interest in those eyes of her, and his senses in that area were fairly refined. He guessed he just wasn't her type.

Idly, he reached for an ivory carving on her desk. "I'm sure—"

"Please don't touch anything," she said with a hint of panic.

"Sure, whatever you say."

The high minister composed herself. "You understand, I like to keep my office purified—not to insinuate that you are a carrier of germs."

"I've probably got my fair share of bugs."

"There is the matter of religious freedom, Inspector. If your daughter chooses to walk the Platonic path, there's nothing either you or I can do about it, legally speaking."

"Legally speaking, High Minister, if you don't produce my daughter, I'm going to have you and assorted members of your faithful flock charged with kidnapping a minor."

"I doubt you would be able to do that, Inspector. However, I'll do what I can to locate your daughter. I'll notify you as soon as I have any information."

"By tomorrow at the latest, High Minister."

"Certainly. What is your daughter's name?"

"Cat—Catherine Dane. There's a video image in the public DIRS file if you need it. Oh, and she might be using the name Callisto. She got that from you people."

"Good day then, Inspector."

"Yeah, have a good day yourself. Thanks for your time."

NOAH TORE THROUGH HIS MEAL WITH THE ENTHUSIASM OF A BUZZ SAW. HE'D BARELY bothered to throw off his coat and activate his grid screen before wading fork-deep through his chile relleno, enchilada, beans and a trio of tacos. He hadn't eaten all day, and he didn't let the fact that Marilyn sat across from him watching slow him any. She wore an expression of astonishment, almost as if she were mesmerized by the ballet of his gluttony.

"Do you have to eat like…like that?"

"Like what?" he replied with disinterest, his mouth being otherwise occupied.

"Like that. Like a pig."

"I bet you've never even seen a pig."

"I have too."

"Yeah, some programmer's cartoon version I bet."

"You must think I was born yesterday."

"Weren't you?"

The celebudroid turned her head, ignoring him. "I don't think it's healthy for you to eat that fast."

"Healthy? There's nothing healthy about this. But it sure is tasty." Noah took a swig of his beer and ran the back of his hairy hand across his mouth. "I say you've got to live life with gusto, or it's not worth living."

"You've got quite a stock of those sayings, don't you?" Marilyn got up from the table and walked over to examine his flora.

Mid-chew, Noah looked up at his screen to find a program on modern dance. His consumption slowed as he became intrigued with the dancers. When one of them executed a particularly unusual arm movement, Noah, almost without thinking, tried to mimic the move, still sitting at the table, fork in hand. It didn't feel right to him, though. He wasn't doing it correctly.

"What's this?" asked Marilyn.

He'd forgotten she was even in the room. Like a little boy caught peeping into the girls' locker room, he switched to another program.

"This tiny little white flower by itself here," Marilyn continued when he didn't answer right away. "It's very different."

"It is," Noah responded. "That's my Martian moss lily—cost me quite a chunk of credit."

"Is it really from Mars?"

"Why do you think it cost so much? The seedling and soil came straight from the fields of the Marineris colony."

"'Consider the lilies of the field,'" Marilyn recited, "'how they grow. They toil not—'"

"What?"

"I don't know where that came from," Marilyn said, looking confused. "I remember it, but I don't know why. I don't know where I heard it before."

"It must be hell having a patchwork memory like that," Noah said, sounding like he felt sorry for her. "It's tough enough when you have to deal with—"

"You have an incoming call." His screen flashed the message to coincide with the audio. "You have an incoming call. The caller has been positively identified as Georgia Benson Browne, formerly George Benson Browne, official capacity with the San Francisco Police Department designated as—"

"Open the call."

Georgia, still in her lab coat, appeared on the screen.

"Working late, Georgia?"

"Only for you, sugar," she said, finger-flipping her hair. "I found something I thought you'd want to know about. I can't believe I missed it before."

"What is it?"

"I was doing a final scan of Tim Huang and discovered he had an implant."

"An implant?"

"Yes, on the back of his neck, right under the tattoo. That's why I didn't see it before. It plugs straight into his spinal column."

Noah scratched his chest. "What in the name of the four virgins of the apocalypse is that all about?"

"I can't tell you, sugar. I have no idea what such a device would be used for. I'm putting it out there for the biotechs to look at, but..." Georgia raised her hands in resignation. "I thought you'd want to know, though."

"Yeah, thanks."

"Toodles, Noah. I've got a date with a big, fat mocha milkshake."

Georgia cut the link, and Noah turned to his partner.

"This is right up your circuits. Any ideas?"

Marilyn frowned. "The tattoo and the implant must be related—but how?"

"That's the diamond-studded question, isn't it?"

22

SWEET NOTHINGS

CHASTITY HAD BEEN SITTING IN FRONT OF HER MAIN SCREEN FOR MORE THAN AN HOUR. Not that she had any idea how much time had passed. The audio was muted, and she hadn't paid much attention to what was on. In her lap was a box of raspberry truffles. It was half empty.

She was unfocused, dispirited and hollow—devoid of anything meaningful. The only scrap of emotion she discerned was a nebulous anger. It churned and festered but had no direction.

She was angry with herself for being such a good girl, such a puppet, dancing to the strings pulled by her father for so long. She regretted not having forced the issue years ago.

She was angry with him, and not only because he'd lied to her all these years. He'd betrayed her. He'd deprived her of something so basic, so elemental, she felt as if a piece of her soul had been carved out and tossed away like so much carrion.

And she was angry with the world in general. Though what part it played in her wretched state of mind she couldn't pinpoint.

About the same time the truffles faced extinction, Chastity resolved to cease her wallowing and take a more direct, more constructive course of action. She tossed the box of surviving chocolates aside and snatched up her pad. The information was out there, somewhere, and research was something she knew. Once the idea manifested itself, she fed upon her own determination. She'd find her mother—the woman who donated her eggs—whether she was living or dead. She'd find out everything she could about the woman, about her family. She'd know where she came from, no matter what or how long it

114

took.

Empowered by purpose, she was anxious to begin. But where should she start? Chastity's hand found its way to the base of her neck as she pondered a strategy to uncover her mother's identity. First, she decided, she'd learn everything there was to know about in-vitro fertilization. She could ask her father—

No, she wasn't going to ask him anything. She'd identify all the medical facilities licensed for artificial birthing, and cross-reference his name. Then she—

A piercing cry interrupted her line of thought, and she looked up from her pad to see Angel peering up at her with blue cat eyes.

"Angel, what's wrong?" Chastity had never heard her make a sound like that. "What are you crying about?"

The feline wailed once more for good measure, fell to the floor and began rubbing one side of her body against the carpet. The contortions continued as she flipped herself over and squirmed off in a different direction. Chastity was so distracted by the queer little dance she forgot her mission for the moment.

"What are you doing, you silly kitty? You're acting very strange."

Chastity reached down to touch her, and as soon as she made contact, Angel rolled onto her stomach and thrust her hindquarters into the air. As Chastity stroked her, she kept wiggling forward, tail in the air.

"I don't know what's got into you—"

"Ms Blume, David Mandala of building maintenance is at your door, inquiring if you are at home."

"Oh? All right, deactivate security."

"Shall I respond to his inquiry, Ms Blume, or grant him entry?"

"I'll do it," Chastity said, getting up.

When she opened her door, David seemed surprised to see her. "Oh, Ms Blume—I mean, Chastity—I didn't know you were home. I thought maybe you'd be at work. I didn't want to bother you if you were at home. That's why I asked your homeminder if you were here."

"I didn't feel like going to work today."

"Are you sick? I shouldn't be bothering you if you're not feeling good."

"I'm not sick really. What did you want?"

"I, uh, watered your plants the other day like you asked, but they were so dry I thought I'd better come back today and water them down again. Some of them aren't in too good of shape."

"You're so thoughtful, David. Come in, come in. Why don't you sit a minute? The plants can wait. You can sit a minute, can't you?"

"Sure, I guess so." David looked around and chose the closest armchair. He set his water container on the floor next to him.

"Can I get you something to drink or—"

"No, thanks, Ms—Chastity." He smiled, and she laughed.

"I guess calling me by my first name will take some getting used to."

"Yeah, I'm not used to that."

"Here, have a truffle," she said, holding the box out to him. "They're really delicious."

"I don't think I've ever had a truffle before. Looks like chocolate."

"It is, but flavored. These are raspberry."

He took one, and as he bit into it Chastity found herself staring into his eyes. She'd never looked at them closely before. Like the truffles, they were a rich, dark brown, and there was a tenderness to them, a forthrightness she found quietly appealing. For a moment she thought she saw him looking at her. Really looking—like a man looks at a woman. It was a brief notion she abruptly rejected as wishful thinking.

"These are really good," he said. "Of course, there's not much that's better than good chocolate."

"I love it," Chastity agreed. "Does your mother like chocolate?"

"Sure. Who doesn't?"

Chastity opened a drawer and pulled out another candy box. "Here, I want you to take these to your mother."

"Oh, you don't have to do that," David said, waving his hand in the air.

"Of course I don't, but I want to. You take these to her—no argument."

David accepted the box. "Thank you, Chastity. I'm sure she'll like them even more because they came from you. She's a big fan, you know. She watches your show all the time. She even brags to her friends that I work in your building."

"How's your mother doing?"

His smile faded, and he looked at the floor. "She's not doing all that well right now. It's getting harder for her to get up and get around by herself. The arthritis is really bad, and her bones aren't as strong as they used to be. I'm afraid she'll fall and break something."

"That's too bad. Isn't there anything the doctors can do about her condition?"

"Not really. They've got some new, experimental medicines they wanted to try, but she says she doesn't want anyone experimenting on her. Besides, they're expensive."

Chastity made a mental note to look into it and see what kinds of medicines there were. Maybe she could help.

"I'd better get to watering your plants," said David, standing. "I've got some other work to do."

"Ms Blume, Leeland Powell is at your door requesting your presence."

"Leeland? What's he doing here?"

"If you got company then maybe I'd better go," David said.

"He's my, uh...boss, David. I don't know what he wants. Maybe you'd better go ahead and do your other work. You can water the plants tomorrow if you have a chance."

"Sure, I can do that. Thanks for the candy."

"You're welcome," said Chastity, opening her door.

Leeland was standing there. He looked from her to David, and there was an awkward moment as David started out the door and stopped because Leeland was in his way.

"Leeland, this is David...I'm sorry, David, I forgot your last name."

"Mandala."

"David Mandala, Leeland Powell."

David nodded. "Hello."

Leeland returned the nod and stepped aside to let the maintenance man pass.

"Goodbye, Ms Blume."

Chastity felt a twinge of guilt that she was glad he'd reverted to her last name in front of Leeland. She called after him, "Goodbye, David," and turned to Leeland. "What a nice surprise, Leeland. Or are you just checking up on me? Come in."

"When our top talent calls in sick, I come out with the chicken soup."

"Really? Where's the soup?"

"Damn, I knew I forgot something."

"That's all right, I'm not really sick. I just had to deal with some other things today. So, why are you really here? Is this about the other day with the marketing people?"

"That?" Leeland chuckled. "I rather enjoyed that. No, this has nothing to do with business. I purposely wanted to speak with you away from all that."

Chastity wasn't so preoccupied that she didn't know where the conversation was headed. It was the last thing she needed to deal with right now. She was busy formulating excuses in her mind when he gently but firmly grabbed hold of her and kissed her.

She was too stunned at first to do anything but go with it. Even in the midst of her emotional disorder, she found it enjoyable, though not so much that she was about to completely surrender herself to the pleasure of it. He sensed her lack of passion, pulled away and looked hard into her eyes.

"Chastity, you can stop the act now. It's just the two of us here—no cameras, no audience."

"What act?"

"Your coy act. The preservation of your public image."

"It's not an act, Leeland. That's who I am."

He looked at her like he still wasn't buying it. "I don't want to play games any longer. I want a real relationship, and I want it with you. I'm not the kind of man who stands back and waits for something to happen. I need to know how you feel. If I'm wrong, tell me. If I'm not…"

He reached for her again, but she casually stepped away, turning away from him and pulling at her dress.

"I don't know if I can answer that, Leeland," she said, turning back to look at him. "I can't say that part of me doesn't find the idea appealing, but…"

She was, indeed, tempted by his offer. She'd been attracted to him since the day they'd first met. The idea of being with someone, not being alone all the time, had its allure. Still, what if he knew the truth? Would he still want her? She wondered if her reputation was part of the attraction. It wasn't her fault she'd been branded with that name. She'd never made any claims. What would Leeland think, what would her faithful fans think, if that label were written in scarlet letters?

"But what?"

"There's too much going on right now, Leeland, too much on my mind. Personal things—things I can't explain to you. Not now." She tried to laugh, but it was a weak attempt. "I'm in no condition to commit to any kind of relationship now. I'm sorry."

He looked at her like he didn't know what to say. Then, as if he'd resigned himself to a decision, said, "I'm sorry too, Chastity. I was hoping we could…well, anyway." He turned and walked straight to the door. "I'll see you tomorrow?" he asked, his tone decidedly professional.

"Yes." She wanted to say more, but "yes" is what came out.

23

HERE TODAY, GONZO TOMORROW

NOAH WASN'T SURPRISED WHEN A PLATONISTA LACKEY CALLED TO TELL HIM WHERE HE could pick up Cat. He didn't 'jecture the "religious freedom" of one lost little girl would be worth the exposure he'd threatened Redstone with. Of course, how he was going to deal with his daughter was a different matter. Still, he was anxious to check in at the Hall, sign out a pod and go get her.

The Mag pulled into his stop on time for a change. He made his way out of the train car along with a gaggle of other commuters, many of whom he noticed were wearing those V-Real visors. It was getting so you couldn't go anywhere anymore without seeing someone with one of those things or talking about V-Real, or running into some holoboard ad. Noah wondered how long this particular craze would last before the next one took over.

"Hey, PD man!" It was Snip, standing right there, her bad eye seeming to wink at him. "I've got the word."

"What is it, Snip? What are you doing here?"

"You ask for the Thrash, you gots the Thrash."

"The leader of the Scorpions? He'll meet with me?"

"Meet he will. Grand Master Thrash says now or never. He's waiting at Pier 39, next to the virtual carousel. Won't wait long."

"I can't go now." Noah thought about Cat, and how likely it was she might slip away from her theological guardians once she realized he was coming for her.

"You wants to talk, has to be now—just him, just you. You'd better slither on if you want truce."

"All right." He'd have to hope they'd hold on to Cat until he got there. "Let

119

me get you something to eat first."

The street clone ran four fingers through her shaggy Mohawk. "Thrash already fed me. I'm crucial, tiptop."

"Do you trust this Thrash bikeroo?"

"Me? I don't trust. Not nobody."

Noah smiled. "Smart girl. Don't trust anyone."

"Maybe I trust PD man a little." She put her hand on his arm, and Noah sensed genuine affection in the touch. "If you gots to meet with Thrashmaster, then you gots to. But lurk low and keep eyes back of head."

"Okay, Snip, I will. Thanks."

PIER 39 WAS USUALLY MOBBED WITH KIDS AND TOURISTS. HOWEVER, ON THIS EARLY morning in February it was practically deserted. Some of the shops were just opening, though the kiddie rides and game booths were still locked shut. Noah made his way down the pier, past the security cam array to where the virtual carousel was located. When he was a boy, it had been a real carousel with fiberglass horses and unicorns you could climb aboard and ride round and round. He didn't see the sense in the technological upgrade. How much better could virtual be than the real thing?

He heard a stifled sneeze and turned around. Standing a few yards away, wearing an electric-blue derby, a fancy silk brocade vest and no shirt, was a guy who had to be Thrash. Noah performed a quick visual reconnaissance of the surrounding area but didn't spot any other bikeroos. So he closed the gap until he stood just the other side of an antique wooden barrel from the leader of the Blue Scorpions. The barrel was a touristy thing from better days, now a trash receptacle.

The first thing he noticed about the gang leader was the large blade sheathed at his belt. It was partially concealed by the vest, which was woven with a peculiar spaceship design. He was surprised at how short the bikeroo was—nearly a foot less than himself. But Thrash was bulldog built; his heavily-tattooed arms were monuments to either a monster workout regime or steroidian devotion. Noah did a quick check of his neck. No collar-like tattoo there. Just the prerequisite tat of a blue scorpion crawling across his Adam's apple.

Without warning, the bikeroo unsheathed his blade and in a single downward chop sank it into the top of the barrel. It was a wicked-looking thing at least twenty inches long, curved, but not like any knife Noah had seen.

He had reached for his own weapon; however, he didn't draw it. Instead he rested his hand on the butt, considering the significance of the gesture. Moving slower, to make sure his intent was clear, he pulled out his gun and set it next to the knife.

"That's quite a hammer you have there," the bikeroo said through thin lips, making no attempt to touch the gun. He had a voice that could rub sandpaper raw. "You don't see many like that."

"Mark XIX .50-caliber Desert Eagle with a six-inch barrel, titanium carbon finish."

"Nice. No wonder my boys got holes the size of handlebar grips in them."

"That's an unusual blade you've got there yourself."

"Klingon mek'leth. Had it special made."

"Klingon?"

"So, you're Dane," the Blue Scorpion said, ignoring his query.

"And you're Thrash."

Noah knew the game, and he was playing from the position of power. So he waited for Thrash, but didn't have to wait long.

"Snipper says you want to open hailing frequencies. I can cope with the merits of that. Sure, I'm five bikes down, but I'm not one to cry over spiked milk." He sneezed and went right on. "Dim-witted spokeheads were off track anyway. They're always doing this when I'm telling them to do that. I tell you, they're the pain of my existence, they are. You just can't find any streeters with any real smarts these days. I've already got a tussle with the Razorbacks, so I don't need more conflict. You want a truce, I say make it so." Thrash rubbed his eyes. "Damn allergies, they start earlier every year. Here it is not even March yet and my eyes are itching and watering. You got allergies?"

"No."

"You're lucky there. They're a damn nuisance."

"All right then, it's agreed. Your boys stop trying to turn me into mulch, and I stop sending them to bikeroo heaven."

"You won't be giving us any drudge either."

"I've got other items on my agenda. Speaking of which, you can line our new relationship with rose petals by telling me about the diamonds."

"Diamonds?"

"Don't go coy on me now, Thrashmaster, I was just starting to like you. You know what I'm talking about. The diamonds your bikeroos were after the day I flattened three of them."

"That's a Horace of different color. Now you're talking business, and I really can't talk business. I have a certain fiduciary responsibility to my clients."

"You mean the responsibility to try and rip them off?"

Thrash smiled, flexing his right bicep. "There is that. All right, Dane. There's not much to tell anyway. This guy—"

"What was his name?"

"Name? I don't know. Long, Dong, Bong—one of them Chinese names."

"Huang?"

"Maybe. Yeah, that might have been the mump. Anyway, I hear this guy had cut himself a slice off the top of his employer's gems, so I pass streetword that I could find a buyer."

"Who was this employer?"

"Couldn't say."

"What about the other guy—the guy with Huang. What was his name?"

"I don't know. Probably some muscle he hired for protection."

Noah scratched at his chest and retrieved his gun. Thrash pulled his blade from the wood and sheathed it.

"In the spirit of our new relationship, I'm sure if you hear anything else about that transaction, or anything else about diamonds, you'll get word to me, won't you?"

"I will make it priority one," said the bikeroo, a more than mischievous glint in his eyes.

"Well then, nice chatting with you, Thrash." Noah backed away out of habit before turning to head for his pod.

"Live long and propagate," Thrash called behind him.

Noah waved the back of his hand and kept on going.

HE WAITED AND WATCHED AS TWO GRAY-ROBED ACOLYTES ESCORTED CAT DOWN THE LONG corridor toward him. He looked for any telltale signs she might bolt, but all he saw was resignation. They'd evidently already informed her that she'd have to go with him.

"I'm Deacon Lacrosse," said the elder of the two when they stopped in front of him, "and this is Deacon Browar."

Noah nodded in reply.

"I'm going to have to ask you for formal identification before I can release her to your custody," he said, holding out a portable idisk.

Noah placed his hand on it and declared his name. The Platonic deacon examined the results, then said to the teenager, "Go with God, Catherine Dane." Both of the men made the sign of the inverted pyramid.

She scrunched up her face at the deacon in a magnificent frown even Noah had to admire and walked right past him toward the sanctuary's exit.

Once outside, she didn't know which way to go, so she stomped to a halt as if she weren't taking another step.

"I don't know why you're here. If you take me home, I'll just run away again."

"Cat," Noah said with exasperation. "You've got to go home, so make the best of it. Your mother's worried about you, you've got to go back to school, and—"

"Mother is worried about all of her husbands, and what they'll think if she can't control me."

"That's not true, Cat. Your mother is worried about you. I know. And I'm sure your other fathers...er...the rest of your family is, too."

"I hate it," she said, her blue eyes as innocent-looking as they were angry. "There's always somebody telling me what to do. Some group parent who thinks they're the boss."

"Well, I, uh..." Noah stammered and shifted his feet. "I guess that's the way those poly...poly-whatever families work."

"I want to live with you."

Noah had to catch himself so he wouldn't fall. Live with him? Where did that come from? He was still trying to get used to her new hair color.

"You can't live with me, Cat. I mean—"

"My name's Callisto, and why not?"

"For one thing..." His brain froze on him. For the life of him he couldn't think of anything to say.

"If you take me to Mother's, I'll run away again. I swear I will."

Noah knew she would. He also knew what Sheila would say when she heard about this.

"Okay, we'll try it. But there are going to be rules, and if you don't follow them it's back home with your mother. The first rule is, you're going back to school." He noticed her tense body visibly relax, though she still wasn't about to free up a smile. "One other thing." He reached in his coat pocket and tossed her his pad. "*You've* got to tell your mother."

"You can have this room," Noah said, opening the door.

"What's wrong with the lights?" Cat asked, looking into the gloom.

"Nothing, you just have to flip the switch," he said, demonstrating.

"No auto-lighting? That's crusty," she said, walking in and looking around.

Noah ignored the remark. "There's a bed, a desk, some drawers. I've got some of your things stored in the closet, games and clothes that you used to…I guess you've outgrown most of what I have. We'll have to go by your mother's and get some of your stuff, I guess."

"I don't care about that."

"Then we can get you some new stuff. You can fix the room up however you want."

"Where's the screen?"

"There's no grid linkup in here, but we can fix that too. You can come out and watch my big screen in the den."

"No thanks, I'll just stay in here."

"Okay." He turned to leave. "I was going to order in some Mexican food, your favorite. What do you want? Some tacos or—"

"I don't like Mexican food anymore."

"Why the hell…? Okay, what do you want to eat?"

Before she could answer, the door chime sounded.

"Who the drudge could that be?"

On the way to the door, he 'jectured it had to be his neighbor. Not exactly crucial detective work. No one else ever came by.

"Mrs. G, what can I do for you?"

The old woman's hair was a slightly different shade of red than he remembered. A tint closer now to pink than orange.

"I wanted to warn you," she said, adjusting her glasses.

"Warn me about what?"

"Warn you about the mutants I've seen lurking about your place. Late at night, I saw them. You'd better be careful."

"I'm always careful."

Cat chose that moment to poke her head into the entryway, and Mrs. Grabarkowitz let out a cry of surprise.

"Don't worry, Mrs. G, this is my daughter, Catherine. She'll be staying with me a while, so you might see her around. Cat, this is Mrs. Grabarkowitz. She lives next door."

"Oh, well, that's nice. Catherine, what a lovely name."

"My name's Callisto." Having seen what she needed to see, Cat withdrew.

"You be careful with her," said Mrs. Grabarkowitz, emphasizing the point with her finger. "Don't let the mutants get her like they got my Charlie."

"I'll be careful, Mrs. G, don't worry."

"All right then." She turned and hobbled down the stairs as though he were no longer there.

Noah closed the door and discovered Cat had made herself comfortable in his favorite chair and had activated his screen. She'd found an installment of *Gridspeak* with that Blume woman and was engrossed by whatever claptrap she was selling.

"So what do you want to eat?"

"I just love Chastity," Cat replied, ignoring his question. "Don't you think she's great? I think she's crucial. How do you get the 3-D to work on this screen," she said, studying the pad.

"It doesn't have 3-D."

Cat sighed as if she would resign herself to dealing with his inadequate grid screen and turned her attention back to the program.

Noah decided he'd leave her alone and go find something to eat in the kitchen. First, he poured himself a drink—a little Jack would take the edge off what had been a particularly thorny day. He hung up his coat and unstrapped his holster. When he closed the closet door he considered whether he should get a lock for it, now that Cat was in the house.

He saw himself in the mirror, and the image didn't look like much of a father figure. He wondered how big a mistake he'd made, bringing Cat home with him. It was a little late to be attempting to make up for lost time. Still, he could give it a try. He inspected his hairline from a variety of angles. It was in full retreat. He had less hair every time he looked.

When he turned around, Cat was there, staring at him.

"Change your mind about some food? We can order in whatever you want, or I can make something."

She shook her head.

"What then?"

"You've got an incoming message and it's interrupting my program."

Noah accessed the message link. It was Marilyn.

"I'm sorry to bother you at home, Noah. I'm glad to hear you found Catherine, though."

"Yeah, she's staying here with me. Sorry I didn't get back to you. What's up?"

"Georgia got a report from the biotechs. They don't know what to make of the implant found in Huang's neck. They've never seen anything like it. All they can tell us is that it looks as if it's used as a plug for some kind of input directly into the spinal column."

"That's it?"

"Yes. Georgia says it appears the implant was inserted before the tattoo was imprinted, but I don't think that helps us much."

"Not that I can see." He scratched his chest and shook his head. "We're still nowhere on this. Let's get a fresh start in the morning."

"All right," responded Marilyn.

"You know, you're still welcome to stay here if you want."

"Thank you, Noah, it's nice of you to say so. I think, though, you should probably spend some time alone with your daughter. Don't you?"

"Yeah, sure." He looked and found Cat wandering into his arboretum. "I'll see you tomorrow."

"Goodnight," Marilyn said, cutting the link.

"You sure have a lot of plants," said Cat in a tone that made it clear she thought all the vegetation was peculiar.

"Careful with that!" shouted Noah as she bent the stem of his *Lotus maculatus.* Then, calmer: "Those damage easily. It doesn't take much to kill them."

"Sorry," she said as if she really wasn't. "Was that your girlfriend?"

"Who? You mean Marilyn? No, no, no. She's my partner."

"Are you sure? She's awfully pretty."

"She's not even a...She's an android."

"Really? An android?" Cat continued to check out the various plants, stooping occasionally to smell a blossom that caught her eye. "So, who *is* your girlfriend?"

Noah sighed. This daughter thing was going to take some getting used to.

24

DÉJÀ CLUE

H E WAS DOING HIS BEST NOT TO WORRY ABOUT CAT. IT HAD ONLY BEEN ONE NIGHT, AND they'd gotten along fairly well, considering. It had even gotten to the point where she was following him from room to room, as though he might somehow vanish if she didn't keep an eye on him. So, he had no reason to think she wouldn't come home from school. He had to get his focus back on the case. Cy's killer was still out there somewhere, and that was unacceptable.

On his way down from the pod bay he crossed paths with the ERT in full body armor. He actually smelled them before he saw them.

"What's the heat, Sergei?" Noah asked a member of the team he recognized.

"We got a tip about a Loftur attack at the Golden Gate. Turned out to be another false alarm."

"That's why you get the big bucks, right?"

Sergei responded with a look that said he failed to see the humor.

"What's that godawful smell?"

"On top of everything else, we had to slosh our way through knee-deep sewage. Another pipeline break. Damn city can put cams on every street corner but can't replace its old sewage lines," the ERT officer complained, and fell back in with the rest of the team.

Before he got to the squadroom, Noah spotted a cluster of cops in the auxiliary communications room. He stuck his head in to see what was going on. Harper waved him over.

"Dane, you've got to see this."

They were all huddled around a small screen. Most were laughing, but trying not to do it too loud. On the screen was video of Captain Raevski, dressed in full football gear, helmet in hand, standing on a chair and speaking to a lockerroom full of football players.

"What the drudge is this?" he asked no one in particular.

"It's a bogus vid Sloanne over in cybertech is working on for the captain's retirement party," responded Harper.

"She's not retiring for months yet, is she?"

"Yeah, but Sloanne's still got a lot of work to do on it. This is just the first part—it's a 'win one for the little grand Lings' speech. Isn't it crucial?"

"Shit and frijoles, how did he do that?" marveled Noah. "How did he get her body in that uniform and make her talk like that?"

"Hell, they can do anything they want nowadays and make it look real. Sloanne calls it digital light processing or some such drudge. Don't you love it?"

"Captain's going to pass a melon when she sees that."

MARILYN WASN'T AT HER DESK WHEN HE GOT TO THE SQUADROOM, SO HE TOOK A MOMENT for something else he'd been thinking about. He accessed the link he had for Heather. He hadn't been himself during their last encounter, and that didn't sit well with him at all. He was going to make it up to her in a big way.

"Noah," she said, seeming surprised to see his image on her screen.

"I thought I'd check in and take your temperature."

"I was on my way out, Noah."

"That's okay, I wanted to see if you were available tonight to—"

"I can't tonight. I've got a date with my V-Real."

"Your V-Real?" Noah couldn't believe she was giving him the brush-off.

"Yes, I've got the new *Deep Blue* undersea exploration version. I can't wait to put it on. It's better than chocolate, you know."

Noah was certain she was playing with him. "Look, Heather, I know I wasn't exactly at my best last—"

"Sorry, Noah, I've got to run. Talk to you later."

She cut the link, leaving him staring at his screen icons. He felt like shaking himself. He scratched at his chest. He couldn't believe what he'd heard. Not that he hadn't ever been turned down before. But this was a woman who usually couldn't wait to get her hands on him. Surely it wasn't because he'd had that little problem last time. Maybe she was trying to get even for all the times he'd turned her down.

He realized, inwardly, part of him was relieved by her dismissal. Promptly he rejected the feeling as cowardly. It wasn't like him at all.

"What do you think?"

He looked up and saw his partner.

"Think about what?"

"My new clothes." Marilyn spun around to give him the full three-sixty. "I told the captain you thought my clothes were inappropriate for police work so she arranged for me to go shopping. Do you like this outfit? I think it's just hunky-dory."

She was wearing loose pants, a simple blouse and a dark jacket. The outfit wasn't especially attractive on her, but Noah had to admit she looked more like real police now. Then again, part of him missed the glamour queen look.

"You look fine. The new clothes are...They're just right."

"I've got some other outfits too. There's one I'm just crazy about. Would you like to see?"

"Not right now. What's that smell?" Noah moved closer to his partner and found himself enveloped in a cloud of floral fragrance. "Shit and frijoles! What have you got on?"

"It's the latest perfume," Marilyn said. "They told me where I bought my clothes that all the girls are wearing it."

"It reeks."

Marilyn looked downcast. "I thought you'd like it."

"You're not supposed to take a bath in the stuff."

"Did I use too much? I can't smell it, so I wasn't sure."

"Well, go wash it off would you? Then—"

"Dane!" It was Captain Raevski. She had this serious-times-five expression welded onto her face as she approached. "We've got another murder, and I want you on it."

"Captain, I'm already on a case that's got more loose ends than a bordello."

"I don't care, Dane. This one's in Snob Hill. It's high profile and I want my top playmaker—that's you. I don't even want to think about what the grid response on this one is going to be, but I don't plan on being blindsided."

"Who the hell is it?"

"Hurley Hutchinson."

"Who the hell is that?"

"For the love of Jerry, Dane, sometimes I wonder if you live in a box. Hutchinson is the most recognized VR designer in the world. He practically invented virtual reality software. I suggest you and your partner pull up some background on your way to the scene. Use that augmented reality of hers and join us here in the real world, would you? Now get out there and pound it out."

She stalked away without waiting for an answer. Noah pushed his chair back, stood and waved his hands in a gesture of surrender. He looked to Marilyn.

"I'm already accessing," she said.

FINDING THE RIGHT APARTMENT PROVED EASY—BLOOD TRAILS LED THE WAY FROM THE elevator. As they walked down the hall, the abstract tracks became more obvious shoeprints that led them right to Hutchinson's door.

It was a tiny unit for the posh Nob Hill district, and inside the furnishings were so scarce the place was practically empty. Only a bed, one dresser, a couple of lounge chairs near a big screen, and a huge computer desk console scattered with printouts, disks and stinky old food containers occupied the space.

The body was facedown near the desk. Blood was everywhere.

"For a big-time designer, he didn't have much of a life, did he?" said Noah after glancing around. "Looks to me like he traded his reality for virtual emptiness."

"Noah, sugar, you gorgeous hunk of man you," squealed Georgia so loud the two uniformed officers turned to stare. "Hi, Marilyn honey. I didn't know you two caught this case."

"Yeah, better than catching a case of the clap, but—"

"But not as much fun," Georgia replied, finishing the old axiom for him. "Don't you worry, sugar, I'm as sterile as a hot cup of black coffee. You should try a sip."

The officers chuckled as if to some joke of their own.

Noah scowled. "I think I liked you better when you were George."

"Now, there's no call to be insulting a girl."

Georgia resumed adjusting her crime scene omnicam while he looked around.

"What have you boys got?" he asked the officers.

"Not much. Neighbors didn't hear anything, but one of them spotted the bloody prints going down the hall and called us. None of them really seemed to know the guy. Said they hardly ever saw him."

"Did they see anyone coming or going from here recently?" Marilyn asked.

Both the uniforms ignored her, and their attitude wasn't wasted on Noah. He took a single, menacing step toward the pair.

"Answer the detective's question."

"They didn't see—"

"Don't tell me, tell her," ordered Noah. "She's the one who asked you." Reluctantly, the first officer looked at Marilyn. "No one saw anything or anybody."

"Can we go now?" asked the other officer.

Noah flicked his hand. "Get out of here."

"What was that all about?" asked Georgia when the uniforms were gone.

"I guess word about my new partner has gotten around," he said, bending down next to the corpse. "Apparently, they don't care for the idea of a droid getting promoted over them."

Georgia adjusted the tight little zebra-striped skirt she had on and flashed him an accusing look. "Not very open-minded of them, is it?"

Noah didn't take the bait. He did look over at his partner, though, to check her reaction. She wasn't paying attention. She was scouring the apartment for clues, like a good detective.

Georgia knelt and inspected the corpse. "Surface streaking of the face and abdomen, discolored veins, gas blisters—all signs of early putrefaction. I say he's been dead almost forty hours." She turned the body over, revealing a long gash across the throat.

"The cause of death is pretty obvious," Noah said.

"The killer knew what he, or she, was doing, that's for sure, sugar. Strong, too—probably a man. It's a deep cut that caught both the carotid and the jugular. This poor boy bled out in minutes."

"Butchered up-close and personal," said Noah.

"The killer has to have gotten blood all over him," added Marilyn.

"Whoever he was, he took time to search the place," Noah said, taking notice of all the open drawers. "Was it a straight-out robbery or was he looking for something?"

"You can see the bloody handprints," Georgia said, "but nothing we can use. He was wearing gloves."

"Should I check his grid files, his link records?" Marilyn asked.

"Sure." Noah continued to look around. "Of course, he might have been trying to make it look like a robbery. By the looks of all these containers, it appears our world famous VR designer had most of his meals delivered. That's probably how the perp got in."

His pad vibrated for attention. He accessed the incoming message. He 'jectured it had to be Captain Raevski, but it was Cat.

"What are you doing?" she asked nonchalantly.

"I'm working, Cat. Is something wrong?"

"No," she replied as though her attention was divided, "nothing's wrong."

"Do you want something?"

"No, I was just seeing if your link worked."

"I'm busy, Cat."

"When will you be home?"

"I'm not sure. You go ahead and make yourself something to eat when you get hungry."

"Okay," she said, looking at something other than the pad.

"Are you sure there's—" She cut the link before he could finish. He wondered what that was all about. He turned around and almost stepped on one of Georgia's crime scene autovacs. It squealed like a rodent as his foot came within an inch of crushing it. "Sorry."

"Heavens to Ray Charles," Georgia exclaimed as she placed a speck of something into an evidence container. "I've got something here, sugar."

"What is it?"

"I'm going to have to get it back to the lab to be sure, but I'm fairly certain this is more of that bat excrement. It's in a couple of these bloody shoeprints."

"Bat shit? Like you found at Huang's place?"

"That's right, sugar. If it is, I'd say your two cases are connected. Of course, I'm no police inspector."

It took him a few moments to disengage from the perplexity that confounded him. This was no coincidence. It wasn't like they were talking about pigeons. You didn't find bat droppings on every street corner. But how in the name of...

He scratched his chest, deep in thought. If Huang had this crap on his shoes, it followed that maybe his partner did, too. Which meant it was possible the same guy who killed Cyrus aired out Hutchinson. But what was the connection? What was the killer doing here? Who sent him?

"Check the victim's shoes—the ones in his closet, too. See if that shit is anywhere else in this place." Noah leaned back down over the body. "No tattoo, no implant. Hutchinson must have had something this guy wanted. Something of value, or something we weren't supposed to find."

Marilyn got up from the desk where she had activated Hutchinson's console. "It looks as if every file in here has been deleted from the system."

"I'll have Sloanne take a look at it," Georgia said. "If there's any way to retrieve what was there, he'll do it."

"The only thing I found was the log of his most recent grid links," said Marilyn. "There are some restaurant food delivery entries—the Pizza Palace, Wong's Way-Out Takeout, the Clean Sweep maid service, some link to the Lucidity Corporation—"

"Lucidity? That's one of the largest companies in the world. That must have been who he was selling his VR designs to.

"They'll probably take us nowhere, but we're going to need to follow up on all those links. Keep a record of them of them, Marilyn. Good work," he added almost as an afterthought.

"I can be smart when it's important," Marilyn replied, her childlike voice taking on a different tone, "but most men don't like it."

"What are you talking about?"

"Sorry, that was a line from *Gentlemen Prefer Blondes*. It slipped out."

"I know what gentlemen prefer, honey," Georgia said with a wiggle of her prominent hips, "and it's got nothing to do with color."

"There's another recent link here," Marilyn said, changing the subject. "It's some place called the Hyacinth House."

That caught Noah's attention. "The Hyacinth House? Haven't been there in a while. We'll check that one out first."

25

MUMBO-JUMBO AND OTHER RITES

"Imagine yourself flying through the endless black void of space, six thousand light-years from Earth. To your left looms the red giant Betelgeuse, on your right the great Crab Nebula, ahead the unknown still to come. You choose an amber-colored planet, and as quick as thought, you're standing on cliff-edge, high above a churning magenta sea. You spot a group of strange creatures approaching you. Are they friendly or hostile? What will you do next? Only you can decide when you take a trip through *Cosmos*, the newest, truest, most crucial virtual adventure from V-Real.

"Don't you think it's time for you to get real? Take that next step, that one step beyond reality, with V-Real. It's better than chocolate."

As they came back from break, she waited for the theme music to play out. She tried to focus on her next question, but her powers of concentration had developed a blemish. She didn't know if it was the topic or her own disordered agenda. She told herself it didn't matter. Either way, she had a show to do.

Despite her resolve, she missed her cue.

"Welcome back to *Gridspeak*. I'm Chastity Blume, and our topic today is 'Homosexuality: Benign Lifestyle or Immoral Wasteland.' We've been speaking with Bishop Abraham Lecroix of the San Francisco Catholic Diocese; Chris Eisenrich, regional director of the Gay Rights Alliance; and Adam Habib, a member of HIGH, Homosexuals Intent on God's Heaven, an organization of religious homosexuals of all faiths.

"First, I'd like to ask Mr. Eisenrich what the purpose of his group is. After all, due to a number of contentious rulings by the judiciary of this country, homosexuals have been granted all the same rights as heterosexuals. So why does the Gay Rights Alliance still exist?"

"That may be true, Chastity, but history has demonstrated that we must remain vigilant. There are always those looking for ways to deny us equality. If we aren't watchful, aren't united, those rights could be taken away."

"Aren't those rights just a license for one more sexual obsession—an excuse for unbridled lust without even the masquerade of procreation?"

"I'd like to say something about that."

"Go ahead, Mr. Habib."

"Homosexual relations are not just about sex. And simply because gay couples cannot procreate in the traditional way does not mean they can't be loving parents. Thousands of gay couples have adopted and cared for the unwanted children of heterosexual liaisons—children in desperate need of love. And, thanks to modern science, gay couples who so desire can now have children produced from their own genetic material. The advances we've seen in the use of in-vitro fertilization and artificial wombs have made this possible."

It was a slap across the face of Chastity's half-hearted attentiveness. But even as the words stirred her reverie, her ability to utter a cohesive thought congealed. Fortunately, no one noticed her paralysis.

"The Church maintains that same-sex unions are gravely immoral and an affront to God," spoke up the bishop. "And, as such, they certainly provide no environment in which to rear a child, not to mention the health concerns involved."

The representative of the gay rights group countered, "That's very quaint, but the Vatican's pronouncements are about as relevant as the rites of Stonehenge. The Catholic Church is still plying the same superstitious mumbo-jumbo it did a thousand years ago. Come on, Bishop, get with the reality program. Your waving of the health flag only further demonstrates the provincialism of your paranoia. Having been on the forefront of the fight against sexually transmitted diseases for decades, studies now show gays to have become among the healthiest fornicators on the planet."

"I agree with that," said the homosexual intent on God's heaven, "but I must disagree with the way you seem to want to paint all religions with the same brush. While the Roman Catholic Church is indeed an anachronism, there are several splinter sects which adhere to more modern, more realistic credos. The same can be said for my own faith, Islam. As a new age Muslim..."

Chastity tried to stay abreast of the debate but failed. It was no longer a priority. She wondered why she'd ever placed so much importance on her show, on her steadfast beliefs. What was really important? Why did she feel so empty? What would satisfy her?

26

LUSTSICK

HYACINTH HOUSE WAS A STATELY MANOR, WITH MULTIPLE CHIMNEYS, SIMPLE IRON latticework terraces and V-shaped roofs jutting out from distinct quarters. Great trellises adorned with ivy nearly obscured its ground floor, and an enormous fountain featuring a rendition of Canova's neoclassical *Cupid and Psyche* greeted visitors in the front courtyard.

From the outside it gave the impression of surviving the 19th Century untouched. Inside, however, the dignified simplicity gave way to a gaudy display of lush silk pillows, heavy drapes and rich upholstery stylized with a nymph-and-satyr motif. Reds and oranges were the dominant hues, and grand tapestries that told tales of passion and playfulness adorned the walls. The blissful ambience was further enhanced by the sounds of light music and laughter.

"Don't you love the smell of this place?" Noah said, more to himself than to his partner.

"I can't smell, remember," Marilyn reminded him.

"Yeah, right."

"What does it smell like?"

"It smells like...lust."

As if on cue, a pair of women dressed only in chiffon mini-robes sauntered by—both natural blondes, as far as Noah could tell. One of them paused, smiled at him then turned to Marilyn.

"You've got a great look. Are you working?"

"Why...no," Marilyn replied, looking bewildered.

"She can't do what you do, doll, believe me," Noah said. "What's your name?"

"Noah, you big galoot." A husky, lilting voice chastised him from behind. "What's the matter—you can't even take a moment to say hello before you start going after my girls?"

He and Marilyn turned and looked up. Descending the plush-maroon-carpeted staircase was a petite though robust woman whose age hadn't yet cloaked the classic beauty of her full lips and perfect cheekbones. She came down the stairs with confident steps, head held high, a handsome, scantily clad young man on her arm.

Noah moved to greet her, and she motioned the young man off. He joined the pair of blondes, and the three of them wandered away.

"Betty, you're looking ravishing."

"You should know, you old ravisher," she said, greeting him with a kiss and whispering in his ear, "I'm sorry about Cyrus."

She was plumper than he remembered, but on her it looked good. One thing that hadn't changed was the familiar hint of cinnamon about her. She took a step back and shook her head. Her dark-blond curls, highlighted with lighter streaks, bounced and fell back into place.

"Who's your friend?"

"This is Marilyn—Marilyn Monroe."

"Well, of course she is," Betty said, turning to Marilyn. "You're a celebudroid, aren't you, honey?"

"Yes."

"It's nice to meet you. I'm Elizabeth Fontaine, Betty to my friends. Welcome to Hyacinth House."

"How did you know?" wondered Noah.

Betty took Marilyn's hand. "I'm a big fan of your movies. I loved you as Cherie in *Bus Stop*. You were so real, so down-to-earth as the country girl turned chanteuse." To Noah she said, "I recognized her immediately. I've used celebudroids for parties and such.

"So what are the two of you doing together? Getting kinky in your old age, Noah?"

"Don't you wish, you lusty old wench." He gently grabbed her derriere. "Marilyn's my new partner."

"You mean your police partner?"

"Yeah."

"Just when you think you've seen it all…and I thought times were tough for me."

"Don't tell me business is bad." Noah laughed.

"It's not funny." Her green eyes narrowed. "The bordello business hasn't been this slow since we went legal."

"Is it the new STD scare?"

"Maybe. I'm betting the Platonistas are behind that. I don't think there is a new disease. I think it's just a way to keep their holier-than-thous in line. But that's not the only thing. Some of my regulars—and I mean regular regulars—aren't coming in at all. And it's not just straight sex either. Most of the girls work the links, have their own grid sites, do vid work on the side, and it's all on the wane. I mean, what's this world coming to when you can't sell a little love?

"So, are you a paying customer tonight, or...?"

"Actually, we're here on police business, though maybe after..." Noah's voice trailed off as his gaze followed a coquettish vixen who smiled at him in passing.

"We found your grid link in the records of a murder victim," Marilyn spoke up, cognizant of Noah's distraction.

"That's awful," replied Betty. "Who was it?"

"Hurley Hutchinson."

"Hutch! Oh, my."

"You knew him?" Noah asked.

"Sure, he was here all the time. He really had a thing for Meadow. I thought the two of them might end up together. Poor kid."

"We'll need to talk to Meadow."

"Of course. She should be down in a minute. Hutch was such a good guy. Who would want to hurt him?"

"That's what we want to find out," said Marilyn.

"That's what we *will* find out," Noah added.

"I can't imagine him being in any kind of trouble. He seemed like such a nice, normal guy."

Noah sniffed. "Everyone seems normal until you get to know them."

"When was the last time he was here?" Marilyn asked.

"A few days ago—Sunday, I think. I was actually wondering why I hadn't seen him in a while. Lately it seemed like he was here almost every day. The last time he saw Meadow he gave her a diamond necklace."

"Diamond?"

"Yes, it was a beautiful little thing, and real. I took a close look at it. If it's one thing Mama Fontaine knows, it's diamonds. They're a girl's best friend, right, Marilyn?"

Marilyn responded not so much in agreement, but as if she were remembering something. "Yes, that's right, Betty."

"You women are so mercenary," Noah joked.

"Only because you men are such animals," Betty replied in-kind. "Here comes Meadow. Let me break it to her, okay?"

He nodded, and Betty moved to intercept a trio of girls coming down the stairs. Two were wearing enormous strap-ons and nothing else, the third a simple silk robe. It was the third, a thin, fragile looking young Asian girl that Betty intercepted. She escorted her to a nearby divan where they both sat.

Noah and Marilyn waited where they were as Betty delivered the bad news. The dark-haired girl dropped her face into her hands and sobbed. Betty consoled her for a moment and then rejoined them.

"Please take it easy with her, Noah. Why don't you let Marilyn talk to her? I think that would be best right now."

"Okay." Noah shrugged. "Go see what you can find out. We can always talk to her again later if we need to."

Marilyn sat next to the girl and slid an arm around her. She waited until Meadow finished crying before saying anything.

"So, what else can I do for you?" Betty asked, putting her arms around Noah's waist and turning his attention from his partner.

"I can think of several things without working up a sweat."

"But working up a sweat is the fun part," Betty replied, releasing him from her grasp. "I think I can find someone young and energetic enough to keep up with that power tool of yours."

"You know I'd love to, Betty, but I'm working."

"That never stopped you before. Are you getting old, Inspector Dane?"

"Old?" He reached for her, and she playfully spun away.

"Okay, if you're just too tired, I'll tell Rosie you couldn't spare a moment to say hello."

"Rosie's here?"

"Yes, though I think she may be a little piqued at you for staying away so long."

"I'd like to see her."

"I thought you would. I'll call her down."

Betty caught the attention of one of her employees, said something to him then activated her console. Marilyn, meanwhile, finished speaking with Hutchinson's girl and rejoined Noah.

"Anything?" he asked.

"She's pretty upset. I don't think she knows anything about the murder. Hutchinson never mentioned any trouble. She said they were going to get married soon."

"What about the necklace?"

"I told her we'd have to take it, temporarily. She said Hutchinson told her he'd made it special for her, and that there were a lot more where those came from. Do you think he was just bragging?"

"I'm sure he had more credit than he knew what to do with, and it sure didn't look like he spent much on himself. He probably meant he had plenty of money to take care of her."

"She thought he meant more diamonds."

"Anyway, we've got two things now that connect Hutchinson and Huang— diamonds and bat shit—though how the hell they fit together crashes my brain."

"He might have just bought a diamond necklace," Marilyn countered. "It might not have anything to do with the ones you found on Huang."

"My nose says different. I smell a connection. I just don't know what the drudge it is."

Betty returned, smiling at Noah.

"She's upstairs. She says to come on up and she'll forgive you if you're nice to her."

"Uh, yeah, okay. Tell her I'll be right there."

"Are we going somewhere?" Marilyn asked as Betty returned to her console.

"I am, you're not. Look, Marilyn, I'm going upstairs to see an old friend. You wait for me down here, get that diamond necklace, and I'll be back in a while. Okay?"

"All right, Noah," Marilyn said, studying him with those heavily lidded eyes of hers. "I'll wait here for you."

ROSIE WAS GLAD TO SEE HIM. SO GLAD SHE DISPENSED WITH MANY OF THE USUAL pleasantries and went right to work, so to speak. Noah's first reaction was to acquiesce wholeheartedly—Rosie could take a man's mind off the apocalypse. He knew he should be concentrating on the case, knocking down doors to find Cy's killer, but he wasn't going to let himself worry about that right now. He wasn't going to worry about the little problem he'd had with Heather either. He wasn't going to think at all.

Except he was thinking.

Initially, Rosie's ardent affections hardened his resolve. However, as his mind wandered from her ministrations, anxiety took a firm hold and quashed her forthright endeavor. She redoubled her efforts but soon surrendered to the inevitable. She slid up to snuggle next to him, planting a kiss on his hairy chest.

"It's all right, Noah. It happens."

Abruptly he sat up, pulling away from her embrace. "Not to me it doesn't. It's never—I mean *never*—happened before."

"You've probably got a lot on your mind, what with Cyrus getting killed and everything."

"I didn't get Cyrus killed!" he said, almost shouting.

"That's not what I said," Rosie replied, rolling over and climbing out of bed.

"Yeah, I guess you didn't. Sorry, I didn't mean to snap at you."

"You'll be okay, Noah. It'll just take time."

"Yeah, time." He reached for his pants. "I'd better get back to it. My partner's waiting downstairs."

HE LOOKED AROUND, BUT MARILYN WASN'T WHERE HE'D LEFT HER. HE ASKED THE HOSTESS near the entrance, and she told him his partner had gone outside. He wanted to say goodbye to Betty but couldn't find her, so he left Hyacinth House to find Marilyn. The sun had set, and the wind was beginning to bluster. He looked at the sky. No storm clouds were evident.

Marilyn was right outside, standing at the main gate and talking with someone sitting on a bicycle. As he got closer, he saw it was her friend. The smart-mouth with the wild hair and black leather pants.

"What's the garbage man doing here?" he asked in a tone that was crabbier than he intended.

"I didn't expect you so soon," Marilyn responded. "I contacted Jim because Betty told me I'd have a long wait."

"Well, it wasn't that long, was it?" snapped Noah. "So what—you just went on the grid and told him to come over?"

"It was an easy ride, man," the celebudroid said. "I was just out cruising around, taking the highway to the end of the night. It's not too far from here you know."

"I didn't have to use the grid," said Marilyn, "Jim and I have this link from when we worked together. All of us were conjoined in that way—kind of like the com link that connects you and me, only my link with Jim isn't verbal, it's binary."

"Yeah," Morrison added, "it's like the scream of the butterfly."

"You can stay out here with Jimbo and chase your butterflies if you want. I'm going home to my daughter."

"Yeah, come on, Marilyn. There's still one place to go. Come ride with me. Can you picture what we'll be, so limitless and free? We'll write proclamations—watch the day destroy the night and the night divide the day."

Marilyn faltered as if considering the proposition. Noah tried to imagine it. The two of them, biking through the city until dawn. The absurdity of it made him smile.

"You're a grown droid," Noah said. "Do what you want."

"Come on, baby," encouraged Morrison, "this is no time to wallow in the mire. The time to hesitate is through. Come on, try now, we can only lose."

"Not tonight, Jim," said Marilyn reluctantly. "I've got some research I need to do on the case we're working. We'll do it some other time, okay?"

"Oh, man, deliver me from reasons why." He pushed off on the bike, pedaled away in a circle and held his arms out like wings. "I'd rather fly."

"Goodbye, Jim," she called.

Proceeding up the street in a drunken zig-zag, Morrison called back to her, "Tell all the people that you see, to follow me, follow me down!"

He pedaled off into the night and Marilyn stood watching until he disappeared. Noah thought he saw a look of regret pass over her face.

"Well, are you ready to go?" he asked.

"I'm ready, Noah."

27

A GIRL'S BEST ZEN

FOR A MOMENT, FORGET ABOUT DOCTRINE AND SIN AND CEREMONY, AND THINK ABOUT the time to come when the Lord God gets in your face and asks you, 'Well?' What are you going to say? How will you defend your existence here on Earth? He put you here. He gave you the time and resources. What did you do with them? Are you going to be able to look Him in the eye and say, 'I was a good person, a productive member of society, a vessel of physical and spiritual purity?' Are you?"

High Minister Rebekah Redstone looked down at her congregation, her gaze sweeping over the crowded tabernacle. From her seat near the end of an anterior row, Chastity saw the high minister's gaze lock on to her for a moment before continuing across the assemblage. As it was, she felt the high minister's words had somehow been directed at her. Maybe she was imagining it. Maybe Minister Redstone hadn't even noticed her sitting there. Maybe each parishioner had felt the high minister staring at them individually.

"You probably won't be able to say all of that, especially if you're eyeball to eyeball with those omnipotent orbs of His."

Chastity joined much of the congregation in a responsive chuckle.

"I know, you probably think you're a good person, a productive person, but that part about purity, oh, that's the tough one isn't it? We all try to be pure, in thought and deed, but it's not always easy, is it?"

Heads throughout the audience nodded in agreement.

"The key word there is *try*. We must constantly strive to remain pure, to think pure thoughts, to do the right thing."

When Redstone invited her to this evening's rites, she hadn't known the high minister herself would be delivering the word. It was rare she actually ascended to the pulpit herself anymore. Most of her sermons were delivered via the grid. However, Chastity found that being in the tabernacle soothed her, helped clear her mind of troublesome bits of refuse and tattered remnants of soul searching.

"And speaking of the right thing, remember, purity begins with your tithes, so think plenty of pure thoughts as you are scanned and enter your donations."

There was more laughter, and then applause as Minister Redstone waved and exited stage right. Space-age jazz enveloped the immense hall, and Chastity rose to leave with the rest of the congregation. However, before she'd gone far, a deaconess approached and, without speaking, handed her a note. It was from the high minister. It read "Please come visit with me. This young lady will lead you on the right path."

The deaconess motioned for her to follow.

They made their way easily through the tide of exiting parishioners, who, in deference, made way for the gray-robed deaconess. Once past the throng, as she was led through corridors lined with camera sentries, Chastity wondered if she should tell the high minister about the dream she'd woken from that morning. The dream about David, the maintenance man. No, she couldn't. It was too shameful. Just thinking about what she'd done in the dream mortified her.

Eventually, they came to a part of the sanctuary she'd never visited before, and her guide directed her into a room she guessed was part of the high minister's private quarters. The deaconess left without uttering a word, closing the door behind her.

The room's furnishings were luxurious, comfortable-looking and immaculately clean. However, the white-and-chrome theme in effect in Redstone's office had metamorphosed here to midnight blues and passionate purples, accessorized by copper-red metallics.

Chastity had only a few seconds to look around before Minister Redstone walked in wearing a gold silk kimono, cut to mid-thigh and belted with forest-green felt. The silver headband she made a point of wearing whenever in public still held her sable tresses in place.

"Chastity dear." Redstone greeted her with a kiss on the cheek that surprised her. "Come, sit with me. Tell me what you've been up to since we last spoke."

Chastity joined her on an indigo leather divan and tucked her legs underneath her as she sat.

"I'm anxious to hear if you've spoken with your father."

"Yes—yes, I did."

"Well?"

Chastity ran her fingers first up then down her neck, considering her reply.

"It's hard to say, High Minister."

"Please don't call me 'High Minister' when we're in private," Redstone said with annoyance. She stretched out and slumped down into the divan. "You don't know how exasperated I get hearing 'High Minister this' and 'High Minster that.' It can be very tiresome. I want us to be friends." She reached over without moving from her comfortable spot and rested her hand on Chastity's knee. "I don't really have anyone I can be close to—that I can talk to. So call me Rebekah, and tell me everything."

"My father told me," Chastity began hesitantly, "that I never had a mother, that I was conceived through artificial insemination and born from an artificial womb."

Redstone sat up straight and took a moment before she replied. "I'm sure that was unexpected. But you sound bitter, dear. Aren't you happy to finally know the truth? Isn't that what you wanted?"

"I wanted to know who my mother was. Instead, I discovered I never had a mother, just an egg donor."

"So what?" inquired Redstone with a harshness that caught Chastity off guard. "So you're different. Aren't we all? So you never had a mother. It doesn't really matter if it's biological, sociological or just fate. Many children in the world grow up without a mother or a father—sometimes both. Think of what you do have." Redstone moved closer to her and put an arm around her shoulders. "Think about all the good things in your life. Don't wallow in self-pity. What would the Most Pristine Plato say about that?"

"You're right, Hi...Rebekah," Chastity responded, properly chagrined. "I have no right to be so disconsolate."

"It's not a matter of 'right,' girl. We all have the right to be sad, mad, glad...you just have to pick your spots better. I think you should rejoice that you know the truth. Think of yourself as special, not different."

"I'm going to find her—my mother. That is, the woman whose egg I...I want to know who she is, what the rest of her family—my family—is like."

Redstone contemplated this before she replied. "That could be good—both for you and her. Still, you have to remember that, if you find her, you'll have to consider her thoughts, too. It's not only a matter of you finding her. She may not want to be found. She may be happy with her life as it is. You need, first, to reflect on the possibility that learning about you might not be the best thing for her."

"You're right. I've thought about that. My first step is to find her, if I can. If I do, then I'll decide whether I should approach her or not."

"I think that's wise." Redstone removed her arm from around Chastity and stood. "How about a glass of wine? Let's both have one to celebrate the accomplishment of modern science which introduced you to this world."

Chastity laughed in spite of herself, and pulled her pale-blue chiffon dress down over her legs.

"So," Redstone began as she set out two glasses and poured, "have you had any more of those urges you were telling me about?"

The conversational shift untracked Chastity momentarily, but she was feeling at ease now, and relieved that she'd shared her secret. Rebekah—it was still strange to think of the high minister by that name—made her feel so comfortable, so safe.

"Yes, yes, I have. There are these two men—"

"*Two* men?" Redstone said with exaggerated emphasis.

Chastity laughed at her tone. "It's not what you think."

"Really? Tell me what it is, then," Redstone said, handing Chastity her glass of wine. "After that you can tell me what it is you think I'm thinking."

28

GOING ROUND IN CIRCLES

"A RE YOU REALLY AN ANDROID?" CAT ASKED, POKING HER FINGER INTO MARILYN'S ARM. "I've never met an android. I mean, I've seen them and everything, but I've never actually met one."

"Yes, I am," Marilyn responded with a smile, ignoring the rude finger. "It's nice to meet you, Cat. Or would you prefer that I call you Catherine?"

"Call me Callisto—that's my new name."

"Your name is Catherine Anne Dane," Noah called from the kitchen where he had been listening. "You can change your name when you become an adult. Until then you're Cat."

The teenager let out an exaggerated sigh, purposely loud enough so her father could hear. She looked Marilyn up and down, appraising her. "You're supposed to be some famous vid star or something aren't you?"

"Yes, I was in many movies, uh…I mean I was modeled after Marilyn Monroe, the movie star."

"Never heard of you," Cat said bluntly, staring at some program on the screen.

Marilyn sat next to her. Cat continued to watch her show, and Marilyn squirmed, uncomfortable with the silence.

"What are you watching?"

"It's *Gridspeak with Chastity Blume*. I just love her, don't you? What she says about sex and abstinence is so jell, don't you think? Do androids have sex?"

"Nice girls don't talk about such things," Marilyn replied.

"Chastity does, but I guess she does it in a nice way. She's crucial."

148

"Your father and I spoke with Ms Blume the other day."

"What?" Cat jumped out of the chair, freckles dancing across an animated face. "You didn't tell me you met Chastity!" she exclaimed accusingly as Noah looked in to see what the shouting was all about. "Why didn't you tell me? You talked with Chastity? That's ultra crucial. What's she like?"

"She seemed like a pleasant young woman," Marilyn said.

Noah snorted as he placed a tray of food on the table in front of his daughter. "She's just another talking head trying to mind-drudge everyone with her freak philosophy. I don't know why you think she's so special."

"Oh!" Cat said, too exasperated for words. "You think you know everything, but you don't know anything." With that she stomped off to her room, slamming the door shut.

Noah looked at Marilyn. "She didn't have to take it personally." He picked up a half-empty glass of whiskey from the tray and took a drink.

"It must be hard to grow up," said Marilyn. "There's so much to learn."

"We all have to do it," Noah said, taking off his coat and throwing it over the nearest piece of furniture.

"I didn't, of course—grow up, I mean. I know the original Marilyn grew up, but I have no memories of being a child. Either my makers had little of my early history to work with, or they didn't think it was important."

"You're right about growing up," he said. "Sometimes it's like being a dandelion in a hailstorm. My mother was a stripper. I was raised backstage by a gaggle of dancing girls." Noah smiled, remembering. "It was actually a great way for a boy to grow up."

"What about your father?"

Noah picked up his glass and took another drink. "I never had a father. At least not one that I ever knew." He made a sandwich out of some of the bread and cold cuts he'd brought out, and took a bite. "The funny thing is," he said, still chewing, "at the time I wanted to be a dancer when I grew up."

"A stripper?"

"Nooo! I wanted to dance on Broadway—modern dance, jazz, that kind of thing. But I grew up to be such a big, awkward behemoth that I jectured pretty quickly I wasn't going to be no elegant hoofer. So I played football instead. I didn't really like it that much, but I was damn good at it. It was a way to fit in." He took another drink. "Sometimes that's what growing up is all about. Just finding out where you fit in."

"Since Celebuwares went out of business, I've often wondered where I fit in," Marilyn said. "I don't think I fit anywhere."

"Welcome to humanity," Noah responded sardonically. "Sometimes you just have to pick a direction, elbow your way in and make a spot for yourself."

"If you don't have a direction, you just keep going round in circles."

"What's that?"

"I don't know. It just popped out. I think maybe it was another line of movie dialogue."

"Well, right now you've got a place with me, working an important case."

"It's important to you because you feel like Cyrus's death was your fault, isn't it?"

Noah stared at her. He couldn't believe what she'd said. Not that it wasn't true. He just couldn't believe she'd said it like that.

"When your partner gets killed, it's always your fault."

29

WORDS DISSEMBLE, WORDS BE QUICK

H E REALIZED AS SOON AS HE WOKE THAT HE'D HAD SIX OR SEVEN TOO MANY THE NIGHT before. He struggled to rouse himself and tried to remember if he had any more Hangoverin in the medicine cabinet. For some reason that made him think of Cat. He needed to make sure she had a small credit line, so she could buy some things for herself. He'd do that before he left, and give her a grocery list to fill, too. It would be good for her to have some responsibilities.

He staggered out of bed, pulled on some clothes and discovered much to his lament that he was indeed out of Hangoverin. He'd have to remember to put it on the list for Cat.

He wandered out of his room and found his partner sitting where he'd left her, watching the grid screen. He trudged over and fell into his chair.

"Good morning," Marilyn greeted him.

He grunted in reply and turned his attention to the screen. What he saw made him wonder for a moment if he was still asleep. There, wearing the funniest little hat, was his partner—no, not his partner. The real Marilyn Monroe.

"What's this?"

"*Bus Stop*," Marilyn replied without turning her attention from the screen. "I remembered your friend Betty mentioning how much she liked it, so I found the right link and thought I'd access it. It's funny, in a way it's like looking at my memories come to life. Sort of a video scrapbook."

"Yeah, well, that's nice," Noah muttered. "I'm glad you found a way to keep yourself occupied."

"Oh, that's not all I've been doing. I've spent quite a bit of time searching the grid. You were right. Hurley Hutchinson did design games and virtual adventures for the Lucidity Corporation. Or, should I say, for one of its subsidiaries, V-Real. He is credited with creating, alone or in conjunction with others, all of the virtual reality scenarios currently marketed by V-Real."

"Very interesting." Noah yawned and scratched at his chest in thought. "So now we not only have bat drudge and diamonds connecting the dots between our two corpses, we've got V-Real."

"I discovered one other thing," Marilyn said. "I don't know how helpful it is, but the tattoo pattern imprinted on Huang's neck isn't a design, it's a language. It's Troloxian."

"Why would he and his buddy get a bunch of troll lingo tattooed on their necks? Not to mention that fembot who took a shot at us." Noah considered it for a moment. "Hell, maybe they just liked the looks of it. Or maybe they were too drunk at the time to care. What does the tattoo say?"

"I don't know. There's no Troloxian language translation available anywhere on the grid."

"Okay. Who do we know that speaks troll?"

As they waited outside V-Real's main gate for security to usher them in, Noah watched his partner going through some strange gyrations. He stared for a moment before blurting out, "What in the twelve days of Christmas are you doing?"

"I was just remembering the steps from a dance number I did in *Ladies of the Chorus*. I guess I was—"

"You're with the police, right?" Another guest awaiting an escort spoke up timidly. He'd already been standing there when Noah and Marilyn identified themselves to the gate guard.

"Yeah," Noah said, "I'm Inspector Dane, this is Detective Monroe. What can we do for you?"

"It's my wife. She works here. I'm waiting to see her. Only…Only, she's not my wife. I mean…she is my wife, but she's not the same person anymore."

"I suppose some plant pod has taken over her body?" Noah replied sarcastically.

"No, really, she's not the same at all. I don't know what's happened, but—"

"Look, fella, we'd love to help you, but this doesn't sound like our jurisdiction. Maybe you should try a marriage counselor, or a nice late-model theratech."

"You don't understand. I—"

The gate activated with a loud grrrunch and slid open.

"Inspector Dane, Detective Monroe," said one of the two security guards who approached them, "we're supposed to take you to Mr. Kess's office."

"Sorry, fella, wish we could help."

As Noah and Marilyn fell in step to follow their escorts, Marilyn turned to look at the pathetic figure of the man who had approached them.

"He's not the first guy to feel that way about his wife," Noah said. "That's what marriage can do to you."

"Oh, sometimes it's not so bad."

"How would you know?"

"I've been married before—both in real life and in the movies," Marilyn assured him, then caught herself. "You know what I mean. I mean Marilyn Monroe was married. I can remember them though—the marriages, that is."

"Good for you."

It was a short walk to the main building, and after winding down a couple of corridors, the guards showed them into an empty office.

"Mr. Kess will be here in a minute," one of them said. "He said to make yourselves comfortable."

Their escorts departed, and Noah took the opportunity to nose around. However, there wasn't much to see except for a desk and a bookcase thick with hardback volumes. No knickknacks or souvenirs, no pictures on the walls, no videographs of the little trolls at home. Noah was about to see what kinds of books lined the case when the diminutive Walter Kess walked in.

"Inspector Dane, Detective Monroe, what a joy it is to see you both so soon again. To what do I owe this unexpected pleasure?"

"We won't take up too much of your time, Mr. Kess. We just have a couple of questions for you."

"'Ah, 'tis better to be brief than tedious.'"

"Are you familiar with the name Hurley Hutchinson?"

"Of course. I've never met Mr. Hutchinson myself, but I am certainly aware of his work. We fabricate his virtual reality creations right here in our factory."

"So you personally have had no contact with Hutchinson?"

"As I said. My understanding is that Mr. Hutchinson was never an actual employee of V-Real, but was contracted for his design work. A freelancer, as you say."

"Maybe you can help us with something else," Marilyn said, pulling the printout from the purse around her shoulder. "Could you translate this for us?"

Kess accepted the document and looked it over. His red eyes studied the image only briefly, but in that instant Noah observed the nostrils of the alien's broad, flat nose flare open.

"This originates from an ancient Troloxian proverb which means, roughly, 'Loyal and devoted pet.' May I ask where you found this?"

"It was tattooed on Timothy Huang," Marilyn replied.

"Oh, yes, the former V-Real employee you inquired about the other day."

"Any idea why a man, a human," Noah added, "would have such a thing tattooed onto his skin?"

"Who can say, Inspector?" The troll held up his right hand, splaying his fat thumb and trio of fingers. "'To gild refinéd gold, to paint the lily ...'"

"What the drudge does that mean?"

"Only that there is often no rhyme nor reason for what men do. Don't you find that to be so? Isn't that the fascinating part of your primal nature?"

Noah looked at the alien as if he couldn't fully assess him, which he couldn't. "If you say so."

"Or, as another Dane once said, 'there are more things in heaven and earth than are dreamt of in your philosophy.'"

"Yeah, uh, thanks for your time. I don't think we need to bother you anymore."

"No bother, Inspector," he said, handing the printout back to Marilyn. "Feel free to come back any time."

"Don't worry, we will."

30

LOVED HIM LIKE A SON

CHASTITY HAD HER DRIVER LET HER OUT SEVERAL BLOCKS FROM THE RESTAURANT. SHE was telling the truth when she told him she felt like walking, but the main reason was that getting out of the stretch Mercedes was always such a scene, even at an upscale restaurant like Chez Cachet. Few could afford such transportation, so it was bound to draw attention, and attention was the last thing she wanted, especially tonight.

Her father, sounding almost contrite, had asked her to meet him for dinner—a rare occurrence in and of itself. She was certain he wanted to make peace, and that was fine with her. She was wholly unused to such inner conflict, and the burden of it was beginning to wear on her. She would gladly accept dinner as a way to calm the waters.

She arrived at the restaurant feeling like the walk in the blustery fresh air had done her good. Brief as it was, the exercise had relaxed her. She hadn't realized how tense the prospect of seeing her father had made her. Nevertheless, her relaxed state didn't last long. Floating down the promenade near the restaurant was a holoboard flashing its silent message in a gaudy rainbow of colors. It was the content of the message that twisted Chastity's stomach into knots again.

The video display read, "Find out what America's Favorite Virgin has to say about masturbation. Link *Gridspeak* tonight—see what's crucial—input your own jectures. *Gridspeak* with Chastity Blume." The words dissolved into a likeness of Chastity as the holoboard drifted by.

She shook her head disdainfully. It hadn't taken them long. Then again, she'd known it wouldn't. She just hadn't expected to run into their new

155

marketing campaign face-first. They'd even capitalized it as if it were some grand title, like she was some sort of new age grid royalty. She wondered what the ratings would be for tonight's taped gridcast. If they spiked, she knew Chesty/Chelsea and her ilk would take the credit.

She paced up and down the promenade for a while to compose herself. When she paused and looked up, intending to stargaze, she was staring into one of the city's security cams, mounted high above her. It should have made her feel safer, but for some reason it had the opposite effect. It sent a chill of apprehension through her. It was one more prying eye sneaking a look at her life. At least none of the people she passed appeared to recognize her. She was glad for that.

It wasn't until the maitre d' escorted her inside that the whispers of recognition began. Even in a place as expensive as Chez Cachet there were those with enough tactless indiscretion to point. Fortunately, her father rated a table that was at least semi-private, up a few stairs on a separate level overlooking the restaurant floor proper.

Henri Blume didn't acknowledge the arrival of his daughter. He simply watched as she gathered her long burgundy lace dress so she could be seated. When the maitre d' left he said, "You're late."

"I went for a walk."

"You shouldn't be out walking by yourself at night. It's dangerous. The streets are full of perverts and terrorists."

"That's not true, Father. It's a perfectly lovely night, and I wanted to walk."

"Your business, I guess. I've already ordered for both of us—assiette de saumon fume, la caprese salad, and chateaubriand. Is that all right?"

"Sure, that's fine." Chastity allowed herself a subdued laugh. "You know, you always used to order for me when I was a little girl, too."

"You can change it—order what you want." Her father raised his arm to signal a waiter.

"No, no, that's fine, Father. I love chateaubriand."

Henri Blume dropped his arm and picked up his glass. "Try the wine, it's a Coppola merlot. I find it mellow yet complex."

Chastity obliged and found the taste satisfying.

"I hope..." He hesitated, fumbling with his forks as he did. "I hope you're okay now. I mean, after our talk the other day. I trust you've gotten over the...over my disclosure. Are you—"

"I'm fine, Father," Chastity responded without letting him finish. "It was a bit of a shock at first, but I've accepted it now, and I'm moving on."

"Good, good. You've always been a strong girl. I raised you that way."

"I'm going to find her—the woman who donated her eggs."

"You're *what?*" Henri Blume set his glass on the table so forcibly the red wine splashed up over the lip and onto the plum linen tablecloth.

"My mother—the woman who would have been my mother—I'm going to try and find her. I want to learn all about her, her family, where she comes from..." Her voice trailed off as she saw her father's face beginning to flush, swelling with animosity.

"No! I forbid it!" He lashed out so loudly some of the patrons below looked up to see who was causing the disturbance. Realizing his outburst had attracted attention, he lowered his voice. "You can't do this. You mustn't. There were stipulations, contractual provisions that—"

"You don't care about the legalities, Father. Why don't you want me to know about the woman who's my biological mother? Why does it upset you so much? It can't hurt you."

Henri Blume put his hands on the table, gathering himself. Just then the waiter approached, and her father emphatically waved him away. He tried to calm himself, but Chastity saw the seething rage looking for a means to vent.

"You don't know anything about hurt. I can tell you about hurt, about anguish so intense it makes you vomit. I'll tell you why you don't want to know about her, whoever she is. I'll tell you something about mothers.

"You think having a mother would be nice, would make you happy, don't you? You want to know about your family? Let me tell you about your family, about my mother—your grandmother." He faltered momentarily, as if the words couldn't escape his mouth. "Oh, she was so nice, so loving. She said she loved me so much. So much that she made me sleep with her every night. Every night until I was sixteen. That's when I finally got the courage to go to the police, to tell them what she'd done, what she'd been doing for as long as I could remember."

Chastity opened her mouth to say something, to utter some sympathetic platitude, to make some commiserative nonsensical sound, but she was struck dumb. It was a startling revelation, but at the same time it shed new understanding of her father.

"Do you want me to tell you all the things she did, the things she made me do all those years? Do you still want to know all about your family, Chastity? Should I describe my boyhood in loving detail?"

She shook her head slowly. "No, no. I'm sorry, I..." She had no concept of what to say. What could she say that would make any difference?

Calmly, Henri Blume took another sip of his wine. He looked for the waiter, motioned to him and sat back as if he'd been talking about the weather.

"What happened to her—your mother?"

"She went to jail," he said matter-of-factly. "Later, they transferred her to an asylum. She spent the rest of her short, sordid life there. I made sure of that."

A pair of waiters arrived with their salads. Her father looked as if he were ready to enjoy his meal, but eating was far from Chastity's mind. She stared surreptitiously at him, wondering what emotions must be churning inside him, what scars he must bear. She understood now why he never married. Why he chose to have a child the way he did. Even why he raised her as he did.

Though he'd divulged his long-buried secret with the intention of dissuading her from searching for her biological mother, he'd only affirmed her desire to learn more about where she came from. At that moment she wanted nothing more than to discover a less tainted tributary to the genetic pool that spawned her. The thought shamed her.

31

CUPCAKES & FIREWORKS

IT WAS SO QUIET WHEN NOAH AND MARILYN WALKED IN, HE WORRIED THAT MAYBE CAT had run away again. He went directly to her room. The door was open, and to his relief his daughter was lying on her bed. She had one of those V-Real visors on, and the lens was glowing like a hot ember. She was so preoccupied with it, she hadn't even heard him come in. He noticed, too, that she'd changed her haircolor—if you could call pink and orange haircolors. Well, maybe that meant she wasn't "Callisto" anymore.

"Cat, I'm home." When she didn't answer, he said it louder. "Cat, I'm home."

"I'm busy, Daddy."

"I can see that. What do you want for dinner?"

Immersed in her own unreality, she didn't answer right away.

"I'm not hungry."

"Okay, you're on your own then." He waited, but she didn't respond. "Well, uh, have fun."

Noah returned to the living room where Marilyn was waiting.

"Is everything all right?"

"Yeah, she's got one of those V-Real games or adventures or whatever it is. She seems pretty engrossed in it."

"They say it's better than chocolate."

Noah tossed his coat over a chair and undid his holster. "That's what they say."

"I'm crazy about chocolate," Marilyn cooed, tucking her fists under her chin like a little girl. "I used to eat it all the time—when I could eat."

Noah didn't take notice of his partner's girlish enthusiasm. His mind was still on Cat.

"At least she's not watching some transcendental drudge, or that virginity zealot. Maybe she's over it. Maybe it was just a phase."

"You don't approve of the Platonic philosophy, do you?"

"I try to ignore it."

"Any mention of it seems to make you angry."

"Angry? Maybe. Hell, they want to take all the fun out of life. I've heard they believe in having sex only for procreation. What are they thinking? It's the best thing life's got going, and they want to turn it into a biological routine." Noah grabbed his watering can. "Some of the real fanatics want to eliminate it all together. Can you imagine that? A life without pow-whammy?"

"My makers didn't include any sexual experiences in my memories," said Marilyn almost wistfully.

"I thought you were the sex goddess of your time?"

"I was. At least that was Marilyn's image. Image was everything in Hollywood in those days. It was a place where'd they pay you a thousand dollars for a kiss and fifty cents for your soul."

As he began watering his chantilly lace begonias, Noah glimpsed his reflection in one of the windows surrounding his little arboretum. He was bent over, and the pose exaggerated his bulging waistline to a degree that made him straighten up. He put his free hand to his stomach as he inhaled to minimize it.

"What's it like?"

"What's what like?" Noah asked, preoccupied by his own thoughts.

"Making love," she answered shyly. "I know I once made a movie called *Let's Make Love*, and I remember there were many men in my life, but I don't have any memory of what it was like. I try not to think about it, because when I do it's like this great big hole inside me." She almost sounded sad. "What does it feel like?"

"It's..." he started then stopped, not sure how to put it. "It's a lot of things, a lot of different things. I'm not sure how to describe it exactly. It's a powerful, primal force that sort of overwhelms your entire being. Sometimes there's this moment during it all—it may only last ten or twenty seconds, but it's this moment where you know...you just *know* life doesn't get any better. For those few seconds it's prime, and you want to absorb the sensations through every pore in your body. At least, that's the way it is with me. When you're doing it right, there's nothing like it."

"Of course, it's not always cupcakes and fireworks. Otherwise, when it's special, it wouldn't be…you know…special."

"Was it special with Cat's mother?"

"Sure, for a long time it was. Then we changed. People change, things change, there are problems. The trouble with women is, they all become bossy in the end, like they think they own you. There's nothing I loathe more than a bossy woman. Hell, there have been times I made up my mind to give up women completely, go cold turkey. Fortunately, the rest of my body never agrees. That demon pow-whammy keeps calling me back."

He glanced at Marilyn, and experienced a flash of incredulity that he was trying to explain this to a woman who, at least on the exterior, looked so incredibly sexy. Not a woman, he reminded himself, a droid.

"I'm not helping much, am I?"

"No," she said, smiling. "Thanks for trying, though. I guess it's something you have to experience for yourself."

"That it is."

"Did you and your friend Rosie…?"

Noah jerked his watering can and splashed some on the floor. Frowning, he bent to wipe it up. "Let's change the subject, okay?"

32

COURTESAN OF APPEAL

THE GRID SEARCH SHE INITIATED USING THE TERM "ARTIFICIAL INSEMINATION" HAD resulted in a variety of options, not all of which seemed relevant to her interests. The ensuing list included everything from bovine reproduction to the art of creating hybrid flowers. She was going to have to narrow her search, be more specific in order to cull the listing to a manageable number.

Perhaps, instead, she should begin with her own medical records. Using the efficacy of the Health Rights Act of 2009, Chastity believed she could force the disclosure of all records concerning her birth. That should, at the very least, establish at which facility the event took place. It would be another matter to retrieve the name of her donor.

She was about to modify and resubmit her search request when one particularly odd listing caught her eye. It read *Cyber Courtesan, Talk, Laugh, Play, Indulge.* She wondered what it was. The term was unfamiliar. What was a "cyber courtesan?"

Curiosity got the better of her, and she selected the "male" link, not certain if they were referring to her gender or...

The link was established instantly. A door appeared on her screen. It opened. Standing there was a man with soulful green eyes and long, wavy dark hair that nearly fell to his shoulders. He was dressed simply in an open white shirt and black pants, and his smile was as inviting as the sweeping gesture he made with his hand. His movements were graceful, his features so handsome as to be dazzling.

"Welcome, welcome. Please come in," he said with a slight Italian accent. "I am Antonio, and it would be my pleasure if you would join me."

The moving video effect was such that Chastity felt she had stepped inside. She watched as "Antonio" closed the door behind her. Inside was a lavish home, rich with inlaid marble floors and plush but tasteful furniture.

"Won't you please activate your audio input and tell me your name so that we may get to know one another," Antonio pleaded, his eyes as captivating as the seductive tone of his voice. "I can't wait to learn more about you, about your innermost thoughts and desires. I long to touch your soul and delve deep into the woman that is you. Please sit, and together we'll while away the hours."

Chastity was intrigued. She reminded herself that this Antonio was only a video representation of a specialized program, but still she was enticed. She activated her audio input but stayed silent.

"Ah, I can hear you breathing now, and the tremulous beating of your heart. Like a little bird it beats, excited but full of trepidation. Won't you please tell me your name?"

"National grid poll's up," said Tanya, sweeping into the office with the overnights and assorted hard copy.

Chastity severed the link, watching the elegant face of Antonio vanish, and the screen pixels reform in grid search mode. She squared herself and cleared her throat.

"What's the topic?" she asked as she ran her fingers over the screen to link with the polling site.

"Special task force to deal with terrorists," Tanya replied. "I'm voting for it. Will and I are worried about Loftur. It's scary to think our children aren't safe. Who knows where they'll strike next, or what kinds of atrocities they'll commit. We need to stop them."

"We've heard quite a bit about Loftur threats and violent acts believed related then later denied, but I don't remember the last time there was actually an incident attributed to them. Do you?"

"Sure," Tanya said, "there was that…oh, what was it? I can't recall right now, but I know they're dangerous. We wouldn't be so scared if they weren't dangerous, would we?"

Chastity looked over the basic issues and tenets on the polling site.

"I guess you're right. It's just strange that for all the rumors and reports, there haven't been more acts of terrorism."

She contemplated it for a moment and decided to vote later.

"How was the family reunion?"

"It was great. I didn't get to relax much, what with the kids, but it was still fun. It was nice to get away, even for a couple of days. Billy's uncle gave him one of those V-Real visors, but now I can't get Will to stop playing with it. He's like a big kid anyway."

Chastity switched back to the state medical database.

"I want you to do some research on in-vitro fertilization for me. I want to know how it's done—the science, the technology—just the basics. And I want to know about related laws or regulations governing the privacy of the various parties involved. I'm going to focus on the facilities where the process is actually carried out."

"Is this for a new show I don't know about?" Tanya wondered. "Because I'm right in the middle of preparing for the group marriage show. I've got—"

"I want this to be your top priority right now. I'm not certain whether it'll work into a topic or not. That's why we're going to do the research."

Tanya looked frustrated. "But we've got the group marriage show coming up next week and I haven't even—"

"I don't want to waste time discussing it, Tanya. I want you to do what I asked. The sooner you get it done, the sooner you can get back to the other, right?"

"All right. Whatever you say," Tanya replied. Clearly Chastity's demand had thrown her. "I'll get on it now."

Her snippy tone was obvious, and Chastity felt bad at how she'd handled it, even if Tanya did work for her. However, she paid little attention to the look her producer gave her before retreating from the office. Her subconscious had summoned up the image of Antonio, the cyber courtesan. She recalled what the antiquated term described. The more she thought about him, the more eager she was to recall the link and find out where he would—no, where *it* would lead her.

But not now. She wiped the image of Antonio from her mind with a slight shake of the head and turned her attention back to the screen. She busied herself sorting through the subheading of the database until she became lost in her work, thoroughly involved in finding the trail that would lead her to her own family reunion.

33

DRUDGE HAPPENS

"WHAT'S ON YOUR MIND, NOAH?" THE THERATECH'S FEMALE IMAGE SET HER NOTEPAD aside as if moving the conversation to a less formal level. "I can tell something's bothering you."

"What do you mean? I'm fine."

"You're not your usual belligerent self. Is there something you want to talk about?"

There was something on Noah's mind, but he didn't want to talk about it. Especially not with a woman. Then again, she wasn't a woman, was she? She wasn't even a real person. It would be like talking to his azaleas, wouldn't it? Hell, he might as well get it out there.

"I've been having some trouble getting it up."

"Getting it up?"

"You know." He paused, then blurted out, "for sex."

"That's nothing to be worried about, Noah."

"That's easy for you to say, Gertie. A fresh set of gigabytes and a little reboot and it's bliss city for you."

"Impotence is a common occurrence, especially among older men. There are—"

"I am not older," he huffed, cutting her off. "At least not that old."

"As I was saying, there are a number of biochemical remedies for the condition that work quite well."

"I don't want to pop a pill every time I get a whiff of pow-whammy. You don't get it. This has never happened to me before. *Never.*"

"Why do you think it's happening now?"

165

"I don't know."

"Are you sure? Think about it." The theratech's image retrieved her notepad and began looking through it.

"You're the doctor, Gertie, you tell me."

"All right. Do you remember in our first session, when you were talking about Cyrus's death, you said, 'I should have been there for him. I should have protected him'?"

"No, I don't."

"Would you like me to replay the conversation?"

"No."

"It's clear you feel an enormous amount of guilt over your partner's death. You admitted as much."

"So, I feel guilty. What does that have to do with the price of peanuts?"

"I believe there's a direct correlation between that guilt and your inability to achieve erection."

"That's drudge!"

"Is it? You said you should have been there for Cyrus. Where were you?"

"I was down the street a ways—not that far."

"Why weren't you with your partner? What were you doing?"

"I was…" He remembered exactly what he was doing. He thought of, and discarded, several ways of saying it. "I was chasing down this girl on skates."

"Why were you doing that?"

"It seemed like the thing to do at the time."

"Was this police business, or were you engaged in making a sexual advance?"

"It wasn't police business," admitted Noah.

"I see."

"What do you see?" he asked defensively.

"I believe, Noah, whether your conscious mind realizes it or not, your subconscious has directly connected your sexual drive with your feelings of guilt. Because you were attempting to engage in a sexual activity at the time you believe you should have been with your partner, your subconscious is punishing you by denying you that very activity."

He considered it. He had to admit it made a kind of sense, in a twisted psychobabble sort of way. But that didn't mean he was necessarily buying into it.

"I believe we've set the table with enough food for thought for the time being," the theratech stated. "Why don't we schedule another session in a few days, and we'll speak again after you've had a chance to think over what we've talked about."

Noah pulled himself out of the thickly cushioned chair. "All right. Link you later, Gertie," he replied flippantly. Inside, however, his thoughts were anything but brash.

He wanted to cling to the idea nothing was wrong with him, despite the theratech's theories, but his grasp of that particular reality wasn't nearly as tenacious as it had been.

CAPTAIN RAEVSKI USHERED HIM INTO HER OFFICE, AND HE NOTICED THE STALE FRAGRANCE of ganja was especially strong in her hair. He 'jectured retirement probably couldn't come soon enough for her. She didn't wait to get behind her desk before starting in on him.

"Dane, have you seen the results of the latest local grid poll? Of course you haven't. I'll tell you what it says. It says the public believes I've dropped the ball. They don't think I should have let you have this case. They say you're off your game, in a slump, pressing because you're too close. They're blaming me, Dane. For the love of Jerry, this thing's getting more coverage than Loftur. I need a heads-up, Dane. How close are you to bringing in Budd's killer?"

"Not close enough to know who he is," Noah stated flatly.

"You've got to know something," Raevski insisted, picking up her zapper and eyeballing the floor for unauthorized intruders.

"It's a hardscrabble case, Cap. We've got pieces, but they aren't fitting together." He proceeded to tell her about the tattoos and the implant, the military lasers, what he knew about the diamonds, and the bat shit. Raevski was paying more attention to her scan for roaches until the last part.

"Bat shit?"

"Guano, to be exact, Cap."

"What in the holy roller play does that have to do with this case?"

"We're not exactly sure."

"Not sure? What are you doing, waiting for the case to make itself? Throw your game plan out the window if you have to, audibilize, make your own breaks. It's time to start playing with a sense of urgency."

"Cap, we've—"

A knock on the open door salvaged Noah's prefabricated excuse. He was saved by the belle of the ball—Georgia, dressed in a high-waisted, filmy white chiffon halter dress with a plunging V-neckline. Noah thought she looked like somebody's idea of dessert. She didn't wait to be invited in.

"Marilyn said you were updating the captain on your case, so I thought I'd just sashay in here with my findings."

"Browne," Raevski stated disapprovingly, "what is that you're wearing?"

"Don't you just love it?" Georgia spun around so they could both get a good look. "Marilyn gave it to me. It's a little snug in places, but I think it's cream and cake. What do you think?"

"Just perfect," Raevski muttered acerbically.

"I was thinking of wearing it to the Exotic Erotic Ball, but they've cancelled it this year. Can you believe that? Cancelled due to lack of interest. What's this world coming to?"

"You come in here dressed like that, and you're asking me?"

Georgia's expression turned serious, her eyes an entreaty focused on the captain. "I just want to be me."

Raevski exhaled in mild exasperation and glanced at Noah.

"So, what have you got on the case?" he asked.

"I've got the same species of feces," Georgia replied, giggling. "*Myotis lucifugus*, commonly known as the little brown bat. The guano was a definite match."

"More bat shit!" Raevski ranted. "What kind of a case is this?"

"This shit's from the VR designer's condo," Noah explained. "Same as Georgia found at Huang's place. That's not all. Hutchinson apparently got his hands on some diamonds recently. We don't know if there's a link there yet. We're having the diamonds examined by an expert."

Captain Raevski dropped her zapper on the table and fell more than sat back in her chair.

"Are you telling me, Dane, that these two cases are connected?"

"It appears they are, Cap. We think the same guy who burned Cyrus and partnered with Huang killed Hutchinson. We just don't know why."

It took several seconds for the implications to soak in, but when they did, Raevski erupted.

"For the love of Jerry, don't tell anyone about this—not until you've got this guy locked up. If the public finds out, they'll crucify me in the next grid vote."

"I wasn't planning on sending out any news releases," Noah responded dryly. "But just tell me one thing, Cap. Who the hell is Jerry?"

"Jerry? Oh, you mean Jerry. Jerry Rice, the greatest receiver in the history of the NFL. Played his entire career right here in the Bay Area."

He gave her an odd look.

"What? It's an expression I picked up from my grandfather. So? So what are you both standing there for then?" Raevski's attempted bellow came out as a high-pitched screech. "Get going. Flush this guy out of the pocket and close this case before my retirement party becomes a lynching!"

MARILYN WAS IMMERSED IN WHATEVER IT WAS SHE WAS DOING; SHE DIDN'T NOTICE WHEN he returned from the captain's ritual reaming. He 'jectured his partner was deep into her AR, but he could also see a conglomeration of tiny parts on her desk.

"What are you doing?" he asked her.

She turned to him but wavered momentarily, as if completing some unseen task.

"Was the captain...?"

"Yes," he answered, not needing her to finish the question. "What's that?" He nodded at the pile of loose parts.

"Last night, after you went to sleep, I decided to disassemble that V-Real visor I got."

"Why?"

"I just wanted something to do. First I tried to use it, but it didn't work for me. I guess the visor doesn't interface properly with my neural nodes. Anyway, I decided to take it apart to see if I could figure out how it works."

"Well, did you?"

"No. I don't really have the technical programming necessary to—"

"Great. Well, let's get back on this case, okay? The captain is burning my butt. I'm one sports adage away from a meltdown. Let's see what DIRS has on our perp."

"But wait, I did find—"

"Later. Let's see the vid."

Marilyn let out a sigh of frustration but complied. She accessed the surveillance video from outside the complex where Hutchinson lived. Unfortunately, it was brief, and gave no positive indication of where their suspect might have gone next. As for the identity of the killer, the only clear frames they had were profile, and from slightly behind. Still, it was enough for Noah.

"That's him."

"How can you be so sure?" wondered Marilyn. "There's no full shot of his face."

"Call up the other video and compare if you want. All you have to do is look at his frame, the rigid way he carries himself, that heavy-footed strut. It's him." He turned back to his own desk. "Make sure you add this to the DIRS alert on this guy. Every scrap the recognition system has on file makes it that much easier to find him."

"All right. Can I tell you now?"

"Tell me what?"

"What I found out about the V-Real visor."

"If it'll make you happy.

"First, I learned that a diamond is a good semiconductor material for some electronic applications because of its chemical stability, strength and heat conduction properties."

"So what?"

"I found a diamond chip inside the visor."

Noah didn't respond right away. "So you're thinking our diamonds and V-Real are related?"

"Well, I don't know, *Inspector*," Marilyn replied with more than a hint of sarcasm, "you're the real detective, not me."

"We need to get that chip to our expert," he said, ignoring her tone, "so he can compare them all. But even if they match up, that doesn't put us any closer to our killer."

"There's one other thing. I did some more research on it, and I was just double-checking my figures. If a thing's worth doing, it's worth doing well, and, well, I'm sure I'm right."

"What is it, already?"

"This virtual reality device—the diamond and the parts that are used to build it have a higher aggregate cost than the retail price of the visor itself."

"That can't be right. How can you stay in business selling something for less than it costs to make? Why would you if you could?"

Marilyn had nothing for him but a blank look, like she could throw all this drudge at him and then deactivate herself. When was this case going to start making sense? When were they going to catch a break? He 'jectured it was like the captain said. They were going to have to make their own.

34

HEAVEN AROUND THE CORNER

C HASTITY HAD FINISHED COMPILING A LIST OF WESTERN HEMISPHERE IN-VITRO CLINICS and had begun to expand her search worldwide when she decided to take a break and stretch her legs. So she made her way down to the street, and headed for her favorite little shop, The Sweet Boutique. It was around the corner from the IGN building, a tiny place not much bigger than her closet space at home. Nevertheless, its display cases were laden with every kind of confection she could imagine, and some she would never dare. Simply walking inside and smelling the pervading aroma of chocolate made her pause and take a deep breath.

Chocolate, candy, sweets of all kinds had been forbidden by her father when she was a little girl. She'd never really understood why, but she'd had fun ever since, making up for lost time. The Sweet Boutique had become her Wonderland, and she was Alice all grown up.

Marigold, the shop's owner, was used to her stopping by. Chastity guessed she was the store's best customer.

"Would you like to sample our new dark/light mix, Ms Blume?" Marigold asked. "It's simply divine."

"I…Oh, excuse me a moment," she said as her pad notified her of an incoming call. Few people had access to her personal link, so she wasn't that surprised to see High Minister Redstone identified as the caller. She accessed the link.

"High Minister, what can I do for you?"

Redstone was dressed in her ceremonial robes and silver headband.

"Now, Chastity, it's Rebekah, remember?"

"I'm sorry, force of habit."

"I'm going to have to break you of certain habits if we're going to be friends." Redstone's smile emphasized her exquisite cheekbones. Chastity caught herself wondering if they were implants.

"You're right, Rebekah."

"I know you're probably busy, so I won't keep you. I wanted to see if you'd like to have dinner with me this evening. Just the two of us, here in my quarters."

"I'd love to, but I have too much to do right now. I might be working all night."

"That's all right, we could make it a late dinner."

Chastity considered the offer. "I'd better not, not tonight. I'd love to some other time, though."

"Fine," Redstone responded, no trace of disappointment in her smile, "we'll do it another time. Don't work too hard, dear."

The high minister broke the link, but Chastity didn't have much time to ponder the unexpected invitation before her pad chimed with another call.

"Yes, Tanya?"

"I'm transmitting the research you asked for." Her producer still had a hint of glower on her face. Her cadence was coolly professional. "It includes a detailed outline of the in-vitro process in layman's terms and the pertinent regulations from both the Revised HIPAA and the National Privacy Act of 2012. I have to go pick up Billy and Shannon from their afterschool mover lessons now, if that's all right with you. If not then I can—"

"Of course it's all right. Thanks for getting all that done. Go home and I'll see you tomorrow."

Tanya broke her link, leaving Chastity smarting from her tone. She second-guessed herself for directing Tanya to help her with this. Yes, it was her producer's job to do whatever Chastity needed, but she felt a modicum of guilt because the research had nothing to do with her show. It never would. This was personal. She'd never expose the details of her life to the public as so many of her guests did. If that made her a hypocrite, so be it. She certainly wasn't going to dwell on it now.

She was fueled by her own tenacity. Each step took her that much closer. More than anything, now, she was determined to finish what she started. She would know if her true mother was alive, and if so, who she was. Whether that knowledge would satisfy her she couldn't say. She had plenty of work to do before that question could even be asked.

But first…there was so much to choose from, so many different shades of chocolate, so many varieties of flavor.

"I'll try that sample now, Marigold."

35

DÉJÀ VIEW

Noah didn't believe in umbrellas. They were fine for women and Dainty Dans, but they weren't for him, despite his aversion to rainstorms and their meteorological accomplices. Consequently, he was soaked and sullen after his jog from the Mag-Lev station to the Hall of Justice.

He pulled off his long black coat and hung it over the back of his chair. His pants felt too tight so he tugged at the waistband. Either the damn things were shrinking, or his belly was taking in boarders. He unholstered his Desert Eagle to wipe it dry, and as he did his nostrils picked up a peculiar scent.

"What the drudge are you eating, Chen?"

"Chang wang."

"What?"

"Egg noodles, bean curd, pig intestines and assorted veggies."

"Shit and frijoles, is that what you nightshift boys eat? What are you still doing here, anyway?"

"Just catching up on the file work. You know how the brass hats love their gigabytes."

"Yeah. Well lap up that slop or take it downwind, would you?"

"Eat my badge, Dane."

He ignored the offer and looked for his partner. She wasn't in the squadroom, though she'd decided to stay there for the night to do some "personal research." What that was he had no idea, and didn't really care. But with her AR ability, she could have done the same research anywhere. He wondered if the real reason she hadn't come home with him was that she didn't want to complicate his ever-so-slowly budding relationship with Cat.

Not that she would have interfered with anything. His daughter had taken to spending most of her time in her room, playing with her V-Real. But at least Cat seemed to have discarded the notion of running away to be a disciple of Transcendental Platonics.

His ear began to itch. He holstered his gun and pinched his lobe.

I'm getting us a pod, meet me up here.

"What's the hurry? What's up?"

The Digital Imaging Recognition System just reported an eighty-three percent-probability hit on our suspect.

"Get an IRIS out there. I'm on my way."

THE POLICE POD HAD BARELY CREPT OUT OF THE LAUNCH WHEN THE FIRST BOLT OF lightning illuminated the gray skyline. Noah flinched so noticeably that Marilyn turned to look. She was watching him as he tensed, bracing himself for the inevitable violent crack of thunder. The seconds were interminable. The relief was plain on his face when the dreaded sound was so far-off as to be hardly discernable.

"What's wrong?" she asked.

"Nothing," he said without much conviction. "Nothing's wrong."

"You don't look like nothing's wrong. Are you feeling okay?"

"I'm fine, I'm—" Another flash of lightning punctuated his denial. "I'm all right."

She eyed him like she wasn't buying a word.

"Okay, okay," he relented. "You want to fly? Then take over the controls. You've been yammering on about how you can operate this thing, so go ahead."

Marilyn took over, not that she had much to do at the moment but monitor their progress. The pod was set on autopilot, its destination already input. She wouldn't actually do anything until they were ready to land, and Noah knew it would be easy enough to take control if needed. Watching her, though, he didn't think that would be necessary.

It wasn't likely their perp would be out in this weather, so they'd have to search all the neighboring buildings—he had already called for reinforcements. The grid recognition factor of this case was high enough to give him the clout he needed to muster a small army of uniforms. They'd be waiting at ground zero. He cursed himself for not using his juice to requisition more than one IRIS.

When they arrived at the location where the DIRS hit had registered, they circled the area for a quick scan. It revealed no activity at all. It was a residential neighborhood, and everyone was staying inside, out of the weather.

"Anything from IRIS?"

"Nothing," Marilyn replied. "I'm linked, so I'll know the moment it makes an identification."

They were about to land when his pad came to life, demanding attention.

"Hi, sugar." It was Georgia, looking unusually serious but odd with a V-Real visor pushed up on her head. "I've got another body."

"And...?"

"Well, I'm here with Harper and Brunelli. They've got a professor who was strangled."

"Good for them. I've got my own problems. Why are you telling me?"

"Honey, you're not going to believe this. It's really *Bizarre del Mundo.* I've found more traces of guano here. I thought I'd better tell you."

Noah looked at Marilyn as if for confirmation of what he'd heard. "Where are you?"

"It's a house in Glen Park—545 Arlington."

"That's right down the road from here. We're on our way. Don't let that ape Brunelli trample anything before we get there."

"Hurry up, sugar, I want to get home so I can play *Cosmos.*"

"Cosmos?"

"It's the latest, greatest virtual adventure. Don't you get real with V-Real? It's better than—"

"Than chocolate, I know. Just secure the scene."

He deleted the link and resumed control of the pod. "I'll take it," he said without even a glance at his partner. "Link up with whoever's in charge of our search squad down there, and tell them to start without us.

"Anymore of this bat drudge and we're going to have to bring in every wannabe vampire in the city for questioning."

"WHAT THE HELL ARE YOU DOING HERE, DANE?" SNARLED BRUNELLI, HIS UPPER LIP twitching angrily.

Noah was busy examining the front door, which had obviously been forced.

"Didn't Georgia tell you? This is my case now."

"Like drudge it's your case." Harper was already moving in between them. "What's that transie got to do with anything? This is our case, so you and your droid queen can play with each other somewhere else."

Noah didn't take the bait. He knew he had the upper hand here, and played it cool to stoke Brunelli's fire.

"You think I want your stinking leftovers? Check with Raevski if you want. She's already planted this one in my pot, so go piss somewhere else."

"I'll take off your head and piss down your neck," Brunelli blustered as his partner shepherded him away.

The rant continued in a series of mumbled curses, but Noah ignored them. He followed Marilyn into a back room where Georgia was taking a sample off the face of the white-haired guy on the floor. It was a workroom of some sort, with discs, papers, books piled everywhere. Marilyn proceeded straight to the desk and activated the grid unit.

"What have you got?"

"I'm not sure," Georgia said, sealing the swab. "There's a light residue on his face. It could just be his own sweat. Livor mortis had barely set in when I got here." She checked her pad. "Body temperature ninety-four degrees. I'd say he was killed less than two hours ago."

"Who is he?"

"Professor Wu Chun Wei, according to Harper. A professor of what, I don't know."

"How'd they find him?"

"Security alarm was tripped when the front door was broke open."

"Are you positive about the bat shit?"

"As positive as I can be until I get it back to the lab, sugar. Though I've surely seen enough of it lately."

"I don't suppose he has any tattoos or implants?"

Georgia shook her head. "And it looks like whoever strangled the poor old guy was wearing gloves, so the chance he left any trace DNA is unlikely."

"Like with Hutchinson."

A uniform stuck his head in the door and said, "Inspector, we've got some guy out here who says he's the professor's assistant. He just showed up at the front door."

Noah followed the officer back outside, where he saw Harper and Brunelli on their way out. He 'jectured they must have confirmed with Raevski that they were off the case.

"Leaving without saying goodbye?"

"You can have it, Dane, along with your droid and your transie," Brunelli said, stalking out the door. "Let's get out of this freak show."

"He says his name is Peri Wayton," said the officer, pointing at the thin, mop-haired figure waiting on the couch. "I checked, he's in the system. His name is Peridot Thomas Wayton."

Noah could tell this Wayton fellow had already been given the bad news. He looked dazed, genuinely in shock. Not that he could have been a suspect in Noah's mind. He was too small, too frail to have strangled the old guy.

"Peridot Wayton?"

He stood as Noah approached him. "Yes, that's me. It's awful. Do you know what happened? I mean, who would do such a thing?"

"We don't know yet. Do you know anyone who might want to hurt Professor...?"

"Wu."

"Yeah, Wu. Did Professor Wu have any enemies?"

"No, of course not. I mean, he didn't really socialize or anything. He was busy with his research most of the time, and teaching his classes, of course."

"Where did he teach?"

"Berkeley."

"What exactly is he a professor of?"

"Sociology."

"Any students you know of who might have had a grudge?"

"No. I never heard him mention anything."

"Did you help the professor with his work?"

"Oh, no, I'm sort of his man Friday. I do the housekeeping, shopping, laundry, run his errands—that sort of thing."

"Okay," Noah said, not hearing anything he hadn't expected. "Come with me."

He led the professor's assistant into the workroom and moved aside so the kid had a clear view of the body.

"Oh, my God."

"Is that Professor Wu?" Noah asked as Wayton turned his head away from the corpse.

"Yes, yes, that's him."

"I found something interesting," Georgia said, handing whatever it was to Marilyn so she could look it over. "It's a stickpin, a little sunburst or something. Very expensive—looks like platinum with gold edging. I didn't see it until I pried open his fist."

"That's not the professor's," Wayton said. "I mean, I've never seen it before."

"Probably too fancy to be some fraternity pin," Noah said, taking it from Marilyn.

"I found something, too," Marilyn said. "Or, I should say, I found nothing. This hard drive has been wiped clean. Every file has been deleted."

"Just like with Hutchinson." Noah turned to Wayton. "Do you know what the professor was working on?"

"Oh, dear, no. I would have no idea. I know he was in here a lot, and didn't like to be disturbed."

"Okay, Mr. Wayton, you can go. This is going to be a crime scene for a while so no cleaning up. Go home. We'll contact you if we need anything else."

"All right." He took a last look at the body, as if in fond memory. "Poor Professor Wu. I just don't know what this world's coming to."

Georgia closed her case and collapsed her omnicam tripod. "I'm done in here. I'll call for a pickup," she said, following Wayton out of the room.

"Somebody's covering up something, but I'm damned if I know what it is," Noah muttered.

"We need to find out if there's any connection between Professor Wu and Hurley Hutchinson," Marilyn added.

Noah's pad vibrated with an incoming call. He didn't recognize the ident code.

"Inspector Noah Dane?"

The face wasn't familiar, but the caller was wearing an Army uniform and the silver oak leaves of a light colonel.

"I'm Inspector Dane."

"Lieutenant-Colonel Frank Caswell, sir. I'm attached to the CID unit at Fort Irwin. I'm calling about the weapon you found. We want to thank you for reporting it, and we'd like to come pick it up."

"I can't turn it loose just yet, Colonel. It's part of an ongoing investigation. Have you boys come up with anything on your end about how it might have found its way into civilian hands?"

"We don't have any hard evidence yet, Inspector. However, a non-commissioned officer with access to some missing weapons went AWOL a few months ago. We think there might be a connection."

"What's his name?"

"I'm afraid that's currently classified, Inspector."

Noah let out an annoyed grunt. "Look, Colonel, I've got three murders already, and there are at least two of your weapons still out there in criminal hands. One of them killed my partner, and the other took a shot at me. Now, I'm not looking to put any of this on the grid, but I need to know this guy's name."

The Army officer wrapped his hand around his forehead and scrunched his face up like he was in distress.

"All right, Inspector," he relented. "Sergeant Brock E. Kutzler."

"Thanks, Colonel. If we come across him, we'll let you know."

"Thank you, Inspector." The colonel made a move to cut the link.

"One more thing, Colonel. Just how many of these lasers of yours are missing?"

Noah could tell by the officer's expression that he didn't want to say.

"Two dozen, including the one in your possession."

The link was severed, and he put away his pad.

"Shit and frijoles," he muttered. "Two dozen of those things."

"At least we've got another lead now—a name," Marilyn said hopefully.

"Yeah, but if the Army hasn't been able to track this guy down in months, we're not likely to do any better."

They did a quick walk-thru of the house but found nothing that spoke of disorder. The killer knew exactly what he wanted this time, and where it was. Back in the main room they found Georgia sitting quietly in a chair, her V-Real visor pulled down over her eyes. Its narrow lens was alive, flickering like a fluorescent ruby. It appeared now even she was hooked on this new fad.

Well, thought Noah as he absentmindedly played with the stickpin Georgia had found, at least she's not hitting on me anymore.

He fumbled with the pin, almost dropped it then caught it inches above the floor. In doing so, he somehow activated a holographic display, though he didn't immediately realize it was projected from the pin. It was a young woman, standing, smiling sedately.

He gawked at the inert projection, blinking his eyes to clear his vision. It took him a moment or two, because the face in the projection was much younger—maybe nineteen, twenty at most. But when he finally recognized her, he was certain.

The holographic image was that of Chastity Blume.

36

BETWEEN A BIKEROO
AND A HARSH PLACE

THE HORIZON THREATENED ANOTHER STORM AS THE SUN DROPPED INTO THE PACIFIC. Sinister thunderheads gathered as if in a council of war, nearly blotting out the fire of the ruddy sunset. The wind whipped through San Francisco's streets like demon sprites on missions of mischief.

Chastity pulled her beige jacket around her as a particularly determined impish gust blew it open. She stared up at the inscription on the edifice before her. It read BRAZIER INSTITUTE OF FERTILITY. Next to the inscription was a round dish with flames growing out it.

So this is where she was conceived. Conceived, gestated and delivered unto the world. It hadn't been as hard to track down her birthplace as she thought. She was mildly surprised it was right here in the city, and that her father hadn't whisked his sperm away to some clandestine foreign laboratory.

She didn't waste any time on memories she didn't have. She passed under the exterior security cam, went inside and confronted the receptionist, who immediately recognized her. Her fame gained her admission to the office of one of the institute's associate executive directors, but that was as far as its influence went.

"I'm sorry, Ms Blume," the executive said for the third time, even more apologetic than he had been for the first, "we are not allowed to divulge that information to anyone, not even the resulting offspring. It's a matter of both contractual agreement and state law. I empathize with your desire to locate your natural mother, but I just can't help you."

Chastity had tried charm and supplication, so she fired away with a new stratagem.

"Tell me, Dr. Hughes, if I were to make the institute the focus of my next investigative report, looking into any possible health code violations, financial mismanagement or the like, would that help you bend the rules any?"

She could tell he didn't like the sound of that. He twitched nervously, taking hold of a pad from his desk and fumbling with it.

"I'm certain there's nothing to be gained from such an investigation, Ms Blume," he said stiffly, trying to disguise his anxiety with indignation. "We're very meticulous with our procedures, and our compliance with all government regulations. I doubt you'd find anything of interest. Regardless, I can't reveal the identity of your egg donor. Now, if you'll excuse me, I have other business to attend to."

Chastity knew a wall when she ran into one. She left the institute without any further attempts at coercion. Nevertheless, she wasn't about to give up that easily. She just *might* look into the institute's dealings—there could be something, despite Hughes's assertions. If she had to, she could use her show, offer a reward for the donor to come forward without identifying whose parent they were looking for. Of course, then she'd have to use DNA testing to sort through all the loons looking for attention or quick credit.

She'd been inside the institute longer than she thought. It had grown dark, the only illumination the soft coral glow of the streetlights and a single public grid screen pulsing with some marketing inanity across the way. She retrieved her pad from her purse to call for her car then realized she wasn't alone on the street.

A trio of bikeroos, alternately resplendent and ragged in their striking blue colors, leaned on their bikes just yards away. She hesitated with her pad, and as she did, four more gang members coasted to a stop near her. They were all around now, leering at her with countenances both curious and threatening. Some of the faces were so young—too young, she thought, to be on the street. Belatedly, she considered activating her pad's emergency link.

A bikeroo approached her from behind and snatched the pad from her grasp.

"You won't need this," he said, smiling almost politely.

"See what else she's got in there," called another one, gesturing at her purse with a blade that glimmered in the dim light.

The first bikeroo held his hand out expectantly. Part of her wanted to slap it away, but the part that was in control right now was terrified—terrified and angry. She was angry at herself for being so preoccupied, so stupid as to put herself in this position. After a few seconds hesitation, she handed over her purse.

That's when another trio of bikeroos pedaled in, the lead biker skidding to a stop so close she was about to jump out of the way. This guy was older than the rest, bare-chested except for a fancy vest that looked small on his barrel frame. Chastity couldn't make out the designs, but she could tell his heavily muscled arms were covered with tattoos.

She gathered from the way the other bikeroos wavered that this was their leader. He got off his bike, let it drop and looked her over with deep-set eyes under beetle brows. His stare was disconcerting.

She nervously pulled on her pale-lavender skirt and took a step back. The gangster tilted the bright-blue derby he wore back from his forehead and smiled like a kid at Christmas. A glint of silver ignited his grin.

"Chastity?" he asked in a gravel-toned voice. "Chastity Blume? Damned if it isn't really you."

She was used to being recognized, but this time she was caught unawares. It took her more than a moment to grasp how this bikeroo knew her name.

"I'm mega-fan numero uno. Haven't missed a single program—no, not a single one."

Still flabbergasted, Chastity didn't know if she should feel relief or not.

"You dim bulbs know who this is, don't you?" Only a few appeared to have caught up with their chief. "This is Chastity Blume, America's Favorite Virgin, a dyed-in-the-bull celebrity. You know, from that show *Gridspeak*."

Signs of recognition surged through the group, though a couple still remained dumbfounded. Even so, those who weren't sure nodded in agreement. Chastity's panic amplitude racheted down a notch, though she was too confused to feel safe.

"I'm Grandmaster Thrash, captain and president pro tem of the Blue Scorpions," he said, taking off his hat and extending his hand to her. "You can just call me Thrash."

She took his hand, meaning to be polite but brief, but he grabbed hers and shook it with the enthusiasm of a pit bull.

Suddenly, he yanked an enormous blade from his waist and pointed its curved edge at the bikeroo who had her purse and pad.

"Is that hers?" he demanded.

The chagrined gang member nodded.

"Give it back, you mump," Thrash ordered, and the other did so instantly.

"Thank you," Chastity said, placing her pad back into her purse.

"I spin my wheels trying to manage them, trying to teach them right, but they don't listen," he said, turning to fire frowns of disappointment at several of his cadre. "I'll tell you, Chastity, it's no bed of posies leading these spokeheads. But, you know what they say about birds of a feather traveling as the crow flies."

Chastity's expression said she wasn't sure, so he went on.

"Be that as it mayonnaise, what in the name of James Tiberius Kirk are you doing out here? Don't you know it's dangerous on the streets at night? We could have just as easily been Razorbacks—then you would have had a real red alert. You can't be too careful these days, what with all the crime and the Loftur everywhere. Never know what they could be up to."

"I was just trying to get some information from this clinic," she said, motioning to the building behind her. "They weren't very helpful."

"What was it you needed to know?" Thrash asked, squinting one eye so as to remind her of a pirate.

"It's personal, a family thing. I'll have to find out some other way."

"You mean they've got the goods, but won't give them to you?"

She nodded. "They're just following their rules."

"You know, rules give me a colossal rash right down where it matters most," Thrash said, sheathing his huge knife. "Who'd you talk to?"

"A Dr. Hughes, but—"

"I think I'll have a little parley with Dr. Hughes, see if I can help you out."

Chastity's imagination painted an unpleasant picture. "Oh, no, you can't. I mean, you don't need to do that. It's fine, it's okay."

"No, no, I insist. Don't worry, we won't cause any trouble—won't need to." He smiled that roguish smile again. "We'll just go in there with phasers on stun and convince Dr. Hughes that he lives in the land of milk and money, and that this isn't the time for him to be the flea in the ointment."

Her protest was cut off by his upraised hand.

"Don't worry." With that, he pointed at a pair of his bikeroos, who bounded up the steps of the institute, and said to the rest, "You mumps take care of Ms Blume here."

Chastity wanted to stop him, but at the moment didn't feel like she was in a very formidable position. She didn't fool herself into thinking the leader of the Blue Scorpions was going to sway the doctor with reason alone. She only hoped no blood would be shed. She smiled at her ragtag honor guard as a light rain began to fall, and moved closer to the building for cover.

In a few minutes, Thrash exited alone.

"It's jell. The boys are inside with Dr. Hughes, and to make a wrong story short, he's agreed to cooperate with your inquiries. Told you I could take care of it. The Thrashmaster is a bikeroo of his word. Just send my boys out when you go in. I know you need your privacy."

"Thanks." She didn't know what else to say.

"Just tell me one thing first. You're not really a virgin, are you? That's hype, right? It's all special effects, isn't it?"

Shocked by his bluntness, Chastity faltered before deciding why not?

"If I tell you, you have to keep it a secret. Just between you and me, okay?"

"Understood," he replied, and for some reason she couldn't substantiate, she didn't doubt he would keep his promise.

Chastity stepped closer and whispered in his ear. He grinned, but all he said was "Better get inside, looks like it's going to rain cats and hogs."

Indeed, the tempo of the rain had increased, and the bikeroos were mounting up and beginning to circle, waiting for their chief.

"Thanks again," Chastity said. She hurried up the steps without looking back.

The receptionist gawked at her but said nothing. Once she was inside Hughes's office, the pair of bikeroos departed.

An expression of dread lingered on the associate executive director's face. Chastity wondered what they had said to him, what sordid threat they had made. It was better she didn't know.

As nonchalantly as she could, she said, "I believe you have a name for me."

37

IMPRESSIONS OF YOU

A S THEY WAITED FOR THE NETWORK'S SECURITY PROTOCOLS TO UNRAVEL, MARILYN BEGAN to hum. What the tune was, Noah didn't know and didn't care. His eyes narrowed as they aimed a disapproving blue glint at his partner. She was so preoccupied with either the song in her head or some other deep droid thought that it was half a minute before she noticed his squint of annoyance.

"What?" she asked.

"Knock off the humming."

"Was I humming? Oh, I guess I was. I didn't even realize I was doing it out loud. I was just remembering a song—'There's No Business Like Show Business'—from a movie I...well, a movie you-know-who starred in."

"Just knock it off, okay? Let's focus on what we're doing here."

"Okay, Inspector Spoilsport." She pouted and looked away from him.

A lithe redhead in a security uniform opened an inner door and called them.

"Inspector Dane, Detective Monroe, this way please."

Another time he would have given the security officer the twice-over, despite the fact she leaned to the twiggy side. Instead, he realized he was going out of his way to ignore her. He sensed his own trepidation, and didn't at all like the way it made him feel. This whole performance anxiety thing was new to him, and it was careening out of control. He tried to forget it, tried to concentrate on the questions he wanted answers to.

Even before they turned into the office proper, he caught the familiar scent of lilacs.

The redhead stood in the doorway and tried to announce them. "Ms

Blume, the police officers are here. Inspector Dane and—"

"Yes, we've met before. Thank you. You can go." Chastity Blume got up from her seat and greeted them coolly but professionally. "Inspector, Detective, what can I do for you today? Please sit down."

She sat, so they did. Noah could see they weren't exactly welcome. Which was too bad. Any other time he would have marveled at those finely chiseled cheekbones, been caught up in the feral swirl of her hairstyle, anxious to press those perfect lips. She was one crucial commodity, and…

And what was he doing? His runaway craving deflated like a pin-pricked balloon. He was here to do a job, to find Cyrus' killer, not—

"We found something we'd like to show you," Marilyn said, snapping him out of his reverie. Seeing him sitting there like some mind-drudged mump, she'd taken the lead. "Have you ever seen this before?"

Marilyn handed the sunburst stickpin to Blume. She looked it over, and Noah, having disengaged from his inner devils, thought he saw a flicker of recognition in those seductive green eyes.

"No, no, I don't think I've seen anything like this before." She returned the pin to Marilyn.

"Are you certain, Ms Blume?" Marilyn activated the holographic projection. "That's you, isn't it?"

Noah studied the grid star as she stuttered a reply, planting her hand nervously at the base of her neck. "Uh…yes, yes it is. Where…Where did you get this?"

"We found it at the scene of a murder," Noah said, still gauging her reactions. "We think the victim pulled it off his killer. Any idea why someone would have an expensive little bauble like this, with your holograph?"

"I…I don't have any idea. I mean, I have—that is, my show has— millions of viewers. Certainly some of them are more…zealous than others. Maybe one of them had this made with my likeness."

"Why would they use this much younger image of you?" Noah gestured at the display. "And where would they get access to such an image?"

"I have no idea," Blume responded. "You don't know how extreme some devotees of celebrity can be, Inspector."

Noah heard her summoning up a firm tone of irritation to replace her earlier hesitation.

"I've seen much more determined acts of fanaticism than that. As for the old image, I don't have a clue where it was found, but I'm sure it wasn't difficult to locate for someone persistent enough. I've been the subject of several biographical profiles and such. Any one of them may have used the same image, I don't recall. Can't you use fingerprints or DNA or something to find out where it came from?"

"It was clean, except for the victim's DNA," Noah said as Marilyn turned off the projection. "Do you know a Professor Wu Chun Wei?"

"No, I don't believe I know that name."

"Maybe he was a guest on one of your programs, or you took a class from him at Berkeley?"

"No, I didn't attend Berkeley, I went to Wellesley College in Massachusetts, and I'm certain I never had a Professor Wu on any of my shows."

Noah pulled out his pad, called up the file and showed it to her.

"Do you recognize this man?"

"No, he doesn't look at all familiar. Was he the one who was killed?"

"Yeah, that's Wu." He put the pad away and stood. Marilyn followed suit. "We're done here. Thanks for your time."

"Sorry I couldn't be of more help to your investigation," Blume said, getting out of her chair. "Do you have any suspects?"

"Not yet." He was already heading for the door. Blume moved as if to come around her desk, but he put up his hand. "We'll see ourselves out, thanks."

"We'll let you know if we need anything else, Ms Blume," Marilyn added, following him out.

A half-dozen steps down the corridor Noah said to her, "She's lying."

"She looked up and to the right when she told us she'd never seen the pin before," Marilyn agreed.

He smiled.

"You might make a good detective yet, Monroe. The question now is, why was she lying, and what's the connection between America's Favorite Virgin and a dead sociology professor?"

38

THE MINUTIAE OF MURDER

VERY GOOD, THEN. MS BLUME, YOUR FATHER SAYS YOU CAN GO RIGHT IN. AND MAY I SAY that's a very lovely outfit you have on today. I've always favored the color green."

"Thank you, Michael," Chastity responded as the android held the door open for her.

"Have a nice visit," he added.

Chastity offered a spurious smile in reply. She'd never thought of her visits with her father as nice—not since she was a little girl.

Henri Blume looked up from his work. His eyes were bloodshot, but she couldn't read his face. Not that she ever could. Whatever he was thinking, was feeling, he usually kept locked inside.

"What is it, Chastity?"

She fondled her purity chain and straightened her skirt as she sat.

"A pair of police detectives showed up at IGN this morning to question me."

"About what?" A shadow of interest crossed his face.

"A murder."

"Why would they think you know anything about a murder?"

"Father, where's the stickpin I gave you—the one with the holograph?"

"What does that have to do with anything?"

"The police found it at the scene of the murder. They think the killer was wearing it. The victim was a Professor Wu Chun Wei from Berkeley."

"That stupid—" Her father grimaced before cutting himself off and resuming his stolid posture.

"Do you know this professor?"

"Never heard of him."

"How would the killer have gotten your stickpin, Father?"

"I imagine he found it, or bought it from someone who did. I lost it some time ago, or it was stolen. I don't know."

"You never told me."

"I hadn't really given it much thought, Chastity," her father said with obvious annoyance. "I'm a busy man. I haven't got time for minutiae."

"I see." She stood, telling herself it would be childish to be hurt by his attitude.

"What did you tell the police?" he asked with more curiosity than she thought he wanted to let on.

"I told them I'd never seen the pin before, and that one of my fans must have made it."

"Why did you say that?"

She stared at him. "I said it so you wouldn't be involved, Father. I'm certain you're too busy to be bothered by the minutiae of a murder investigation."

"Well, that's true," he replied. "I guess it's best you kept my name out of it."

Abruptly, Chastity turned to the door. "Goodbye, Father."

As she passed through his office door, she heard him call out, as if his thoughts were still elsewhere, "Goodbye."

She marched through the outer office so quickly Michael almost missed her exit.

"Have a nice day, Ms Blume," the android called as she was disappearing round the corner.

Chastity wasn't sure why she felt so indignant. Maybe it was because she couldn't escape the feeling her father wasn't telling her everything he knew. Something she'd said had almost provoked him. Did he know Professor Wu? Did he actually know anything about the murder? She couldn't believe that was it. He couldn't have anything to do with that. Why would he? But she was certain of one thing—he wasn't telling her the whole truth.

39

THUNDERSTRUCK

I GOT THE DIRS TRACE YOU WANTED ON CHASTITY BLUME, BUT THE WARRANT FOR THE grid tap was disallowed," Marilyn said as she got into the pod. "I didn't think we'd get it," Noah replied. "We'll just have to see where she goes and who she talks with, and hope that leads us somewhere. That's one cold fembot, I'll tell you—uh, no offense."

Marilyn flashed him a disapproving look but said nothing.

"Anything on the diamonds yet?"

"We should have the test results soon," she said. "Do you think they're important?"

"I have no idea. Pretty soon something's got to make sense in this case. There's a connection between these three murders, we just haven't made it yet. And it's more than bat shit."

He eased the pod out of the bay and, despite the reduced visibility of the rain-streaked shieldglass, wasted no time in soaring around the Hall of Justice, preparing to circumnavigate imminent air traffic. A hint of twilight lingered behind the dreary cloud curtain—another Pacific sunset shrouded by the hostile tempest that had seemingly taken up residence over San Francisco. Noah was anxious to get home before the storm got worse.

"Isn't that the girl you spoke to before? There, by the south wall."

Marilyn pointed at a figure huddled next to the building. He could barely make it out in the rain but slowed and brought the pod down to where he could see. It *was* Snip.

"Those android eyes of yours are pretty sharp."

"That poor girl. Why doesn't she go home and get out of the rain?"

191

"Doesn't have one," Noah said matter-of-factly as he landed the pod.

"What are you going to do?"

He didn't bother answering. He opened the hatch, took a moment to steel himself and bounded out into the rain. He ignored the unbridled tremor that passed through him like a quake of muscle memory and held his hand out to the soggy waif.

"Come on, Snip. Let's get you out of the rain."

She peeked up at him with one eye—the mongoloid one—her once jaunty Mohawk now a sodden dog tail.

"Hey, PD man, what's the sliggy?" She tried to make it sound casual, but a shiver distorted her last word.

"Come on. Get up."

She took hold of his hand, and at the same instant he felt her touch a bolt of lightning split the sky so close overhead its thunderous ovation shook the air around them. Noah dove forward, covering the diminutive street urchin with his own massive frame. He felt himself cower uncontrollably on top of her, too rigid with fear to move until she said, "Knew you liked me, PD man, but how about you get a girl a hot meal 'fore you jump her bones?"

Hearing Snip's voice settled him. It also embarrassed him. He got up quickly, helped her up and hustled her into the pod. As he guided her into the rear compartment, another nearby lightning strike rattled the vehicle. A reflex jerk shook him, but he grabbed hold and fell into his seat. Marilyn looked at him with curious eyes, but he faced straight ahead.

"Let's go," he said. "You take the controls."

THE LITTLE STREET CLONE HAD CURLED UP AND FALLEN ASLEEP BY THE TIME MARILYN SET the pod down in front of Noah's house. The backlit overcast had faded to black, and the rain had slowed to a timid drizzle. Marilyn cut the running lights.

"What now?" she asked, looking at Snip.

"Go ahead inside. I'm going to see if my neighbor will take her in."

"Why don't you let her stay with you?"

"Are you kidding? I mean, not that I give a damn what people think, but do you know what it would look like if I have her living in my house? I mean, me, with my…reputation. You know what they would think. Besides, I've got Cat to consider. We're still on delicate footing, getting to know each other and…and this is no time for me to bringing home a stray. You know what I mean?"

Marilyn nodded. "I understand." She looked at him like there was something else, something she couldn't quite figure.

"What is it?" he asked, acknowledging her unspoken query.

"Back there, in the rain, the lightning, there was a moment...I've noticed it before. You don't like it, do you?"

He snorted more with sarcasm than mirth. "You could say that."

"How come?"

"It's personal," he said, reaching for the hatch release. "The only one I ever told about it was Cyrus." He wavered, pulling his hand back from the hatch controls. Cyrus, his friend, his partner who was burned down in front of him, who died because he wasn't there, and whose killer was still on the loose because he hadn't done his job.

"I'm your partner now. Why don't you tell me?" Marilyn looked at him with those naive bedroom eyes of hers, and he 'jectured what the hell.

"I was seven, maybe eight years old. Me and some friend were playing down around this old dock. It started raining, but, you know, we were kids, we didn't care." He looked away from her as he told the story, as though it were being replayed for him in the darkness outside the pod. "I ran down the dock for some reason. I don't remember why. That's when it happened.

"There was this flash of pure blinding light, and a searing pain that bucked through my whole body, kind like I'd been rubbed down with jalapenos. The next thing I knew, I was sucking down seawater like it was air. I didn't even know what had happened, but I knew I was drowning.

"I passed out, woke up some time later in the hospital. My friends had pulled me out of the water and called for help. When they told me I'd been hit by lightning, it jogged my memory. It was only an instant, but I remembered the flash, the pain." He glanced at her. "So that's why I whimper like a whipped puppy every time it starts to rain."

"I can't imagine what it must have been like."

"Yeah."

"But you ran out into the storm to get her anyway."

"It seemed like the thing to do at the time."

"You know, you're not so bad, Noah. Not so tough and grim as you act."

Snip mumbled something in her sleep, kicked one foot out and fended off an imaginary nemesis with her hands. Noah flicked the hatch release and reached into the rear compartment to roust the unconscious girl.

"Come on, Snip. Time to wake up. No more nightmares for you."

MARILYN WENT IN TO CHECK ON CAT AT NOAH'S REQUEST, WHILE HE WAITED FOR SNIP. IT took her several minutes to fully wake and relax with her surroundings enough for him to explain where they were. She must have been exhausted. He thought he'd give her another minute to adjust to the idea of going into a stranger's home, so he pinched his lobe to converse with his partner.

Yes? Marilyn responded almost immediately.

"Is Cat okay?"

She's fine. She's curled up on her bed with her V-Real visor. I'm not sure if she's asleep or not. She looks very peaceful, happy.

"All right. Thanks."

Noah didn't know if he liked the idea of his daughter hooked up to that virtual reality thing night and day, but at least she wasn't one of those religious pecans anymore. He scratched his chest and 'jectured there would probably always be something she was doing that didn't sit well with him. Part of being a parent, he guessed.

"I'll see you in a while," he told Marilyn and pinched off.

Snip was already beginning to scoot out of the pod, so he helped steady her. She stood there, looking around, unsure, a wild animal in unfamiliar terrain.

"Come on, Snip, you'll be fine."

He started up the walk to Mrs. Grabarkowitz's house without checking to see if Snip was following. He knocked on the door, waited, knocked again then pressed the doorbell. He saw the curtains of a nearby window move, and heard someone press against the door.

"Who is it?"

"It's me, Mrs. G, Inspector Dane. Noah Dane from next door."

She opened her door to peer out, a pair of chains still providing her with some sense of security. She looked him up and down with a suspicious glare.

"Oh, it's you. Sorry. Between those Loftur terrorists and all the mutants running free in this city, a woman can't be too careful." She closed the door enough to slide the chains and opened it again. She still had a broom in her hands, holding it like a pugil stick. "Did you come to pay the rent?"

"No, Mrs. G, I've got someone I want you to meet."

On cue, Snip sidled around from behind him. The young girl and the old woman sized each other up with equal uncertainty.

"She's not a mutant, I swear, Mrs. G, she's—"

"Of course she's not," Mrs. Grabarkowitz said emphatically, propping her broom against the inner wall. "She's a dear child."

She stepped out and took Snip by the hand.

"I was hoping you could—"

"You come with me, dear," she said, ignoring him. "What's your name? You can tell me over warm cocoa and cookies, and then we can vote on that grid poll about the city council. Most of them are mutants, you know." She led Snip into her house, passing Noah as if he weren't there. "My goodness, you're soaking wet. I've got some clothes somewhere that might fit you, but you're such small little thing."

Snip looked back at Noah and smiled her genetically flawed smile before the door closed in his face. He 'jectured they weren't going to need him to get acquainted after all.

40

MOTHER, MAY I?

CHASTITY HUGGED THE BOX OF CHOCOLATES APPREHENSIVELY AS HER CAR PULLED INTO an expansive driveway. This was the address she'd found for her mother. It hadn't been difficult to locate; What had been difficult was resisting the urge to learn more about her on the grid. Still, she'd decided she wanted to meet her mother first. Learn all about her in person. That was the point of searching for her in the first place.

She couldn't help but worry. She worried she might not be welcome. Still, she could understand that. Here she was, inviting herself into the life a complete stranger—no warning, no mother-may-I. She allowed herself a giggle at the childish phrase that skipped into her head as the car pulled round the Victorian fountain that was the centerpiece of the circular drive and stopped at the entrance.

Chastity looked out her window and was surprised to see a grand old manor, several stories high. Its lower facade was rich with ivy, and the grounds were immaculate. Either her mother was very wealthy, or this was some sort of theme hotel she lived in.

She activated the intercom. "Geoffrey, are you certain this is the right address?"

"Yes, Ms Blume."

"All right. I need you to wait for me, but I don't know how long I'll be."

"That's fine, Ms Blume. I just got the latest V-Real—you take your time."

Two men and a woman were coming out the front door as she was going in, so she lowered her gaze to lessen any chance they'd recognize her. One of them held the door for her, and she mumbled, "Thank you," as she entered.

When she looked up she was astounded by what she saw. Her guess of a theme hotel wasn't far off, but she wondered what the theme was.

The interior design was a garish fusion of vivid reds and fiery oranges, the high walls draped with lurid tapestries while strategically placed statuettes stared at her from compromising poses. The place was a virtual tempest of bawdy brilliance. She heard laughter coming from somewhere, a brief bit of singing from somewhere else, and light music pervading it all. She was so taken aback by the scene, she hadn't even noticed the girl who stepped forward to greet her.

"Welcome to Hyacinth House. How may we serve you tonight?"

"Serve me?" What was this place? It wasn't a restaurant. She looked at the girl who had approached her. A hostess of some sort, apparently, but she wore an open thigh-length magenta silk robe, and only enough under it for modesty—hers, not Chastity's.

"Are you here for the Masturbation Ball?"

"Uh, no. I'm, uh…I was looking for Elizabeth Fontaine. Does she…?" Chastity didn't finish her query.

"Elizabeth? I don't think we have any girls named Elizabeth," the woman replied.

A young man Chastity found strikingly attractive—almost pretty—joined them. He was dressed with similar casualness in a velour robe of imperial purple. He smiled at her and whispered something in his co-worker's ear. The girl nodded then, before he could leave, asked, "Do you know anyone here named Elizabeth—Elizabeth Fontaine?"

"Sure, that's Betty," he said and continued on his way.

The hostess turned back to Chastity with an expression of realization.

"Oh, you want Betty. Just a moment, I'll see if she's available."

A number of things ran haphazardly through Chastity's mind as she waited, not the least of which was that she should turn around and leave—immediately. However, she didn't give in to her cowardly impulse. Instead, she watched two half-naked girls as they led a man older than both of them combined up an elegant staircase with varnished maple handrails and lavish wine-colored carpeting. All the way up the trio fondled and groped each other.

It was only then that it dawned on her that she was in a brothel. The realization consumed her with anxiety. She tugged on her skirt with both hands then nervously clasped one hand around her throat. Just as she was reconsidering a retreat, an older, somewhat buxom woman with highlights in her hair and an expression that heralded a quick wit appeared.

"Welcome to Hyacinth House," she said. Chastity caught a hint of cinnamon flowing from her. "I'm Betty. How can I be of service?"

She studied the woman before answering. She observed the almond shape of her vibrant green eyes, the slightly upturned nose, her prominent cheekbones, and concluded she could see herself in the woman's face.

"Are you Elizabeth Fontaine?"

"Yes, I am. And I recognize you," she said, her tone not as friendly, her greeting smile freezing into an expression less charming. "You're Chastity Blume. How can I possibly be of service to America's Favorite Virgin?"

Chastity opened her mouth, but the words stuck in her throat. She contrived several phrasings but dismissed them all, finally blurting out, "I think you're my mother."

After recovering from her initial shock, Betty collected herself and directed Chastity through a gaggle of hedonists to her office. There, Chastity attempted to explain her desire to find her natural mother, and what had led her here. She talked about her father's incestuous upbringing, as if that would shed some light on why he'd opted for an in-vitro child. When she finished, she collapsed more than sat back in her chair.

Betty Fontaine considered what she'd heard and stated simply, "I did it for the money." She looked at Chastity to gauge her reaction. "I was young, broke, without any real family of my own, no outstanding career prospects. Then I learned about this opportunity.

"It sounded too good to be true. I'd be paid a tremendous amount of money to undergo a simple procedure and allow my eggs to be harvested. I presumed I was helping some infertile couple have a child. I talked myself into it by saying I was actually helping someone. Of course, the money talked, too. I used it to start this," she said with a wave of her hand took to indicate the brothel. "It's all mine. I built it from nothing, I manage it, and I mother three dozen girls and ten or so guys in one way or another. I'm a business woman, and business has been very good to me. Of course, lately, you and your Platonistas have cut into profits somewhat."

Chastity looked dismayed, but Betty just smiled and opened the box of chocolates. She took one and held out the box to the woman, who followed suit.

"I guess we could get tested if you wanted to be sure," Betty said. "But looking at you now, it's pretty obvious."

"I don't think we need to do any tests," Chastity replied. "Unless you want to."

Betty shook her head and bit into the chocolate confection. "I just love chocolate," she said. "There's nothing better...well, maybe one thing." She flashed a knowing smile at Chastity, but when it wasn't returned, she changed the subject.

"Of course I never knew about you, but I always wondered, you know? Wondered if I had a child out there somewhere—or children. I guess it was the same for you. Only you did something about it. You found me."

"I've wanted nothing more than to know about my mother for as long as I can remember," Chastity said, "but now..."

"But now you find out your mother is a whore."

"That's not what I was thinking," Chastity protested. "I was just wondering, what now? I know you didn't ask for this. I just barged in here and said 'Here I am.' And you're right. All this, what you do, it does conflict with my beliefs. As much as I wanted to find you, I don't know how to accept this."

"I can't say this doesn't open some old wounds for me as well. Maybe we should both just think about it. Let the idea simmer for a while before we say anything else."

"You're probably right." Chastity stood. "I guess that's my first-ever bit of motherly advice."

They exchanged halfhearted smiles.

Chastity walked to the door and took hold of the antique brass knob. She paused, looking at the floor. She turned and asked, "Why this? Why...?"

"Why did I choose this business?" Betty finished the question, thought about the answer then shrugged. "Sometimes you don't do what you want to do, you do what you have to do. Not to say there's anything wrong with it. It's a good life. I make a lot of people happy. Not everyone can say that."

Chastity nodded as though she understood, but she didn't. She turned back to the door and walked out.

41

MIXED SIGNALS

THAT'S VERY INTERESTING. TELL ME, NOAH, ARE YOU SEXUALLY ATTRACTED TO YOUR partner?"

Noah scowled. "She's an android."

"Yes, on the inside, but don't you find her outer appearance attractive?"

"Shit and frijoles, of course. What do you want me to say? Yeah, she's my type. She'd be one nuclear taste of pow-whammy if she were real, but she's not. She couldn't shudder if she wanted to."

"Then you are drawn to her in a sexual way?"

"No, I'm not! I don't think you get it, Gertie. Looking like something is one thing, but giving it up is another matter. She's not a woman. I can't drive her beyond her own limits of ecstasy and send her soaring over the cliffs of bliss…because she's not built for it. It's not part of her program. And even if it was, it wouldn't be real.

"That drive, that challenge is what I want. That's what it's all about. If I can't do that, then why bother? Sure, a woman who's built like a rocketship is going to twist your head and suck your eyeballs out, but that doesn't mean she's going to blast off. It's the orgasmic soul that really counts. Marilyn, poor thing, doesn't have one."

"I sense you've come to like her."

"Yeah, she's okay. She grows on you, you know? She's turning out to be pretty decent police. Of course, the drudge hasn't started flying yet, but I think she's going to be okay."

"Have you experienced any further episodes of impotence since we last spoke?"

"It hasn't come up—I mean, I've been too busy working the case," Noah snarled. "I haven't had the chance to test the equipment. I thought I'd let it ride, give it a chance to forget about what happened before."

The theratech image shifted in its seat, looking contemplative. "That's a very healthy strategy, Noah. Dwelling on such…incidents could lead to severe medomalacuphobia."

"What in the world of Jack Daniels is that?"

"That's the clinical term for the fear of losing an erection. In extreme cases, it can lead to genophobia, a total fear of all sex."

"Thanks for that bit of vocabulary, Gertie."

"As I was saying, the most constructive thing you can do is put it out of your mind. So the next time you attempt to engage in a sexual act you're not concerned with your ability to establish an erection, and—"

"Can we drop the subject already?" bellowed Noah.

"Certainly."

The vid image spent a few moments straightening its purple pantsuit while he simmered. He knew it was just the computer's way of formulating a new line of discussion.

"Regardless of your mindset, Noah, you're still going to have to deal with the guilt that led to your…difficulties. You can't continue to blame yourself for Cyrus's death."

"I don't blame myself…not exactly. That's not the way it works."

"Oh? Explain to me how 'it works.'"

"Police get killed, it's one of the hazards of the job. Yeah, maybe I could have been there, maybe things would have turned out different, but I don't go around blaming myself for it."

"Maybe not consciously, Noah, but subconsciously, on some level, you think his death is your fault."

"If you say so, Gertie. I don't know what's going on with my subconscious, that's your department. All I know is that Cy will be able to rest in peace when I even the score."

"Are you talking about revenge?"

"You could call it that, or you could call it justice. Either way they're just words. Actions speak louder, wouldn't you say so, Gertie?"

"Yes, that's generally true. However, I'm concerned. Are you talking about taking the law into your own hands?"

"I would never say that, Gertie. You know if I told you I was going out to throttle this guy personally, you'd have to suspend me from duty, wouldn't you?"

"Yes, I'm afraid I would."

"See, that's why I'd never say such a thing."

When he got back to the squadroom the first thing he saw was the last thing he needed to see. It was his partner, bent over her desk, wearing a professionally demure, if rather tight, skirt. The provocative view of her, albeit artificial, derriere sent mixed signals to his brain. As he sorted through the cerebral transmissions, trying to shelve them in their proper places, he couldn't help but recall his theratech session.

Then he noticed Lapchick and Martin leaning out from their desks to get a better view of the same lush vista. He slammed his fist on Lapchick's desk as he passed, startling both men.

"Don't you mumps have anything better to do?"

"Jesus, Dane!" replied Lapchick.

Martin smiled. "You can't blame a guy for looking."

"I can when it's my partner you're staring at," he said, adding an icy glare.

"All right, all right." Martin turned back to his work.

Noah grunted and moved on.

"What have you got?" he demanded gruffly as he approached Marilyn. "Anything new?"

"What are you so grumpy about?"

"Nothing. It smells like it's going to rain, that's all."

"The forecast calls for sunny skies today."

"Sunny in Kansas maybe." He tapped his finger against his right nostril. "The nose knows. So, do you have anything new or not?"

Marilyn stood. "One of the neighborhood's security cams got something near Professor Wu's house."

She restarted the video, a long-range view of a large man crossing a green lawn and continuing down a sidewalk. She paused it, created a still image and maximized the view of the man's face. It was a blur—just enough distortion to disguise his major features.

"This is the best shot of about thirty seconds showing him leaving the professor's house and traveling by foot northeast on Arlington before he turned southeast onto Richland and out of camera range."

"He's wearing a falseface," Noah stated flatly.

"Yes, but look," Marilyn said, pointing at the fellow's neck, "you can see the tattoo clearly."

"The same 'loyal pet' tattoo as Huang," he muttered contemplatively. "But whose loyal pet?"

"I compared the body types with the man from your street shooting," said Marilyn. "I'm certain this is Huang's partner."

"So now we've got more than just bat shit to connect these killings."

"I think you just like to say it," Marilyn admonished.

"Say what?"

"You know." She hesitated as though the words were something to be avoided. "Bat shit."

"I don't get my shudders that easily, and there's nothing about this case I like."

"I haven't said anything about it before, but I don't care for that kind of language."

"What kind of language?"

"You know what kind of language I'm talking about," Marilyn huffed.

"Well, excuse me," he replied sarcastically, "I didn't know droids were so sensitive. Let's go see if Georgia's found anything for us."

They found Georgia lying on her autopsy table, a V-Real visor covering her eyes. It was shimmering blood-red.

"Georgia, what have you got for us?"

The forensics specialist was so rapt in virtual reality, she didn't stir.

"Georgia!" Noah nudged her roughly.

She sat up and removed the visor.

"Can't a girl even take a little break to go solar-wind surfing through the aurora borealis without being interrupted?"

"What did you come up with on the professor?"

"Sugar, you've just got to try this. It's out of this world." Georgia moved to put the visor on Noah, but he grabbed it from her and scowled.

"All right, all right. I do have a couple of choice tidbits for you," she said, sliding off the table and picking up her pad. "That wasn't just perspiration on the professor's face, it was saliva—not his, the killer's. At least, I presume it must have been the killer's. I ran it through the DNA registry and bingo." She handed him the pad. "I got a match. Your killer is one Brock Edward Kutzler. There's not much information on him, except that about ten years ago he joined the—"

"The Army." Noah finished it for her.

"How did you know?"

"He's the one who stole those lasers and went AWOL. But if he was in the

203

military then his face should have been on file with DIRS."

"I wondered about that, too," Georgia replied. "I compared the image picked up by IRIS from the scene with his military ID. Look at this." She held out her pad.

"It doesn't look like the same guy at all."

"Evidently, he's had some work done," Georgia said, "and by a surgeon who's willing to bypass DIRS protocols."

"For a price, I'm sure," Noah offered.

"If he's in the registry, he could still be identified by idisk scans," Marilyn said hopefully.

"Unless he's using a blind, which would be my guess," Noah responded, handing the pad back to Georgia. "We know he was wearing a falseface, so I'm guessing whoever he's working for has supplied him with all the latest tech dodges."

"How do you know he's working for someone?" Georgia asked.

"There's something bigger going on here than just what this mump is up to. Otherwise, it doesn't make any sense. Someone is using him to cover their tracks."

"Still," Marilyn suggested, "we should put out an alert on the idisk system. I mean, in case he gets sloppy."

"Yeah, go ahead," Noah said, nodding. He knew by his partner's reactions she had activated her augmented reality feature and was doing just that.

"There are numerous records for Brock Kutzler, but the most recent is almost two months old."

"He's got a blind, all right," Noah said. "Keep a record of those recent hits. If we get desperate, we might have to backtrack that far."

"There's something else," Georgia said. "I don't know if it means anything or not, but the trace substance I found on the floor near Professor Wu's body was a mixture of bat guano and Troloxian excrement."

"Troll shit and bat shit?" asked a puzzled Noah.

Georgia nodded her head, and Marilyn shot Noah a disapproving glance.

"She brought it up," he said defensively, gesturing at Georgia.

Marilyn frowned in response, and he couldn't help but smile.

42

MYSTERIOUS WAYS

WHAT IS IT, CHASTITY DEAR? YOU LOOK ABSOLUTELY FRAZZLED," MINISTER REDSTONE said, taking her by the hand. "Come, sit. You look as if you could use a drink. Have some of this marvelous Sabra I've just discovered. I'm told it's from the Holy Land."

Chastity sat as Redstone poured her some of the dark, viscous liqueur.

"Here. It tastes like chocolate, and I know how much you love that."

She took a sip, found it agreeable and took another. It was like dark chocolate with a hint of orange.

"I need to pray for guidance, High Minister."

"What happened to Rebekah?" inquired Redstone, sitting next to Chastity.

"Right now I think I need spiritual guidance even more than I need a friend."

"Can't I be both friend and advisor all at once?"

"I don't know. I'm confused." Chastity took another drink, and said abruptly, "I found my mother."

"That's wonderful, dear. Is that why you're so upset?"

"Yes, I mean, no—not because I found her, but because..."

"Because what?" Redstone's penetrating brown eyes sought and held hers.

"My mother's business is...sex. She profits from lust."

The high minister nodded her head as though she understood.

"I want to get close to my mother, learn all about her, but what she does goes against everything I've been taught. The things I believe—"

"But what does *she* believe? You must realize that while our Platonic creed teaches us one thing, others have different beliefs." Redstone moved closer and put her arm around Chastity. "You poor girl, I've tried to tell you that sex in and of itself is not evil, despite what your own father may have taught you. The human sexual urge is a gift from God. It can be a powerful expression of the spiritual quality of love if not misused.

"What's more important than how your mother's beliefs may differ from your own is whether or not she's a good person. Does she help people or use them? Is she honest and caring, or abusive? Not everyone lives by the same standards."

Chastity finished the last of the drink and put her glass down. "You're right, I know. I'm not accusing her of anything. It was just such an unexpected revelation. I was prepared to meet my mother after so many years, but I wasn't prepared for that."

"It's such a shame," Redstone said, "that a beautiful girl as yourself had such an ascetic upbringing. You know, it's okay to be yourself, to be a woman."

Chastity felt the high minister's hand slide down and brush against her breast. It was a casual touch that she didn't give a second thought until the hand went back up, stroking the breast again. Or was she just imagining it? That drink had left her slightly muddled. Maybe...

"It's an unfortunate irony," Redstone continued, "that your celebrated virginity only makes you more attractive."

"It does?"

Redstone laughed. "Certainly, my dear. You're not that naive, are you? Maybe you are." She moved closer, brushed aside Chastity's hair and whispered in her ear, "You're a mystery, dear Chastity, an enigma to be solved, a wild mare to be broken and tamed."

Chastity's first reaction was to move away. Her second was to put her hand on Rebekah's bare leg. She did neither. Instead, she pulled on her skirt, covering her knees.

"What if I wasn't really a virgin?" she asked, trying to read Redstone's expression. "What if it was a lie?"

"The church teaches us to be honest with ourselves and with others," Redstone replied, then whispered in her ear again. "Is it a lie, Chastity?" She followed the whisper with a kiss, and Chastity surrendered to the sensation, a sensation that swelled as hands touched her and lips caressed her own. She grew dizzy. Was it the drink? What was she feeling? What was she doing?

Chastity pulled away. She stood and fought to regain her balance.

"This isn't why I came here? It's not what I—"

"Why *did* you come?" Redstone asked, sounding slightly ruffled.

"I came here for guidance."

"That's what I'm doing," Redstone said, holding out her arms. "Trying to guide you the way I think is best."

"But...this?"

"God moves in mysterious ways, His wonders to perform."

"I can't," said Chastity. "I can't—it's a lie."

She turned away from the high minister and rushed out of the room.

43

A COP, A KILLER AND A DROID
GO INTO A BAR...

Iᴛ ᴡᴀꜱ ꜱᴛᴀʀᴛɪɴɢ ᴛᴏ ʀᴀɪɴ, ʙᴜᴛ ᴛʜᴀᴛ ᴡᴀꜱɴ'ᴛ ᴛʜᴇ ᴏɴʟʏ ʀᴇᴀꜱᴏɴ Nᴏᴀʜ'ꜱ ᴍᴏᴏᴅ ᴡᴀꜱ ꜱᴏᴜʀ. He was waiting for something on this case to come together, something to make sense. He'd never had so many little clues, and so little clue how to frame the big picture.

Now they'd gotten a DIRS hit on Kutzler near the east end of Trolltown. He was surprised the mump would be out in public without his falseface, but that's how criminals usually got caught. They'd get overconfident, sloppy, sometimes downright brazen, as if they were daring you to catch them.

As soon as they'd gotten the word, he had dispatched four IRIS units to the scene, despite some grumbling about "allocation of resources" from the dispatcher. They also had a number of uniforms on standby. Nevertheless, he wasn't hopeful. Chances were, especially on a night like this, their target would be on the move, and long gone before the IRIS units arrived.

"Ready?" he asked Marilyn. "I'm going to come in quick, maybe spook this guy if he's still in the area. Let's hit the ground running."

She nodded and pulled her stunner out of her bag as he dropped the pod like it was in freefall. Despite the breakneck trajectory, he landed them with barely a jolt. He flipped the hatches and they both emerged, weapons in hand, scanning the area for any movement.

It was raining harder now, limiting their visibility.

"Let's go." he ran for the nearest cover, and Marilyn followed. "Anything from IRIS?"

She didn't respond, but he was getting used to her phasing in and out of her augmented reality link without it looking like she was doing anything. He waited, noticing a hoverboard floating unattended over the empty streets, promoting that *Bizarre del Mundo* show. They were hawking some musical trio called "The Singing Assholes." A literal description, he gathered.

"Nothing," Marilyn said.

A bolt of lightning and its accompanying blast of thunder struck several blocks away. Noah flinched like he was ready to hit the pavement. Chagrined, he looked at Marilyn, but she was pretending not to have noticed.

He gathered himself, straightening up to his full six feet, six inches.

"The remotes can cover the area out here better than we can, but there's a dive near here our boy may have gone into. Let's play a hunch."

It was down one street and around the corner. They put away their weapons and made for the entrance. Despite the intermittent rain, there were several men hanging around outside the front door of the Grotto Sotto. Noah checked the faces they passed and didn't find the one he was looking for.

They weren't two steps inside when he balked, throwing his hand up to his face.

"Shit and frijoles," he snarled, frowning. "Consider yourself lucky you've got no smeller. This place reeks." He shook his head, as if the motion would ward off the odor. "All right, stay close and keep your eyes open for our guy."

The place was roomier than it looked on the outside, but packed. There must have been forty or fifty people crammed in elbow to elbow. There wasn't much light to work with, but he could see well enough to tell the patronage was evenly divided between humans and trolls. There were few women in the place, and most, if not all of the men, locked lustful stares onto Marilyn then sized him up as though they were thinking of locking antlers.

The aliens ignored them both. However, Noah found it difficult to ignore them. The stench that assailed him was, for the most part, the same one he'd noticed at the V-Real factory. He wondered if it was something in the Troloxian's diet that gave them that gamey scent. What did they eat?

He saw two mumps in the corner dealing jazz juice but ignored them. He was interested in only one particular perp right now.

Marilyn spotted him first. "Over there," she said. He should have 'jectured the dimness wouldn't bother those android eyes of hers.

He followed her gaze to a spot near the end of the bar where a fellow nearly as large as himself was gabbing away with a couple of bored-looking trolls. It was him. A high-collared coat covered his neck, but Noah didn't need to see the tattoo there. Even in this light, he remembered the face.

He reached inside his coat, rested his hand on his Desert Eagle and eased his way through the press of bodies. He was only a few steps away when he heard a loud, drunken voice behind him slobber, "Hey, missy, come have a drink with me."

He looked back and saw the drunk accosting Marilyn. The geezer had his hand on her arm like he didn't want to let go. He'd been so loud everyone in the vicinity was looking. Including, apparently, Kutzler, because when Noah turned back to find him, he was gone. He'd either recognized Noah or been spooked by the sight of a fineline like Marilyn in such a hovel.

He hadn't gotten far, though. The sound of breaking glass alerted Noah. Kutzler was scrambling back toward the entrance on the business side of the bar. He'd knocked the bartender into a row of bottles in his rush, creating the clamor.

Noah took off without looking to see if Marilyn followed. Pushing one body, throwing a forearm into another, he felt like he was linebacking again, trying to make his way downfield to the quarterback. But it was more than a sack he had in mind.

By the time he neared the entrance, the bar patrons were clearing a path for him. Instinct and habit slowed him at the open door. He wasn't about to go rushing out into the line of fire. He pulled his Eagle and cautiously eased out into the wind-churned rain.

The bystanders were gone, but he saw his man running down the street. He propelled himself into pursuit, certain he had the mump now. A half-dozen strides, and he was closing the gap on his lumbering suspect. Kutzler looked back, saw him coming and brought round his arm to aim.

Noah's plunge took him face-first into a shallow pool of water. The silent laser stream flashed overhead, off to his right, missing him by a good four feet. He emerged from the pool firing. Two .50-caliber rounds shattered the benign patter of rain. But Kutzler was gone.

Noah was up and on the move again when his ear started itching. He activated his com on the run.

Noah? Are you all right?

"I'm fine. In pursuit. Call in the backup."

Where are you?

He was too occupied to answer. He slowed around the corner where Kutzler had vanished but couldn't find him. Shit and frijoles! He couldn't have lost him already. Ahead of him he heard sloshing footsteps. He accelerated, trying to track the sound. Kutzler had turned to the right twice now, and it looked like he was veering that way again. He was circling, headed back around the bar, deeper into Trolltown.

The splatter of the footfalls stopped. So did Noah. He saw the flash and fell back. The beam caught the corner of a utility box. Its paint crackled and blistered. Another sound caught his attention. He looked up and spotted one of the IRIS units—it had locked onto the laser flash and was headed for the source. Noah gave it to the count of five to close in. He hoped it would distract Kutzler. Then, at a full sprint, he raced down the narrow walkway.

He was still twenty yards away when he saw the IRIS erupt in a violent display of spark and ozone. It gave him both the moment he needed and the illumination to spot his target. He fired.

Kutzler was taking aim again when the bullet tore into his side and spun him around like a windvane, but it didn't bring him down. Instead, he took off running. Then, after a few wobbly strides, he slipped trying to turn too fast and fell.

Noah was on him in seconds. The titanium carbon barrel of the Desert Eagle drew perpendicular to Kutzler's chest. The killer still had hold of his laser, but his survival sense told him Noah would aerate him before he could aim and fire. Laying partially propped against a wall, Kutzler dropped the laser and held his empty hands out for Noah to see.

Still Noah's gun bore down on him, his finger snug on the trigger. He didn't say anything He stared at Kutzler as if by sheer force of will he could incite him into making an overt movement.

He wanted to end it right there. Do it for Cyrus. Do it for Cy's family. Do it for himself. He must have had that look, because as he stared down, he saw fear in Kutzler's eyes. With the look of a trapped animal, the man glanced to where he'd dropped the laser but couldn't summon the nerve to reach for it.

Noah wanted to do it. He couldn't think of a good reason not to. Yet he couldn't manage to pull the trigger. He lowered the weapon and saw the relief on Kutzler's face. Something passed overhead, and he looked up to see a second IRIS unit had arrived on scene.

That was the exact moment a jagged dart of lightning ripped through the sky so close the thunder shook buildings and men alike. Noah fell back in a cringe, throwing his arm across his face protectively. It was all Kutzler needed. He rolled over to retrieve his laser weapon and took aim at the still-dazed police inspector.

Noah had just enough time to assess his peril when he heard a high-pitched whine. It was almost imperceptible, but the effect on Kutzler was immediate. He doubled over in pain, forsaking the laser and grabbing his stomach.

Noah glanced up as Marilyn moved in to pick up the laser and powered-down her stunner. Kutzler appeared about to lose consciousness. She turned to Noah. He was already straightening up and putting away his gun.

"Are you all right?"

"Yeah. I guess I owe you one."

"Actually," Marilyn said with a smile, "I think we're even now."

He nodded.

"How'd you find me that quick?"

"I linked into the system. Through the IRIS I saw the laser fire, triangulated your coordinates from my position and, well, I took a shortcut."

Noah nodded, saw Kutzler begin to stir and pounced on him. He grabbed him by the collar and slammed him up against the wall like a rag-stuffed scarecrow.

"Who do you work for? What are they up to?"

Kutzler still looked dazed from the sonic stunner and made no attempt to speak. Noah wrapped his fingers around the bull neck and squeezed, pressing his thumbs deep into the tattoo design over the man's windpipe.

"I'm going to tear off your scrotum and feed it to my African sundew if you don't start singing—and it had better be in tune."

Kutzler grabbed at Noah's wrists but was too weak to pull away the hands locked around his throat.

"You know, he can't talk if you're choking the life out of him," Marilyn scolded.

"That's okay, too," said Noah, continuing to squeeze.

She put her hand on his arm, not trying to pull it away but just making contact.

"Stop, Noah. Let's see what he has to say."

Reluctantly, Noah eased off and let go. Kutzler gasped for air and collapsed. When he'd caught his breath he looked up at his captors with a fatuous grin.

"Doesn't matter. You don't matter," he rambled irrationally. "Too many people. Too crowded. Soon enough you'll be gone."

"What are you babbling about? Why did you kill Hurley Hutchinson and Professor Wu? Who told you to?"

"The professor knew. He knew. Couldn't let him tell. It's a secret. A secret plan."

"What plan, you psychotic…" Noah made a move to grab him again, but Marilyn intervened. She pulled Noah aside and spoke to him in a hushed voice.

"Listen to how he talks," she said. "He doesn't sound right."

"Yeah, he sounds brain damaged."

"It's almost like he's a child. He doesn't sound like someone the Army would give access to classified weapons. Something's happened to him. Someone's done something to him."

"Or he's just playing the pecan to fuck with us."

Marilyn frowned at his choice of words so he turned away to avoid her expression of disapproval. It was enough for him to see movement out of the corner of his eye. Realizing what it was, he shoved Marilyn away even as he fell backwards and reached for his Desert Eagle. He heard two shots and sensed as much as felt a pair of bullets whizzing through the space they'd just occupied.

Guided by reflex alone, he returned fire, a single shot that caught Kutzler as he was turning to run for it. The impact sent him sprawling headlong through the air for another six feet before he hit the pavement with an abbreviated thud.

Marilyn had her stunner out and hurried over to the body. It didn't stir, so she reached down, picked up what looked like a military .45 and showed it to Noah. He shrugged and replaced his own weapon in its holster.

"Well, at least now we don't have to bother with a trial."

THE CALVARY ARRIVED LATE, AS USUAL, BUT NOAH WAS HAPPY TO LET THEM MOP UP. Georgia was there, along with the investigators who handled officer-involved shootings. The rain had finally stopped, but it was still a soggy scene. He and Marilyn sat in one of the police pods, waiting to deliver their reports to the inspector in charge.

"I'm so sorry, Noah," said Marilyn. "I messed up. I didn't follow basic procedure. After I picked up the laser I didn't think to check him for any other weapons. It's my fault."

"Don't let it sweat you. We all make mistakes—I've made some whoppers in my time. Hell, I was there, too. I should have thought of checking him. He got what he deserved in the end, so it's no big deal."

"But we needed to question him more, find out who he was working for. Now we're—"

"Forget about it. It's done."

They sat, neither of them saying a word for some time, until Noah broke the silence.

"I thought I'd feel better," he said, talking more to himself than his partner. "I thought once I'd nailed Cy's killer I'd..."

"They call it closure, don't they?" offered Marilyn.

"Yeah. I guess I won't have it until I find out who Kutzler and Huang were working for. Who pulled their strings."

"We may never find out. What then? You'll have to let it go—I mean, eventually."

He didn't respond, so she stayed quiet. Neither of them said another word until they saw Georgia approaching. She was wearing a slick hot-pink, mini-raincoat and matching go-go boots. Beneath the coat, revealing her long muscular legs, was an even shorter chartreuse skirt. It all made her relatively demure white blouse seem out of place.

Noah gestured toward the forensic specialist. "Quite a sight, huh?"

Marilyn giggled.

"You've got another one, sugar. He's got guano all over his shoes and pant cuffs, and it looks like there's one of those implants on the back of his neck. It's right under the tattoo, same as Huang."

"Do you think that's why he talked strangely?" Marilyn asked Noah. "Because of something they did to him through that implant?"

"That would be my guess."

"Who are 'they,' sugar?"

Noah shrugged his shoulders.

"Well, I've got another kink for your hose, honey. I was just about to link you when the call to this scene came in. I got the report back from our diamond expert. Wait until you try to wrap your noodle around this."

"Shit and frijoles, Georgia, what is it, already?"

Georgia feigned a short-lived look of indignance then resumed her animated deposition.

"You're just not going to believe this. First of all, the diamonds in the necklace do not match the others. They're very basic, not high quality stones. Worth a couple thousand. However, the ones you found on Huang, and the sample from the V-Real visor, are alike. Our expert says he's never seen any diamonds quite like them. He says he can't be a hundred percent certain, but he believes, because of their distinctive isotopic signatures, their ratios of carbon-12 and carbon-13, that they're extraterrestrial. Can you imagine that?"

Noah contemplated it for a moment. "You know, that's the first thing in this case that's made any sense."

"It does?" said a surprised Georgia.

"I think I know what you're thinking," Marilyn offered. "Are you thinking what I think you're thinking?"

"Could be, beautiful. Why don't we put our heads together and see what we think?"

Marilyn's smile was too enormous to contain in a single expression. "You've never called me 'beautiful' before."

He found her smile infectious and returned one of his own, despite himself. "Maybe I'm seeing things in a whole new light now. A V-Real diamond, bat guano, laser, alien tattoo kind of light."

She nodded.

"Are you two going to tell a girl what in the world you're talking about?"

44

PUBLIC RELATIONS

A LUNATIC WAS PERCHED ON THE EDGE OF THE PLANET, AND HE KEPT SPINNING THE world in the wrong direction and laughing. That's what Chastity saw in her mind's eye. She hadn't been able to sleep until she took a couple of Sleepeasys.

Even so, the madman played ringmaster to her dreams. Her father was there, talking with someone she couldn't see, saying something she couldn't quite hear. When she moved closer to listen, her father was gone. Instead she saw Minister Redstone in an embrace, sharing a passionate kiss with someone. It was her mother. They broke from their kiss long enough to smile at her then continued. She ran from them, as best you can run in a dream, and the next thing she knew she was talking to David. What was he doing there? He wasn't part of the insanity that had so recently engulfed her.

Then she wasn't just talking to him. He was naked, and she was touching him. Grabbing hold of his...

Chastity didn't want to remember what had happened next. Despite that, her mind clung to the image. Sleepeasy had always given her strange, vivid dreams. That's why she seldom used it. Nevertheless, even with the dawning of consciousness she couldn't rid herself of that feeling she sometimes got with a dream. The feeling that it was real. That what she dreamed had actually happened.

Logic told her such a feeling was ridiculous, but it was there, in the back of her mind, troubling her all morning. Especially the erotic portions, which kept replaying inside her head regardless of self-reprimands.

One vision proved particularly enduring. The more she told herself not to think about it, the more insistent it became. She saw herself, lying on her back, David...

"We're here, Ms Blume."

Chastity looked out the window. She hadn't even realized the car had stopped.

"Will you be needing me for anything else, Ms Blume?" asked the driver.

"No...uh, no, thank you, Geoffrey."

She composed herself as she made her way into the IGN building. She needed to get back to work, back to the stability of what she was sure of. Doubt was depressing. She noticed several people sitting in the lobby wearing V-Real visors. She wondered why they didn't have anything better to do than spend their time in fantasyland. Dreams were bad enough, she thought, then reminded herself she didn't want to remember.

She passed through security and was concentrating so hard on forgetting the dream and thinking about the work she had to do she almost didn't notice the big-eared, flat-nosed little alien that rounded the corner in front of her.

"Ms Blume?"

"Yes? Do I...? Mr. Kess?"

"Yes, 'tis I," the Troloxian said, offering his hand to her. "I congratulate you on your powers of recognition. I know from personal experience how difficult it is to distinguish among individuals of another species. It can be like trying to pick a single cow out of a herd, don't you agree?"

Chastity took his hand lightly in hers, aware of the rough skin and strange feel of his chubby fingers.

"Yes," she laughed, "I guess it is kind of like that."

"Still, I'm certain the more we interact, the less difficulty we'll have. 'Smooth runs the water where the brook is deep.'"

"I'm sure you're right. What, uh, brings you to IGN? Another interview?"

"No, no. Just a little business, Ms Blume. Public relations, you might say."

"Well, it was a pleasant surprise running into you, Mr. Kess. Have a nice day."

"You also, Ms Blume. Good day to you."

The Troloxian was so well-mannered he was disarming, thought Chastity, continuing to her office. If his charisma and intelligence were a sample of what the aliens were capable of, Earth was lucky to have them. She wondered if, indeed, he *was* representative of his race as a whole.

But why did she think of him as a "he?" She considered it, and decided that Kess didn't seem like a she. And "he" was certainly better than "it."

Upon arriving in her office, Chastity found Tanya waiting.

"Mr. Powell said he wanted to see both of us in his office as soon as you got here," Tanya blurted out anxiously. "Do you know what is? What he wants?"

"No, I don't," Chastity said, picking up her pad from her desk. "Take it easy, Tanya. They're not cancelling the show or anything."

"No, no, of course not," Tanya said. "It's just that he sounded so…agitated, I guess."

"All right then, let's go see what he wants."

"I WANT TO SEE IT AGAIN," CHASTITY SAID.

Powell nodded to Vince, who'd been called in along with Chastity, Tanya and a woman Chastity had seen around the network but had never met. Vince activated the replay, and they all watched. Chastity's hand found its way to her neck, absentmindedly running her fingers up and down as she considered what she was viewing, and the ramifications of it.

"I don't know about the way this is edited," she said. "Where's the rest of it? Where's the raw file?"

"Irretrievably damaged," replied Powell. "The cam got caught in the crossfire. We're lucky to have this."

"Where did you get it?"

"It doesn't matter where we got it," Powell said enthusiastically. "This is prime video. It's great grid. I want you to get it on immediately."

"Wait a minute," Chastity objected. "We can't just put this on the grid without getting a response first. We need to talk to those involved, find out what it is we don't see. This is volatile stuff. If we put this up like it is, there'll be repercussions that'll—"

"Exactly!" broke in Powell. "That's why I want to get it on now, before GridVid or some other network latches onto it and blows our exclusivity."

"This is Big-J stuff," Chastity argued. "You have to investigate, find the facts. You can't simply throw it out there and see who signs on."

Powell stood, his expression hardening to match his tone. "I want this on, and I want you to intro it."

She didn't hesitate. It didn't matter if she personally found the guy repulsive, or even if she suspected what the video revealed him doing might be accurate. It was the principle.

"I'm not going to do this," she said defiantly. "Not without comment. Not without hearing the other side."

"Look," Powell started, his exasperation evident, "you've been complaining to me that you want to do something harder, something with a more serious edge. Well, here it is. Here's what you've been waiting for, Chastity. This is your chance. It may not come again. I'm going to put this on the grid in the next twenty minutes, with or without you. Now do you want to take this step or don't you?"

It was a side of Leeland Chastity hadn't seen before. A manipulative, tyrannical side. However, she knew what he was implying. *Don't do this, don't ask ever again. Stick with your talk shows, your interviews.* At least, until they found someone new, someone with a fresh look, a better attitude, someone willing to do whatever it took.

"Okay," she said, "but I'm not going to do it without some kind of disclaimer."

"Fine, whatever. Just get it up and on, and do it quickly."

When he walked out of the room, Chastity knew the discussion wasn't the only thing that had just ended. She also realized she didn't care.

45

ANUS OF THE HURRICANE

THE DAY BEGAN WITH MORE RAIN, AND IT DIDN'T IMPROVE ANY AS FAR AS NOAH WAS concerned. Thanks to standard obtuse procedure, he'd been sitting around most of the morning, having been placed on the usual post-use-of-lethal-force restricted duty. It would take at least a day for the investigators to get all their ducks in a row and restore him to field work. Until then he'd have to deal with the boredom.

Still, while his partner was searching the grid for a clue as to who was behind the killings, he was stuck sitting outside the department's theratech office, waiting for a mandatory chat with Doc Gertrude. A newscast was on the waiting area's grid screen, but he wasn't paying any attention.

> "...continue to deny the spread of a virulent new strain of a sexually transmitted disease. However, the rumors persist, fueled in part by claims that a shipment of bananas from Guatemala was contaminated by Loftur terrorists. Federal officials are investigating those allegations, and promise to reveal their findings soon. As one might expect, the demand for bananas throughout the nation has dropped dramatically."
>
> "I certainly won't be eating one anytime soon, Richard."
>
> "Stay with us. We'll be right back with a look at the latest wisp art show—fog screen pictures you can

walk right though."

"You haven't gone in yet?"

Noah looked up to see Marilyn. "Still waiting. What's up? You look ready to burst."

"I found something very interesting in Professor Wu's files."

"I thought his drive was wiped clean."

"It was, at his home. But on a hunch I got permission from the university to look through his personal items there, and found this disk." She held up the matchbook-size case. "It's got a lot of notes, copies of papers he'd published."

"Anything about who might have killed him?"

"No, no, it didn't have anything like that."

He relaxed back into his seat. "So what, then? What are you so fired up about?"

She sat next to him and took a deep breath, signaling she had a long story to tell.

"First, I found out that he was mostly interested in demographics, factors affecting population—that kind of thing. Two weeks ago he'd published an article on the grid that examined the most recent world census. He stated in the article that, while the accuracy of all the reported numbers couldn't be verified, the figures showed the population of the Earth had decreased by seventy-three million over the last two years, the first significant decline since the 14th century, when the Black Plague spread through Europe."

"What's so fascinating about that? Didn't a bunch of countries sign that Global Population Management thing—what was it, fifteen, twenty years ago? Wasn't that the purpose of the whole thing?"

"Yes, but the point of the article was that not all of the countries experiencing decreases in their birthrates signed the GPM Act."

"I'm still waiting for the point," Noah countered. "What does this have to do with our case?"

"I'm getting to that," Marilyn replied, somewhat piqued. "Hold on and listen a minute."

He motioned brusquely with his fingers for her to go on.

"I discovered in the professor's notes that he was putting together a paper with much more detail than was included in the published article. He had begun to look for the reasons behind what he described as 'unprecedented declines in the birthrate.' He was examining several possible correlations to the declines, which he concluded began about four years ago. One correlation he discovered was between the areas of birthrate decline, which were mostly urban and relatively affluent, and the areas of V-Real distribution."

"V-Real? What possible connection could there be between those virtual reality toys and how many babies are being born?"

"Well," Marilyn admitted, "none that the professor could find. He had apparently dismissed any relationship between the two, and had moved on to other possible causes."

"So, if he didn't think it was anything, why are you telling me?" He looked up at the grid screen, not really paying attention to what was on but as a way of dismissing his partner's rambling.

"It wasn't in the professor's notes, but I checked. Lucidity began marketing its V-Real adventures almost five years ago."

He gave her a so-what look.

"Don't you see? Kutzler was with Huang, who, according to company officials, was a former V-Real employee. We're fairly certain it was Kutzler who killed Hurley Hutchinson who designed the V-Real adventures. The same kind of unusual diamonds Huang and Kutzler were trying to sell are used in the manufacture of the V-Real visors. Then, Kutzler kills Professor Wu, not long after he publishes an article on birthrate declines."

Marilyn looked at him, expecting a response, but Noah only stared at the screen.

"I don't see it," he finally responded. "I don't get what you're driving at."

"V-Real. There's a connection with—"

"Did you hear that?" He cut her off and leaned forward in his seat.

"Hear what?"

"On the screen, they just said something about a special report on our little episode last night."

"Now we turn to Chastity Blume, who, as promised, has a special report on the use of deadly force by the San Francisco Police Department..."

"Despite legislation passed three years ago requiring all new police officers to be trained in the use of nonlethal weapons, some relics within the department continue to arm themselves with obsolete but deadly firearms. One such old-fashioned gunslinger is forty-year-old Inspector Noah Dane."

"Forty! I won't be forty until December. She can't even get her facts straight."

"Last night, in the old Chinatown district, Inspector Dane used the same kind of lethal force that only two weeks ago left him standing over five other bodies."

"She's making it sound like I killed them all."

"In pursuit of a suspect with unspecified charges against him, Inspector Dane gunned down Brock Edward Kutzler, the man he believed responsible for the death of his partner. What you're about to see is actual video of the shooting. Due to damage incurred by the remote police cams on the scene, some of the video is fragmentary. We warn you, this footage may contain scenes of violence unsuitable for some viewers."

"With that kind of tease, who isn't going to watch?" Noah asked flippantly.

The video began with a scene of him chasing Kutzler then cut to a different angle of him firing his weapon and Kutzler running away. The next scene was of Kutzler doubling over in pain as Marilyn's sonic stunner brought him down. Then it cut to Noah choking Kutzler.

"I'm going to kill you. I'm going to tear off your scrotum and feed it to my African sundew."

"He can't talk if you're choking the life out of him."

"That's okay, too."

After some brief static-infused distortion the video resumed with a close shot on Noah as he fired his weapon, followed by a close-up of his Desert Eagle firing not once but three times. The next shot was of Kutzler being hit in the back and falling.

"Did you see that?" complained Noah. "Did you see how they twisted that? I only fired one round!"

"That's not what happened," Marilyn agreed. "They didn't show Kutzler shooting at us, or any video of him holding a weapon."

The final scene was of Noah shrugging and holstering his gun, followed by a quick shot of Kutzler's body before it cut back to Noah.

> "Good riddance. Now we don't have to bother with a trial."

"That's not what I said! Was it?"

"Not your exact words," Marilyn replied as Chastity Blume came back on the screen.

> "In the light of such evidence, we urge the district attorney to prosecute Inspector Dane for this cold-blooded killing. Our police cannot be allowed to bypass the judicial system and take the law into their own hands. Whether the motive be revenge or the concealment of corruption, such brutal actions cannot be condoned. Despite the damning evidence of this video, and whether he believes in it himself or not, our system of justice demands that Inspector Noah Dane be considered innocent until proven guilty. Brock Edward Kutzler was due the same. I'm Chastity Blume, reporting from…"

"Let's go," Noah said, vaulting from his seat.

"Where are we going?"

"Down to IGN. We're going to speak with Ms Chastity Blume and find out where she got that trumped-up tape."

NOAH GLARED AT THE DISPATCHER LIKE THE FELLOW HAD JUST INSULTED HIS AZALEAS.

"What do mean I can't sign out a pod?"

"I'm sorry, Inspector, but you're not on the authorized list today. See?"

He handed his pad to Noah, who looked it over.

"It's that damn restricted duty thing," he said.

"Can I sign it out?" asked Marilyn.

"No, only inspector-grade or higher can get a pod without authorization," answered Noah. "Call Captain Raevski," he told the dispatcher. "Tell her I need it for a personal emergency."

"All right, Inspector."

The dispatcher walked away, and Noah looked at Marilyn.

"Can't you just use that augmented thingy of yours and release one of these pods?"

"That would be against regulations. I can't do that."

"Yeah, okay, just checking for future reference."

"I didn't get to finish telling you everything I found in the professor's notes."

"I'm listening," Noah said, as though he had no choice.

"The countries experiencing the highest birthrate declines were those that already had the lowest population densities, countries with cool or moderate climates like the United States, Australia, Argentina, Canada, Norway—"

"Yeah, yeah, don't give me the whole list. Spike the ball already and tell me what the score is."

"I already told you that the regions in these countries with the biggest declines were the areas with the highest V-Real distribution. Well, when I saw that list of countries, something seemed familiar to me, so I did a grid search. Each of those countries was chosen by the Troloxians for immigration."

"A coincidence?"

She shrugged.

Maybe, thought Noah, but then again, maybe not. Another flimsy piece of the puzzle was not what he needed right now.

He was still trying to collate it all, wondering what was taking the dispatcher so long, when he saw Captain Raevski coming toward them. She wasn't alone. Lapchick, Martin, Harper and Brunelli were with her. Noah scratched his chest and got a bad feeling.

"Dane," the captain barked, her high-pitched voice cracking, "hold it there."

The detectives with her fanned out, and Noah was liking what he saw even less. Brunelli stopped a few steps away. Noah saw he was clutching a sick stick.

"Sorry, Dane," Raevski said, "I need your gun and your badge."

"What for?" he asked without making any move to comply.

"You're being charged with murder. I've got to take you into custody."

"Tell me you're not buying that video drudge, Cap."

"It's not up to me, Dane. There's already a grid poll out demanding your head. The DA is going to indict. She doesn't have any choice. That's the way it is. Sometimes the ball takes a bad hop."

"Captain Raevski, I will testify that Inspector Dane fired his weapon only in self defense—his and mine," Marilyn stated.

"Being an android, you may or may not be allowed to testify, Monroe. That's up to a judge. Either way, it's a Hail Mary. The testimony of his partner, especially one that's a former celebudroid, won't carry a lot of weight."

"Not like a doctored vid, huh?" said Noah sarcastically.

"And," added Brunelli with a smarmy leer, "with your trigger-happy record…" He punctuated the statement with three clicks of his tongue.

"Come on, Dane," the captain urged, her tight almond eyes revealing no emotion, "no false starts here."

Noah saw that all five of them were braced. They weren't sure how he'd react. For that matter, neither was he. But he wasn't about to lay his head on the chopping block and go softly into that gentle night like a good soldier. He hoped they'd hesitate to bring down one of their own, even with a stunner. He 'jectured they would—all except Brunelli, who was enjoying every second.

So, he wheeled to push the slack-jawed baboon out of his way and make a run for the door. He got his hands on him, but Brunelli proved to be more alert than he'd thought and thrust the sick stick right up into his gut.

A sweltering surge of nausea swept through him like a seven-point-five temblor. He doubled over, grabbing uselessly at the stringent knot in his stomach.

His next reaction was immediate and involuntary. His head came up, and out shot a jetstream of vomit, showering Brunelli. Noah collapsed to the floor as Lapchick and Martin moved toward him. Harper, meanwhile, stared at his partner and tried to repress a laugh.

"Goddamn fucking motherfucking drudge! Look at—" Brunelli's rant was stifled when the lights in the pod bay suddenly snuffed out.

"What the…?"

"Get those lights on."

Too sick to realize what was happening, Noah felt someone help him to his feet and pull him through the dark. He could tell by the touch—and the lack of smell—it was his partner. He stumbled several times, but her progress was sure despite the confusion around them. She guided him down a short flight of stairs and out a door into the rain.

"What happened?" he asked, still recovering from the nausea.

"I used my AR link and turned out the lights."

"You? You—who was worried about violating regulations to use a pod?"

"It all happened so fast," Marilyn said, chagrined. "He stuck you with that awful stick and I–I didn't really think about what I was doing. I just reacted. I guess it seemed like the thing to do at the time."

Noah tried to smile, but it still hurt too much. "Well...you've got good instincts...I'll give you that." He tried to straighten up. "But you'd better get back in there before they realize you helped me."

"But I want to help you," she said resolutely. "We have to find out who edited that tape."

"If you do this, they're going to dismantle you when they catch up with us."

"I know." She stood there, the wind blowing her now-damp hair, regarding him serious-like with those bedroom eyes of hers. "Just the idea that they can makes me mad. I don't think I like the idea of being a piece of property. It's not right."

Noah looked at his partner with newfound respect. Maybe there was something to that self-awareness android rights drudge he'd heard some wackadoos raving about.

"Well, that's a discussion for another time. We've got to get going. We're in the anus of the hurricane now."

46

KEEPING THE HOME
FIRES BURNING

"WELCOME HOME, MS BLUME. DID YOU HAVE A NICE DAY?"
"Not particularly, Suzette, but thanks for asking. I see the new social protocols are working."

"Yes," the homeminder system responded in a tone that implied it hadn't needed the upgrade. "Apparently, the protocols have achieved the desired effect."

Chastity withdrew to her bedroom, where the grid screen activated automatically upon her entry. She laid out her robe and began taking off her clothes, paying little attention to the programming on the screen.

"I was compiling the shopping order, Ms Blume. Would you care to check it and add any additional items?"

"Not this time, Suzette. You go ahead."

"Would you like me to make something for your dinner?"

"Not right now, Suzette. I just need to relax. Then I'll think about what I want."

She wasn't really hungry, but even as she thought about it she spied the nearly empty box of chocolates on her dresser and plopped the last one into her mouth. The burst of sweetness revived her. She stepped out of her underwear and pulled the robe around her.

"Should you be eating candy before your dinner, Ms Blume?"

"I'm a grown woman, Suzette, I can eat it whenever I want. I didn't know mothering was included in those new protocols. I'll have to—"

A loud cry, almost a squeal, interrupted her. Angel jumped onto her bed and cried again. The cat threw herself onto her side against the bedspread as if she were trying to rub something off her fur.

"Angel, what's wrong with you? Are you going to start acting up again? Suzette, has Angel been acting strange today?"

"I'm sorry, Ms Blume, but my database has no input relative to the behavior of felines. However, the animal *has* appeared somewhat agitated at times."

Chastity began stroking the cat, who responded by turning onto her belly and sticking her tail end up.

"Remind me to download some files on cats into your programming, Suzette."

"Whatever you say, Ms Blume."

"I don't know what I'm going to do with you, Angel," she said, still petting the cat. "If you keep acting like this, I'm going to have to take you to a vet to find out what's wrong." Something on the screen turned her attention from the cat. "Augment the grid audio, Suzette."

She saw the end of the same video she'd seen that morning. The same one she'd agreed to intro, despite her misgivings. The screen cut to a freeze frame of the police inspector firing his gun then dissolved to a still frame of the inspector.

"...shortly after IGN first made public this exclusive video, Inspector Dane assaulted the police officers who attempted to take him into custody. He escaped, along with his police partner, Detective Special Class Marilyn Monroe, a celebudroid recently assigned to the police department as part of the city's attempt to integrate androids into the workforce."

Chastity looked at the picture of Dane's partner. She hadn't realized she was an android, much less a celebudroid. Now that she thought about it, she realized she did recall the name of a cinematic celebrity named Marilyn Monroe, but didn't remember ever seeing any of her films.

"Standard alerts have been issued for the fugitives, and police officials say they'll soon have the pair in custody. Our grid poll this evening concerns this latest police incident. Please select one of four possible responses for the primary question, 'Based on the evidence of this on-the-scene video, do you believe San Francisco Police Inspector Noah Dane should be prosecuted to the full extent of the law?' Then consider the secondary questions concerning—"

"Suzette, would you select an episode of *The Adventures of Ozzie and Harriet* I haven't viewed recently. I'm going into the sitting room to watch it."

"Certainly, Ms Blume."

Chastity made her way to the outer room, curled up in her favorite chaise and tried to lose herself in the black-and-white world of the time-honored sitcom. Nevertheless, she kept thinking about Minister Redstone—the contradictions she'd posed, the impulses she'd evoked. How could she reconcile the high minister's actions with the precepts of her Platonic faith? How could she justify her own feelings, her own urges?

She found herself trying to imagine Ozzie and Harriet engaged in sex. They had two boys in a time when no medical technological assistance was available, so they must have done it. Unless the two boys were merely actors, and not their real sons. She shook off the image she'd conjured of the pair naked, intertwined in an embrace.

Were Ozzie and Harriet religious people? She wasn't sure if she'd ever seen them invoke a deity or talk of faith. Faith in what? What good was faith when it became tainted? How could it be called faith if you questioned it? Of course, it wasn't the "superstitious nonsense" her father called it. It was simply a philosophy. A philosophy that corresponded a great deal with the way he had raised her.

But how much credence did she actually give that philosophy? Did she really understand it? Chastity wondered if it was the belonging that mattered to her more than the message. To sit shoulder-to-shoulder with kindred spirits had given her strength. Minister Redstone had given her strength. Until...

She thought of Redstone, provocatively clad in white satin, her tanned legs bare to the thigh. She recalled how the high minister's hand had brushed across her breast, and how it felt when their lips pressed together. She could still feel traces of the carnal desire that had surreptitiously invaded her. Was that what she wanted? What if she hadn't felt so guilty? What if she'd just told her the truth?

Chastity closed her eyes, trying to remember the sensations she'd felt in the high minister's quarters. Lost in the moment, she slid her hands down the front of her robe, trailed them across her stomach and between her legs. The dampness surprised her, disrupting her reverie. She sat up straight and tried to focus her attention on the sitcom.

But her thoughts inexplicably veered off in a new direction. She found herself thinking about Antonio, the cyber courtesan. She couldn't help but wonder what kind of satisfaction such a program could provide. Logic said it must offer something, probably to thousands of women, or it wouldn't exist.

"Suzette…" Chastity initiated a request then caught herself.

"Yes, Ms Blume?"

"Never mind, Suzette."

She reached for her pad and inwardly mocked herself for feeling reticent about making the request of her homeminder. Nevertheless, she found the link herself, accessed it and again watched the ornate door open to the charming visage of Antonio.

"You've returned. I'm so glad. Please come in and accept my hospitality."

The program was obviously set up to respond to repeat visitors, storing whatever interaction had taken place.

"I believe you were about to tell me your name," he said as she was once again ushered inside.

"Chastity," she responded, mesmerized by the beguiling stare of his emerald eyes.

"Chastity," he repeated as if tasting each syllable, "it's such a lovely name. Almost as lovely as the woman it has been bestowed upon. Tell me, Chastity, tell me all about yourself. I want to know you. I want to be close to you. I want to feel your warmth as we float gently into the night on clouds of intimacy, and transport ourselves with rapturous ardor into a world of our own making."

"I–I don't know."

"Your modesty is as alluring as your beauty. Yet this is not a moment to let pass quietly in the lonely night. Grab hold of it, dear Chastity. Grab hold and savor the taste of passion."

"You're certainly very persuasive, Antonio, but this…this is so strange."

"There is nothing strange about what a woman desires, Chastity. Share with me what is inside you. Share it with me, and I will guide you across vistas of pleasure, through the mossy hillocks of sensation, and onto sheer plateaus of ecstasy."

"You make it sound so wonderful. I could almost—"

"Ms Blume, David Mandala of building maintenance is at your door."

"Oh. I'm sorry, Antonio, I have to go."

"What? So soon?" His perfectly groomed eyebrows lifted in a display of concern. "If it must be so, then I will eagerly await your return, darling Chastity. Please don't make me wait long."

She cut the link and *The Adventures of Ozzie and Harriet* returned to her screen. She stood, pulled her robe around her and tied it tightly.

"Should I deactivate security, Ms Blume?"

"Yes, Suzette. I'll get the door."

David smiled when she opened the door, but it was a nervous smile. He had something in his hand.

"Hello, David."

"Hi, Chastity."

He stood there blankly, so she asked, "Would you like to come in?"

"Oh, I just brought this." He handed her a small container. "It's a box of chocolates. You were so nice to give those others to my mother, and you said you like them a lot, so…"

"Thank you so much, David. You didn't have to do that. Come in, come in. Sit down and relax a moment. You must work long hours to be going home just now."

"Sometimes I work longer."

"Sit," she said, motioning to her lounge.

He looked reluctant, but sat when she did.

"What's this?" he asked, pointing at the screen.

"That's a very old sitcom—situation comedy—part of my special collection. I love to watch the really old shows. I have hundreds of them. This one's called *The Adventures of Ozzie and Harriet.*"

"I like adventures. What kind of adventures do they go on?" David wondered.

"They're not real adventures, not like you might think," she explained. "They're more about the adventures of being a family. But I know what kinds of adventures you're talking about." She got up, searched her tall bookcase and pulled out a particular volume. "Here, I bet you'd like this. I wanted to give you something anyway, for being so nice to keep my plants watered for me."

"You don't have to do that. I like taking care of your plants." David took the book and read the cover. "*The Adventures of Huckleberry Finn* by Mark Twain. Thank you, Chastity. I just finished my other book, so now I'll have something new to read."

"Did you enjoy *Of Mice and Men?*"

"Yeah, it was pretty good. But sad."

"I think you'll like this one even better."

"I'm sure I will."

As she stood over him, and he continued to examine the book, Chastity was struck by the thought that she didn't have anything on beneath her robe. Her first reaction was to turn and pull it even tighter around her. But even as she did, she got a tingle of excitement being this close to David and nearly naked. She could just untie the belt, let the robe drop and be in his arms in seconds. What would he think? Would he embrace her, or would he be shocked? Did she want him to take her?

She couldn't dismiss the fact she was attracted to him. She was drawn by his quiet manner, his calm voice, his large, gentle hands. With her back still turned to him, she clutched her throat, contemplating what it was she really wanted...and why.

Meeerooow!

Angel let out a mournful wail as she entered the room and threw herself onto the carpet. Once again, she began rubbing herself around on the floor.

"Is something wrong with your cat?" David asked.

"I think so," Chastity replied, "but I don't know what. She's been acting very strange."

He stood, book in hand. "I'd better go. My mom'll be waiting for me."

"Do you have to go already?"

"Yes, I should."

"Okay."

"I sure thank you for the book, Chastity. Now I don't have to go all the way to the library to find another one."

"I hope you enjoy it."

"I know I will. It's fun reading about people I don't know, and visiting strange places."

"Most people don't think about reading as fun, but I think it's great you do."

"Life should be fun, don't you think?"

"You're right, it should. Though I guess it can't always be."

David opened the door, and Chastity was right behind him.

"I'll see you later then," she said.

"Sure, I'll see you."

When he'd gone, she shut the door behind her but didn't move. She half considered going after him. What would she say, though? How could she explain something she didn't understand?

233

47

THE RUNNIN' BLUES

I ALWAYS KNEW YOU WERE CRAZY, BUT THIS? DO YOU KNOW WHAT THEY'RE SAYING ON THE grid? They say you and your android partner murdered someone, and that you assaulted the police who tried to question you. What are doing, Noah? What are you—"

"I didn't call to argue with you, Sheila. You know me. You know I didn't kill anyone."

"Maybe I don't know you at all. Where's Catherine? What's happened to her?"

"Cat's fine. She's at my place. That's why I called. I need you to go get her. I won't be going home for a while."

"Of course, I'm going to get her. Do you think I'd leave her with you after this?"

"Just tell her for me...tell her I'm going to be okay."

"Are you, Noah?" Sheila asked, her expression softening for a moment.

"I can't really say right now. I've got to go, Sheila. Link you later."

He deactivated his pad so it couldn't be traced and put it back in his coat pocket. As he did, he heard the sound of an engine, a cacophonous shifting of gears. An enormous garbage truck turned the corner and bellowed through the pale illumination of a single streetlight.

"Our knight in shining armor," Marilyn said, stepping to the curb and waving as if they weren't the only two people on the street.

The truck groaned as it lurched to a stop. Noah recognized the city seal on the rig's side. It read "City of San Francisco, Department of Sanitation." Beneath the seal another imprint had been added. "Sponsored in part by

Clean Sweep Autovacs."

Marilyn climbed up and opened the cab door. She scrambled inside, and he followed, closing the door behind him.

"Welcome to Mr. Goodtrip's traveling sanctuary," said the driver.

"Thanks for coming, Jim." Marilyn kissed him on the cheek.

"Yeah, Jimbo, thanks," added Noah.

"Strange days have found us, wouldn't you say, mister policeman?" The Morrison droid's tone hinted at mockery. "You got the runnin' blues, and I'm the only solution—isn't it amazing?"

"Yeah," Noah replied, "I guess you never know what kind of riffraff life is going to strew in your path."

Marilyn was about to respond irately but saw both he and Jim were smiling.

"I dig it. The future's uncertain and the end is always near. So what's the gig? We could plan a murder or start a religion," said Morrison with a devilish grin. "Just tell me where your freedom lies." He swept his arm out in a grand gesture, pointing to the road in front of them. "The streets are fields that never die."

"Where are we going?" Marilyn translated unnecessarily.

"I want to have a look around Trolltown. Kutzler was headed somewhere—somewhere he likely picked up those traces of troll sh—" Noah caught himself and peered at Marilyn. "Troll excrement and bat guano."

"I see Miss Manners has been working her etiquette on you, too," Morrison said.

"Yeah," Noah responded, exchanging glances with Marilyn, "she's been very patient with my bad habits."

"She's the lady who waits."

Marilyn smiled and patted each of them on the leg.

"Before we start traipsing around Trolltown, we're going to have to make sure we're not recognized. I know just the guy who can help us with that."

"Take a face from the ancient gallery and walk on down the hall."

"Let's go, Jimbo. I think we can find him in the Haight, by Golden Gate Park."

Morrison revved the engine, jammed it into gear, and the truck pulled away with a whine and a moan.

"The soft parade has now begun," he recited as he wrestled with the big steering wheel. "Listen to the engines hum. People out to have some fun."

"This is it. Stop here," directed Noah.

Morrison downshifted and slowed the truck until it came to a halt. "They'll freak out and come looking for me if I don't get this truck back before the morning shift. I'm going to have to split."

"We'll be fine from here," Noah said, opening the cab door. "Thanks again for the ride."

"Go on, do your thing, man."

"Thank you so much, Jim."

"Any time, lady mine," he said, grinning. The grin morphed into a much more serious expression, and Morrison put his hand on Marilyn's shoulder. "You know, after the streetlights shed their hollow glow and morning comes, the man's going to want his due. I'm not going to lay some heavy trip on you, but what you're up to is throwing a cloud of suspicion on all androids. I won't try to tell you the things that you know, but our cause is getting burned. Do you dig what I'm saying? Unless you can turn the tide of public opinion with some righteous riff, this could be the end of laughter and soft lies."

"I know, Jim."

"I guess I've been singing the blues ever since the world began, but I'm not exaggerating. Dr. King, John, Paul, George and Ringo—everyone's talking about it. It's in the air. It's on the grid. Word is, the man's considering dismantling all of us. It could be a real bummer."

"I can't explain now. I'm not even sure I could if I had the time. I'm doing the right thing, though."

"You drop me a line if you need me," Morrison said as she slid out of the cab.

Noah shut the door. Morrison hit the accelerator and turned the monstrous vehicle within the expanse of the intersection. As he drove past them, he yelled out his window, "This isn't the end, beautiful friend!"

Marilyn stood there waving goodbye.

"What was that all about? What cause was he talking about?" Noah asked as they made their way across the fringes of the park.

"Jim believes in freedom—freedom for everyone, even androids. He thinks we should demand equal rights."

"It'll never happen."

"I bet you didn't think you'd ever have an android for a partner either, did you?"

He smiled at her. "You got me there. Let's split up and look for Bink. He could be anywhere."

He hoped the destitute magician was here somewhere, but he had no guarantee. The last time he checked, this was where Bink spent his nights. Where he went when it rained, Noah had no idea. Fortunately the rain had stopped, though a bone-chilling wind was still howling through the city like a vindictive spirit.

He passed several derelicts, some sleeping, curled up in little cubbyholes, trying to stay warm. Some were even wearing V-Real visors—he was beginning to think he was the only one in the city who hadn't climbed aboard the virtual reality fad.

"'Tis the noble Dane." The sound of the voice turned him. "To what do I owe this unforeseen honor?"

No wonder he hadn't spotted him right away. Bink was dressed all in black. He was even wearing his ebony silk magician's cape, pulled around him for warmth. The cape had seen better days.

"Bink, I need your help."

"Any assistance I can render would bestow upon this poor misguided soul a profusion of delight."

"Do you know what's happened? Have you been on the grid?"

"Alas, my access to said medium has been curtailed of late. Nevertheless, I'm aware that the karmic fires of passion and prurience continue to wane and wither." His coarse, chaotic eyebrows twitched as he spoke. "I fear, Noah, that the ebb and flow of Eros has been disrupted. The Earth cries out to me of its demise."

"I don't know about that, Bink, but I need some idisk blinds and a couple of falsefaces. One for me, and one for Marilyn," Noah said, pointing at his approaching partner. "But my credit's been deleted. I can't pay right now."

"I can be of service in that arena," Bink replied. "Wait here. I'll return as promptly as the powers of my prestidigitation permit."

He was off without another word, his short little stick legs churning along at a speedwalk toward the street. He scurried past Marilyn on his way, said, "Milady," and gave her a crisp circular salute across his forehead without slowing.

"Where's he going?" she asked Noah.

"Hopefully to get us what we need."

Marilyn straightened her rumpled outfit and looked thoughtful. "Are we doing the right thing?"

"I'm doing what I need to do. It's right for me, but I don't know about you."

"When your partner's in trouble, you do what you have to, right?"

Noah made a noise that was part laugh, part derision. "Yeah, but this is one time you should have played it by the book. And what about what your friend Morrison said? This thing is high profile. It could affect more than just you."

"I know," Marilyn said, the distress evident in her voice. "I hadn't thought about that, about how it might cast suspicion on all androids. But I don't know how to undo it." She looked pleadingly at him, as if he could give her an answer he didn't have.

"If we can track down whoever is responsible, the people behind Kutzler and probably my frame-up, then it'll be a good thing, right?" he said, trying to cheer her up. "If justice is served, the real criminals put away, then we come out of this smelling like roses and a lot of people are going to have to change their minds about droids.

"Look at me. I don't even like dealing with automated dishwashers, and you've changed my mind about androids. I think, with a little more experience, you'll make a great detective. You can partner with me anytime."

Marilyn's downcast eyes brightened, and she surprised him by stretching up on her tiptoes to plant a kiss on his cheek.

"I wish I could remember what a rose smelled like," she said.

"A rose smells of sunshine, dewdrops and a child's laughter." It was Bink, whose return was surprisingly prompt. He came back wearing a hat. "The scent of a rose is like the song of the robin redbreast and the soft touch of a woman's lips."

Marilyn giggled. "Thank you, Bink. I can smell it already."

"Any luck?" Noah asked.

"Indubitably," Bink replied and held out his hand. "For the lady, earrings to accentuate her natural radiance." Marilyn took the earrings, and Bink flipped the hat off his head so that it tumbled down his arm and into his hand. "For the gentleman, a rakish derby to cover his troubled brow."

"The falseface generators I take it?"

"Precisely."

Noah looked over the black felt hat as Marilyn put on her earrings. He noted, with some distaste, the hat's gaudy silver band. "Are you sure they'll work?"

"I have no firsthand knowledge of such devices, but I trust my source. No controls are necessary. They are fully activated at all times. And here are a pair of blinds. Two were all I was able to acquire. There's not much credit in the accounts, but I'm told they'll respond to any name you choose to use."

"Thanks, Bink. I owe you."

"Bosh and balderdash. Consider them gratis. You're off to save the world, aren't you?"

"At least my little part of it."

"Then you're simply allowing me to play my meager part in the sublime tableau which is about to unfurl."

"Shit and frijoles, Bink. When you put it that way, you should be thanking me."

"Indeed, indeed."

"Well, I want to thank you anyway," Marilyn said, pecking the indigent magician on the cheek.

Noah slapped the derby onto his head and patted it down snug. "Put a bow on it, Monroe, we're done here."

"One moment," Bink interjected. "I surmised you would require some form of transportation."

"I jectured we'd have to hoof it, but, yeah, a ride would be nice."

"Follow me."

He led them across the park in the direction he had previously disappeared. When they reached the street bordering the park, Noah spied a trio of bikeroos but couldn't see their colors in the dark.

"Business associates," Bink said to allay Noah's concern.

He directed them around the side of a 24-hour cafe that looked deserted, though its lights were on. Seeing it reminded Noah of how hungry he was. He thought about how he could sure use a couple of tacos or maybe real beef steak right about then.

Bink stopped in the shadows clinging to the cafe's exterior and said, with a flourish of his hands, "Your conveyance."

Noah stared at the contraption leaning against the wall then skewered the wizened illusionist with a reproachful gaze.

"Ooooh!" Marilyn squealed with delight. "A bicycle built for two."

Responding to Noah's sullen expression, Bink raised his hands in defense.

"It was all I could procure with such limited forewarning."

"Come on, Noah," Marilyn said, pulling the bike from the wall, "it'll be fun."

"*Fun?* I'm standing on a street corner in the middle of the night with a celebudroid and a has-been magician—no offense, Bink—a dirty look away from some bikeroo's bullet, and a blackmarket falseface malfunction from being locked up for the rest of my life. Do I look like I want to have *fun?*"

"Oh, don't be such a stick-in-the-mud," said Marilyn. "Come on."

He shook his head, more in disbelief at the entire scenario than anything. Well, at least the damn thing didn't have any stubborn microprocessor or sassy circuits to give him any grief.

DAWN FOUND THEM PEDALING TOWARD TROLLTOWN. SEVERAL TIMES THEY BIKED PAST THE watchful lenses of city security cams. He knew there would be a DIRS alert out for both himself and Marilyn, so he could only hope the falsefaces were working. Twice they had to stop when his pantlegs got caught up in the mechanism. Each time he cursed and ranted despite his partner's sour looks. Finally, he rolled up his pants, making him feel more absurd than ever. He'd never been much for bikes.

Right now, he 'jectured, they must look like some eccentric circus act, and the last thing they wanted was to draw attention to themselves. The falseface transmissions might fool the cameras and disguise their faces, but the two of them together could still be identified. He didn't want someone who stared too long to recognize him or, even more likely, Marilyn, now that they'd been all over the grid.

So, as soon as the streets began to repopulate, they ditched the bike and found a small, quiet place on the fringes of the immigrant district to get something to eat. Noah hoped the trouble he had distinguishing between various Troloxians worked both ways.

For appearances sake, Marilyn ordered matzoball soup, but had to settle for a chocolate milkshake when their Troloxian waiter said it wasn't on the menu. She stared at the shake and played with the straw while Noah wolfed down his sausage and eggs.

"What you were telling me before, about the places where the Troloxian ships landed? What were you getting at?"

"Well, nothing really," Marilyn replied, "except that there seems to be some connection between the Troloxians and V-Real."

"Obviously. But where does that leave us?"

The waiter approached their table, looked at Noah's empty plate and Marilyn's full milkshake.

"Yeah, we're done here," Noah said in response to his silent question.

The waiter held out his idisk, and Noah palmed his blind before placing a hand on the scanner.

"Joe Schmo," he stated. No beeps or alarms. Apparently the blind was working, and had enough credit to pay for their meal.

As the waiter cleared away their dishes, Noah asked, "Hey, do you know of a nice jewelry store around here where a guy could find a diamond bracelet for his girl?"

The waiter shook his head and carried away the dishes.

"It was worth a try," he said to Marilyn. "Look, we're in the same neighborhood where we found Kutzler, and the V-Real factory isn't too far away. We know that place is full of trolls, so I say we head that way and see what we can see."

48

TRUTH & CONSEQUENCES

CHASTITY WAITED PATIENTLY FOR SOMEONE TO RESPOND TO THE DOOR. SHE KNEW BY now the security system had identified her. What she didn't know was why it was taking so long. Maybe her father didn't want to see her. But, if so, why didn't he just send Michael to the door to tell her he wasn't home? She realized she hadn't been here in several years, and felt somewhat guilty about that.

She was also feeling guilty about the dream she'd had the night before. It was disturbing yet, at the same time, enticing. In the dream she was naked, rolling around in liquid chocolate until it covered her entire body. She remembered delighting in the fact it was warm, and then licking it off her fingers.

As odd as it was, she didn't know why the dream left her with a feeling of shame.

She pushed the doorbell again and looked the place over. It was drab, not very well kept up, but enormous. It was more mansion than house, and much larger than he actually needed. Yet, except for the numerous cams and other elaborate security devices, nothing about the design of the place was particularly prominent. She wasn't even sure if all the cameras were still active. The grounds appeared untended, and even the paint was peeling in spots. No one would have known that a man who had made countless millions lived here.

She decided to leave and was caught off-guard when the door opened. Her father stood, his shoulders hunched, looking much smaller than he ever had.

"What are you doing here?" he asked, sounding almost suspicious.

"I just came to visit, Father, to talk."

He turned and walked away, the open door her only invitation.

"Where's Michael?" she inquired, closing the door behind her.

Henri Blume's pace was slow but steady. He continued down the hall and spoke without turning. "I sent him on some errands."

"Don't you have anyone else here? Anyone to help out?"

"Don't need anyone. Michael takes care of everything."

"But Michael's an android, Father. You should have people around. I mean, look at this place."

The inside of the house was as austere as the outside—meager furnishings, empty walls, closed curtains that kept the sunlight out.

"What's wrong with it?" he grumbled.

"Well, for one thing, there's no light. You need some color in here, some music, some conversation. It's not a place to be alone."

Blume turned into what was once the study but now looked more like an office.

"I like being alone. I don't need a bunch of noisy people around. Is that why you're here? To pester me about how I live?"

"No, Father, it's not."

He looked tired—exhausted, really—his eyes bagged and bloodshot.

"Can I sit down?"

"Of course."

Chastity sat, but he remained standing.

"I wanted to tell you that I found my mother—the woman whose eggs you bought."

"I asked you not to," he said calmly, turning away from her.

"I had to, Father. I needed to find her for my own peace of mind."

"Oh? And do you have peace of mind now?"

She wavered. "I don't know. I'm not sure."

"I knew it would only mean trouble," he said angrily. He turned to look at her, and she saw an almost deranged gleam in his eyes. "I tried to protect you, to shield you from the licentiousness of the world. That's why I made you stay inside as a child, why you had to play alone. I wasn't going to let you become fodder for someone's sexual cravings.

"The world has gone mad with lust. It's an obsession that's led to nothing but vulgar displays and rampant procreation. The world is a festering sore, teeming with obscenity and ignorant, slavering mobs no better than rutting animals. That's why I agreed to the V-Real modifications. Because something had to be done. I couldn't let it go on that way. I couldn't let you be a part of such a world."

"What are you talking about? You're not making any sense, Father."

"Of course I am," he said, throwing his hands in the air. "I'm the only one who *is* making sense. Mankind's pursuit of sex has driven it mad. I'm just bringing some sanity back to it."

"How? How can you do that? What are you saying?"

Henri Blume's look softened as he sat next to his daughter, yet that glint in his eyes frightened her.

"V-Real, the virtual reality adventures—there's a side-effect. It's going to change the world...for the better. The Troloxians showed me the way. They had the technology. I didn't think it would work, but they showed me. Everything was fine until Hutchinson figured it out. Then that thug stole my stickpin."

"Father, you're rambling. What technology? What side-effect?"

"Sex, Chastity. V-Real dilutes the sex drive. It kills the motivation for all the perverts and pornographers. It means people will no longer waste so much of their productivity in pursuits of the flesh. I did it to protect you, to protect all of us, to change the world."

"But how? How does it—"

"It doesn't matter how it works," he told her with the sudden enthusiasm of a little boy. "What matters is that it does."

Chastity's was alarmed. She didn't know what to say.

"What's wrong?" her father asked. "This is what you want, too. This is what you've prescribed on your show. All I've done is make the message of America's Favorite Virgin a reality."

She couldn't believe what he was saying. That even he used that nickname galled her more than the insanity he was describing.

"You can't play with people's minds, Father. You can't just re-program them like they're some kind of gadget you've invented."

"Why not?"

"Because they're human beings. They have the right to choose for themselves. I can't believe what you're saying. It can't be true. You even tried to give me one of those visors! Why? So you could brainwash me? So I would always be your good little girl?"

The smile vanished from her father's face, replaced by a look of guilt.

"Well, you know what, Father? You were too late anyway. I'm not even a virgin."

Her admission shocked him into silence. To Chastity it was a burden lifted. A burden she'd carried for too long—ever since the night she'd slipped out of the house to go to a high school prom after he had forbidden it. Not her prom—she'd never been allowed to go to school. She'd always had private tutors. It was Bret Leninger's prom.

She'd met him by chance, and arranged to see him secretly whenever she could. That night, Bret had "borrowed" his father's company car and was waiting for her. After the dance, she let him do it. Let him put his hands under her dress. Let him take off her panties. Let him do what he wanted to do. Then, afterwards, after he'd taken her home—that's when it happened. She found out the next day.

On his way home there had been an accident. Bret had been killed when his car collided with a Mag-Lev. As soon as she heard, she knew it was her fault. He died because of the thing she'd let him do, the dirty thing they'd done.

"It's all a lie." Chastity stood. "America's Favorite Virgin isn't as pure as she lets people think. She isn't even a virgin."

Her father remained mute. He wouldn't look at her. That was all right with Chastity, because she didn't have anything else to say. Nothing else mattered. She didn't know if she believed his ramblings about a conspiracy or not. At that moment, she didn't care. All she felt was relief—relief that she'd told someone the truth.

49

SMOKE & MAZES

I'M NOT LOST," NOAH INSISTED. "I'M JUST A LITTLE TURNED AROUND."
He'd spent little time in Trolltown, but he wasn't about to admit to his partner he didn't know where he was. He'd taken a wrong turn somewhere, though; now he wasn't sure which way led to the factory. One thing was certain—they'd wandered into an area primed for redevelopment. Half the area had been bulldozed into humongous piles of debris, and the other half was a collection of rundown hovels that had seen better decades.

Let's see, he thought, the sun's up there, so north is this way, which means the factory must be...

As he mapped out a new route in his head, he saw a pair of bike cops pedaling their way.

"Come on!" He didn't wait for Marilyn to respond but grabbed her by the arm and tugged her back across a debris-strewn field toward a dilapidated shack.

"What are you doing?"

"Quiet."

He wasn't sure if the uniforms had spotted them or not, but he wasn't taking any chances.

"I don't think they saw us."

"Who?"

"A bike patrol. There they go. Let's power down here for a couple minutes, and then..."

The wooden slat he was leaning against was so rotten it crumbled, and the flat of his hand smacked the side of the shanty as he groped for balance. The vibrations created a stir above them. They looked up to see a cluster of bats underneath the structure's eaves.

"Shit and frijoles."

His outburst sent the bats flying. They swooped up en masse, out into the sunlight and down again through a partially boarded window.

Noah and Marilyn exchanged looks that said they were thinking the same thing.

"Should we...?"

"We've been looking for bats, haven't we?"

They made their way around to the back of the collapsed structure, until they found a space they could squeeze through. They had to skirt a plethora of refuse to make their way in. Once inside, Noah hurried to a filth-encrusted window and peeked out while Marilyn brushed the dust off her pantsuit. Seeing nothing outside, he turned his attention to the interior.

"I don't see any bats. Where'd they go?"

"Maybe right here." She pushed aside some pieces of broken furniture with her foot. "Look at this," she said, clearing away more debris.

It was a gap in the floor, cut roughly, about three feet in diameter. Near the top of the hole, Noah saw what looked like handholds.

"My foot slipped right into it," Marilyn complained. "I thought I was going to break an ankle."

He bent down to take a closer look.

"I bet this is part of those old Chinatown catacombs."

"Catacombs?"

He looked up to explain and saw her "in augmented reality" expression. Instead, he peered back into the excavation and said, "I wish I had a light." He picked through the remnants on the floor and found an old table leg. He wrapped one end of it with a torn curtain. He was still searching the floor when Marilyn returned from her brief interlude in cyberspace.

"There are many stories, and even some references in obscure official reports, of such a system of tunnels and caverns," she said as if reading it, "but there is no concrete evidence to prove that they ever existed. The catacombs of Chinatown have long since been relegated to the status of myth."

"What do you say we find a way to light this torch of mine and go investigate this myth?"

AS SOON AS THEY DESCENDED INTO THE MURKY PIT, NOAH DISCOVERED HIS HOMEMADE torch wasn't going to stay lit for long. The curtain material burned quickly, and the wooden table leg didn't provide more than a flicker of flame. Fortunately, before it extinguished completely, they discovered candles set in random niches along what proved to be a lengthy tunnel. They each took one and proceeded to light the others as they came to them.

The hole in the floor dropped ten feet before it hit bottom. It branched off into a narrow but level tunnel, much of which proved to be reinforced with wooden beams. Noah had to take off his falseface hat and hunch over in order to maneuver. He didn't feel particularly comfortable about making his way through such a confined space, especially when they started coming across small cave-ins where unsupported sections of the tunnel had collapsed. He tried not to think about it. Marilyn seemed fine, so he tried to concentrate on seeing through the darkness ahead of them.

They had been winding their way through the tunnel for what he thought was at least twenty minutes when he noticed an odor. It was such a drudge-awful stench that the force of it caused him to stop.

"What's wrong?" Marilyn asked.

"I know you can't smell it, but the stink in here would make a dead man cry."

He covered his nose and mouth with the hat, but it didn't help much. He kept on going, trying to breathe as little as possible.

It wasn't much longer before the tunnel opened into a natural cavern large enough for Noah to stand straight again. He held his candle high to look around. It was twice his height, and maybe twenty feet across. Above, he saw the source of the smell.

"Here's where our bats went," he said, turning enough to see that the entire ceiling of the cave was obscured by bat wings.

"Little brown bats," Marilyn added, "the most common bats in the United States, according to my research."

"I say we're on the right trail," he offered. "Look around, see if there's another way out of here. And try not to disturb the tenants."

They didn't have to look long. There was a smaller tunnel on the ground floor of the cavern, veering perpendicular from the direction they had been traveling.

"We'll have to get on our hands and knees to get through there," Noah said, taking a closer look.

Marilyn examined her clothes. "Well, I'm already filthy," she said. "Let's go."

Progress on all fours was slow, especially since they were trying not to let their candles go out. But they hadn't gone far when Noah got a whiff of something new.

"I'm smelling something else now—not the bats. It's familiar but…" He let the thought go as he continued to crawl through the passageway. He hoped it didn't go on much longer, because he was becoming increasingly claustrophobic, and the thick, musty odor was making it worse.

His tired fingers cramped, and he lost his grip on the candle. It extinguished as soon as it hit. Before he could hand it back to Marilyn to relight it, he noticed a dim violet glow up ahead, so he didn't bother with the candle. He crawled forward until he could see an opening where the illumination was coming from.

When he reached the mouth of the tunnel there was enough room for him to turn back to Marilyn, put his finger to his lips and snuff out her candle. He didn't know what was out there, but the light source looked artificial.

He wriggled through the opening onto a rocky ledge overlooking an immense grotto so deep and wide he couldn't see where it ended, despite the curious illumination emanating from what looked like intermittent patches of phosphorescent goo. The enormous cavern wasn't empty. The expanse was honeycombed like a beehive. Hordes of bats clung to the walls, some occasionally taking flight.

He studied the hive-like formation closer and saw that crammed into each chamber were three, four, maybe five creatures. Troloxians, he quickly realized. Pressed together, bunched like a single entity, naked and apparently asleep. There had to be thousands of them just in the space he could see.

Marilyn crawled out next to him, her face expressing the same astonishment that gripped him.

"I thought I recognized that smell," he whispered. "No wonder they like their privacy. They don't want anyone to see this. It would scare the drudge right out of people."

"Do you think they're dead?" wondered Marilyn.

"Looks more to me like they haven't been born yet. Maybe they're hibernating, or whatever it is they do. That factory guy told us they didn't like open spaces, but this is ridiculous. Canned sardines have more breathing space."

He couldn't tell what the hive was made of. It was cream-colored and looked like dense Styrofoam on the outside. However, the inner chambers, the walls nestling the trolls, appeared more organic.

Marilyn tugged on his coat to get him to turn around. She looked as if something new had occurred to her.

"When I was checking Professor Wu's census figures, he had a separate total for the Troloxians." She paused, and Noah gave her a go-on look. "Well, if there's even one of these…nests in each of the cities where the Troloxians landed, then the census numbers are off—way off. There are likely tens of thousands more Troloxians than anyone knows about, maybe more than that."

He was about to respond when he saw something moving. Apparently, not all of the trolls were napping. He saw several now, moving through the hive on an assortment of ladders and trestles. Maintenance workers or nursery aides, he wasn't sure.

He motioned for Marilyn to follow him, and they scooted along the ledge toward a larger alcove. As they made their way, they passed one of the bright reservoirs of goo. The slimy stuff pulsated, almost like it was alive.

Noah hoped to put more distance between them and the workers, who were ascending to the level he and Marilyn were crawling across. However, it took only one loose piece of rock to make him regret his course of action.

He didn't know if it was Marilyn or him that sent the pebble flying. It didn't matter much. It was a tiny thing, but it made a loud enough ping when it glanced off the trestlework below. One of the trolls looked straight up at them and began chattering in Troloxian. The bleating of his alarm roused several of the sleeping trolls, while others from below began to climb.

"Let's go," Noah said, getting to his feet. He didn't think they could make it back the way they'd come, and besides, he had no desire to get caught in that crawlspace. Instead, he led Marilyn to the alcove he'd spotted. It turned out to be a dead end.

"Look," she said, staring down into the grotto.

Noah moved to the rocky edge and saw what had gotten her attention. A pair—no, a trio of trolls were floating up toward them. Each wore a hefty pack on its back, and he saw they were leaving wispy vapor trails of exhaust.

"Never seen anything like that before. These guys obviously don't know how to share. Maybe—"

His quip was cut short when one of the flying trolls took aim and fired at them. He grabbed Marilyn, and they fell back as the laser stream burned into the roof of the alcove. Noah pulled his Desert Eagle and gestured for her to get to other side of the recess. No sense in making it easy for them.

Marilyn had her stunner out, but it was a defensive weapon, not made for moving targets.

"Keep low. Get on the ground," he called.

Those jetpacks might have been slow, but the trolls using them weren't stupid. Noah was prepared for them to fly up over the edge, but instead they circled the opening and came down from above. Apparently, they moved faster going down.

The first one swooped in at an angle and fired at him, missing him by several feet. The surprise point of attack threw him off, and his shot missed, too; the echo of the small space gave his Mark XIX the boom of a howitzer, and its reverberations had another effect. The second troll, swooping in from the opposite angle wobbled as if he were flying through turbulence. His shot at Marilyn went wide, and before he could correct his flight path, Noah nailed him.

The force of the .50-caliber slug propelled the little troll backward as it ripped through his chest and into the jetpack on his back. A tiny explosion sent sparks flying as the troll slammed into one of the upper chambers of the hive.

It turned out that whatever material the hive was composed of, it was extremely flammable. The sparks from the jetpack ignited several of the chambers. They burst into flames like they were lined with napalm. Scores of trolls woke up screaming. It wasn't a sound Noah ever wanted to hear again.

Panic ensued as hundreds of the aliens tried to escape. They crowded in bunches down ladders and across lean metalworks meant for one or two. The blaze raced to the top of the hive in seconds. The vast majority of the huge structure was beneath the fire; still, the flames were spreading downward, and Noah saw it was going to be one big troll roast unless they had an emergency system that would put it out.

Regardless, the grotto was beginning to fill with smoke, and they had to find a way out, even if it meant backtracking. He looked, but couldn't find the other flying trolls. They must have beat a retreat as soon as they saw the fire.

"Come on." He motioned for Marilyn to follow him back onto the ledge. They'd didn't have any choice. They'd have to get out the same way they'd gotten in.

He was sidestepping carefully along a narrow portion of the ledge, looking down, when he saw another jetpacked troll flying up at them. He reached for his gun, but noticed the troll, blinded by smoke, was rubbing his eyes. Too late, Noah braced for the collision. The troll slammed head-first into the ledge at Noah's feet, and the entire section collapsed.

He fell before he could shout a warning to Marilyn. He hit something hard and realized it was the troll. The alien, or more likely its jetpack, slowed him, but not much. He plummeted in a shower of dirt and rock, only vaguely aware of the panicked sound coming from the hive.

50

MOTHER OF INVENTION

By THE TIME SHE GOT HOME, CHASTITY HAD RECOVERED FROM HER CONFESSION. ONCE she'd accepted the fact her father now knew, that she'd actually been able to acknowledge her indiscretion, she was able to relax and consider what he'd told her. She found it hard to believe her father was involved in some secret conspiracy, that it was even possible to do what he claimed. That look on his face, the timbre of his voice—she was afraid her father was teetering on the brink. It wasn't some mind game he was playing. He seemed to believe what he was saying. It was too incredible, too inconceivable.

"Ms Blume, building security says there's a woman requesting admittance to visit you. Her name is Elizabeth Fontaine. Shall I tell them to grant her entry?"

Her mother? What was she doing here? *How did she even know where I live?*

"All right, Suzette. Tell them she can come up."

Chastity felt like she had enough on her plate right now. She didn't want to deal with this. But what was she going to do? She couldn't turn her away. After all, she was the one who'd made the connection. She'd forced herself into the woman's life.

Nevertheless, she wondered what her mother wanted. Her mother—the thought seemed foreign. Was this woman truly her mother, simply because of some genetic material? Would she ever be more than a distant relative?

It was a complicated, difficult thing to consider at any time, but especially now. It was made even more difficult when Angel began rubbing against her and crying that cry she'd made a habit of lately.

"Angel, what is wrong with you? I guess I'm going to have to take you to the vet, aren't I?"

The cat continued to cry, pulling herself along the carpet with her claws, her hind end protruding upward.

"Your visitor has arrived, Ms Blume. I'm deactivating security."

Chastity opened the door. Elizabeth, her mother—Betty—carrying a spray of flowers, dressed much more formally than she had been when they first met.

"Hello," she said hopefully.

"Come in," Chastity greeted her, "come in."

"I'm sorry to surprise you unannounced like this," said Betty, stepping in and handing the flowers to her, "but after I thought about it, I didn't care for the way we left it before."

"It's certainly all right," Chastity responded. "After all, I barged in on you unannounced. But how did you find out where I lived?"

"Oh, I have some connections, too." Betty smiled. "I figured if you could go to all that trouble to find me, I could do the same."

"Sit down, please," Chastity said. "These are lovely, thanks. I'll put them in water."

Betty walked in, looking around before she sat. "It's a beautiful place you have here. Much homier on the inside than it looks from the exterior. A very nice young man led me to your door—David. He said he knows you."

"Yes, he's very nice. He works here."

"Handsome, too," Betty added as if hoping Chastity would take the bait and respond. She didn't.

When Chastity returned with the flowers in a vase, Betty was petting Angel, who was continuing to act up.

"That cat, I don't know what's wrong with her." She placed the vase on the table and sat. "She's been acting like that for a week. I've never seen her like this."

"She's in season," Betty said simply.

"In season? You mean she wants to...?"

"She doesn't just want to, she needs to." Betty continued to stroke the little feline. "The poor thing can't help it. It's in her blood. She's got the fever. Haven't you ever had a cat before?"

Chastity shook her head. "Angel's my first. My father, well, he never let me have any pets when I was little. What should I do?"

"You've two choices. You can get her fixed so she'll never have to go through this again, and you never have to worry about her having kittens, or you can introduce her to some boy cats who can take care of her needs. You probably don't want to know what I'd suggest."

"Yes, I do. What would you do?"

"Well, it's too late to get her fixed now. You'd have to wait anyway. I'd let her have her fun. Then, if you don't want to deal with a bunch of kittens, take care of her afterwards. Every girl deserves one good fling before she…well, you know, calls it quits."

"Maybe you're right." Chastity looked up from the cat to her mother, trying to examine every wrinkle, every nuance of her face. "You were also right about us taking some time to think—I mean about us. I got to wondering afterwards, whether I have any brothers or sisters. Do you have any children?"

"No," she said, turning her head to look away momentarily.

Chastity tried to read her expression. Was it regret? Guilt? She still wasn't sure when her mother turned back.

"There were times I thought about having children, but after I'd sold that part of me, I never quite felt…I don't know, worthy I guess."

Chastity waited through an awkward silence before speaking. "Well, I'm happy you came by, because I was rude the other day. I'm glad you didn't hold it against me."

"You weren't rude, you were just trying to deal with something unexpected. Something that was happening a little too fast—for both of us. So why don't we take it a slower. Tell me everything about yourself, and then I'll do the same. That is, if you've got the time."

"I've got the time," Chastity replied. "I'd like that."

"Good," her mother said with obvious relief. "Then, when we're done, we'll see if we can find little Angel a devilish tomcat."

Betty peered tentatively at her, unsure how she'd react, but when she smiled and nodded her head, her mother giggled.

"Okay, gee," Chastity said, "where do I start?"

51

BURIED IN HIS WORK

Someone was calling his name. Were they telling him it was time to get up? Was it time to go to school? He was weighed down by so many blankets he couldn't move around in his bed to see the clock. He tried to scoot off the edge but was unable to move. The blankets were covering his face, and he couldn't breathe. He struggled and suddenly the blankets, the bed, everything around him melted. He was deep underwater, thrashing, trying to swim, but the weight on his chest kept him pinned in place.

Panic filled him. His lungs felt about to burst. He gasped for air, and water rushed into his mouth.

Noah choked, coughed and woke with a mouthful of grit. Consciousness returned slowly, but as it did he realized he was lying on his stomach, buried under a paralyzing weight, yet still alive. His whole body hurt, but he didn't waste time testing for broken bones. He began digging.

At first he was barely able to move his hands. The weight on him was almost as oppressive as the fear that he was trapped. As he dug, he tried to squirm forward. Each time, though, more dirt collapsed in his face.

Then his hand hit something that wasn't just loose soil. He grabbed hold and pulled. He was able to leverage himself ahead somewhat, but not much. He couldn't see even a hint of light, but he'd found a small pocket of air. He let himself take a breath and spat out the dirt in his mouth.

He felt around and discovered what he'd latched on to was the troll he'd fallen on—dead, from what he could tell. Reaching out with his fingers, he came across the jetpack on the troll's back. He had no idea how the thing worked, or even if it still did, but he didn't think at the moment he had much choice.

He was head-to-head with the troll, so that meant the pack's exhaust was pointed away from him. He dug around it, ran his hands over it, but couldn't find anything that felt like a control. So he followed the harness around the troll's shoulder to a pad on its chest. He could barely reach it, his fingertips probing, pressing wherever they could until he heard the device power up, sputtering and coughing as if it were congested.

A loud whooosh assailed his ears. Noah felt the mound of earth atop him shake. Then the jetpack died, and nothing he did would revive it.

He still couldn't see, but he hoped the flying device's thrust had created a space for him to work with. He pulled himself along the alien body and found the going easier. He didn't know if it was the work of the jetpack or not, but the weight on him diminished as he struggled forward. If only it wasn't so damned dark. He heard a voice—or thought he did. He dug faster and heard it again.

"Noah?"

It was his partner, but he couldn't answer without getting a mouthful of mud so he kept digging.

"Noah?" The voice was clearer now.

He kept going until a hand grabbed hold of his.

"Noah, it is you!"

He wanted to respond with something appropriately sarcastic, but a face full of dirt kept him quiet. Marilyn let go of his hand and from the sound began digging furiously to help free him. Soon she grabbed both his hands and pulled until he came sliding out of the mound.

"Are you all right?"

Hearing her voice in the darkness, Noah 'jectured she was the only woman he knew who could ask if he was all right and make it sound like an invitation to dance the pow-whammy. Except she wasn't a woman, she was a droid.

He spat most of the remaining grit from his mouth and blew the grime from his nose.

"Yeah, for a mole I'm in great shape. I can't see a damn thing though. Where are we? Where are the trolls?"

"I don't know," Marilyn responded. "I think the cave-in separated us from the main chamber. But there's a tunnel over there." He 'jectured she was pointing but couldn't see her. "I found it while I was looking for you. I tried to call you on the com, but you didn't respond."

"I was probably still unconscious."

"There's a faint light coming from the tunnel. It looks like more of that bioluminescence. I was about to go down there when I heard a noise. What was that?"

Noah ignored her question, still trying to find the tunnel she was talking about. "Where's the light? I don't see anything."

"I couldn't see it until I went a few yards inside."

"Okay," he said, "give me a second and then you can lead me to the tunnel. What about you? Are you okay?"

"I think so," Marilyn replied. "But I feel just filthy dirty. My hair is just...well, I'm glad you can't see it."

Noah's laugh reverberated so loudly he worried for a moment about another cave-in. "We've been shot at, almost buried alive, have no idea where we're at, and you're worried about your hair?"

"A girl should always try to look her best," Marilyn said as though repeating something she'd been taught.

"Does that go for androids too?"

"Yes, it does," she said, and Noah imagined the disapproving look she was giving him. "I do think I might have suffered some damage in the fall. I've tried to activate my AR feature to call for help, but it's malfunctioning. I can't get a link."

Noah checked his pockets but couldn't find his pad. It was likely buried under the rubble.

"I've lost my pad, too," said Noah. "Just as well. What would we tell them? We don't even know where we are. And even if they could locate us, we're still in the same boat we were before. We don't even have a decent theory about what's going on, just a bunch of unrelated factoids. Something's up with our quiet, peaceful little troll friends. I don't know what it is, but I'm sure it's bigger than just blackmarket diamonds." He took off his coat, threw it aside and felt for his gun. It was still in its holster. He pulled it out and made sure it wasn't clogged.

"I've been thinking about that," Marilyn replied. "I've been doing some calculations—estimates, really—but I think they're fairly accurate."

"And?"

"Based on what we saw of that Troloxian nest, I believe their actual birthrate must be at least fifteen times what they've led authorities to believe."

"Shit and frijoles, they must be doing the pow-whammy fandango like crazed rabbits."

"No," Marilyn said, "Troloxians don't...they don't have sex."

"That's right, I forgot. They're like more aphids and ants, aren't they? I even read about this one kind of lizard that's like that."

"It's called parthenogenesis."

"Kind of gives a whole new meaning to 'Go fuck yourself,' doesn't it?"

"Noah!"

"Yeah, yeah, I know, I've assaulted your pristine ears again."

"It doesn't work like that, anyway," explained Marilyn. "It's simply a process where an ovum, an egg, develops into a complete individual without fertilization."

"They teach you all that in celebudroid school?"

"No," Marilyn replied, "I came across it in my research."

"Well, anyway, I can see where, landing on this already crowded planet of ours, they might not want to put a damper on their welcome by advertising their proliferation. But it still doesn't explain anything. Not the murders, not the tattoos, not the connection with V-Real."

"It doesn't make any sense to me, either."

"Sitting here isn't going to answer anything," Noah said, grunting in pain as he stood. He held out his hand in the dark toward Marilyn. "Take my hand. Lead me to this tunnel you found. I could really use a shot of Jack about now, and the service in this dive is lousy."

52

REVELATION

B Y THE TIME HER MOTHER LEFT, CHASTITY WAS FEELING MUCH BETTER ABOUT HER decision to seek her out. In a few short hours she'd been able to relax enough to enjoy Betty's company, even though, on the surface, they were two very different people. The time had also helped her reach a decision concerning her father.

She realized he needed help. She'd try, or she'd find someone who could. If what he told her about V-Real was genuine, then he had to go public with the truth. She had to persuade him it was the right thing to do. Not that she was convinced any of it was really possible. More likely it was something created by a distraught and lonely mind. Well, she was going to make sure he wasn't lonely anymore.

She didn't want to put it off. She felt it was important to begin right away. To let her father know she was there for him. That's why she'd called for her car even though it was late. However, she told the driver not to wait for her. She planned on spending the night in her father's house, and staying with him as long as necessary.

The idisk system recognized her and granted entry through the outer gates, but no one was answering the front door. Chastity pulled out her pad and attempted to contact her father. There was no reply. Where could he be at this time of night? She was about to request that her car return for her when she decided to try the door. To her surprise, it wasn't locked.

The house wasn't completely dark, though the lighting had been dimmed considerably. She stepped inside, made her way down the hall and called out, "Father? It's me, Chastity. Are you here?"

She listened but heard nothing. She turned to have a look in the study and gasped out loud when she spotted a pair of legs jutting out from behind a sofa.

"Father!" She rushed across the room. She bent down and saw that it wasn't her father after all. "Michael. Michael, what's wrong?" She dropped her purse and shook the lifeless android. He didn't respond, but she heard a muffled voice across the room.

"Chastity."

She found her father on the floor behind his desk. She cradled him in her arms and looked for signs of injury. She didn't see any.

"Father, what happened?"

"They...were using me. Just using me."

"Who? Who was using you? What did they do to you?"

"I–I didn't know. I..." He barely got the words out and went limp.

"Father? Father!" Chastity didn't know if he'd just passed out or...

She had to get help.

She laid him gently aside and got up to retrieve her pad. Her panic congealed when she saw three Troloxians standing over Michael's body. She thought she recognized the one in front, the one wearing a suit and holding her purse.

"We were about to pay you a visit, Ms Blume," the alien said ever-so politely. "But this is certainly much more convenient. I understand from your father that he's been telling you some incredible stories. However, his was a countenance more in sorrow than in anger, wouldn't you agree?"

"Walter Kess?"

"Your recognition does me honor."

"I need to call for an ERT. My father's been hurt," she said desperately.

"Yes, it's an unfortunate thing." Kess motioned the other two aliens forward. They approached Chastity from either side. "Your father was a brilliant man in his time. However, 'I come not to praise Caesar, but to bury him.'"

"What are you talking about? He might still be alive."

The Troloxians reached for her. She managed to avoid one, but not the other. He pressed a metallic device against her side.

"We've got to—" She jerked as a shockwave of numbness spread through her. Every muscle in her body imploded, and she collapsed, blacking out before she hit the floor.

53

TUNNEL VISION

NOAH SQUINTED IN THE NEAR-DARKNESS, TRYING TO SEE AS FAR AHEAD OF THEM AS possible. At every turn they had to duck another swarm of startled bats.

"This tunnel's got as many twists as a really bad mystery vid. Do you have any idea what direction we're headed?"

"My inner compass tells me we've been going north, for the most part. But I don't know."

"You don't know what?"

"Ever since that fall, when I lost my connection to the grid, I don't feel right. I feel like I can't be sure of anything."

"Well, these lights tell me we're going to run into something soon. They wouldn't be down here if this didn't lead somewhere."

With him out front, often stooping to pass through parts of the tunnel, they continued, doglegging to the left three more times before they spotted a brighter light ahead. He pulled out his Desert Eagle and cautioned Marilyn to be quiet.

Slowly, he approached what he could now see was the end of the tunnel. At the mouth, he stopped and took a good look around.

It opened into a fully constructed room with a high ceiling and concrete walls. It was lit, though dimly, by standard fluorescent tubes, as opposed to the bioluminescence of the tunnel. The room looked like a large laboratory, though it was crowded with storage crates.

He was about to step out of the tunnel when he heard something and crouched back inside, cautioning Marilyn again. It sounded like a door closing and locks being thrown into place. A pair of trolls emerged from where the sounds had originated and made themselves comfortable on some crates.

The aliens were close to the mouth of the tunnel—too close for him and Marilyn to slip out unseen. He motioned to his partner that he was going to try and sneak up behind the trolls, but she put her hand on his arm to stop him. She pointed at his gun and shook her head no then showed him her sonic stunner. He frowned then nodded agreement.

She eased out of the tunnel as Noah positioned himself to cover her. The trolls were engaged in what seemed a heated Troloxian exchange; Marilyn was almost on them when one caught a glimpse of her. Before either of them could raise an alarm, she fired her all but silent weapon. The aliens were so close to each another they dropped one on top of the other.

Noah crept out of the tunnel and scanned the area for other trolls.

"Let's look around," he said.

Weapons in hand, they began a quick survey of the room. It looked like it had been used as a lab at one time, but whatever work had gone on here was long finished.

"I smell lilacs," Noah said. "Now, why would I smell lilacs…"

Before he could finish, he spotted the answer to his own question. He was looking through a shieldglass partition into a large chamber—not a room, more like a compartment built into the center of the larger space. He realized it wasn't so much a partition as it was one side of the chamber. The other three sides were standard opaque walls.

Lying on what looked like an oversized medical table was Chastity Blume. He remembered then where he had last sniffed lilacs.

"What the drudge is she doing here? Let's get in there and see if she's still breathing."

He took another look around as Marilyn unlocked the chamber door. Inside, she checked Chastity's pulse.

"She's alive."

"Well, wake her up."

Marilyn patted the unconscious grid star's face. "Wake up. Come on, honey, wake up now."

Chastity came to but was decidedly groggy. She looked at Marilyn, then Noah, though she didn't seem to recognize them at first.

"What…What are you two doing here?" she asked, barely coherent. Then, focusing more on her surroundings: "Where am I?"

"We were hoping you could tell us," Noah responded.

"I–I don't know what happened. I was…I was in my father's house. They killed him!"

"Who killed him?" Marilyn asked, holding onto Chastity, who had managed to sit up though still dazed.

"They did—the Troloxians...Kess."

"That Shakespeare-happy troll, Walter Kess?" asked Noah with renewed interest.

"Yes. He was there, in my father's house. My father told me they used him."

"Used him for what? What's the connection between your father and the trolls?"

Chastity grabbed her head as if she were dizzy.

"Your father's Henri Blume, isn't he?" Marilyn asked.

Chastity nodded but seemed too unsteady to speak at the moment. Noah showed no sign he recognized the name.

"Henri Blume is the man who created the grid," Marilyn explained. "He's the president of Lucidity."

"Yeah, I remember the name now," Noah said, holstering his gun. He turned to Chastity. "What's going on? What's your father have to do with this?"

"I'm not sure," she responded. "He told me something about V-Real and how it has these side-effects. I didn't really believe him. He sounded like he was—"

"What side-effects?" Noah demanded.

Chastity took a moment to think, as if her thoughts weren't completely clear yet. "Something about dampening the sex drive, using Troloxian technology. I don't really know. He was talking like a madman."

"'Though this be madness, yet there is method in it.'"

Noah recognized the voice even before he turned.

"Kess."

On the other side of the transparent wall stood the Troloxian, along with a half-dozen other trolls and the fineline they'd chased across Union Square, the one with the neck tattoo who'd shot at them. Even as he reached for his gun, Noah saw the aliens were armed with the military hand lasers.

He never got the chance to reconsider his action. Just as he grasped the Desert Eagle's grip, he felt a surge of pain followed by a blinding flash of light and then nothing.

54

HIDDEN AGENDA

CHASTITY HAD SCARCELY REGAINED HER SENSES FROM THE JOLT SHE'D RECEIVED IN HER father's study when a similar wave of pain shot through her again. The blistering, initial shock was followed by the same numbness, the same brilliant flash of light and then blackness.

Consciousness returned slowly. She woke to the sound of pounding, and peeked under her eyelids to see the police inspector pummeling the shieldglass with his fists. When that proved fruitless, he picked up a small metal chair and slammed it against the transparent wall. No effect.

"Please stop," she said. "The only thing you're hurting is my head."

Noah tossed the chair aside. "They took my gun. They took Marilyn."

"Your gun's named Marilyn?"

"No, my partner, Marilyn. When I woke up she was gone."

Yes, remembered Chastity, her brain fighting through the fog, his partner, Marilyn Monroe, the celebudroid. She looked around the chamber and saw that indeed it was only her and the inspector.

"We're locked in tighter than a nun's lips," said Noah.

Chastity could almost see him reigning in his anger, assessing the situation with a cool eye. She saw him pinch his ear lobe.

"Marilyn? Marilyn, can you hear me?"

"What are you doing?"

"I'm trying to contact my partner. We've got com implants, but she's not responding. What the drudge have they done with her?"

"Can't you call someone else," Chastity asked, "call for help?"

"It's strictly a two-way link, and I've lost my pad so I'm deaf and dumb."

"I won't argue that."

He wasted a scowl on her, then asked, "What about you? Have you got a pad?"

Chastity looked around, but didn't see her purse. She shook her head. "What are we going to do?"

"It doesn't look like it's up to us," Noah said, testing the door once again. Chastity was amazed at the brute force he brought to bear on the door, bracing his leg against the wall and throwing himself backwards as he tugged. The door didn't budge. Chastity saw it was reinforced by a steel frame.

"What do you think they're going to do with us?"

Noah conceded the door and shrugged. He grabbed the chair he'd thrown aside and used it for its primary purpose.

"What was that drudge you were giving us about V-Real and sex? You don't really believe that, do you?"

"You should believe it," said a voice from an overhead intercom system.

It was Kess, standing alone now, on the other side of the shieldglass wall. He had a strange look on his face. To Chastity it appeared to be a smirk, but with his alien features she couldn't be certain.

"It's true," continued the alien. "All that your father told you was true-but he didn't know everything."

Noah stood and threw his chair at the shieldglass for effect. The chair caromed off, and Kess never flinched.

"'Proud man, dressed in a little brief authority, most ignorant of what he's most assured, his glassy essence like an angry ape.' I'm afraid, Inspector, your display of force is a useless bit of bestial bravado. There's no way out of that chamber."

"Where's my partner?"

"The android? We've secured her elsewhere. What we have planned for you two would not be effective with her."

Chastity stepped forward. "What did you mean about my father not knowing everything?"

"Your father's neurotic apprehension regarding procreation proved to be the perfect wherewithal to boost our agenda."

"And what is your agenda?" Noah asked, not bothering to conceal his contempt.

"Why the domination of your planet of course."

55

SLINGS AND ARROWS

IT WAS THE MATTER-OF-FACT WAY THE ALIEN SAID "OF COURSE" THAT SHOT A BURR INTO Noah's butt. He didn't care for smug on a troll any more than he did on a human criminal. That's all Kess was to him—just a perp with bad skin and big pointy ears.

"Don't look so dismayed, Ms Blume," continued Kess. "We're not evil. We're not power-crazed conquerors. We simply needed a place to live. And your Earth is such lovely place, don't you agree?"

"But you already live here."

"I'm afraid, Ms Blume, that we need more, much more. You see, unlike your own, our reproductive patterns are unalterable. The growth of our population is rampant, a byproduct of the innumerable dangers on our native world."

"I've seen one of their nests," Noah told Chastity. "They've kept them underground so we wouldn't know they're breeding like rabbits."

"More like rabbits to the tenth power," interjected the Troloxian.

"It was like a colossal beehive," said Noah, "but it went up in flames like tissue paper."

"So it was you who attacked and destroyed our *pesssstaal.* You killed thousands of us. Did you know that, Inspector?"

"It seemed like the thing to do at the time."

"I don't understand," Chastity said. "What does this have to do with my father?"

"As soon as I met your father I knew he would provide the key to your world. He was very amenable to the idea of blunting mankind's sex drive. He felt your frivolous obsession with lust was a waste of time, as well as a perversion. You yourself have supported such ideas on your program, Ms Blume. Your Church of Transcendental Platonics has been equally helpful in that arena. The only difference between us is a matter of degree. Your father thought the virtual reality devices were modified simply to diminish human sexual desires. He had no idea that, given time, they would eradicate the libido entirely."

"How much time?" Noah asked.

"It varies with the individual, Inspector. After a usage period of, say, a hundred hours or so the effects are more or less permanent."

Noah thought of Cat, and tried to calculate how many hours she'd worn that V-Real visor by now.

"This very chamber you're sealed in was used in our human tests. The development process was rather simple, as it turned out. At first we used direct input into the nervous system. Later we refined our methods. It took only a few years. It wasn't nearly as difficult to devise such a mind-compelling instrument as we first calculated. We discovered most humans have all the tenacious individuality of a flock of sheep."

"This is one sheep who'd like to ram his individuality up your feathered troll ass," fumed Noah.

"Humans," Kess said, pity in his voice. "You're like salmon, swimming upstream all your brief lives only to spawn and die. And then there are those of your kind willing to sell out their entire race for the price of a few baubles." The troll reached into his coat pocket and opened his fist to reveal a handful of diamonds.

"So your plan is to take over the world by putting an end to sex?" Chastity asked incredulously. "That makes no sense. It would take..."

"Decades?" Kess finished the thought for her. "Possibly a century? As I explained to you before, Ms Blume, we are a long-lived race. 'Though patience be a tired mare, yet she will plod.' Patience, you see, is our primary virtue.

"We've used your own Machiavellian contrivances, your marketing and publicity mills, your prejudices and religions, to spew rumor and innuendo that progressively aided our cause. You'd be surprised at how helpful a few random reports of a new, virulent strain of a sexually transmitted disease can be. We even embellished the terrorist threats of your pathetic Loftur cabal so as to give you some demon to focus on.

"You see, we're in no hurry. We're perfectly willing to wait for the day when Troloxians outnumber humans ten to one—a hundred to one. You won't live to see that day, of course, but it will come."

"Why not just develop some real disease that would wipe out only humans?" Noah asked sarcastically.

"Oh, but then there would be all that mess to clean up. Besides, humans will have their uses in the new order of things. I've found, for the right price, they make quite nice pets."

"The tattoos," said Noah, making the connection.

"Yes, the tattoos, which I so graciously translated for you."

"How can a…a simple virtual reality game do this?" Chastity asked in disbelief.

"Not so simple, I assure you. The V-Real visors are designed to use the optic nerve as a conduit to your neural pathways. Its effects have certain pyschotropic properties that…"

As the Troloxian explained the detailed workings of the device, Noah heard another voice.

Noah? Noah, are you there? His com had come to life, or Marilyn had, but he couldn't respond, not without the troll catching on. *Can you hear me, Noah?* He reached up and squeezed his earlobe several times, activating and deactivating the link. *That's you, isn't it? You can hear me, but you can't talk, right? I understand. I can hear Kess.*

"…and by stimulating the frontal lobe—your brain's pleasure center—it elevates the levels of serotonin, thereby creating mental and emotional distress disguised as euphoria. A very addictive euphoria that deadens the natural sex drive."

I don't know where I am. It's like a closet, completely dark. I was unconscious for a while. I don't know what they did to me, or how I got here. I'll see if I can get out.

"An unfortunate side-effect of this loss of libido is an increase in violent behavior. I'm told it couldn't be helped. However, on the positive side, the shriveled desire for procreation also leads to apathy in other areas, such as diminished ambition and creativity. Even mankind's basic survival instinct will stagnate.

"Of course this means there will be no more Shakespeares," Kess said, as though struck with regret, "but then, we Troloxians have learned through the millennia to endure the bad with the good."

"So there never was any religious persecution that forced you to flee your planet."

"As a matter of fact, there was. What I said of that was true, though I may have embellished a few of the details."

"How can you do this?" Chastity's question was almost a plea. "After we took you in, allowed you to join us?"

"Yes, *allowed.*" Kess let the word linger on his tongue. "It was magnanimous of you. Yet, this is a matter of survival—survival of the fittest. I believe that's a phrase you're familiar with. And we are the fittest, Ms Blume, I assure you."

"You said you weren't evil, but you are," shouted Chastity. "You intend to wipe out an entire species, and you do it without a trace of remorse."

"On the contrary, I'm not a savage, Ms Blume. I have my moments of doubt and regret. I've simply tried to make a virtue of necessity. Try to think of it as a shifting of tides. Humans have had their time on Earth, now it is our time. It's not as if we're committing genocide. We're not actually killing anyone."

"You killed my partner," said Noah. "You killed her father, Hurley Hutchinson, Professor Wu, and who knows how many more."

"I admit, a few instances of violent attrition were necessary along the way. Which leads us to our present predicament. I can't very well allow the two of you to go free. Not that anyone would likely believe you, especially you, Inspector. I suspect your credibility is currently nonexistent after that video representation I gave the network, and which Ms Blume was so kind as to gridcast."

Noah threw a look of scorn Chastity's way.

"However, Ms Blume is another story altogether. I can't have her show up dead without expecting an investigation, especially after the recent demise of her father. No, what I think I'll do, since your image is already tarnished, Inspector, is make it appear that *you* killed Ms Blume, and then committed suicide. And with the proper reprogramming, I'm sure we can get your android partner to verify that scenario."

I'll never do it. I wouldn't, Noah, no matter what they do to my circuits.

"But first, you'll have the honor of becoming the initial test subjects for a new process we've developed which will facilitate our endeavor. You see, we currently are at the mercy of many factors regarding our ability to distribute the V-Real visors. That distribution has been uneven at best.

"Our scientists believe they've developed a system that will allow us to disperse the same effects via your global informational internet. By using the grid, another item we have to be thankful to your father for, we will be able to spread our message, as it were, much more effectively.

"I was about to conduct the first test of this system on you, Ms Blume, when, as good luck would have it, Inspector Dane and his partner decided to join us. Now I have two subjects, male and female. It's such synchronicity, don't you think, Inspector?"

"I think you're a full-blown pecan."

"Such eloquence. I'm sure you'd love your pound of flesh, but that is neither here nor there. Let me describe what's about to happen. Soon after I leave—and do I have to depart shortly, I beg your forgiveness—I will issue the order to activate the device, which pervades this chamber. A visual image is not necessary for this application, but you will hear a slight hum. You'll be glad to know, I'm sure, that the dose you'll receive is a highly concentrated one. Within fifteen to twenty minutes you will begin to lose all reproductive urges. In less than an hour, neither one of you will be capable of sexual desire for the rest of your lives—which, of course, won't be long.

"Over the next hour, you will begin to develop residual brain damage. If we were to continue past the second hour, your deaths would be a foregone conclusion. However, we'd like to run a few tests before that occurs. Not that you'll care much at that juncture.

"Now, if you'll excuse me, I must bid you farewell." Kess bowed mockingly with a stage flourish of his arm. "'All our yesterdays have lighted fools the way to dusty death. Out, out, brief candle. Life's but a walking shadow, a poor player that struts and frets his hour upon the stage and then is heard no more.'"

Noah launched his body against the shieldglass. The unexpected violence startled the otherwise composed Troloxian. Noah slammed his fist against the barrier separating them. The savage glint of his blue eyes spoke of unrestrained mayhem.

"I'm going to wrap my hands around your neck and squeeze until your beady red eyes pop like a pair of zits."

Kess regrouped, recovering his stolid composure. "'A tale told by an idiot, full of sound and fury, signifying nothing.'" With that, he strolled away as Noah pounded his fist several more times.

"That's not going to do us any good," Chastity criticized.

Noah struck the barrier a final time. "It's doing me good."

Noah, wherever I am, I can't get out.

"Have you tried your AR link again?"

It's still not working.

"Well, keep trying."

Chastity stared at him. "Who are you talking to?"

"My partner," Noah said, looking around their cage again. Two chairs, the oversized med table, a few odds and ends on the countertop—nothing that would be of any use in getting out of there.

"Do you believe what he said?" Chastity asked. "Do you think they can really stop people from...you know?"

"I guess we're about to find out."

Noah, I'm trying something else. I'm trying to contact Jim—let him know I'm in trouble.

"The garbage man?"

Not knowing where I am, I can't be sure if the link will work. If I'm still underground, I may be out of range. And even if he gets the message, I'm not sure if he can track it to where we are.

Noah turned to Chastity. "Do you have any idea where we're at?"

Chastity shook her head. "I wasn't conscious when they brought me here."

"We know we were close to the V-Real factory. I'm betting that's where we are, under it somewhere. If you get Jimbo, tell him that's where we think we are."

I'll try.

"What are you two talking about?" Chastity wondered.

"Nothing. Nothing that'll probably do us much good."

Noah, I've made contact. Jim's responding.

"Does he get that you're in trouble?"

Yes. He says he'll try to get help.

"They won't believe him. Standard obtuse procedure. It'll take him forever to convince them. We'll be so much dry mulch by then."

As if on cue, a soft but audible hum began. The sound was all around them.

What's that?

"Kess's little experiment just kicked into gear. Well, maybe the cavalry will arrive before they can mess with your circuits."

I doubt that will matter much. Do you think, even if I'm able to tell what I know, that the world would believe such a story from a celebudroid? Captain Raevski stated it rather plainly. My testimony would not mean much, especially now, after I broke the law helping you escape. No, you and Ms Blume must survive, especially Ms Blume. If she exposes this conspiracy on the grid, the Troloxians can still be stopped.

"You're probably right."

Noah, I've been thinking about what Kess said, about how V-Real affects the brain's pleasure center.

"Yeah, so what?"

Well, ever since you explained to me what sex is like, I was...Well, I was curious. So I did a lot of research, read whatever I could find on the grid.

"Yeah, so?"

Maybe I don't know what love is, what it's like for two people, the emotions and all, but I did learn quite a bit about how the human body works. If what Kess told us was accurate, then the one way to combat the effects of the device might be with sex itself.

"What are you babbling about?"

I'm saying that if you and Ms Blume engage in sexual intercourse, it could very possibly protect the higher functions of your brain by putting the primitive part in control. The two of you have to make love.

"I think you've slipped a gasket, partner."

It's the only thing that might work.

"What if it does work? How long could we possibly...? I mean, I could, but what about Miss Prissy?" Even as he said it, as he thought about it, anxiety swept through him. What if he couldn't? What if it was like the last time? He certainly wasn't going to get any help from America's Favorite Virgin. Sure, she was attractive enough, but she was no Rosie in the area of wanton debauchery.

The thought of Rosie only exaggerated his anxiety. He recalled how her best efforts had failed. What was that old saying? About the guy who couldn't get it up to save his life? What if he couldn't get it up to save the world?

And you can't just go through the motions. If it's going to work at all, it must be passionate lovemaking. You must both be consumed with desire, lost in the primal essence of animal lust.

Noah looked at Chastity, who was clearly annoyed at being the third party in a dual conversation.

"What if she won't? What if she can't?"

Then you must use all of your experience, all of your expertise to inflame her passion.

"Yeah? Well, who's going to inflame mine?"

Give yourself a chance. Relax.

"Easy for you to say."

"What if she can't what?" Chastity asked irritably. "Are you two talking about me?"

"My partner has a crazy idea about how we can stop this thing from turning our minds into mush."

"What is it?"

"She says that if we do the pow-whammy fandango, we might get out of this."

"The pow what?"

"You know, make love, have sex, the horizontal mambo. She says if we have our own little jamorama, and shudder enough, we might be able counteract the effects of this alien gizmo until help arrives."

"That's crazy!"

"Well, we agree on something."

56

OUTRAGEOUS FORTUNE

CHASTITY WAS FLABBERGASTED. THE IDEA OF SUCH A THING. HOW COULD THAT possibly…? Her annoyance turned to anger, and she let it consume her so she wouldn't have to deal with the fear that was trying to usurp control. A fear fueled by that steady drone all around them.

"I'm not going to…" She started, but couldn't finish.

"Look," Noah said, "I admit it sounds like an octopus juggling chainsaws, but it makes a kind of sense."

"What kind of sense?"

"Marilyn says if the animal parts of our brains are otherwise engaged, we can fight this thing. And I'd rather fight than sit around waiting to be neutered and mind-drudged. She's made contact with someone on the outside. Help's on the way. But if you and I—no, not me, not after the job that video did on me—if *you* aren't coherent when it gets here then who's going to expose this thing? We can sit here and do nothing, or we can do our damnedest to stop them."

Chastity didn't know what to say. If it was their only chance, what else could she do? Part of her felt responsible, guilty because she'd gone ahead with the broadcasting of that tape despite her misgivings. The inspector's credibility was ruined, thanks to her.

She also thought about her father. He was culpable, too. He was gone now, but she had found her mother. There was so much she still wanted to learn about her.

This would be easy for Betty. She wouldn't be hesitating like this, not with what was at stake. Her mother's words echoed in her head. *You do what you have to do.*

"All right," Chastity said stiffly, "let's do it."

Resolute, she approached Noah, put her arms over his burly shoulders, closed her eyes and kissed him.

It was an awkward kiss, somewhere between a grandmotherly peck and a childish slobber. He tried to kiss her back. Her first impulse was to resist. She felt his hand slide down her back and take hold of her derriere. Again, her natural reaction was to pull away. She fought it.

"This isn't going to work unless you really mean it," Noah said. "You've got to go for it, lose yourself in the moment, or we're history."

Yes, thought Chastity, us and the rest of humanity.

"I know it's the logical thing to do, but..."

"Forget logic, would you?"

"Okay, I'll try."

She redoubled her determination and kissed him again. It wasn't easy. Not that he was so ugly as to be repulsive. He was certainly muscular, though not exactly her ideal of handsome. His powerful arms actually felt good around her. If only they weren't so hairy.

Nevertheless, she couldn't let that or anything else bother her now. She had to get beyond it—way beyond it. Bravely, yet at the same time distressed at what she might find, she reached between his legs.

To her surprise, there wasn't much there, at least not what she expected. What was there lacked a certain...firmness. Wasn't she attractive enough? Was it that difficult for him to want her? Her doubts returned en masse.

57

A LABOR OF LUST

HER HAND CAUGHT NOAH OFF-GUARD—HE HADN'T EXPECTED HER TO BE SO BOLD. However, her audacity only served to stoke his anxiety. He reached for her left breast to bolster his staggering libido. He found it a pleasing handful, soft beneath a thin bra but responding firmly to his attentions.

You must hurry, Noah. It's been five minutes already.

"A little music would be nice," he said.

I could sing. I remember the words to 'When Love Goes Wrong, Nothing Goes Right.

"No."

What about "I Wanna Be Loved By You?"

"No thanks. I don't think that'll help."

Then think of it as acting. You can have conscious preparation, but you must have unconscious results.

"That's where you're wrong. It's not about acting, it's about being."

"What's she saying," Chastity wondered in-between their mutual groping.

"That there's no time for any Tantric teasing."

Without warning, Noah grabbed Chastity's blouse and ripped it off, breaking her purity chain as he did. Shocked, she gasped at the violent motion. Noah didn't stop there. He pulled her bra up over her arms and brusquely snatched at her skirt. It was too tight to pull, so he fumbled for the zipper. She pushed away his hands to do it herself, so he wasted no time getting his own clothes off.

Once they were both naked they embraced again, kissing, touching, though still rather awkwardly.

That's good. It sounds good, Marilyn kibitzed in his ear. *I think she's responding. Keep it up.*

"Hey, do you mind? How about a little privacy? I'm trying to save a species here."

Marilyn didn't respond, so he 'jectured she'd got the message her play-by-play was not helping matters. He was having trouble reading the whispered noises coming from his reluctant co-participant. Would her frosty demeanor allow her to be aroused, no matter what he did? Or were his efforts destined to wilt on the vine?

He knew he couldn't allow that. Boldly, vigorously, he scooped her up and laid her on the med table. In an instant he was over her, continuing his deft ministrations. His hands and lips were here, there and everywhere, doing what they could to rouse the grid star's dormant lust. He became so involved in his task he forgot about his own dilemma.

That negligence proved fortuitous. He felt a slight tremor, a hesitant wiggle. His expectations for success rose. His nose told him that her body, if not her mind, was coming round. He smelled the rut in her and knew he was on the right track. As soon as he was certain she was ready, he forged ahead where no man had gone before.

At least that's what he thought.

58

THE POW-WHAMMY EXPRESS

S O THIS IS WHAT IT WAS. THIS IS WHAT SHE HAD DENIED HERSELF ALL THOSE YEARS. THIS all-consuming, utterly entrancing feeling of pure pleasure. An endless train, rocketing past all the barriers erected by her superego. So powerful, so hypnotic—no wonder it evoked such mania, such hysteria.

"Oh...oh...oooh...oh...oh, God! Yes! God, yes! Ahhhhhh!" The baleful screams rang in Chastity's ears. Was that her voice? Did she make that sound? Before she could decide, another rapturous wave swept through her. It took hold of her and transported her. It possessed her.

How many times now had she...? She had no idea. Several she was sure. But one moment merged into the next, one incredible orgasmic response coalesced into another.

She glanced over her shoulder at the brawny police inspector who so recently had been an object of repulsion. His hands were clamped to her rear, his perpetual motion machine-like. No longer a strange, tactile violation, each thrust now brought her closer to immersion.

That's all she thought of now. That's all she wanted. She'd forgotten about the Troxolians and their insidious plan for world domination. She no longer thought about the device that even now fought for control of her mind. She wasn't thinking about her father, her mother, Minister Redstone, or even her own doubts. She wanted simply to dissolve into this unconflicted pool, to wander aimlessly through this lush garden of bright new sensations.

59

SOARING OVER THE CLIFFS OF BLISS

Noah wasn't sure how much longer he could go on. What had it been? Thirty, forty minutes? More? Marilyn hadn't been in his ear since they started. He 'jectured she didn't want to bother them, but he wished she'd give him an update. America's Favorite ex-Virgin was putting him through his paces. She was an uncaged beast, and every time she came it grew harder for Noah not to join her in blissful release.

Then again, he had a job to do. And he was doing it. He was still rock-hard, still vigorously pumping away, still relishing the feel of her silky torso and savoring her cries of ecstasy. The humming sound continued to surround them, but that damnable alien technology hadn't castrated him yet.

Chastity was on top of him now, showing no signs of slowing. He reached to fondle her nipples and spur her on when his com finally sounded.

Noah, help has arrived. We're on our way to find you. Don't stop until we get there.

He wanted to respond, to ask who and how, but didn't for fear of disrupting the enthusiasm of his partner. What was going on out there? Were the trolls putting up a fight, or had they surrendered in mass? He was itching to get into it himself and knock a few alien heads together.

Nevertheless, now that he knew rescue was imminent, he no longer felt like he might lose control. In fact, he felt like he could go on for another hour if he had to.

However, despite her energetic responses, he didn't think Chastity would last much longer. Experience told him she was just about maxed out. Her body didn't know how tired it was, not yet. But soon it would hit her and she'd want to surrender. He knew he couldn't let her, though. They couldn't let up, not for a moment.

No sooner had he thought about it when...

"Oh, oh, oh, oooooooh!"

...Chastity exploded once more, and when her pulsating contractions ceased, she collapsed on top of him. He gave her a moment, but she seemed unwilling or unable to move. Gently he turned her so he was over her again.

"Marilyn just contacted me. A rescue team is on its way. We can't stop now. We've got to keep going until they get us out of here."

"I don't think," Chastity said, fighting for breath, "I can go on. It's over...overwhelming. I can't...take much more."

"Sure you can. I'll go slow. Concentrate on the sensations."

Noah found he needed to concentrate himself. He couldn't let the distraction of potential rescue deflate his resolve now. Not when they were so close. He had to be certain Chastity remained aroused as well, so he brought his fingers into play once more. At least she was still wet. That was a good sign.

Time lapsed, and presently he was lost once again in the thick, musty trance of fleshy carnality. Sweat-glossed heaving breasts, quavering belly, undulating hips—he suddenly wanted it all. His primal essence called out for satisfaction, for the propagation of the species, for release of the voracious, yearning beast trapped inside him. So he let go. His cries mingled with hers as he shot into her with raw ferocity.

It was over. He was spent. He lay there, struggling for breath, using sheer willpower to suspend himself on exhausted arms so as not to crush her with his full weight. As he did, she opened her eyes and looked up at him, still breathing heavy.

"That was...it was *good,*" she stated simply, like a little girl making a fascinating discovery.

"It was good?"

"You know," she added, "it was *really good.* Wasn't it?"

"Yeah."

He was still dealing with the banality of her praise when he heard another voice.

"Noah? Noah, we're here."

It was Marilyn's voice, right there in the room. He hadn't even heard the door open. He was still catching his breath, too drained to even glance over that way. Likewise, Chastity lay beneath him, her eyes shut again, her heart still beating out a vibrato rhythm.

"Noah, are you all right?"

He managed to turn his head. Standing just inside the door was Marilyn and an odd-looking little guy he didn't recognize. Noah 'jectured he must be from a different precinct, though he'd evidently put away his own weapon in favor of one of the missing military lasers. Marilyn had her sonic stunner in one hand and Noah's Desert Eagle in the other.

"Just in the nick of time," said Noah, smiling. "I'm as wrung out as an old washrag."

"We've got to go," urged Marilyn.

Fighting exhaustion, Noah got up off of Chastity and began putting his clothes on. Chastity lay there another few seconds, then seemed to realize she was naked. She got off the table and began collecting her clothes.

"If we don't get out of here quick-like our circuits aren't going to be worth a hill of beans," said Marilyn's companion.

"The Troloxians are putting up a fight," Marilyn said to Noah. "We lost Elvis and one of the Madonnas on the way in."

"You lost who?" responded Noah.

"Elvis and Madonna," Marilyn said. Seeing the mystified look on his face, she added, "Jim called in all of our celebudroid friends."

"Shit and frijoles! What about the police?" Noah asked as he fastened his pants.

"He tried, but they didn't believe him. They wanted him to come down in person and file a report. By the way, this is Bogie," she said, introducing her companion.

"I'd say it was good to meet you," said Bogie, "but I'd be lying. We're going to have to fight our way out of here, you know."

"Give me my gun," Noah said, not bothering with his shirt. Marilyn handed it to him, and he relished the familiarity of its heft. "So where's Jimbo?"

"I don't know," Marilyn replied, clearly concerned. "He was with Sam Clemens and the Babe when we got separated in the fighting."

"The Babe?"

"You know, Babe Ruth. I'm worried about them."

"I'm sure Jim and Baby Ruth are okay."

Another guy Noah didn't recognize, this one with a mustache and a pair of prominent ears rushed to the door.

"Marilyn, honey," he said, motioning with the antique rifle he had in his hands, "we've got to get out of here, pronto!"

"Wait," pleaded Chastity, "I'm not dressed yet."

"Frankly, my dear, I don't give a damn," the newcomer told her then turned to Marilyn and Noah. "Eastwood and Sinatra are holding the stairs with Dr. King and Cleopatra, but I don't know for how long."

Chastity tossed away her torn blouse and picked up Noah's shirt. "All right, I'm ready."

"Well, shit and frijoles," declared Noah, "let's go save the world."

60

A GIRL'S BEST END

"...SO THE VIDEO I SHOWED YOU THREE DAYS AGO WAS FRAUDULENT, EDITED TO VILIFY THE police department's lead investigator pursuing this vast conspiracy. I must take some personal responsibility for failing to verify the source and accuracy of that video.

"The truth is, the world owes a debt of gratitude to Inspector Noah Dane of the San Francisco Police Department and his partner, Detective Special Class Marilyn Monroe. If not for their diligence, we might never have known of the insidious plot that could have eventually condemned mankind to the fate of the dinosaur.

"However, I can report that once the facts were made clear to city and federal security monitors, immediate action was taken to arrest all known co-conspirators and effectively quarantine the entire immigrant Troloxian population. The same measures are now being taken by foreign nations, according to their own laws and customs.

"The apparent leader of the aliens, known by the human name of Walter Kess, escaped the initial confrontation between National Guard units and the Troloxian resistance." Chastity glanced at her monitor to see if the file video of Kess had been called up. "Kess appeared on this very program two weeks ago, putting a benign face on what was, as we know now, a clandestine plan to gain control of our world.

"I'm told that every attempt is being made to modify the Digital Imaging Recognition System so that its biometric ratios can be used to distinguish Troloxian characteristics. In this way, Kess and other known leaders of the alien conspiracy can be identified and separated from the others.

"As for the fate of the Troloxian people themselves, that is a matter which I'm certain will be discussed and debated by both world leaders and the populace at large. Should all Troloxians bear the blame for what their leaders attempted to do? Will some attempt be made to find a scientific remedy to their rampant population growth? Should they be exiled from Earth, forced to leave in the vessels that brought them here?

"Some, I'm certain, will argue for even harsher penalties. I will make no attempt to answer those questions here and now. I will offer you no opinion."

She noted that the video montage of Troloxians had ended, and that her own image was once again on the monitor.

"As for myself, this will be my last appearance on *Gridspeak*, at least for the immediate future. After taking some time off, I will be pursuing the story of the Troloxians, continuing to investigate the conspiracy and examining the current dilemma. Whether my findings will be made available on the grid is a matter that will be decided by those in charge of this network or others.

"For now, thanks for watching. I'm Chastity Blume, and this is *Gridspeak.*"

That's it, we're out, Vince said in her IFB. *Good show.*

Chastity felt a sense of relief. Not simply because the show was over, and that she'd helped make the public aware of the threat that had faced them— still faced them to a degree—but that she was walking away. She was going to take that time, get her own life in order, then pursue the kind of journalistic work she'd always wanted to do.

She had much to consider. So much that needed rethinking. The world felt new and full of possibilities. Her priority had been to use her notoriety to make certain the conspiracy was exposed. Now she'd done that. She was free to look after herself.

"Chastity." It was Leeland, hurrying to catch up with her as she left the set. "What was that?"

She kept walking. "What was what?"

"About this being your last show? I know you need some time off, but then—"

"There are no buts, Leeland. I'm not interested in being a talking head anymore."

"But with this Troloxian thing, you've never been bigger. Tonight's insta-ratings are going through the roof. The public is going to want more."

"I hope you give it to them, Leeland. I'm sure you will."

"You can't just quit. You've got a contract."

"You can take me to court if you'd like," Chastity said, "but I don't think that would be a wise public relations move right now, do you? Besides, I'm not quitting. I'm taking some time that's due me, and if you want me back, I'll be here to work. But it'll be the kind of work I want to do or…"

He grabbed her arm to slow her. She stopped, but gave him a look that made him let go.

"What about us, Chastity? Aren't we going to…?"

He didn't finish his question because she was shaking her head.

"There's no us, Leeland. I'm sorry, but I don't think there ever was."

She didn't wait for a response. She turned and proceeded to her office. He didn't follow.

When she got there, she checked her messages and found only one she was interested in. It was from Suzette. Chastity activated the link.

"What is it, Suzette?"

"It's Angel, Ms Blume, and the feline companion you procured for her. They don't seem to be getting along at all. The newcomer is very aggressive. He keeps jumping on her and biting her. And the noises they're making…it sounds to me as if they're fighting."

Chastity smiled. "I understand it's like that sometimes, Suzette. I'm sure they'll be okay. I'll be home soon anyway."

"Very good, Ms Blume. But I hope the hostilities cease soon. The noise is playing havoc with my circuits.

"I also took a message from your mother. She would like to adjust the time frame of your dinner plans tomorrow evening from seven to six, if that's possible. She also asked me to remind you to 'live a little.' She seemed to think you'd know what that meant."

"Contact her and tell her the time change is fine, and…no, no, never mind, I'll call her myself."

"Will there be anything else, Ms Blume?"

"Yes. Connect with building master control and see if you can link me to David."

"David? David Mandala, of building maintenance?"

"Yes."

"All right, Ms Blume. I'll see if I can locate him."

As she waited, Chastity tried to reassure herself. She was nervous, but discovered it was a titillating nervousness. The very idea of it was liberating. It was as if the events of the past few days had given her a whole new perspective on things. A clearer perspective she felt, especially on one particular thing. Not so clear, though, that her eagerness wasn't shaded by apprehension.

In the flutter of her anxiety something else occurred to her. It crossed her mind from nowhere in particular that she should introduce Suzette to Antonio. She giggled at the thought. Now there was a match made in cyber heaven.

"Hello? Chastity?" It was David, his ever-pleasant face now curious. "Did you call for me?"

"Hi, David. How are you today?"

"I'm fine. But what about you? I heard what happened to you. I wanted to call and check on you but decided I shouldn't bother you."

"I'm okay, David, I'm great. But I'd be better if you felt like you could call me any time you wanted to."

"Okay," he responded hesitantly.

Chastity could tell this wasn't going to be easy. He might need some motivating.

"David, do you know what's better than chocolate?" she asked coquettishly.

"Better than chocolate? No, I guess I don't."

"I can show you." She found she was embarrassed by her own brazenness. "I mean...I was wondering if you could stop by my place when you were done with work today. Can your mother do without you for a little while?"

"Sure," he said, "her sister's visiting from Tennessee. She's fine. Did you need me for something?"

"Yes...I mean, no, I don't really need you for anything, I just wanted to see you. You know talk and..."

"Oh, I thought maybe you had something you needed me to do for you."

"There is something I'd like you to do for me," she said, a slow grin evolving on her face.

"What's that?"

"Let's just say my plants need watering."

61

RECIPROCITY

NOAH STEPPED IN FRONT OF THE MIRROR AND RAN HIS FINGERS THROUGH HIS SANDY-blond hair. No question it was much thinner than it used to be. Thinner than when, he wasn't sure. He scratched at his chest, trying to remember, then turned to check his profile. The sight of his bulging waistline coerced him to inhale. Too many cheese enchiladas, he 'jectured. Either that, or he was just plain getting old. After all, he was on the dilapidated side of thirty-nine, steamrolling toward forty like a runaway Mag-Lev.

Even so, he wasn't ready for the mulch bag just yet. He still had some fields to plow...some seeds to plant. He wasn't about to start measuring his mortality now. Some bikeroo with a bullet or a streeter hopped up on jazz juice was more than likely to take care of that for him.

Shit and frijoles, he might live to be a grandpa before that happened. That is, if...

He retrieved his pad and accessed the link. Sheila's image came up almost immediately.

"What is it, Noah?" she asked, apparently perturbed he was bothering her.

"I wanted to check on Cat. Is she there?"

"No, she's out with friends."

"Is she...Is she doing okay? I mean, are there any signs she...?"

"She's fine, Noah. Dr. Indira says she seems to have suffered no lasting side effects."

"That's good," Noah said, relieved.

"She's just the same," said Sheila, the exasperation evident in her voice. "She and her friends are into this face painting and chanting thing now. It's

288

quite annoying. You want to take her back with you? You're welcome to."

"No, no, I think she's better off with you, Sheila. But I promised her we'd get together more often, and she can come over whenever she wants. Let me know if she gets to be too much. She and her friends can chant all they want over here."

"Yeah, her dad's the big hero now. I have to go, Noah."

"Okay, tell her—"

Sheila cut the link before he could finish. That's all right, he thought, he'd tell her himself.

He'd meant what he told her about seeing her more often. Of course, she was getting to the age where she wouldn't particularly care to be around her old dad that much.

Thinking about Cat reminded him he wanted to check on Snip, see how she was getting along next door. On his way outside, going through the kitchen, he caught sight of the bottle. The one Cy had given him. The one he had so deliberately avoided the last couple of weeks.

He thought about it, but didn't hesitate. He grabbed it, cracked the seal and shrugged off the thought it was early in the day. Instead, he recalled the jocular image of Cy the day he'd given it to him, and how he'd gone into a detailed explanation of why the Single Barrel blend was so special. With a nod and a quick hoist of the bottle in salute, Noah took a drink. Good stuff, he thought, replacing the whiskey on the shelf.

Once he was outside, he noticed how the weeds had usurped his front yard. He was going to have to set aside some time to get his house in order. But that could wait. He walked next door and knocked.

He hadn't had the chance to check on his neighbor since he'd dropped Snip off that night. He hoped the little street clone hadn't been too hard on the old woman. He had no idea what he was going to do with her now. He didn't want to her to go back to the street life she had before. Was there a decent place for homeless clones? A school of some kind maybe? Should he try to get her a job?

The door opened, and it was Snip, though she might have gone unrecognized if he hadn't been expecting her.

"What's the sliggy, PD man?"

"Snip, you look…so clean."

"Clean as uptown pow-whammy and twice as frisky." She threw her arms around him with a show of affection that surprised him. She hugged him as tight as her skinny little frame would allow, then let go as if embarrassed by her own display of emotion. Still, she took his hand and led him inside. He noticed she was wearing new clothes, too, though they looked like something his neighbor had packed away decades ago.

"Who's there?" a voice called from behind Snip. "Remember what I told you about—oh, it's you," said Mrs. Grabarkowitz.

Seeing them both together, Noah realized the gray in Snip's Mohawk no longer showed. She'd dyed it the same glaring red Mrs. G used on her own hair.

The old woman adjusted her antique glasses and looked Noah over. Trying to ascertain if he were the real thing or some mutant copy, he 'jectured.

"You here to pay the rent?"

"No, Mrs. G., I just wanted to see how you and Snip here were getting along."

"We're fine, just fine."

"Gonna stay here with Frannie. She makes a crucial burger. All the picks I want, too." Snip's mongoloid eye twitched excitedly as she spoke. "Gonna take care of each other."

"Is that right, Mrs. G?" Noah asked. "Do you want Snip to stay here with you?"

"The girl's a wonder around the house," Mrs. Grabarkowitz said, taking hold of Snip's four-fingered hand. "She cleans like a whirlwind, and I'm teaching her to cook. She's a gem."

"You hear that, PD man? I'm a gem. What'd you call me, Frannie? A rough diamond?"

"A diamond in the rough, dear."

"Keep a good lookout for mutants, I do, too," Snip added. She looked at Noah and winked her good eye.

It wasn't what he'd expected—not at all, and he had his doubts. Then again, the two of them made a queer kind of sense together.

"Well, I'm glad you're getting along. You know I'm right next door if you need anything."

At that moment, his ear began to itch. He pinched his lobe out of habit.

Noah? Are you here? Are you home?

It was Marilyn.

"Where are you?"

I'm right outside your house. I didn't know if you were here or not.

"I'll be right out." He pinched his lobe again and turned back to Snip and Mrs. G. "I have to go. I'll check on you two later."

"Slither on, PD man. Stay tiptop."

"You too, Snip."

As he walked out the door, he heard Mrs. G call, "Don't forget the rent next time." He waved the back of his hand in response and continued on.

He didn't have to go far. Marilyn and her buddy Jim were standing over their bicycles outside his front door.

"Hey!" he called gruffly as he could. "No droids allowed!"

Marilyn and Jim both turned and smiled upon seeing him. Marilyn let her bike drop and met him partway.

"What are you two doing here? I thought you had someplace to go."

"We're on our way," Marilyn explained. "We're going to the Android Rights Rally. Jim is going to speak."

"That ought to be good for a couple of laughs," said Noah with a grin.

"Right on, man," called Morrison, raising his fist into the air. "Power to the quasi-people."

"I'm afraid it might rain, though," Marilyn added.

Noah sniffed the air. "I don't think so, not today."

"Since we were going this way," continued Marilyn, "I wanted to stop and tell you I wouldn't be staying with you anymore. We've found our own place— Jim and I and some other former celebudroids."

"You could have just left me a message." He had been thinking about how he'd unintentionally taken on a houseguest, and wasn't sure how to tell her she couldn't stay there forever. So he was relieved she'd found a solution without making him the bad guy. It wasn't like he still wouldn't be seeing her all the time. But being partners only went so far.

"I wanted to tell you in person, and thank you ever so much for inviting me into your home."

Noah unleashed a sly grin. "It seemed like the thing to do at the time."

"I also wanted to thank you for, you know, giving me a chance to be your partner, showing me how it's done."

"You earned the chance. It just took a while for me to input that through my thick skull. Besides, you gave as good as you got, and managed to broaden my narrow horizons while you were at it. You're good police, Marilyn."

She smiled at what she knew was his ultimate compliment.

"There's something else. I'm thinking about changing my name to Norma Jeane. That was Marilyn's real name, before she became a movie star."

"Yeah? Hey, if that's what you want. Norma Jeane, huh? It'll take some getting used to, but I'm game."

"Thanks, Noah. I'll see you Monday then?"

"Sure, three shakes of a tailfeather after the sun does its thing."

She turned to go, but Noah caught her arm and planted a kiss on her cheek.

"Good luck at your rally," he said, his impulsive buss transforming his own face rose-red. In an attempt to rebound from his fluster, he added, "And tell all your droid friends thanks again for pulling my fat out of the fire."

"Why don't you come with us, man?" Morrison inquired. "It's going to be one awkward instant."

"No thanks, Jimbo. I'd like to help, but I've got something more important to do right now."

"What's that, Noah?" Marilyn wondered.

He inhaled, his powerful chest rising visibly, his incandescent blue eyes dancing a rakish jig. "I'm going to go dive into a pile of pure pow-whammy."

END

ACKNOWLEDGEMENTS

The author would like to express his appreciation to those who contributed their time and insights to the creation of this book.

To Carolyn Crow and Linda Bona, long-time readers, editors, and friends, for their thoughtful comments and suggestions—not only for this book, but nearly the complete catalog of my fiction.

Thanks to David Brin, noted author of speculative fiction, for taking the time to provide feedback for an "unknown."

To Captain Tom Cowper of the New York Police Department, an authority on future law enforcement, and to geologists Dr. Pat Abbott of San Diego State University and Dr. G. Jeffrey Taylor of the Hawai'i Institute of Geophysics and Planetology for their expertise.

For her indomitable patience, and the sagaciousness to see beyond the ostensible clichés and recognize what I was trying to do with this book, thanks to my publisher Elizabeth Burton.

And finally, recognition to my muse, Darlene Santori, for many memorable lines that often mutated into dialogue.

ABOUT THE AUTHOR

Satirist, journalist, novelist—Bruce Golden's professional writing career spans three decades. He began as a freelance journalist, publishing more than 200 magazine and newspaper stories ranging from in-depth profiles to feature stories to satirical commentary. He worked for 14 years as an editor, and was the founding editor/art director responsible for the creation of five different publications.

In addition to his novels, Golden has published 13 short stories over the last four years, five of which have been reprinted in anthologies. He was the winner of *Speculative Fiction Reader's* 2003 Firebrand Fiction Award, and a co-winner of the 2003 Top International Horror contest.

ABOUT THE ARTISTS

CERBERUS INC., a book cover illustrating company, was formed in 2004 by native Saint Louis artist/partners Dan Skinner and Nick Fichter. Since its formation, their art has appeared on over five hundred books and magazines of all genres. Their medium—the photodigital, incorporating real models, 3D and hand-executed art—makes their work as texturally rich as the old school paint/ink format but more easily cover-specific and time-expedient. Their influences range from the works of Boris Vallejo to the graphic-intense visuals of video games.

"Art makes big kids of both of us."

MARTINE JARDIN has been an artist since she was very small. Her mother guarantees she was born holding a pencil, which for a while, as a toddler, she nicknamed "Zessie"

She won several art competitions with her drawings as a child, ventured into charcoal, watercolors and oils later in life and about 12 years ago started creating digital art.

Since then, she's created hundreds of book covers for Zumaya Publications and eXtasy Books, among others. She welcomes visitors to her website: www.martinejardin.com.

Printed in the United States
116987LV00004B/259-264/A